Praise for *The Affair of the Mysterious Letter*

"I haven't been so enchanted and del... the literary equivalent of being wrapped in a blanket and being driven in a horse-drawn carriage through a magical park filled with the most amazing things happening all around, and feeling safe and loved all the way through. A sheer delight from start to finish, and the most perfect blend of gentle humor, wild creativity, and love for the feel of Sherlock Holmes."　　　　—Emma Newman, author of *Atlas Alone*

"*The Affair of the Mysterious Letter* is a witty, enjoyable, extravagantly imagined slant on the Sherlock Holmes canon. Hall nails the Holmesian aesthetic in marvelously amusing ways while taking us on an extended romp through a wild range of alternate universes with a bizarre cast of characters. Don't miss this fun, queer, clever intrigue!"

—Malka Older, author of *Infomocracy*

"Extraordinarily imaginative. This is the most fun I've had between two covers in a while!" —Lara Elena Donnelly, author of *Amberlough*

"I *really* enjoyed this book. It was absolutely delightful, like a chocolate box, full of unexpected and brilliant references, sparklingly witty."

—Genevieve Cogman, author of *The Invisible Library*

"It's difficult to express my delight in *The Affair of the Mysterious Letter* without falling back on semicoherent exclamations that John Wyndham would want to discreetly summarize in gentler language. This book is so far up my alley that I discovered new, non-euclidean corners of the alley that I didn't previously know existed. The world has heretofore suffered from a sad lack of queer consulting sorceresses, prudish yet romantic Azathoth cultists, existentially surreal urban planning, and postcolonial Carcosan politics."

—Ruthanna Emrys, author of *Winter Tide*

Praise for Alexis Hall's other work

"Simply the best writer I've come across in years."
—*New York Times* bestselling author Laura Kinsale

"Devastatingly beautiful. . . . Biting humor even at the darkest moments, this book made me laugh out loud while sobbing."
—*USA Today* bestselling author Jessica Scott

"Hall brings his gift for vivid, cleverly constructed language to this adventurous tale . . . cheeky effervescence, humor, and unexpected pathos."
—Heroes and Heartbreakers

"Brilliantly written, dangerously good, immensely satisfying."
—*New York Times* bestselling author Suzanne Brockmann

The Affair of the Mysterious Letter

ALEXIS HALL

ACE

NEW YORK

ACE
Published by Berkley
An imprint of Penguin Random House LLC
1745 Broadway, New York, NY 10019

Copyright © 2019 by Alexis J. Hall

Library of Congress Cataloging-in-Publication Data

Names: Hall, Alexis J., author.
Title: The affair of the mysterious letter / Alexis Hall.
Description: First edition. | New York, NY : Ace, 2019.
Identifiers: LCCN 2018054500 | ISBN 9780440001331 (paperback) |
ISBN 9780440001348 (ebook)
Subjects: | BISAC: FICTION / Fantasy / Historical. | FICTION / Mystery &
Detective / Women Sleuths. | GSAFD: Fantasy fiction.
Classification: LCC PR6108.A453 A69 2019 | DDC 823/.92—dc23
LC record available at https://lccn.loc.gov/2018054500

First Edition: June 2019

Printed in the United States of America
1   3   5   7   9   10   8   6   4   2

Cover images by Shutterstock
Cover design by Adam Auerbach
Book design by Elke Sigal

The
Affair of the
Mysterious Letter

Acknowledgements

These reminiscences could not have been compiled without the tireless and faithful support of my editor, Mr. Horatio Slapbiscuit; of my publisher, Braddon & Welles; and of the many friends and acquaintances who have served to remind me of those details upon which my own memory is sadly deficient. To my long-suffering husband I offer both my thanks and my apologies. I fear I have repeated several unkind comments Ms. Haas made about you, but I have done so in order to preserve an accurate record of events as they transpired, not in any way as an endorsement of those remarks. And, of course, neither this text, nor any other aspect of my life as I know it, would have been as it is had I not the privilege of knowing the incomparable Ms. Shaharazad Haas. I have faith that we shall someday meet again.

CHAPTER ONE

Captain John Wyndham

That I must begin these reminiscences with a description of myself and my origins is a necessity that runs contrary to both my character and my upbringing. My editor, however, tells me that my readers will wish to know how a man of my unremarkable public reputation came to be associated with so extraordinary a person as the sorceress Shaharazad Haas. I shall endeavour, therefore, to assuage your curiosity by outlining a little of my early life, particularly the circumstances that led to my arrival in Khelathra-Ven and to my falling into company with the woman who would become my most trusted confidant and truest friend.

I was born in the Kingdom of Ey during the four hundred and sixty-seventh year of the reign of the Witch King Iustinian. My earliest memory of childhood is being summoned to sing "Alas! Must I in Torments Dwell" for one of my parents' friends. Such gatherings were frequent at that time and I never thought to question their purpose, though they occurred always after nightfall and were conducted with an air of peculiar secrecy. In any case, I performed poorly, and my father was disappointed, as he so often was.

As for my father himself, I will simply say that he was a man of strong principles and unswerving faith. He fought valiantly for his beliefs and, unlike so many of his contemporaries, practised in private what he espoused in public. Although his role in the revolution and subsequent part in the formation of the Commonwealth afforded him great power and influence, we continued to live simply and spend our days in contemplation of the Creator's mercy and thankfulness for His blessings.

While I cannot say his stewardship brought much joy to his children, I am nonetheless grateful for many of the lessons he taught me. While some would argue that this world has little use for humility, loyalty, and diligence, I have found them to be constant sources of strength. But, to my shame, I have not the serenity to be thankful to him for his efforts to instil in me the virtues he felt becoming of his daughter. To this day, I am not sure how I would have endured my childhood were it not for my mother.

She shared many traits with my father, including his revolutionary fervour and his unyielding resolve, but she leavened them with kindness. It was of her devising that I was sent to the Honoured University of Khel at the age of sixteen. And it was there that I received my bachelor's degree in transubstantial sciences and was able to be, for the first time, myself: John Wyndham.

Following my graduation, I made one attempt to return home. Although I had been away only four years, the Commonwealth and I had both changed significantly; I had left a kingdom unsettled from revolution and still bearing the wounds of five centuries of tyranny. I returned to a nation in the midst of renewal. Thomas Latimer, the man for whom I had sung so badly so long ago, had been appointed Lord Protector and established an advisory council known as the Chamber of Regicides. My father's disappointment in me, however, was unchanged.

It quickly became apparent to me that my future did not lie in Ey. Centuries of fear followed by a decade of transformation had left the people of the Commonwealth unwelcoming of anything that seemed to them foreign or mysterious. And I, with my varsity ways and my

Khelish habits, was both. Ironically, in Khelathra-Ven I had always been too provincial, my friends mocking me for my prudishness and my adherence to my father's faith, despite my having long since learned the Creator was likely little more than a mindless ball of protoplasmic fire that dwelt in a dead star at the heart of the cosmos.

Thus it was I came again to Khelathra-Ven and, like so many outcasts before me, sought refuge with the Company of Strangers, that queer but valiant battalion of soldiers founded some two centuries past under the joint auspices of the Kaiserin of the Hundred Kingdoms and the Uthmani Sultan. It was rare indeed for those two great powers to agree overmuch on anything, but the existential peril presented by the forces of the Empress of Nothing demanded a united response and the company was structured in such a way that it could owe no loyalties and, thus, would never be distracted from the conflict that rages from the Unending Gate. I believe most people, or at least most people who are familiar with such matters, know at least a little about that ceaseless war. They know, for example, that it takes place primarily across a kaleidoscope of ever-shifting, otherworldly battlefields and that our enemy is by her very nature unknowable and unconquerable. They may even be aware that the conflict has its origins in the events surrounding the fall of ancient Ven. None of those facts, to my mind, are pertinent. My experiences during my time with the Company of Strangers are difficult for me to describe and I do not think they would make for edifying reading. I will not, therefore, attempt to describe them. Suffice to say that I am, even now, uncertain what it was that I hoped to find in pledging myself to such a cause. Perhaps little more than purpose and what passed for an honourable death. But there, in those strange and sunless lands, I soon learned that no death is honourable. Unlike many of my fellows I survived and rose, more thanks to circumstance than merit, to the rank of captain.

Just as I was beginning to contemplate the opportunities my unexpected successes had placed before me, I was struck down by an extratemporal jezail, a fiendish weapon whose bullets displace themselves in time and space, meaning the injuries they cause recur unpredictably. Although I am quite well most of the time I shall, on occasion, be afflicted with a stabbing pain in my shoulder or my leg or, most peculiarly, by the recollection of such a pain in the distant past, long before I had even thought of going to war. Such a condition made me unfit for military service. And so it was that I found myself returning to Khelathra-Ven with little more than my clothes and the meagre savings I had accrued during my tour of duty.

CHAPTER TWO

The City of Khelathra-Ven

My arrival in the city, following my demobilisation, was an unfortunately shambolic affair. Not having anticipated my injury, I had been unable to make any arrangements for accommodation ahead of my arrival. The only lodgings I had been able to secure at such short notice, a tiny unfurnished room above a dyer's shop, proved both exorbitantly expensive and to reek of various unsavoury substances that I shall not name for fear of causing distress. From there I was able to move temporarily into the sitting room of an old university friend who, since graduation, had made a successful career for herself as an interdimensional metallurgist. Although she was most welcoming and her home infinitely more comfortable than the room above the dyer's, I was ill at ease imposing too long on her charity.

My first order of business was to secure for myself some semblance of an income, and with the assistance of one my former tutors, I was able to take up a position as dispensing alchemist at the Little Sisters of Thotek the Devourer Hospital in Athra. My remuneration for this role was not entirely generous and I soon realised that I would be forced to choose between living in one of the least reputable parts of the city—and potentially taking my life in my hands on my daily walk to work—or else making an earnest effort to find a housemate. Even this strategy proved less fruitful than I had hoped. Many desirable properties remained unaffordable and many affordable properties remained undesirable. Furthermore, my Eyan origins rendered my company unpalatable to a number of the city's residents. Having been raised with a rigid sense of propriety, I fear I may have given some of my prospective co-tenants the impression that I begrudged them the freedoms that I, in truth, envied.

One morning, when I was coming quite to despair at my situation, I was perusing a local broadsheet when I came across the following advertisement: *Co-tenant required. Rent reasonable to the point of arousing suspicion. Tolerance for blasphemies against nature an advantage. No laundry service. Enquire S. Haas, 221b Martyrs Walk.* I confess that I was not without my reservations, but Martyrs Walk was enticingly close to the hospital, and with my injury sometimes rendering perambulation discomforting, that was not an insignificant consideration. Therefore I resolved to present myself the very next morning.

Before I narrate the details of that fateful meeting, however, my editor suggests I should present for the benefit of my less cosmopolitan readers a brief introduction to the nexus city of Khelathra-Ven. I pointed out to him that there were many texts available on the subject and that interested parties would be better served seeking out one of Ms. Zheng's excellent travel guides. He was not moved by this argument, maintaining that the public in general mislikes being referred to secondary materials in the middle of a serialised narrative and that part of my duty as a chronicler is to describe not only events as they transpired but also the background against which those events occurred. Those already familiar with the great city may wish to turn immediately to the next chapter.

Khelathra-Ven is a tripartite municipality composed of the city of Khel to the south, separated from the city of Athra in the north by some six miles of open sea, which can be traversed by the great Rose Gold Bridge. The ruins of Ven lie beneath the waves and are inhabited by strange but not unfriendly creatures native to that environment, and by those unfortunates forced by circumstance to seek lodging in the few air pockets that persist, through the intervention of engineering or sorcery, in the remains of that once-proud metropolis. During my student days, I lived for two months in a coral-strewn garret in one of Ven's more accessible districts. And although the lifestyle was not without its sense of romance, the inconvenience of coming and going by submersible soon came to outstrip the savings that I made on the rent.

It may seem strange to an outsider that a city that is little more than a scattering of ancient and waterlogged ruins could be so integral a part of a thriving, modern nation. The outsider, however, reckons without the influence of the Eternal Lords of Ven, who are the last immortal survivors of an empire that once spanned galaxies. With their blessing, the dimensional gateways through which they had once walked the length and breadth of the cosmos became again stable thoroughfares allowing the passage of trade from not only distant lands but distant worlds and, indeed, distant times.

Today Khelathra-Ven is famed throughout several realities as a haven for innovators, libertines, and, above all, merchants. Many caravans come by land from the Uthmani Sultanate to the south, and a wide expanse to the northeast of the city is given over to the winged beasts and flying machines that make up an increasingly significant part of trade in the modern age. But the bulk of the city's wealth comes from the sea and from the strange portals that lie within it. Hundreds of ships pass through the strait every day, and thousands of travellers from across the infinite potentialities of all that is pass daily through the docks to visit or to trade or to seek their fortunes. Standing on the quayside of an evening one may converse with people from origins as diverse as the Hagiocracy of Pesh, the People's Republic of Carcosa, the red deserts of Marvos, or the dawn of time itself. Whether one would survive these conversations, however, is another matter entirely.

CHAPTER THREE

✤

Ms. Shaharazad Haas

Number 221b Martyrs Walk turned out to be part of a handsome terrace in a clean, geometrical style that had been fashionable a little less than a century earlier. It sported large, square windows and a neat iron balcony that matched the gate and the rail that ran up the steps to the front door. This last was open, but I knocked regardless and received no answer. I thus found myself in something of a quandary. I would never under normal circumstances have entered another person's home uninvited. However, the curious attitude of the door and the silence within caused me genuine concern.

I glanced up and down the street in the hopes of seeing a neighbour or attracting the attention of a Myrmidon—for those readers unfamiliar with the city, the Myrmidons are the peacekeepers of Khelathra-Ven, once tasked with enforcing the will of the ruling council and now primarily concerned with the prevention and punishment of crime—but saw that I was quite alone and unsupported. Tightening my grip on the walking stick (for which on that day I had blessedly little need), I pushed the door wide and entered.

A narrow hallway led me to a well-appointed but chaotically maintained sitting room where a woman with light brown skin and a cascade of black hair sprawled on a chaise longue. No sooner had I entered than she levelled a pistol directly at my heart.

"If you have come to rob me," she said, without so much as glancing in my direction, "you will find that I have nothing worth taking. If you have come to murder me, you will find that I am dead already."

I thought it best to move little and speak calmly. "I have come to do neither. I have come in response to an advertisement."

She swung herself into a sitting position, which better enabled me to observe her, although the bulk of my attention was still occupied by the firearm, which remained trained unerringly upon my person. Ms. S. Haas, assuming it was she (and hindsight vindicates this assumption), was a tall, striking woman of indeterminate age and background. She was dressed in a heavily flounced skirt of emerald-green satin; a gentleman's shirt, somewhat stained with tobacco; and a charcoal-grey tailcoat. There was something of the chimera about her, being leonine of jaw, aquiline of nose, and lupine about the eyes—though, presently, they were dulled by an undiagnosable cocktail of narcotics and intoxicants.

"Perhaps," I suggested, "I have come at a bad time?"

"Young man, I have danced with the gods at the dawn of creation and watched seas swallow worlds at the end of all things. My perspective on time, good or bad, is I suspect very different from your own."

"Am I to understand, then, that you are not looking for a cohabitant?"

"I already have a housemate, as infuriating as I—" She stopped and was silent for the better part of a minute. "Or did he leave? Or die? Or both. And, if both, in which order?"

"Shall I fetch you a glass of water?"

"Water, in its pure form, is far too valuable a reagent to waste on thirst. You may pour me a brandy and you may be quick about it."

I did not think it advisable for her to add alcohol to whatever she had already taken. On the other hand, she did have me at gunpoint. "Would you mind lowering your weapon? It disquiets me rather."

Ms. Haas stared at the pistol with a look of genuine surprise. "Sorry. Forgot I had that."

She cast it casually to the ground, where it discharged into the wall, sending up a spray of plaster dust and shaking loose an incongruously cheerful watercolour of a country cottage. Stepping carefully around piles of books, papers, and discarded syringes, I crossed the room to an ornate sideboard, where rested a selection of fine decanters and glasses. I poured the lady the beverage she had requested and passed it to her with as much composure as I could muster.

She regarded it warily for a moment and then tossed it back with the proficiency of a sailor on shore leave. Then she stood, shaking out her skirts, and while I consider myself neither especially courageous nor especially cowardly, I thought it best to take a step back. She turned the glass in her hand, watching the light catch upon the crystal, and, when she had satisfied whatever curiosity drove her, returned it calmly to its fellows.

"The rent is due monthly," she said, as if continuing a conversation I was fairly certain we had not been having. "It comes to seventeen Athran florins, twelve Khelish rials, an equivalent value in seed pearls, sourced from wherever you wish, seventy-eight Eyan shillings, a Marvosi trade dagger, or three and a half lines from a Seravic chant of commerce. You may pay it to me or to the landlady directly. Her name is Mrs. Hive, and she infests the attic. Do not enter it without permission on pain of agonising death. There is no laundry service."

"Yes. The advertisement mentioned that fact." That is, it had mentioned the lack of laundry service. The possibility of agonising death, although present for one reason or another in a number of rented properties in Khelathra-Ven, was habitually elided from public notices.

She moved to where the picture had fallen, picked it up, appeared to consider rehanging it, and finally put it down again. "It is a matter of tremendous inconvenience to me."

"I am quite capable of washing my own shirts."

Ms. Haas's eyes glittered in a manner I did not find entirely comforting. As it transpired, my misgivings were justified, for, within the week, I would become responsible for all of the household laundry and would remain so for the entire duration of our relationship. I should clarify for those readers who may be shocked by this situation that there were certain items of clothing I refused to handle, and for which Ms. Haas made her own arrangements into which I did not enquire.

"When can you move in?" she asked.

At this, I hesitated. While it is true that my circumstances were dire I was not certain that I had sunk so low as to share rooms with quite so singular an individual. Despite the reputation of my countrymen, I endeavour to refrain from judging others. However, this lady seemed to spend her days lying in a drug-addled haze with the front door open, casually discharging pistols into the wainscoting, and I did not believe that these were desirable traits in a housemate.

I cast about for a diplomatic way to extricate myself and settled on, "Do you not wish to ask me for references or question me as to my character or background?"

"Why would I need to do that?" She swung round, her skirts knocking over a precariously balanced collection of alchemical apparatus and a human-looking skull. "You were born in the Kingdom of Ey sometime before the revolution, raised in the Church of the Creator, educated abroad, probably in Khel, perhaps in Dvesh, but not Marvos or Carcosa. You have returned recently from military service in the Company of Strangers, where you acquitted yourself well but were forced into early retirement by injury. Your instincts run towards kindness and you are not easily startled. You are fastidious in your personal habits but tolerant of those who are less so. All of which suggest that you may, perhaps uniquely amongst the inhabitants of this city, be able to put up with me."

"My goodness," I exclaimed. "How could you possibly know such things?"

She stared at me speculatively for longer than most people would have considered polite. And, just when I was on the verge of protesting, she flung herself back on the chaise with greater animation than she had hitherto demonstrated. "I must thank you, Mr. . . . I'm sorry, I didn't catch your name."

"It is Wyndham, madam. John Wyndham."

"In which case, I must thank you, Mr. Wyndham. I had expected to spend today imprisoned in the chancery of my own mind, havering between ennui and self-destruction. But you have quite perked me up."

I was slightly at a loss. "Oh, good."

"Since you expressed an interest, I shall explain to you how I know the things that I know. Or at least, some of them. The rest would drive you insane."

She dug between the cushions of the chaise longue and retrieved an ornate, pearl-handled pipe. A nearby table held a stack of the daily papers and the assorted accoutrements of my new associate's various habits, amongst them a packet of tobacco that bore the name of the popular brand Valentino's Good Rough Shag. She pulled some out, packed it into the bowl, and spoke a word in a tongue so ancient and alien that it made my stomach twist and my eyes water. A flame flared briefly into being at the end of her pipe. Khelathra-Ven has few cultural taboos, especially when compared to my homeland, but the outright and flagrant practice of sorcery is one of them. I thought it polite not to mention this.

"Now then. To your question." Ms. Haas brought the holder to her lips and inhaled deeply, smoke billowing forth with indecorous excess. "Your origins are simple to discern. You dress plainly, avoiding any form of ornamentation. Your clothes are fastened with hooks rather than buttons and your accent is decidedly northern. This marks you as a member of the Reformed Church of the Creator and a native of Ey. That you have left the kingdom and are presently seeking to take lodgings with a sorceress suggests you are not a zealot. That you nevertheless abide by the strict sumptuary laws of your homeland suggests that your manner of presentation is a habit formed in early childhood. Since the church would have been illegal in Ey until you were at least eleven or twelve it follows that your parents were revolutionaries. From here, the matter becomes what you are doing in Khelathra-Ven. People from your part of the world are a rarity in this city, but you have the look of one who is accustomed to us and our ways. This suggests that although you have retained the habits in which you were raised you have been exposed to other ways of life and modes of thinking. A foreign education, then, almost certainly here, or else you would have returned to the city in which you had attended university."

"Why, this is extraordinary. But how did you know I had served with the Company of Strangers?"

"My dear man, it's written all over you. Most obviously, you have the kind of pallor that a person only acquires living for a considerable period of time in the lands around the Unending Gate, where the sun never rises. Further, you hold yourself with military bearing, and you did not flinch when I pointed a pistol at you, nor when the weapon discharged. This suggests not only experience in battle but also several personal qualities that would all but guarantee your advancement. You were clearly injured, since you walk with a stick. The fact that you do not at present seem to need it suggests that your wound was courtesy of one of the peculiar weapons favoured by the legions of the Empress of Nothing."

Somewhat disconcerted, I looked for somewhere to sit. I removed what I hoped wasn't—but feared was—a dead dog from the seat of a wingback chair and lowered myself gratefully into it. Of course, I would normally not have sat in the presence of a lady without direct invitation, but I had reached the conclusion that waiting for Ms. Haas to observe such niceties was a doomed endeavour. Again, this instinct was proven correct by better acquaintance. In all the time I knew her, Ms. Shaharazad Haas never showed the slightest regard for the rules of society, the laws of the land, or the inviolable principles of the cosmos.

The ash from her pipe drifted to the carpet, where it was lost amongst the carnage. "This brings us," she continued, "to the rather trivial matter of your personality. Much of this can be inferred from the conclusions I had already reached about your history, upbringing, and education. The rest from the way you reacted to encountering a strange woman clearly out of her mind on a staggeringly dangerous and transparently illegal collection of alkaloids, opioids, and mystical tinctures threatening you with a firearm and inviting you to come and live with her."

Thus it was that I moved into 221b Martyrs Walk and began my long acquaintance with the sorceress Shaharazad Haas.

❦

CHAPTER FOUR

221b Martyrs Walk

Number 221b Martyrs Walk was, and to the best of my knowledge still is, a comfortable townhouse boasting two well-appointed bedrooms, a spacious sitting room, facilities that I shall not detail but which proved adequate for one's daily ablutions, and a kitchen wherein I prepared my meals and Ms. Haas made occasional sacrifices to dark gods.

My editor has suggested to me that, since some readers may hail from worlds whose local physical laws and native occult practices differ from ours, it might be prudent to outline for them the precise manner in which Ms. Haas's sorceries manifested themselves. It became quickly apparent to me during our acquaintance that she was an adherent of no specific arcane discipline but rather had acquired an eclectic and terrifying collection of rites, rituals, secret names, and forbidden bargains that permitted her, in the proper circumstances, to achieve such diverse effects as conjuring spirits from the beyond and returning them thereto, speaking with the dead, commanding wind and weather, surviving near-fatal injury through the never-to-be-courted intercession of blasphemous deities, effortlessly locating missing socks (a power she would often refuse to use for my benefit despite my full knowledge of her possession of it), altering her appearance at will, springing locks with a touch, striking her enemies with debilitating afflictions, talking to cats, the invocation of flame ex nihilo via the True Words of Shaping (this being one of the most spiritually taxing and closely guarded mysteries of the cosmos and the one she had flagrantly used to light her pipe when we first met), and sundry magics of guiding, seeking, warding, and guarding, the broad utility of which she would use to supplement her other activities.

Ms. Haas's supernatural experimentation, like many of her habits, had a tendency to make a mess of the fixtures and, like many of her habits, earned her the displeasure of Mrs. Hive. It was some days before I made the acquaintance of our landlady, and the meeting was sadly not auspicious. She was, at the time, occupying the corpse of a stevedore, which I learned she had purchased from a resurrection man the month before. During my time in the sunless lands I had faced numerous horrors and flatter myself that I maintained my composure appropriately, but the wasps crawling from the body's empty eye sockets left me rather uncertain where I should, in civility, rest my gaze, which presented a hopefully understandable impediment to social intercourse. Mrs. Hive had wished to confront Ms. Haas about the poltergeist which my housemate had unleashed in the most recent of her rituals, but finding the lady in a drug-addled stupor, she had come to me for an explanation instead. Hoping to smooth matters over, I reassured her that Ms. Haas had been able to bind the spirit within a hatstand before it could cause too much damage to the property, and opined that the occasional trembling from the newly haunted item of furniture could perhaps be seen as giving the hallway a pleasing air of mystery. This line of reasoning did not satisfy her, and she was very cold with me for several days afterwards.

As for my cohabitant, the initial weeks of our acquaintance were, on my part, a process of rapid acclimatisation and, on her part, a process of occasionally remembering my existence. Having lived with both students and soldiers I had long since ceased to expect others to abide by the conventions of the society in which I was raised. Over the past decade I had become well used to people speaking the private names of deities, inviting unchaperoned guests into their rooms, and openly discussing matters that, in Ey, would be considered unassailably private. I was less accustomed to a companion who staggered home at three in the morning, her skirts stained with blood, and who would then proceed to engage me in a two-hour conversation about the distinguishing characteristics of certain fungi, before finally falling asleep on my bed. This last habit of hers meant that I had, in a sense, gone from living in my friend's sitting room to living in my own.

At times she would disappear for a day or more and return either full of stories or full of silence as the mood took her. One afternoon, she burned that awful watercolour in a fit of rage, the cause of which I never discovered, then promptly retired to her chamber, whence she did not emerge for long enough that I sincerely feared she may have died. At any other stage of my life I would have never transgressed the boundaries of a lady's boudoir but, on more than one occasion over my long friendship with Ms. Haas, I was required to set propriety aside and check that she had not smothered herself in the night or transported her spirit to some other plane of reality. I generally found her quite well. At times she was grateful for my concern. Upon others she would assail me with missiles or curses. In summary, my tenure at 221b Martyrs Walk was often frustrating and frequently terrifying but never, ever dull.

A peculiarity of Ms. Haas's lifestyle was that, although I knew for certain she had a variety of colourful friends and associates, she seldom invited guests to the house. It was, therefore, a matter of some curiosity to me when one evening, a little over a month after I moved in, a lady called for her.

CHAPTER FIVE

Miss Eirene Viola

I was first alerted to the presence of our visitor by the ringing of the doorbell and the buzzing from the attic as Mrs. Hive forced her way into one of her cadaverous puppets.

"It's quite all right," I called, rising from my armchair. "I'll go."

Perhaps it was presumptuous of me but, even in Khelathra-Ven, a dead body full of wasps did not cut a welcoming figure.

Opening the front door, which I had finally persuaded my companion that we should keep locked, I found upon the step a lady of notable beauty, dressed in a manner that spoke of taste but not extravagance. While I lacked Ms. Haas's unusual perspicacity, I did not require it in order to recognise that our visitor was in a state of considerable agitation.

"Where's Shaharazad?" she demanded.

"I fear she is indisposed."

"Then redispose her. I must speak to her at once."

I stood aside to allow her ingress, and she swept past me into the sitting room. My efforts over the last weeks had rendered it somewhat more habitable, although I had been able to do little about the bullet holes and scorch marks, or the pervading scent of tobacco and wormwood.

"Please do sit," I said, "well, anywhere that you can."

My concerns for the lady's comfort proved to be unfounded. She draped herself over the chaise longue as though she belonged upon it. By the light of the standard lamp, I could see that she was approximately the same age as myself. Her hair was dark, as was common in the city, and twisted into some feminine knot that I could neither describe nor reproduce. Most arresting of all were her eyes, which were a brown so pale as to be almost yellow and caught the lamplight strangely.

While I would normally have offered refreshment, I thought it best to fetch Ms. Haas with the utmost expediency. I first attempted to achieve this by knocking politely but firmly on her bedroom door. She ignored me. I called her name twice and, when she continued to pay me no mind, resigned myself to entering.

I found her lying crosswise over her bed, in a somewhat immodest position, propped on her elbows over a large, leather-bound tome, her ankles plainly visible behind her and adorned by bracelets.

She didn't look up. "It is impolite, Captain, to enter a lady's bed-chamber uninvited."

"I attempted to announce myself, but you did not respond."

"I hoped you would go away."

I fortified my equanimity. "You have a visitor, Ms. Haas."

"Tell whoever it is that they may wait if they wish. But they are likely to starve."

"The lady seems most insistent."

"Mr. Wyndham. I am currently attempting to encompass the secret names of the star-demons of Vz'att. This I find interesting. You and your mysterious guest I currently find boring. Persuade me otherwise."

Later in our relationship I would be well versed in those things that would capture Ms. Haas's attention and those that would not. At this time, however, I was forced to take a proverbial shot in the dark. "She asked for you by name."

"I am the sorceress Shaharazad Haas. The whole city knows my name. And those citizens who do not wish me dead and, come to think of it, some of those who do have frequent need for my services."

"She is in a state of some distress."

Ms. Haas turned the page. "How sad for her. Tedious."

I was starting to feel a little desperate. "She's very pretty?" I tried.

"How pretty?"

"I am not sure I'm accustomed to quantifying these things." Indeed, there were few things I was less qualified to judge. "Her eyes, I think, are quite fine. They are an unusual shade."

Her head came up. "Blood red? Viridian? Wholly crafted from copper and emblazoned with sigils of warding? Like unto a window over an endless void wherein stars gutter and die eternally?"

"Um." This was not going to end well. "More sort of light brown?"

"Yellow-brown or grey-brown?"

"Yellow-brown."

She leapt up in a billow of purple silk. "Honestly, Wyndham. Why did you not mention this before? Sometimes I think you are intent upon wasting my time."

She made for the door.

"Surely," I cried, "you are not intending to greet this lady clad only in a dressing gown?"

"How right you are, Captain." Pausing by her dresser, which was strewn with a wild tangle of items, several of them mine, she selected a single earring—a modest pearl on a golden chain—and affixed it to her ear. "There."

And, with that, she pushed past me into the corridor.

Having done my duty, I repaired to my room, only to be violently roused moments later by the sound of shouting from the sitting room. It was against my instincts to pry, but the debate sounded so acrimonious that I honestly feared for the safety of one or both parties.

I made my way cautiously downstairs, where I found our guest standing in the middle of the room, while Ms. Haas paced its confines with the energy and menace of a caged panther.

". . . frankly insulting," she was saying, "that you consider it possible I would do such a thing."

The other lady retained her composure where many would surely have faltered. "What else am I to think? I know of three people you have personally murdered, one you drove to madness for slighting you, six you left to die in the ash wastes of Telash-Ur, and at least four you fed to the Princes of the Mocking Realm."

"Indeed, I have done all of these things, and more. And yet you still believe that I would resort to blackmail in order to prevent you from marrying a fishmonger?"

At this, the stranger lost all self-possession. Pulling a long pin from her hair, she flicked it at Ms. Haas with uncanny speed and unerring accuracy.

My cohabitant raised a hand, allowing the missile to embed itself into her palm. "That," she said, "was uncalled for."

"Cora is not a fishmonger. She is a member in good standing with the Ubiquitous Company of Fishers."

"She's a tedious little bourgeois." Blood began to pool in the centre of Ms. Haas's hand and she watched it with an air of studied detachment. "And you deserve better."

"I love her, Shaharazad. It's not something I'd expect you to understand."

With an exasperated sigh, Ms. Haas drew the pin slowly from her flesh and licked the tip. "Not even poisoned, dear. I'm not sure if that means you really do care or you really don't."

"Neither am I." Our unexpectedly intemperate guest returned to the chaise longue and arranged herself decorously upon it once more. "But it seems I do need your help."

"Then you shall have it." Ms. Haas settled into the wingback chair and stuck the pin into the arm, where I was quite certain it would shortly do someone an injury. "And as for you, Mr. Wyndham, since you have nothing better to do than hover in doorways, you might as well make yourself useful."

She picked up a notebook from a pile at her feet and flung it towards me. I caught it with only a mild twinge from my shoulder and claimed the other chair. In truth, I wasn't sure what use I could be, besides note taking and moral support, but it was oddly pleasing to be included. Having resolved the immediate crisis of my accommodation, and my journey to the hospital being so much shorter than it once was, I had found my evenings curiously empty. There are, of course, a great multitude of diversions available in the city of Khelathra-Ven, but my temperament and upbringing left the vast majority of them either unappealing or inaccessible. Growing up in Ey, I never developed the habits of drinking, dancing, visiting the theatre, or, indeed, engaging in any pastime that did not involve venerating the name of the Creator. And, while I have no strong objection to such activities today, it is difficult for me to engage in them without the excuse of a companion.

Crossing one leg over the other, Ms. Haas produced a packet of tobacco and retrieved her pipe from where it had rolled under the chair. "Perhaps introductions are in order. Eirene, this is Captain John Wyndham. He's from the Commonwealth, which explains most of it, and has lived with me for a month, which explains the rest. Mr. Wyndham, this is Eirene Viola. I first met her after she was forced to flee Carcosa some dozen years ago. We . . ."

Here Ms. Haas described in far greater detail than was necessary the nature of her prior relationship with Miss Viola. Modesty forbids me from repeating any of it in these pages.

When my companion showed no sign of concluding her discourse, I awaited an appropriate pause and enquired, "What manner of assistance did you require, madam?"

"She's being blackmailed."

At this, Miss Viola turned a sharp gaze upon my companion. "She's also capable of speaking for herself."

"Then by all means tell the good captain what you have already intimated to me." Ms. Haas lit her pipe, this time without the use of forbidden sorcery, and put it to her lips. "I shall endeavour to amuse myself."

I readied my pen and bade Miss Viola tell me her story. The substance of it was thus. She had come to Khelathra-Ven following the popular uprising in Carcosa, that strange city so ancient and so famed that I am given to understand its notoriety has reached even the most backward of realities. Immediately following her arrival, she had fallen in with a bad crowd, of which I understood Ms. Haas had been a part. The lady was vague on the details of her life since, but I had a strong sense she had been a thief and an adventuress and had dabbled in sorcery. Any one of these would have disqualified her from marriage to any respectable person, even in Khelathra-Ven.

In the last year she had met and fallen in love with a warden of the Ubiquitous Company of Fishers (which, for those unfamiliar with the social and commercial institutions of Khelathra-Ven, is one of the city's many influential trade guilds) by the name of Cora Beck. Miss Beck's family had already expressed misgivings about their daughter's engagement to a Carcosan immigrant, and Miss Viola was concerned that any hint of scandal would destroy all hope of their formal union. The blackmail material had so far consisted of a single anonymous letter demanding that Miss Viola break off the engagement on pain of certain secrets being made public. This letter she produced and handed to me for my perusal.

CHAPTER SIX

The Mysterious Letter

To the Lady Eirene Viola Delhali, daughter of the late Count
of Hyades,
You are to break your engagement with Miss Cora Beck or
else she, her family, and all society will learn precisely what
happened to Benoit Roux.
Do not try me. Do not test me.
I hold your future in my hands.

"If I might ask," I said, having examined the epistle, "what *did* happen to Benoit Roux?"

Ms. Haas opened her eyes. "He was one of the four."

"The four?"

"Do pay attention, Wyndham. The four persons Eirene accused me of feeding to the Princes of the Mocking Realm. She neglected to mention she was as much a part of that affair as I was."

"I was seventeen," protested Miss Viola. "I had just fled my homeland and was hiding in fear for my life from armed and fanatical militants. You were two decades my senior and I truly believed I was in love with you."

"You can hardly hold *me* responsible for *your* youthful follies."

"But I can hold you responsible for persuading me that my surest chance of evading my pursuers was to strike a pact with the lords of a psychedelic otherworld."

Ms. Haas blew a perfectly formed smoke ring. "Well, it worked."

I glanced once more at the letter and then at my notes. "Might we perhaps further address the question of the gentleman you murdered?"

"He wasn't a gentleman," drawled Ms. Haas. "He was new money at best. And a thoroughly unpleasant fellow."

"I'm not sure that makes it right to kill him."

"How dare you, Captain. I certainly did not kill him. Eirene and I simply contrived a situation in which Master Roux, of his own free will, exposed himself to extradimensional forces that tragically consumed him. Had he been less venal, he would be with us today. Not in this room, of course. Ghastly man."

As I've said before, and will say again over the course of this manuscript, I strive never to judge others. I was nonetheless given serious pause by the content of this conversation. And, in truth, I am not entirely certain why I remained part of it or continued to keep company with Ms. Haas afterwards. I can only say that I have never made excuses for my friend's behaviour and do, on some level, know that she has done heinous things. But I have also never known her to act without purpose nor with wanton malice, and I believe I must have understood this fact even then. Besides which, to be in the presence of the sorceress Shaharazad Haas was to glimpse a world more beautiful, more terrible, and more limitless than anything I could hitherto have imagined.

Miss Viola drew another pin from her hair, letting the whole mass of it come tumbling down, and then began the complex work of re-binding it. "So you see why I came here. Apart from you and I, very few people know what happened to Benoit."

Tapping out her pipe on the cover of a blameless volume of Ilari love poetry, Ms. Haas rose and snatched the letter from my hand. "Twelve years ago, precisely three people knew: you, me, and du

Maurier. All it takes is for one of us to have told one person at some point over the past decade and, suddenly, we have no idea who knows what."

"If I might ask," I asked, "who is du Maurier?"

"Another ghastly man," returned Ms. Haas. "Although he is the chief servant of the Princes of the Mocking Realm, they have thus far failed to devour him. He runs an extradimensional fleapit of a theatre called Mise en Abyme."

Miss Viola gave a little sigh. "He's also an inconceivable braggart, which means he could have told anybody. Which means the letter could have come from anybody."

"Not anybody." Ms. Haas turned the letter over and peered closely at its obverse. "Just not necessarily someone directly connected to that incident. You know, you've been a wonderfully naughty girl over the years. I'm sure you've left a veritable legion of jilted lovers, double-crossed associates, and good old-fashioned victims who'd relish the opportunity to even the score."

"Which means," said Miss Viola, rather sharply, "that you've narrowed the list of suspects down from 'everyone' to 'everyone I've ever annoyed.' I'm so glad I came to you, Shaharazad. Your reputation is nothing if not deserved."

"Are you like this with the fishmonger? If so, a little blackmail is likely to be the least of your matrimonial impediments."

"You bring out the worst in me. As you do in most people."

"You flatter me, dear." Ms. Haas took a turn about the room. "But to return to your current problem, it is a simple matter of triangulation. We know that whoever sent this letter has reason to wish you harm and has access to at least a small amount of personal information, some of which must have originated at Mise en Abyme. Further, the specific harm they seem to wish you speaks volumes as to their motives. No attempt has been made to extort you financially, suggesting that they have no especial need for money. Nor have they threatened you with violence, suggesting someone comfortable with casual cruelty but held back from more direct interventions by conscience or cowardice. Finally, we know that this individual is right-handed and expected you to recognise their script. It is really very straightforward."

My own pen had been near flying off the page as I attempted to keep pace with Ms. Haas's rapid exposition. "I wouldn't use that word exactly, but I believe I can follow your reasoning," I said. "At least until you reached the subject of handedness."

"Whatever is the matter with you, Mr. Wyndham?" She spun round to confront me. "Was it not obvious the moment you looked at the letter that the writer had used the hand they did not favour? Why do such a thing if not to disguise your handwriting from the intended recipient? And since the sloping of the ascenders and descenders is quite characteristic of the use of the left hand, it follows that our blackmailer is ordinarily right-handed."

I took the note back and considered it with fresh eyes. Now it had been pointed out to me, I could indeed discern that the writing was shaky and ill formed, as if written with the off hand, and that the letters sloped backwards. It would simply never have occurred to me to see such details as significant. Over the coming years, I would learn to observe things a little more as Ms. Haas did, an exercise from which I have derived both satisfaction and utility, although I never attained her facility.

Setting the paper aside, I asked, "Is there anything else we can conclude from the letter?"

"Not by casual examination. The paper is of ordinary quality and could likely have been purchased from any stationer's in the city. The ink likewise. There was no postmark so I assume it was hand delivered, but messengers are only a little more expensive than . . ." And here, I am sorry to say, Ms. Haas made a most inappropriate comparison that I would prefer not to repeat. "If you think yourself able,

Captain, perhaps you could employ your professional training to test this letter and the envelope for any alchemical traces that may indicate who has handled it or where it has come from."

"I should be glad to."

She retrieved her tobacco and refilled her pipe. "Meanwhile, Eirene, I recommend you return home and begin compiling a list of possible suspects. Start with everyone who might want to harm you, and then eliminate those who are in no position to do so or who would choose to do so by other methods. Of those who remain, discard the ones who are left-handed or who have never written you a letter."

Having given us our instructions, Ms. Haas retired abruptly.

CHAPTER SEVEN

The Five Names

I scarcely saw Ms. Haas for the next day or so, although I heard her moving about 221b Martyrs Walk at odd hours. For my part, I took the letter into the hospital and began the lengthy process of testing it alchemically for any clues as to its origin. To my considerable regret and frustration, all of the spiritual residues—the transubstantially detectable traces that all sentient beings leave on everything they touch, interact with, or, in extreme cases, think too much about—I was able to distil were quickly identified as belonging to either myself, Ms. Haas, or Miss Viola. Having concluded my shift, I hurried home to report my findings.

I discovered Ms. Haas in the sitting room, surrounded by an undulating cityscape of newspapers, reference works, and handwritten notes. "Ah," she said, "Captain. What news?"

I settled into the wingback chair. "Very little, I fear. As you suspected, the paper is of very ordinary manufacture and my analyses revealed no evidence of the letter's having been handled by a third party."

"And what does that tell you?"

"It would have been difficult to write, seal, and deliver a letter without leaving any alchemical trace of your presence. This would suggest that the blackmailer took great care and may even have had specific knowledge of the transubstantial sciences."

She gazed at me for a moment. Having grown accustomed to her personal habits, it was startling, and a little unsettling, to find myself the subject of her unwavering scrutiny. "That is certainly one explanation," she murmured.

"Are there others?"

"Always, Mr. Wyndham. In my world, to disregard the impossible is to limit oneself needlessly. In this case, however, we shall begin with what is merely probable." She indicated the carnage of printed matter scattered about her. "I have narrowed Eirene's accomplished list of enemies to the five most promising names. The sixth file"—she gestured to a slew of papers piled haphazardly against one wall—"concerns the associates of Miss Cora Beck. While it is most likely that our blackmailer comes from our client's past, we cannot rule out the possibility that they are, in fact, targeting her fiancée indirectly."

Having served in the Company of Strangers, my life has not been wholly without incident, but warfare, in my experience, is long periods of tedium punctuated by flashes of terror. What I now felt was something rather different: the sense that one was about to embark upon a true adventure. Of course, I was cognisant of the fact that my present excitement was possible only because Miss Viola found herself in a thoroughly unpleasant situation, a reflection that tempered my enthusiasm less than it should have.

I leaned forward a little in my chair and enquired, "Will you tell me a little of your findings?"

"I suppose that I could." For all the nonchalance of her tone, Ms. Haas launched eagerly into an exegesis. "Charles du Maurier is the first, most obvious, and least interesting suspect."

"Because he knew of the unfortunate Mr. Roux?"

"That, and because he's . . ." Here Ms. Haas gave me a detailed and unflattering summary of Mr. du Maurier's character in terms sufficiently colourful that I would not even attempt to put them before my readers. "Which," she concluded, "makes him exactly the sort of person to stoop to blackmail. He considered both Eirene and me his protégés at one time or another, a belief in which, I should stress, he was profoundly mistaken, at least in my case. Before I even met the man I had stolen curses from the Elder Witches of the Hundred Kingdoms and caught spirits in nets spun from moonlight. And while he was drinking cheap brandy and bothering actresses I was walking the Vitrine Road and reading the tales of the Other Kind of Glass. He's a petty, grasping, arrogant coward who, in a rare display of good taste, was briefly obsessed with Eirene. Trying to ruin her marriage is exactly the kind of uninspired excuse for spite I'd expect from him."

As it seemed likely that my companion would extemporise on the gentleman's faults indefinitely, I thought it best to move the matter on. "You mentioned that he operated a theatre?"

"Of sorts. Mise en Abyme is a one part playhouse, one part nightmarish pseudoreality ruled by capricious, thought-devouring ungods."

"That must make it difficult to attract an audience."

"You underestimate the Khelathran love of spectacle."

She passed me a playbill advertising a production of *The Exceeding Violente, Piteous & Unnatural Fayte of Goode King Leontius's Virgin Daughter*, and I could not help but notice Miss Viola's name beneath the title. "But this looks like the worst kind of salacious, unimproving, improper—"

"Yes, so you can see why it's so popular." Ms. Haas grinned with disconcerting relish. "The small risk of having one's soul devoured just adds a little extra frisson."

"I find it hard to believe a lady like Miss Viola could appear in such tawdry entertainment."

"Mr. Wyndham, if you're going to be shocked every time you discover that Eirene did something unsavoury, this is going to be a *very* long conversation. Besides, as I recall she was rather good. Of course"—she handed me another flyer—"he has since acquired a new heroine. A Miss Katrina de la Martynière."

"If," I suggested, "Miss de la Martynière is an intimate of Mr. du Maurier might she not also wish harm upon Miss Viola?"

"You forget that our blackmailer expected Eirene to be familiar with their handwriting."

I blushed. "Of course, how foolish of me."

"Pay attention, Captain, and I'm sure you'll improve with time. Now, let us move on."

My discomfort at my recent error was somewhat ameliorated by the notion that Ms. Haas foresaw a future in which she did not tire of me. "Who is our next suspect?"

"One Mr. Enoch Reef."

"Enoch Reef!" Although there were more notorious criminals in Ven, the infamy of Mr. Reef was sufficient that even I, with my relatively limited exposure to the seamier side of the city, had heard of him. His star had been somewhat on the rise while I was at university and, when I had rooms in Ven, his name was spoken regularly, usually in the context of a fellow student seeking to supplement their income by selling this or that item of gossip on the open market. "I find it hard to believe a lady like Miss Viola could—"

Ms. Haas retrieved her pistol from close at hand and discharged it into the ceiling. "Mr. Wyndham, I gave you *quite explicit* instructions. Eirene Viola is, or at the very least used to be, a delightfully wicked woman. She has done many delightfully wicked things. Live with it."

"But she comports herself so respectably."

"And therein lies her charm. And, indeed, a large part of the reason she was so useful to Mr. Reef for so many years."

"Given his position on your list, I take it that they did not part on good terms?"

She absentmindedly reloaded the firearm and tossed it onto a pile

Prescott Public Library
www.prescottlibrary.info
(928)777-1500
Renew Items: (928)777-
7476

- Checkout Receipt -

Patron Barcode:
Number of items: 2
Barcode: 31449005365962
Title: The affair of the mysterious letter
Due: 04/22/2022

Barcode: 31504000603468
Title: Hot pots : container gardening in
the arid Southwest
Due: 04/22/2022

04/01/2022 10:40:22 AM

of discarded papers. "Indeed they did not. Some years ago Mr. Reef acquired a confidential client list belonging to the Ossuary Bank."

"Good heavens," I exclaimed. "That seems a dangerous thing to possess."

"But immensely valuable."

That it would undoubtedly be. The soul-changers of the Ossuary Bank embodied two of Khelathra-Ven's most despised and most indispensable professions, being at once bankers and necromancers. They offered loans at competitive rates of interest, asking only an eternity of service after death as collateral. This in turn gave them access to a veritable army of spirits with which they could secure their vaults and discourage their opposition, and who the city's wealthier luminaries were able to hire at a princely sum for sundry unthinkable purposes.

"Unfortunately for Mr. Reef"—Ms. Haas rose from amongst the detritus of her researches, stretching with immodest enthusiasm—"the bank has very efficient mechanisms for safeguarding its secrets."

"I'm surprised Mr. Reef survived the experience."

At that, she turned to me with a faintly mocking smile. "The Ossuary Bank has a thoroughly terrifying reputation but, as I know well from personal experience, the great advantage of a terrifying reputation is that one seldom needs to act on it. The bank learned long ago that bribery and subversion are far more effective means to achieve their goals than armies of shambling corpses and shrieking spirits. They simply paid a large but tolerable sum of money to one of Mr. Reef's associates, and she stole the list back for them."

"That associate being Miss Viola," I remarked. "It would explain why Mr. Reef might wish her harm. But surely such a man would have both the means and the inclination to seek more violent retribution."

"My dear Mr. Wyndham, it seems that in your world there are but two sorts of person. Those who are incapable of any vice and those who indulge wantonly in all of them." Stepping over a pile of newspaper clippings, Ms. Haas retrieved a decanter from the sideboard and, having recently smashed all the tumblers in a fit of distemper, drank from it directly. "Many an upstanding citizen has resorted to murder for profit and many a licentious reprobate has stopped short of it."

This would not be the last time that Ms. Haas gave me occasion to reflect on assumptions I had not hitherto examined. Although her approach to morality was often disturbingly flexible, I realise now that my own—for all my attempts to move beyond the rigidity of my father's teachings—was, in many ways, shamefully limited. Over the long course of our acquaintance, she introduced me to a bewildering number of new perspectives and experiences. Many of them were near fatal but, taken as a whole, I sincerely believe they made me a better man. And for that I shall always be thankful to the sorceress Shaharazad Haas, wherever she may be.

"Besides," she went on, "Reef trades in information. It is his most precious commodity and his most dangerous weapon. Should his thoughts turn to vengeance, there would be no better way for him to pursue it."

My wound, which had given no difficulty at all these past several days, suddenly jabbed me in the ribs. I adjusted my position to compensate. "Then it seems we have two promising leads."

"Quite so, and the remaining three are scarcely less promising. The first, Mrs. Yasmine Benamara, is a poetess of some small repute and the wife of a noted barrister-priest. She and Eirene had a rather disastrous affair that severely damaged both her husband's career and her marriage. She apparently swore to Eirene that she would ruin her future happiness by any means at her disposal."

That Miss Viola had been so brazen as to seduce a married woman once again startled me. But, the pistol still being nearby and the ceiling having suffered quite enough for one day, I made an outward show of equanimity. "A marriage for a marriage seems a plausible motivation, but would a barrister's wife really have the means to uncover the fate of Mr. Roux?"

"She moves in artistic circles. Her set are more conventional than those found at Mise en Abyme, but I'd be amazed if there was no overlap. On top of which, she has an income and it wouldn't be so very difficult for her to hire an investigator or an informer." My companion, who I was fast learning could not abide stillness, began pacing in front of the fireplace, pausing occasionally to sip from the decanter. "That just leaves the prince and the vampire."

I spluttered. "I beg your pardon?"

"One of Eirene's former lovers was the Contessa Ilona of Mircalla. My sources inform me that she has recently returned to the city and, vampires being notoriously possessive, I think it highly probable she would have concocted some scheme to win back Eirene's affections. She appears so far down my list only because blackmail seems an uncharacteristically subtle strategy for such a creature."

Since the Witch King Iustinian had counted a number of vampires amongst his court, and the church taught that they were unholy abominations in the sight of the Creator, I was inclined to concur but, having been recently chastened for my ethical simplicity, I said simply, "I am sure I would not know."

"I mean they vary, of course, like any species, but the typical modus operandi is something rather more along the lines of 'fly in on black wings of night, slaughter everybody you care about, and carry you away to a terrifying isolated castle.'" She paused, seemingly caught in something I could have sworn was nostalgia. "Nasty letters and veiled threats are so lacking in panache. But we live in changing times, and even the undying nobility have difficulty keeping their standards up these days."

"And the prince?" I asked.

"Icarius Castaigne. Not technically a prince, but one must be allowed a little artistic licence now and again. Before Eirene left Carcosa she was betrothed to a scion of another of the great houses. For the last decade, she's believed that he died in the revolution—either killed in the fighting or executed as an enemy of the people—but she discovered recently that he had survived, renounced his previous lands and titles, and accepted a position within the party."

Hailing from a revolutionary background myself, I had followed the story of the popular uprising in Carcosa with some interest and had, in all candour, mixed feelings about the affair. The ancient regime had been a byword for decadence and corruption throughout the cosmos, but the stories one heard of the new People's Republic were hardly less disturbing. There was talk of disappearances, of secret police, of labour camps and show trials. I was not sure what I thought of a man who would willingly serve such an administration, but perhaps he was only doing what was necessary in order to survive.

"But why," I wondered aloud, "would somebody who had gone to such lengths to distance himself from his former life go to still greater lengths merely to ruin the happiness of a woman who now lives in another reality and of whom, in all likelihood, he has not thought in years?"

Ms. Haas's attitude remained somewhat wistful. "Back in the good old days, Carcosan court intrigues were fabulously intricate, to say nothing of being tremendous fun. I mean, for the people who weren't driven mad by them. I'll admit it's an outside chance but, in my experience, betraying your peers to a hostile power that threatens your entire way of life, vanishing mysteriously for a decade, and then pursuing your former fiancée with cryptic blackmail letters is *exactly* the kind of thing that Carcosan nobility used to do all the time."

This was not the first time, even given the relative brevity of our acquaintance thus far, that Ms. Haas had demonstrated an understanding of "fun" that differed not only from my own (as, in fairness, did those of most people) but from everybody else's as well. It would certainly not be the last. I elected not to draw attention to the fact at this juncture.

"And which of these individuals," I asked, "do you think most likely to be the culprit?"

Ms. Haas cast herself upon the chaise longue and draped an arm across her brow. "Du Maurier. He has the most direct connection to the events described in the letter; his character fits a blackmailer perfectly; he has no need for money; and he is petty." She sighed. "It would be so much more interesting were it to be somebody less obvious. But criminals seldom value originality."

"I'm sure Miss Viola would prefer that the matter be straightforward rather than interesting."

"Mr. Wyndham, I'm a consulting sorceress. My job is to do what my clients cannot. Their happiness is not my concern."

I was forced to concede that, on some level, she had a point. Although I could not shake the feeling that on another, more fundamental level she had missed it entirely. "So, are we to bring our suspicions to the Myrmidons?"

"Certainly not." She flicked her fingers in a languid, dismissive motion. "Firstly, Eirene, whose feelings you apparently care about intensely, would not wish it. Secondly, the last thing this case needs is a gang of jackbooted thugs like Lawson, Roberts, or Garibaldi blundering around interfering with my work."

"Then what are we to do?"

"*You* are to change immediately."

"Might I ask why?"

"We are going to the theatre and you are most inappropriately dressed."

❧

CHAPTER EIGHT

Mise en Abyme

In truth, I did not own anything that would be suitable for such a venture. The theatre had been banned in Ey since shortly after the revolution and while I had gone occasionally as a student I had always found the experience a little unsettling. I attributed this partly to the aversion one must naturally feel when undertaking an activity that is illegal in one's homeland and partly to the equally natural hostility that the theatrical set expressed towards people of Commonwealth heritage.

Nevertheless, I attempted to comply with Ms. Haas's instruction and promptly changed into my best quality doublet and polished the buckles on my shoes and hat. Emerging from my room, I found Ms. Haas already waiting for me, attired in a burgundy frock coat, embroidered with a pattern of gold roses, and matching breeches. Lace cascaded from her cuffs and collar, and her ivory silk waistcoat was worked with hummingbirds. I did my best to avoid looking lower, for her stockinged calves were clearly visible, but I found it difficult to ignore her frankly remarkable shoes, which were dark red satin, adorned with bows, their tall heels set with diamonds.

"I thought," she said, "I told you to change."

"I have changed. This is wool, not worsted, and I'm wearing new cuffs."

Her gaze swept disapprovingly across my person. "You know, your kingdom used to be a really fun place for a party."

"With all due respect, ma'am, while I have no doubt that there were pleasures untold at the court of the Witch King, the rest of us spent our lives hiding from the dreadwraiths and toiling in fields."

"Whereas now, presumably, they toil in fields and hide from the witch hunters."

"The witch hunters spare the innocent. The wraiths did not."

"Fair point. I suppose Iustinian did kill rather a lot of people over the years. I personally try to stay out of politics. It's usually boring or fatal, and rarely anything in between." She offered me her arm. "Shall we go?"

We went, but I did not take her arm and she did not seem offended. In retrospect, I wish that I had accepted the gesture. I did not realise at the time how infrequently Ms. Haas made such overtures to people she was not intending to seduce. In the moment, however, my thoughts still very much on my homeland, my sense of decorum prevailed.

Mise en Abyme was located in Wax Flower Hill, a fact which did not surprise me, given what I had heard about both the establishment and the area. Like many parts of Khelathra-Ven, its history was somewhat obscure. To the best of my knowledge, wax flowers had neither grown nor been made there. At the time of our visit, as today, it was a tangle of narrow, sloping streets, accommodating a mixture of galleries, theatres, and garrets of dubious provenance, all primarily occupied by artistic persons in either the ascending or descending phases of their careers. These establishments (along with others, the nature of which I shall not discuss) made the region popular with a certain class of student, a certain class of aristocrat, and, if I may speak freely, a certain class of charlatan.

The building itself was an unassuming, rather ramshackle affair with shuttered windows and overhanging eaves. The words *Mise en*

Abyme appeared in faded yellow paint above the door and a poster, with peeling edges, announced that tonight's performance would be *The Moste Lamentable and Bloodie Tragedie of the Laste Wyfe of the Madde Duke Orsino.*

"As you can see," said Ms. Haas, "du Maurier's tastes are quite tediously lurid. Expect strapping stable boys, dewy innocents, sundry beheadings, and at least one wholly unnecessary ravishment."

While I found many of the strictures of the Commonwealth to be gratuitous and stifling, I was beginning to think that the ban on theatre had its merits. "Could we not simply speak with Mr. du Maurier without attending this production?"

"No, the man is impossibly vain. And will give audience only to those who endure his, for want of a better term, *art.*"

A small, fashionably attired crowd had gathered in the street outside. The air was sticky with anticipation as we waited with varying degrees of patience for the doors to open. When they did, we were ushered into an already darkened atrium by a sylph-like youth and an (I presume) equally appealing young lady. A moment later, a shaft of brilliant light shone down from above, illuminating a hitherto unseen figure. It was a tall, somewhat bulky man, whose age I could not quite discern beneath his stage makeup. He was dressed in black velvet in a style that vaguely suggested the past without being tied to any specific era and surveyed us with hard, kohl-darkened eyes.

"I . . ."

Here he paused for a duration I assume coincided with the conventions of this medium.

". . . am the Mad Duke Orsino. And you, gentle guests, are soon to bear witness to the treacherous, murderous, and lascivious misdeeds that I shall visit upon my lovely new bride."

Another light blossomed, this time revealing a raven-haired beauty in an inappropriately diaphanous white dress. She brought a wrist to her forehead in an exaggerated gesture of sorrow.

"But worry not," continued the Duke, "for ours is a most moral and improving tale that warns most correctly of the dangers that await those who indulge in vices, iniquities, and debaucheries. Rest assured that bloodiest retribution shall fall upon every evildoer and that no detail of this just and proper punishment shall escape your virtuous eyes."

Ms. Haas moved her mouth close my ear. "I cannot believe I engaged in connubial activities with this gentleman. But I suppose I was very young."

As a matter of record, I should add that the words "engaged," "connubial," "activities," and "gentleman" were not, in actuality, used by Ms. Haas at this juncture, but I have taken some licence in representing her use of language in order to protect the sensibilities of my readers.

The Duke extended an arm as if plucking fruit from an imaginary tree and held the pose. "One small matter more, gentle guests. Our most marvellous and most wondrous theatre straddles the border between this world and another. If you are to go safely in this most mysterious place three rules must you obey without fail."

"This bit"—Ms. Haas elbowed me sharply—"is actually important. Be careful."

"One: never must you look across your left shoulder. Two: never must you look into the eyes of your own reflection. Three: should a voice call you by name, on no account should you answer. Should you break but one of these most vital prohibitions, disaster beyond imagination will befall you. Now . . ."

He gave another of his, to my mind, somewhat excessive pauses.

". . . follow me into the castle of the Mad Duke Orsino."

Then came a crack of lightning that made the audience gasp. In the brief flare of white, we saw a door at the back of the room, through which the Duke was swiftly vanishing. The crowd pushed excitedly forward to follow him.

Ms. Haas's hand closed about my arm with surprising strength. "I should probably have mentioned earlier that we'll be separated. But keep your wits about you and don't break any of the rules."

I very much wished that she had, in fact, mentioned it earlier. It was, however, too late to inform her of this as the press of the crowd carried me through the door and I found myself quite alone in a hall of mirrors.

✤

CHAPTER NINE

The Castle of Mad Duke Orsino

Taking our host's warnings very much to heart, I stared fixedly at the floor in order to avoid even inadvertently catching the eye of one of my many reflections. I could hear voices from deeper in the maze and decided that this entire affair would be most swiftly resolved if I moved towards them. As I progressed the mirrors fell away, and I stood instead in a vast and shadowy castle such as might feature in the sort of sensational pamphlets they sold from street corners for a penny. Not that I had ever personally partaken of them. My father would not have approved.

I should clarify, for the benefit of those readers who may not have encountered such phenomena, that there was no means by which the space I presently occupied could possibly have existed within the building I had entered just minutes earlier. I was not without experience of travel to other realities, although I had done so almost exclusively in a military context, and this, combined with the outlandish nature of my surroundings and the unsavoury character of my host, left me wary.

The voices I had heard belonged to the Mad Duke Orsino and his delicate bride. They entered through a heavy oak door, which slammed ominously behind them. Casting off his cloak, the Duke declaimed, "And now, my bride, you shall at last be mine. My pain, my woes, my torments all are thine. Your dreams did end the moment we were wed. For now I take you to our marriage bed."

The young lady I had seen in the vestibule flung herself wretchedly to her knees. "My lord, I hope that in some tender part. You find a shred of pity in your heart. My life, my soul, my virtue all to save. Or, I, alas, shall plunge into my grave."

"Nor grave nor freedom shall you ever see," intoned the Duke, clutching her to him in a manner I found quite unacceptable even in artifice, "but day and night do service unto me."

My editor informs me that under the Creative Works (Uses, Abuses, and Recombinations) Act, Third Year, Twelfth Council, I am not permitted to share any more of the text of this production. I confess that I consider this very much a blessing. Suffice to say that, for the best part of the next hour, I wandered the halls and galleries of the Mad Duke Orsino's castle, bearing witness to all manner of ghastly scenes. I did my best to avoid the bloodiest and most lurid but nevertheless saw far more than I was comfortable seeing. I should emphasise, for the benefit of readers in the Commonwealth and other similarly conservative societies, that Mise en Abyme is not wholly representative of the theatre as an art form and I have, in my later years, had occasion to find some plays most enjoyable.

Eventually I came upon a long and winding stair and, ascending, encountered the Mad Duke Orsino a few paces ahead of me. He was in the throes of a soliloquy about the pleasures he imagined would await him in his lady's bedchamber when, quite unexpectedly, he stopped and turned towards me. His image shimmered and his face seemed to move out of focus for a moment. When my eyes adjusted, I saw in his place the young actress who had, up until this point, been personating the Duke's innocent bride.

"Help me," she whispered. "He's keeping me here."

I was insufficiently experienced in matters either of the theatre or of rescuing damsels to be entirely confident that this was not simply part of the production. This left me hesitant to say anything lest I give offence.

She clasped her hands together in a manner wholly unlike the flourishes that had hitherto characterised her performance. "It's du Maurier. He won't let me go. There's a door behind you. That way." Her eyes darted to her right, as if she feared to give any more obvious direction. "I can't go through it unless you come with me."

Just as I was about to look, I remembered the impresario's warnings and carefully kept my head facing forward, turning my whole body clockwise instead. There was, indeed, a door that I am certain had not been present a moment before. I had, by then, come to the conclusion that either the lady was sincere or this interlude was a part of the play in which I was required to interact with her as though she were. Reaching behind me, I clasped her arm and led her onwards.

Beyond the door lay a disordered room, its edges seeming to flicker and recede as one looked at them. Racks and overspilling trunks of what I presumed to be costumes lay scattered about, alongside tables littered with props, shards of glass, and hastily annotated scripts.

"Where are we?" I asked.

"It's a kind of staging area. We can speak freely here."

I turned to face the lady. She appeared to be eighteen, perhaps twenty, and well suited for the role in which she had been cast. "What is du Maurier doing? Are you in danger?"

"Not I." She gave a slow smile, blinked, and then her eyes were mirrors.

And I saw within them my own startled face looking back at me.

CHAPTER TEN

The Mocking Realm

Even at this point in my career I was not a stranger to the attentions of otherworldly beings that wished to devour me. I was, however, unarmed and wholly ignorant of the natures and the weaknesses of the entities I now confronted. I had gleaned a little insight from my experiences thus far at Mise en Abyme, and Ms. Haas saw fit afterwards to explain a trifle more about the Princes of the Mocking Realm. My editor suggests to me that informing you at this juncture of conversations which can only have taken place after the experiences I presently describe robs the forthcoming narrative of any sense of tension or uncertainty. I personally do not understand this complaint. You, the reader, must surely know that I am writing this book many years after these events and, while it is true that some popular memoirs have been penned by the deceased (Miss Evadne de Silver's *Life Amongst the Bone Cults of Lei* being a particularly fine example of the genre), such texts remain a rarity and are normally composed by persons with access to and knowledge of powerful necromantic arts.

In any case, after this encounter (during which you may accurately conclude I did not die) I learned that the Princes of the Mocking Realm are phantasmal beings equal parts illusion, delusion, and memory who build themselves and their worlds from the thoughts and fantasies of mortals. It was for this purpose that they desired sacrifices and it was in their power to offer such gifts as to make the procurement of said sacrifices worthwhile for an ambitious or aspiring sorcerer. When one was drawn into their realm, as I was about to discover, they constructed a feeding ground of sorts shaped from the depths of their victim's mind.

The moment I inadvertently caught the eye of my own reflection in the eyes of the actress, who I later identified as Miss Katrina de la Martynière, the world around me instantaneously shattered into a thousand tiny and jagged points of light that presently resolved themselves into the image of what was now called Industry Square back in Ey. The scene that the Princes of the Mocking Realm had seen fit to conjure before me was the execution (although this is not entirely the right word, for reasons that should soon become apparent to those for whom they are not already obvious) of the Witch King Iustinian. It was not an occasion that came to mind often but represented one of my most formative memories. I recall to this day the utter silence as a thousand onlookers waited, uncertain what horrifying curse the Witch King might even then be capable of visiting upon his subjects.

The king himself stood upon a platform, impaled on seven spears. The spears were attached to chains bolted fast to the ground. The rings to which they were affixed remain to this day. He was muzzled like a dog in order that he might speak no words of power, but, through heavy-lidded eyes, he watched us with a terrible serenity and an almost unbearable sorrow. On a scaffold above him a searing fire was lit beneath a crucible of soon-to-be-molten iron. The method that had been chosen for the execution was partly symbolic—the Creator is a being of fire and thus flames of all kinds are considered sacred in Ey—but partially in concession to pragmatic concerns. The Witch King is immortal, no wound will last upon his person, and even severed his members will retain life and malice and seek to return to wholeness. Encasement in metal, therefore, was deemed the only practical means by which he could be neutralised. I understand that later he was interred in a location known only to the Lord Protector Thomas Latimer and select members of the Chamber of Regicides.

Having experienced this day once, I was less than enthusiastic about the possibility of doing so again and was thus relieved to observe that the scenario had been presented, as it were, in tableau. Or almost in tableau, for a wind I could not feel stirred the long dark locks of the Witch King's hair, and I was sure I saw him blink. Elsewhere in the crowd, a few scattered figures moved also. I recognised Latimer and my mother by his side, and some distance from them, my father and a child I knew to be my younger self, though none of us seemed quite as I remembered.

"Welcome," said my mother, in a voice that was most certainly not her own. "This will be painless."

"Though not swift," added Latimer.

The child gave me a sharp-toothed smile. "And not actually painless."

"Pain is an illusion." I thought that was my mother.

"Then again," remarked my father, "so is everything else."

My family began to close in on me. I could already feel a strange sense of unravelling, as though my thoughts and dreams and self were being teased gently apart. I tried to run. But I did not try to run. I stood like a dreamer, aware of what should be done but unable even to attempt it. Their voices swirled around me.

Hold still—In the Creator's name it shall be so—It has been so long since we—Perhaps it would be best if you left the Commonwealth—You can rest now—Father, I can't—

Quiet now—I call you to service and ask only your faith—Be calm—Let us help you—Freedom—Surrender.

A gunshot shattered the haze of whispers. And, suddenly, there was space around me. The Witch King shook off his chains, the spears melting like mist from his flesh, a smoking pistol in his free hand.

Latimer stared up at him. "You are not welcome here."

"I'm not really welcome anywhere." I'd never heard the Witch King speak, but I was relatively certain he did not speak like that. "But don't worry, I'm not staying long."

My child self drifted forward, the long plaits I remembered infuriating me sliding from beneath the bonnet about which I recalled similar feelings. "You came to our realm. You are ours now."

"Not this one." My father caught my young likeness by the arm. "She's too much bother."

"That's the nicest thing anyone's said about me all day." The Witch King's image blurred and when my eyes cleared, Ms. Haas, still resplendent in burgundy and still very much armed, stood in his place. "Now do step away from my companion or I shall be forced to speak the Nine Lies and Five Truths that bind the Dreaming God in the Cyst of Unyielding Recollection."

"She's bluffing," said my mother.

"You wouldn't dare," said my father.

Ms. Haas raised a single finger. "That those things which are lost may someday be regained." She put up a second. "That a lover's face is a mask of peeling wax."

The ground shook beneath our feet.

And Ms. Haas's third finger joined its fellows. "That this world is real."

The sky began to fall. I appreciate that this phenomenon may prove difficult for some readers to visualise, but I fear that, since I mean it literally, it is hard for me to explain it in any other terms. Flakes of what I can only call firmament descended from above and settled upon the crowd like pieces of blue-tinged, star-dusted eggshell. It was oddly beautiful in the way that only ruination can be.

"That," continued Ms. Haas, "the Sleeper may dream without knowing and may wake without—"

"Stop." The cry was a cacophony of many voices.

Latimer shoved me roughly in Ms. Haas's direction. "Take him and go and do not return."

"You really think I care about your pissant little subreality?" She caught me by the hand. "Come, Wyndham. We're done here."

CHAPTER ELEVEN

Katrina de la Martynière

Our exit from the Mocking Realm was as abrupt as my entrance had been. We returned, however, not to the castle of the Mad Duke Orsino, nor to the peculiar staging area to which Miss de la Martynière had led me, but to a thoroughly dingy room of quite ordinary proportions. I presumed that this was the physical building housing the liminal space between worlds wherein du Maurier and his company gave their performances. We were, for the moment, alone. And for that I was thankful.

Ms. Haas gave a heavy sigh. "Honestly, Captain. There were three rules. I'm beginning to think I can't take you anywhere."

"In my defence, I believe I was deliberately deceived into meeting the gaze of my reflection by a thoroughly dishonourable actress."

"Acting is a dishonourable profession. Then again, honour is overrated. And if you tried to ——" And here again I shall not repeat her language. ". . . the bride of the Mad Duke Orsino during a production of *The Most Lamentable and Bloody Tragedy of the Last Wife of the Mad Duke Orsino* you really have nobody to blame but yourself."

I can honestly say I was quite taken aback by so outrageous a suggestion. "Madam, I made no such attempt. The young lady told me that she was being held against her will and I made an effort to rescue her. That is all."

"My dear man." And here Ms. Haas paused to laugh heartily but not wholly unkindly. "Frankly, that is even worse. A little piece of advice for your future life. If you are ever told something by a professional liar in a place built of lies and overseen by supernatural beings that have the concept of falsehood built into their name and whose very breath is deception: *don't believe it.*"

"I have no doubt you think me very foolish. But I shall always offer aid to those who may need it, and on this principle, I shall not compromise."

Ms. Haas put one hand to her face and the other upon my shoulder. "You are going to get so utterly killed."

It is, of course, true that my life was endangered many, many times during my long acquaintance with the sorceress Shaharazad Haas, although, despite her chiding me often for my naive altruism, she was usually there to extricate me from any predicament in which I might find myself. Indeed, it is somewhat ironic that, as I write this, I have almost certainly outlived her.

At this juncture, we were interrupted by the sudden arrival of Miss de la Martynière. Judging from her demeanour and language she was most upset at my survival and possessed, in truth, little of the modesty she had counterfeited during our earlier meeting. Indeed, her speech was so colourful that I have found it difficult to reproduce without including at least allusion to the various oaths and curses she scattered so liberally throughout her discourse. I have done my best to conceal the substance of the offending terms from my audience while preserving the clarity and character of the lady's speech. If you are easily shocked you may wish to turn to the end of this segment.

"Who the —— are you? And what the —— do you think you're doing? Have you any idea of the —— you've caused and what a ——ing mess I'm in now?"

"Perhaps," I offered, "you should have considered that eventuality before throwing in your lot with a pack of face-stealing demons."

She curled her lip at me. "Well, what the ——— would you know, Mr. Blessed Are the ———ed. You were falling out of your smock to help me out when you thought I was getting ———ed up the ——— by a dirty old man. But now you know I'm doing something about it, you're all 'know your ———ing place.'"

"Madam, you did attempt to murder me."

"Saw an opportunity." She shrugged. "Took it."

"I understand. Perhaps I would have done the same had my circumstances been as yours."

To my surprise, she did not take this reassurance in the spirit in which it was intended. "Oh, go ——— yourself, you ———ing piece of god-bothering ———. You do not get to ———ing forgive me or pretend you ———ing know where I'm coming from. I tried to ———ing kill you and I'm not ———ing sorry. At least do me the ———ing courtesy of being ———ing angry about it."

"This," declared Ms. Haas, "is so much better than that dismal play."

That seemed to distract Miss de la Martynière a little. "Tell me about it. Charlie's ———ing obsessed with these blood 'n' bosoms numbers."

"On the subject of the good Mr. du Maurier"—Ms. Haas concealed her pistol within the folds of her frock coat once more—"I'm afraid I do need to speak to him rather urgently."

"Well, that's going to take a while, seeing as how you and your friend here ——— near pulled this whole place down round our ears. He's out front giving refunds, and he hates giving refunds."

"How unfortunate. I feel rather the same way about waiting." Ms. Haas cast Miss de la Martynière a look that I would have considered inappropriate in most circumstances but felt was even more so given that the lady in question had so recently attempted to orchestrate my demise. "Perhaps you could help me instead."

"Depends what's in it for me."

"While I respect your independent spirit, I fear you have grossly misjudged the balance of power in this situation. Did it not escape your notice that I just plucked your sacrifice from the depths of the Mocking Realm with, though I say so myself, very little effort?"

Miss de la Martynière's shoulders slumped. "Oh ——. You're Shaharazad ——ing Haas, aren't you?"

"Currently only Shaharazad Haas, but I could be ——ing if you play your cards right."

"For someone with your reputation, you've got some really ——ing cheesy lines."

"I have two modes. Flirting and turning your blood to boiling lye within your veins. Which do you prefer?"

The actress rolled her eyes. "Fine. What do you want?"

"You're clearly sleeping with du Maurier. And I know for a fact that he's even more monstrously braggadocious when he's refractory. Has he told you anything about a woman named Eirene Viola?"

"He was doing her, or leastways trying to, for a while way back when. Said she was an ungrateful, lying, cheating, thieving little ——."

"Yes, that sounds like Eirene." Ms. Haas braced her lower body against a rickety wooden item that may once have been a table. "Did he say anything else?"

"Not a lot. He's not paying much attention to what goes on outside the theatre these days. Sometimes I think he don't know what year it is."

"The moral of that story is never move into an alternate reality that you cannot unmake."

Miss de la Martynière seemed to be growing restless. "We done yet?"

"I believe so." Ms. Haas came languorously to her feet again, smoothing her coat. "If you hear anything, you'll let me know, won't you?"

"Do I have a choice?"

From some interior pocket, Ms. Haas retrieved a mother-of-pearl card case, carved with symbols that seemed to writhe obscenely as one stared at them. And, from that, she produced a plain white calling card, offering it along with a terribly ambiguous smile. "We always have choices. That's what makes life so unpredictable."

And so we departed Mise en Abyme and returned, via autonomous hansom, to 221b Martyrs Walk.

For the benefit of those readers who felt, quite understandably, that they would do best to avoid Miss de la Martynière's testimony entirely I can summarise thus: that she expressed great anger towards me personally, showed no remorse for attempting my murder, and was slow to recognise Ms. Haas but was nevertheless persuaded, having realised her error, to assist us in our enquiries. Owing to her intimate relationship with Mr. du Maurier she was in a position to inform us that while he bore a great deal of ill will towards Miss Viola he had made no immediate plans to inconvenience her.

During our ride home, I enquired with Ms. Haas whether, given her admonitions about the inadvisability of trusting professional dissemblers, she felt that we should take Miss de la Martynière at her word on this matter, and she told me she thought we could. The young woman was plainly ambitious and had no love for du Maurier. Further, the fact that she had attempted to kill me strongly implied, according to Ms. Haas, that she had plumbed some of the deeper secrets of the Mocking Realm. Such knowledge is acquired only by du Maurier's very personal favourites and only by those who are capable of handling the man with discretion and finesse. Such an individual would never permit the distraction that would inevitably ensue should du Maurier rekindle his interest in a former protégé, even if such interest was vindictive or vengeful in nature.

I must admit that I was rather pleased that Mr. du Maurier did not turn out to be our blackmailer. Although it would, of course, have set Miss Viola's mind greatly at rest to know the identity of her persecutor, I was beginning to enjoy both the sense of mystery and the sense of adventure that came with working alongside the sorceress Shaharazad Haas and would have been disappointed for it to have ended so soon. I did not, as it transpired, need to worry on that account.

❧

CHAPTER TWELVE

The Ubiquitous Companies

In the days following our return from Wax Flower Hill I was not in the best of spirits. The matter of my near devourment by the Princes of the Mocking Realm was itself of little consequence, but the details of the experience had nonetheless brought to the forefront of my mind certain recollections upon which I preferred not to dwell. Ms. Haas, either out of sympathy for my mood or indifference to my existence, permitted me the space to marshal my reserves, making no attempt to engage my attention for almost a week.

This state of affairs changed abruptly when I returned home from the hospital to find her waiting impatiently in the hall.

"What are you doing, man?" she said. "You're not even dressed."

I hasten to clarify that I was most certainly dressed and that her comment referred to the fact that I was clad in my habitual workwear while she was attired in an extravagant court dress of the style fashionable in the Uthmani Sultanate. That is to say, layers of flowing silk, in jewel-bright colours, trailing sleeves that would be considered sinfully impractical in Ey, and voluminous trousers, the ankles of which were plainly visible under her skirts.

Removing my hat, I attempted to place it on the hatstand, only for the furnishing in question, still unfortunately haunted, to shuffle out of the way. "Dressed for what?"

"For the ball. We are late already."

"I was not aware of any ball."

"Really, Wyndham." She made a sign of warding in the direction of the hatstand. It gave one last shudder and stopped dead. "Must I tell you everything? The Grand Ball of the Ubiquitous Companies is an annual event, and surely it must have occurred to you that, should we wish to seek information regarding the peers, associates, and rivals of Miss Cora Beck as they might pertain to our current investigation, we would be well advised to attend?"

I did not think it entirely fair of Ms. Haas to expect that I would make quite so significant a leap unprompted. "My apologies. I shall change directly."

Returning a few minutes later in my best tunic and collar, I drew an exasperated look from Ms. Haas.

"Were we not," she drawled, "about to attend a gathering of glorified shopkeepers I should insist you allow me to supply you with a more suitable ensemble."

Given my companion's own sartorial choices, that was not an eventuality to which I looked forward. There was not, however, opportunity to protest, for Ms. Haas hurried me out the door and into a waiting hansom. As we were whisked through the cobbled streets of Athra towards the counting hall of the Ubiquitous Companies I risked asking whether we actually had an invitation.

My companion gave me a condescending look. "I am the sorceress Shaharazad Haas. Being uninvited is sort of my thing."

"That seems like it could get one into rather a lot of trouble."

"Getting into rather a lot of trouble is also my thing."

The veracity of this statement was fast becoming apparent and it gave me, at the time, some cause for concern. I had, after all, been raised to see the value in living as unobtrusive a life as possible. Over the years, however, getting into trouble became very much our thing. And although Ms. Haas was nigh invariably the instigator of our adventures, and I never quite came to share her delight in chaos, I would not have traded my part in them for the world.

The counting hall, like many of the city's most ancient buildings, was an eclectic mishmash of architectural styles and features. Its facade had been renovated within the last century, following the damage caused in the unrest following the Khelathran secession from the Uthmani Sultanate, but the original building—designed in high Athran style, emphasising pointed arches, vaulted ceilings, and needle-like spires—was much older. Indeed, the catacombs beneath the counting hall were said to date back all the way to ancient Khel, whose empire had dominated much of the northern seaboard for several hundred years. Presently it was illuminated with a great many lanterns and alchemical lights, which made the ornate stonework gleam golden against the night sky.

Owing to the sheer number of carriages and conveyances all presumably headed to the same location as ourselves, it would have taken us almost as long to travel the last few hundred yards up Alderman's Way as it had taken to make the whole of the rest of the journey. Never one to exhibit the virtue of patience, or for that matter propriety, Ms. Haas insisted that we disembark and proceed on foot. This earned us disapproving looks from the uniformed gentlemen who waited by the doors, verifying the identities of would-be entrants.

"Name?" said one of them in the resigned tones of a person who has been doing a tedious job for some while and expects to be doing it for some while yet.

"Shaharazad Haas and John Wyndham."

He checked his papers. "You're not on the list."

"No, I'm not." And with that, my companion walked confidently into the building.

In some confusion, I trailed after her and the doorman trailed after me. We had made it only a short distance into the spacious and sumptuously decorated atrium when we were descended upon by a number of serious-looking individuals who I took to be guards. I could not help but think that, for a mission whose purpose was to covertly reconnoitre the event, we were making rather a scene.

"You have to leave, miss," insisted the doorman. "Otherwise we'll be forced to summon the Myrmidons."

Completely ignoring him, Ms. Haas instead called out across the hall to a diminutive dark-skinned woman in a gown of the most remarkable cobalt blue, accented with complex patterns in subtly different shades that made her look for all the world as if she was wearing the entire sky. "Perdita, could you help me out of a spot of bother?"

The woman turned and gave Ms. Haas a look I would see again many, many times over the years. It was a look that said "Although it is monstrously inconvenient for you to impose upon me in this manner at this time, I am sufficiently indebted to or respectful of you that I will choose not to emphasise the fact." She swept towards us, her sizable entourage following. "What is it this time, Shaharazad?"

"My friend and I need to get into the ball, and by some terrible mischance our invitations have gone astray."

"What a terrible oversight." The newcomer folded her arms and I had the distinct impression she was not much convinced by Ms. Haas's story. Then she sighed. "The Ubiquitous Company of Dyers will vouch for these two."

The doorman bowed, only slightly resentfully. "As you wish, mistress."

"I am sure"—the lady's attention landed heavily upon my companion—"that they will do nothing to make us regret our generosity."

"Regret is such a waste of energy," returned Ms. Haas. "Come along, Wyndham."

We proceeded into a vast and crowded hall. Like the exterior of the building, it was a marvel of the architecture of its day, with ornate columns and high arched windows more reminiscent of a religious institution than a civic one. Of course, I suppose, in its way it was a temple of sorts—one dedicated to commerce and industry rather than to anything so impractical as a god. From a gallery above us came music I did not recognise to which the guests were performing dances also unfamiliar to me. Although since dancing at all was strongly discouraged in Ey, while dancing in public with mixed company was flatly illegal, this was not, perhaps, surprising.

My companion caught me by the sleeve and dragged me behind a pillar. "Now," she said, "I shall circulate and see if I can pick up anything about the good Miss Beck. You should find Eirene and keep an eye on her."

"To what end?"

"Mostly, I just think it will annoy her."

"Madam," I protested. "I hope we have not come all this way and infiltrated a gathering of some of the most influential persons in the city merely out of a peevish desire to vex our client."

"Not merely. That's just an added bonus. But if you can, see how they are with each other and let me know if you think Miss Beck is the kind of person to concoct an elaborate charade in order to disentangle herself from an unwanted engagement."

I blinked. "I'm not sure I know what such a person would be like."

"Quite a lot like Eirene, now I come to think of it." Ms. Haas tapped her chin with a finger. "You might also try to get in with the family. If it's not Miss Beck it might easily be one of her parents."

"Get in?"

"Ingratiate yourself. Be charming. I have every faith in you, Captain."

Having thus instructed me, Ms. Haas spun on her heel and disappeared into the crowd. This left me somewhat at a loss. None of my experiences to date had prepared me for searching a room full of strangers, all extravagantly attired and moving in complicated patterns, in search of a woman I had met once and from whom I understood I would be expected to conceal myself. Falling back on my training and treating the hall as a site of potential enemy activity, I put my back firmly to the wall and skirted the perimeter. I was very conscious that this behaviour, coupled with my attire and general demeanour, made me somewhat conspicuous and proved not to be entirely suitable to my purposes. Although I was able to get a very thorough sense of the layout of the room, including potential sources of cover, hiding spots, and firing platforms, I was not able to locate Miss Viola. I did overhear snatches of a number of conversations, mostly regarding highly technical issues of trade that I could not repeat even had they been pertinent.

"If you're a spy," came a voice at my elbow, "you're doing a terrible job of it."

I turned to see a slight, delicate-featured young man with waist-length white hair and thick glasses. The discreet silver brooch pinned to the lapel of his charcoal-grey suit marked him out as an agent of the Ossuary Bank. As, for that matter, did the presence beside him of a six-foot-tall animated corpse in footman's livery, its eyes and lips sewn shut with copper thread. I was, on a rational level, aware that the Ossuary Bank provided numerous valuable services that underlay the entire economy of the city and much of the wider world. On a more visceral, personal level, however, I could not help but recoil from a man, however winsome he appeared, whose profession required him to routinely violate the sanctity of the grave.

Inching slightly farther from the gentleman, I endeavoured to explain myself. "I'm just looking for somebody."

"You probably won't find them stuck to the wall."

"Ah. No. I daresay I shall not."

"Don't worry. I'm terrible with balls too." The young necromancer flushed. "Sorry. That came out all wrong."

This conversation was fast reaching a point at which it would have been uncomfortable even without the looming shadow of the ambulatory cadaver. "No matter. I'm afraid I really must—"

"You're not Eyan, are you?"

"Well, yes, as it happens I am. But I really must—"

"That explains the pallor. I mean, not that it's bad. I actually rather like it. I mean, not that I like pale things in general. I mean, I'm not into corpses. Not that you look like a corpse." He paused and pushed his glasses back into place. "It's just, being with the bank—people get the oddest ideas."

I couldn't quite prevent my gaze from alighting on the gentleman's deceased associate. "I'm sure I can't imagine why."

"Really? Well, I suppose it's got something to do with the fact that we traffic in sorceries which transgress the most sacred taboos of most cultures and religions." He blinked and his face fell. "Wait. Were you being sarcastic?"

I confess that this shamed me a little. My intent had been to balance condemnation with diplomacy, but it appeared I had succeeded only in being arch. "I am sorry. That was unbecoming of me."

"No, I understand. The truth is, I mostly work in currencies. But then, I suppose I still spend more time conjuring forbidden darkness from beyond the veil of night than the median citizen."

Apart from that small detail, he seemed a very pleasant fellow, if a trifle odd. And the bright green of his eyes behind his glasses gave him a certain disarming quality to which I was not insensible. Still, I could not shake the awareness that he openly practised the same arts that had held my people in thrall for five centuries.

"Without wishing to give offence," I said, "I fear I am prohibited by my religion from having any dealings with necromancers."

He looked downcast. "I was only going to ask if you wanted to visit a coffeehouse. There's a lovely place by the docks in Khel where they serve these honeyed pastries."

I had not quite expected the conversation to take this turn.

Obviously I had been for coffee with gentlemen before, the beverage being relatively unknown in my homeland and therefore not proscribed. But, by some quirk of either my culture or my character, I had little facility in identifying when an invitation might be forthcoming. On this occasion, I cannot deny I was flattered, but nevertheless I baulked. "That is very kind of you, but I must decline."

"Oh." The young man removed his glasses, buffed them against his sleeve, and put them on again. "I suppose it would be a bit awkward what with your nation hating everything I stand for. Probably I should have thought of that earlier. It's just you seemed so nice, even though you were scuttling around the ballroom like a confused octopus."

"I beg your pardon, I was not scuttling. And I'm not sure octopuses scuttle."

He thought about this for a second and then perked up visibly. "Well, if you weren't scuttling and octopuses don't scuttle, then you were, in fact, scuttling like an octopus."

That hurt my head a little but I was eventually forced to concede the logic of it.

"Anyway," continued the necromancer, *"Blingfeather's Manual of Etiquette* is a bit silent on how to deal with somebody who tells you their god won't let them speak to you at a party. But it's probably polite to leave you alone."

In truth I was a little conflicted. The theological position on this matter was clear but, notwithstanding his terrifying servant, the gentleman was not without his charms. "Um. Yes. That's probably appropriate."

He bobbed a hurried bow and offered me a small square of ivory-coloured card. "In case you change your mind," he said. "Or need financial advice." Before I could reply, he pivoted and hurried away into the crowd.

The card read: *Mr. Jeremiah Donne. Money Changers and Sin Eaters. The Ossuary Bank.* Although I anticipated little need to contact the gentleman, I stored the article about my person and continued my sweep of the perimeter.

Finally, by utter happenstance, the crowd shifted at exactly the right moment and in exactly the right configuration to grant me a clear view of Miss Viola dancing a waltz with a lady I took to be her fiancée. They made a handsome couple, though Miss Viola was the more striking of the two with her Carcosan eyes and auburn hair. Miss Beck, however, complemented her well, having something of the quality of an Athran rose, her fair skin a little blushed and lightly freckled.

I fear that even with my long exposure to Khelathran social mores I found the waltz a rather shocking dance, necessitating as it did such an intimacy between the partners. Nevertheless they moved gracefully together and appeared to possess a comfort with each other that I momentarily envied. Miss Viola had a lightness about her that I had not observed on her visit to 221b Martyrs Walk, a certain ease of manner that made her look, for want of a less bald term, happy. I was then aware of a growing sense of shame at my intrusion and, discomforted by my mission, ducked behind a gentleman in a green waistcoat.

From here I was uncertain as to what I should do next. While Ms. Haas's instructions had been specific, I could see little to be gained by continuing to spy on the two ladies. Certainly, there seemed no strife between them and it would have been most improbable that Miss Beck would suddenly break off in the middle of a dance and exposit an item of useful information that I could report to my companion.

It was at this juncture that, despite my best attempts to remain unobtrusive, I was approached by a shaven-headed woman whose eyes and mouth were filled with roiling celestial fire. She wore a gown trimmed with rich ermine and cockatrice scales, indicating that she was almost certainly a representative of the Ubiquitous Company of Skinners.

"Care to dance the next?" She held out a hand. Her expression was difficult to read owing to the strange illumination of the star-white not-flames that emanated from within her.

"Thank you, but I have not the character nor the practice."

Her smile cast her features briefly into shadow. "You should acquire them. Without dancing, these balls are all business."

"I'm just here looking for a friend."

"As you wish." She dropped a neat curtsy and left in search of a more suitable partner.

I returned my attention to the crowd and realised I had lost all sight of Miss Viola. Then an arm slipped through mine and I found myself being manoeuvred deftly into one of the more discreet corners of the hall. My manoeuvrer, as the astute reader may already have surmised, was none other than the lady herself.

❦

CHAPTER THIRTEEN

Miss Cora Beck

"What are you doing here?" she demanded, with no trace of her former sanguinity. "And, more to the point, what's she doing here?"

I was beginning to recognise in both Ms. Haas and Miss Viola that the one would adopt a particular tone when speaking of the other. Thus I was in no doubt as to the identity of the "she" to whom my interlocutor alluded. "Ms. Haas felt it best to eliminate your fiancée and her associates from our enquiries."

"Well, she can go home. It's not Cora, and I will not have her ruin the very thing I am trying to protect."

"I'm sure Ms. Haas will do nothing to jeopardise your happiness."

"She has no interest in happiness, mine or anybody else's." Her gaze flicked nervously over her shoulder. "Please leave, Mr. Wyndham. This isn't helping me. It's just some game of Shaharazad's."

Despite the fact that Ms. Haas had told me quite explicitly that she considered the opportunity to discomfort Miss Viola a positive benefit of this course of action, I nonetheless found it difficult to believe that she could truly be so callous. "I find it difficult to believe," I said, "that she could truly be so callous."

"Then you're an even bigger fool than you look."

"I do not believe it foolish to see the best in people." With as much politeness as I could manage, I extricated myself from her hold.

"And while your faith in Miss Beck is commendable, might she not have enemies or even allies who would not wish to see her married to you?"

Before Miss Viola could make reply, we were interrupted by her fiancée.

"There you are." Miss Beck seemed wryly amused at having temporarily misplaced her intended, and knowing what I did of Miss Viola, I suspected it was a not uncommon occurrence. "If you wanted to lurk in a dark corner, you could've just asked."

Miss Viola smiled as she had on the dance floor. "If I wanted to lurk with you in a dark corner I'd pick one that wasn't already occupied and wasn't in a formal banqueting hall filled with half the dignitaries of the Ubiquitous Companies."

"Och, where's your sense of adventure?"

The two ladies shared an embrace, Miss Viola having shed utterly all of the suspicion and hostility that had characterised her manner since she first accosted me.

"I'm sorry for vanishing on you," she said. "I just spotted Mr. Wyndham here. He's a wool trader lately arrived from Ey. I happened to meet him in town and I realised that we haven't yet arranged for a blessing in the name of the Creator at the wedding. After all, if anyone would know the proper rituals, it would be an Eyan."

As a lie it had the uncomfortable virtue of being plausibly close to the truth. Khelathrans, especially those amongst the Ubiquitous Companies, have a somewhat transactional relationship with the gods, and it is considered both wise and propitious to arrange for any significant undertaking to be blessed by as many deities as possible. And I would, in fact, have been most happy to provide such a service for Miss Beck and Miss Viola. All that being said, the facility and alacrity with which our client concocted so unfalsifiable a deception gave me pause.

"Good thinking, Eirene. We can probably fit him in between the offering to Thotek the Devourer and the Scourge-Priest of Vu." She loosened her grip on Miss Viola and turned towards me. "So what brings you to Khelathra-Ven, Mr. Wyndham?"

"Um, well, that is, I . . . I mean . . ."

"While we can't expect Mr. Wyndham to give away trade secrets," Miss Viola cut in, sparing me further mortification, "I believe I overheard one of the tailors speculating that there would be a surge in demand for wool in the coming months owing to the emergence of new markets in the Silver Byways of Farath-Lein."

"But of course," I added, endeavouring to deceive as honestly as possible, "I couldn't possibly comment."

Miss Beck nodded emphatically. "I quite understand, Mr. Wyndham. You never know who's listening at these kinds of events."

There followed a moment's awkward silence. This is my perennial experience of large social gatherings but was, in this instance, further exacerbated by the awareness that I was required not only to subtly interrogate Miss Beck regarding the possibility that she, or a close associate, might in fact be a nefarious blackmailer but to do so in the persona of a wool merchant. I knew then, and know now, nothing about wool.

"Might I observe," I said when the lull in conversation had long passed the point of acceptability, "that you make a very handsome couple?"

"You might." Miss Beck flashed me a grin that put me somewhat in mind of Ms. Haas in one of her more wicked moods. "Go on, then. Observe it."

I flustered. "Well, you . . . um . . . you make a most handsome couple."

The ladies laughed, although I thought I caught a look of suspicion just fleetingly in the eye of Miss Viola. "Aye, I struck lucky with this one," continued Miss Beck rather proudly. "Not that my parents see it that way."

"They object to your choice?" I flattered myself that my gambit had worked rather well. And another flash of warning from Miss Viola suggested that such flattery was not wholly unwarranted.

"You know how it is," Miss Beck replied with the air of one who confidently assumes that you will indeed know how it is no matter how manifestly divergent your circumstances are from her own. "They think everyone from Carcosa is a malingering lotus eater taking food from the mouths of hardworking Athrans."

Miss Viola pressed a fleeting kiss to her fiancée's cheek. "Some of us are even stealing your women."

"I prefer to think of it"—Miss Beck had that wicked look again—"as a long-term investment in an emerging market."

I seemed to have lost the ladies' attention, for they were, once more, quite rapt with each other. Under any other circumstances I should have left them to enjoy their evening, but I was conscious of a certain pressure to return to Ms. Haas with useful intelligence. "In Ey a lady would never dream of marrying a person of whom her parents disapproved."

Of course, in Ey a lady would never dream of marrying another lady. Then again, perhaps I was being naive. I have, after all, myself lived a life that the culture of my homeland holds unconscionable.

"Eh." Miss Beck shrugged. "They'll come round. In Athra, you can get away with anything as long as it's not bad for business, and Eirene's been very open about her past. She was adventurous and a bit disreputable when she was younger, but it's not like she's murdered anyone."

I cleared my throat, which had gone unexpectedly dry. "That would—"

Fortunately, or perhaps unfortunately, I was spared the embarrassment of either affirming or denying the veracity of Miss Beck's somewhat misguided assertion for, at that moment, a tremendous commotion occurred on the other side of the hall. Turning, I saw Mr. Donne—the representative of the Ossuary Bank who had asked me so forwardly for coffee earlier in the evening—standing over the prostrate body of his undead servant. As the crowd parted around him I saw also that he stood opposite the sorceress Shaharazad Haas, her multicoloured silks gleaming in the lamplight, one hand raised, an incantation dying on her lips.

❧

CHAPTER FOURTEEN

A Disagreement

"You just destroyed my revenant." Mr. Donne's tone was less that of a powerful necromancer incandescent with fury and more that of a man who has left a restaurant to find that the hubcaps have been stolen from his carriage.

Ms. Haas lowered her arm and wiped what appeared to be a bloodstain from her palm with a fine handkerchief. "Your powers of observation, sir, do credit to your order."

"You know the Charter of Sepulchres gives me the right to strike you dead on the spot for that."

"And"—my companion gave a broad and frankly worrying smile—"you are most welcome to make the attempt."

In all candour, the gentleman did not seem wholly enamoured of the idea of engaging Ms. Haas in direct magical confrontation. However, as the only representative of the Ossuary Bank in the vicinity, it fell to him to demonstrate that his employers were not lightly crossed. "Right. Well. Then. I'll be doing . . . that."

"Oh, do get on with it. Or I shall have expired from boredom before I have the opportunity to show you what a titanic error you're making."

Mr. Donne looked down, pressed his fingertips together, and began to speak in the language of ancient Khel. The room grew at once darker and colder. Indistinct figures began to appear amongst the guests and, to my distress, I felt a ghostly presence at my shoulder. Hesitant to look but sensible of the dangers of ignorance, I glanced behind me. The apparition took the form of my younger brother Thomas, named for Thomas Latimer, now Lord Protector; a boy of about seventeen in whom I saw a little of myself and much of my father. He had died of some sudden and virulent illness while I was away at university, and I had not been invited to the funeral. I reached a hand towards him, but if the spirit saw me at all he paid me no mind.

With a certain awful fascination I took note of who amongst the assembly had their own spectral attendant. Most, it seemed, had somebody, although there was no pattern or uniformity to them. Some were old, some young, some bore the marks of violent death, many were children. Miss Beck was flanked by a man and a woman, both of advanced years. They had the look of family about them although they seemed no more sensible of her presence than my brother was of mine. By contrast, Miss Viola stood quite alone, a distinction she shared with the flame-eyed skinner who had asked me to dance earlier in the evening. Ms. Haas, however, was surrounded by a veritable throng, who swirled around her so thickly that it was impossible to discern individuals amongst them.

The hall had gone, for want of a less obvious term, deathly still. Some of the guests were weeping softly and there came the occasional stifled shriek. Then the necromancer spoke a word of command and every spectre in the room descended upon my companion with a terrible keening. Chaos broke loose as members in good standing of the Ubiquitous Companies fled for the exits, overturning chairs and scattering immodestly expensive tableware as they did so. Miss Viola, I noted, caught her fiancée quickly by the hand and led her swiftly but calmly towards the least occupied part of the room with the air of one who had decided upon an optimally efficient escape route well ahead of its being required.

This did, at least, obviate the necessity of my continuing in the persona of an Eyan wool merchant, but I was not certain of the means by which I could be of most assistance to Ms. Haas. Moving against the flow of the crowd, it took me some moments to reach Mr. Donne and, even when I had, I was not wholly willing to strike the man down without warning. In my time beyond the Unending Gate I had, on occasion, been required to resort to ambush in order to preserve my life and the lives of my fellows, but this was not some fathomless agent of the Empress of Nothing. He was a man whose name I knew, and who had asked me for coffee not half an hour before.

I raised my cane, which the earlier twinges in my rib cage had inspired me to bring along, in a threatening attitude.

"Sir," I said, "cease this at once."

Mr. Donne twisted partially around, his expression fading from imperiousness to mild discomfort. "Oh, it's you. Um, look. I really do have to do this. It's forbidden for outsiders to interfere with the business of the order. And, anyway, I'm not entirely sure I can stop it."

The spot where my companion had been was still a maelstrom of ectoplasmic fury. "What do you mean you can't stop it? What kind of necromancer are you?"

"I'll thank you not to question my professionalism. If you'd bothered reading my card"—he sounded a little hurt—"you'd know that I'm a sin eater. I work primarily with spiritual burdens and I'm afraid the lady is, in a very real sense, doing this to herself."

"That," I retorted, "is abhorrent."

He looked bemused and adjusted his glasses. "Really? I always found it had a pleasing equipoise. It's so much better when things add up. And hitting me with that cane won't change anything."

"Nonetheless, I feel I would be justified in striking you very soundly indeed."

"I have the laws of this city on my side and you"—Mr. Donne

pulled himself to his full height, which was not, in honesty, all that high—"are a very rude man."

At this, the storm of spirits collapsed inwards, revealing Ms. Haas, her clothing torn open and a symbol that I recognised as the same marking that bound the poltergeist within our hatstand carved bloodily into her chest.

"Boys, boys, boys." She sighed. "If you've finished flirting, I have to show this little bean counter what real witchcraft looks like."

Mr. Donne was staring agape at my companion's décolletage, although I'm certain his interest was academic rather than inappropriate. "What have you done?"

"You know very well what I've done. I've trapped a hundred and forty-seven angry ghosts in my heart."

"You're insane."

"No, my dear. I just really like to win." She gave a twisted smile and a chill wind swept through the hall, slamming the doors and windows firmly closed. Then came a rasp of tortured metal and the incongruously jaunty jangling of glass as one of the chandeliers tore itself free from the ceiling and hurtled towards Mr. Donne with malicious precision.

While I was not best pleased with the gentleman, I wished for neither of us to be crushed. So, catching the necromancer about the waist, I pulled him aside and threw us both to the ground, covering him on pure instinct with my body.

He gazed up at me, his eyes very wide. "I, um. Gosh."

"Mr. Wyndham," drawled my companion, advancing on us as the shattered remains of the light fitting rose once more into the air and arranged themselves into a deadly array of sharp points, "we must really have a conversation about your rescuing my mortal enemies."

A piece of twisted iron shot past me and embedded itself in the floor inches from Mr. Donne's head. "Ms. Haas, I am concerned that you have not fully considered the consequences of your actions."

"On the contrary. I have considered them in depth. I simply don't care."

I strongly suspected that Ms. Haas's behaviour at this juncture was at least partly caused by the malign influence of the hundred or so wrathful spirits currently inhabiting her body. Although, in truth, it was not so very out of character for her. Rising, I helped Mr. Donne to his feet and placed myself between him and my companion. "I'm afraid I cannot be party to the murder of a"—I paused—"more or less innocent person."

"He started it." Ms. Haas crossed her arms in a manner I personally thought rather huffy.

"I think actually," said Mr. Donne, peeking over my shoulder, "you started it when you disanimated my revenant."

"No, you started it when you reanimated the body of Klaus Lafayette."

Mr. Donne was standing a little closer than he, perhaps, needed to, but I put this down to his nervousness. "That was in accordance with a lawful contract and also we've never met."

"Neither of those are my problem. Now kindly step out from behind my housemate so I can kill you."

Before Mr. Donne could either comply with her request or assert his intention not to do so the doors of the hall burst open and the room was flooded with grey-uniformed Myrmidons.

✤

CHAPTER FIFTEEN

The Myrmidons

For the benefit of those readers who are not familiar with the idiosyncratic system of legal enforcement in the great city of Khelathra-Ven, I should perhaps clarify who, precisely, had just interrupted the altercation between Ms. Haas and the necromancer. The Myrmidons owe their origins to a time shortly after the unification of the cities of Khel, Athra, and Ven. The early years of independence proved tumultuous as the cities' various power blocks and interest groups vied for authority and influence. An especially vexed question in those days was that of the legitimate application of force. It would plainly not do for every guild, temple, aristocratic house, and popular movement to maintain its own private army and for those armies jointly and severally to act with the full weight of the state behind them.

Thus, it was determined that when violence became necessary within the boundaries of Khelathra-Ven it would be carried out by mercenaries whose loyalty was specifically to the Council of Interested Parties—that ill-defined, not to say anarchic convocation of lawmakers, luminaries, and lunatics who have governed the city for a hundred and fifty years—rather than to any one of the institutions represented upon it. Organisations and individuals were, of course, still permitted to keep their own guards (and any attempt to impose restrictions on the Eternal Lords of Ven was likely to have been nominal at best), but should there arise any circumstance in which it was necessary that a person be held against their will or, as sometimes happened in the early days, cut down in the street or burned alive in their home, that duty would fall to the Myrmidons. The institution has evolved since, being now concerned far more with detection and prevention of crime and far less with the bloody murder of dissidents. But the name, and some of the military trappings, remained.

One such trapping was the routine equipment of Myrmidon officers with some form of armament. Several of the persons who now moved to encircle us drew pistols, a fact which caused Mr. Donne and myself to raise our hands in a conciliatory manner; a gesture that Ms. Haas did not, apparently, feel compelled to mirror. Although the experience of being held at gunpoint by agents of law enforcement was a novel one to me it was not so startling as to distract my attention entirely from the Myrmidons' leader.

Her colouring was unusual for Khelathra-Ven (insofar as anything could be unusual in that cosmopolitan city), since she was fair haired and possessed piercing blue eyes, but what most struck me was that she was dressed in the garb of the witch hunters of Ey. This sight was shocking to me for two reasons. Firstly, because ours is a small and insular country, both literally and metaphorically, and we seldom travel far from our homeland unless driven from it. Secondly, and more pertinently, because the Faithful Society of Witch Hunters does not admit ladies.

"I am Augur Extraordinary Joy-in-Sorrow Standfast," she announced, "and you are all under arrest for making an affray by means of sorcery. Any of you do anything that even looks like witchcraft, everyone gets shot in the head."

It was an uncompromising strategy but, to the best of my understanding, exactly the one pursued by witch hunters in my own country. Since magic, by its nature, is heterogeneous there is no single, reliable countermeasure that can be taken against it other than the sudden, and sometimes preemptive, termination of the sorcerer. I hoped that at least one, and ideally both, of my co-arrestees would refrain from escalating the situation.

Ms. Haas bowed theatrically and in a manner which appeared calculated to draw attention to the occult markings carved into her chest. "My dear Standfast, I'm so glad you could make it. You're about to witness something wildly illegal and quite apocalyptic."

"I will give you one opportunity to rescind that threat and then I will order my men to open fire."

Though my experience at that point was limited, I thought it unlikely that Ms. Haas would rescind anything. Resigning myself to enduring a hail of gunfire, I scanned my immediate surroundings for cover. The chandelier would provide some protection, though little concealment, and I was within a short dive of an overturned table, to which I might be able to drag whichever of the others proved most tractable.

"Madam"—Mr. Donne stepped forward with surprising confidence—"you shall give no such order. I am a representative of the Ossuary Bank and you have neither cause nor authority to employ force against me."

To the best of my knowledge, the gentleman had the right of the situation. Being located on an island in the strait, the Ossuary Bank was not strictly part of the city and enjoyed, therefore, an element of independence from its laws. This technicality, however, did not seem to move the Augur Extraordinary.

"If your employers have a problem, they may register a complaint at New Arcadia Yard. Right now, all I see is a coven of witches calling up cursed spirits against innocent citizens."

I had no doubt that this was indeed how she saw it. In Ey we had learned the hard way that magic, if left unchecked, could subvert and strangle and corrupt anything it touched. We had responded by burning it from our lands with sacred fire, and it appeared that Augur Extraordinary Standfast was keen to do the same to Khelathra-Ven.

"You see?" said Ms. Haas with an air of self-satisfaction that I felt the situation far from warranted. "What we have here is a dreary little jobsworth with delusions of fanaticism. She will never be reasonable. Therefore, our only logical course of action is to kill her and all of her soldiers."

Any hope I had entertained that Mr. Donne or I might be able to de-escalate the situation evaporated. The second explicit death threat proved beyond the tolerance of Augur Extraordinary Standfast, who, at once, ordered her officers to fire. Having time to pull only one of my companions to safety and reasoning that Ms. Haas would not thank me for interfering with her confrontation, I pushed Mr. Donne to the floor for the second time that evening and we sheltered ourselves behind the overturned table I had previously identified. Mr. Donne was holding my hand rather tightly, but I attributed this to the anxieties inherent in our circumstances.

The air was filled with the crackling of gunshots and the screams of angry spirits. Not wishing to expose myself to either hazard, I looked out from my hiding place only cautiously. The Myrmidons, including their leader, were being violently assailed by ghostly figures, a contingency that rendered their aim somewhat inaccurate although I still saw fresh blood staining the silk at Ms. Haas's shoulder and ribs.

Beside me, Mr. Donne shut his eyes and began murmuring verses I couldn't follow in the language of ancient Khel. A few moments later, the apparitions vanished and a chill I had stopped noticing faded from the air.

Ms. Haas whirled upon our makeshift barricade. "I was using those, you presumptuous little corpse-prodder."

At which point Augur Extraordinary Standfast, having recovered her composure far more rapidly than her fellows, stalked forward and pressed her pistol to my companion's temple. "Shaharazad Haas, you are under arrest for making an affray by means of sorcery, for assaulting officers of the Myrmidons by means of sorcery, and for resisting arrest by means of sorcery."

"Oh, just shoot me and get it over with," sighed Ms. Haas. "I've had a long day."

"I would dearly like to, but the law ties my hands and the Creator commands us to obey the law no matter how misguided." The Augur Extraordinary snapped her fingers in the direction of her followers. "Put them in irons. All of them."

Two of the less incapacitated Myrmidons seized us and hauled us out from behind our somewhat bullet-scarred table.

"I must protest," protested Mr. Donne.

Augur Extraordinary Standfast's attention did not waver from my companion. "Noted."

"I . . . that . . . this is outrageous."

It was certainly rather troubling. But, given the Augur Extraordinary's demeanour, I considered resistance a wholly futile endeavour. Besides which, while I found it no small embarrassment to be arrested, I remained secure in the knowledge that the law was on my side and that my innocence would doubtless become apparent sooner rather than later. As for Mr. Donne, despite his moral culpability in the proceedings, he was entirely correct in his assertion that the Myrmidons had no authority over him except that which they exacted at gunpoint. Only Ms. Haas, I feared, found herself in real legal jeopardy, a state of affairs which appeared to cause her no concern whatsoever. Indeed, for a woman with a pistol at her head, who was bleeding from multiple lacerations, and who had until recently been possessed by more than a hundred furious ghosts, she evinced a quite startling air of boredom.

"You could at least let that one go," she remarked, waving a languid hand in my general direction. "He's clearly neither threat nor use to anybody."

This was a little hurtful, but I chose to assume my companion's intentions were, in context, benevolent.

It did nothing, however, to placate the Augur Extraordinary. "Silence, witch. Bring them."

One of the burlier officers produced a set of manacles and was about to fasten them about my wrists when he was checked by the sudden entrance of a newcomer—a tall and, if you will forgive the indiscretion, rather handsome gentleman, with an intent, solemn look that, I confess, inspired in me an unexpected sense of fellowship. From the shade of his skin and eyes, and, for that matter, the fact that his left hand was a remarkable contraption of metal and gemstones, I assumed him to hail from the city of the Steel Magi far to the south, beyond El'avarah and the boundaries of the old caliphate. This assumption proved incorrect on deeper acquaintance, but my editor informs me that I am diminishing the tension of this interlude by such digression.

His expression, as he beheld the scene before him, was not encouraging. "If this is even half as bad as it seems, every single one of us is in for a world of vexation."

Neither I nor any other member of the assembly could have been surprised that Ms. Haas was the first to respond. "Second Augur Lawson," she purred. "And to think, until now, you've done such a fine job of enriching this evening by your absence."

"Can it, Haas. I don't even know what's happening here, but I know it's definitely your fault."

The Augur Extraordinary seemed no more inclined to lower her weapon than she had before the arrival of the stranger. "Stand down, Lawson. These three are all implicated in offences under the Sorcery Act, First Year, First Council. You have no jurisdiction here."

"And neither do you. That man"—he pointed at Mr. Donne with a mechanical finger—"is clearly wearing the sigil of the Ossuary Bank. If you arrest him, it'll cause an almighty—"

And here, the gentleman addressed as Second Augur Lawson employed a colourful meteorological metaphor suggesting a wide-ranging and indiscriminate unpleasantness.

Augur Extraordinary Standfast at last took her eyes off Ms. Haas, but only to glare at Lawson. "That is a matter to be resolved between the necromancers and the Office of Augurs Extraordinary."

"I think you'll find," piped up Mr. Donne, "that particular matter was resolved a century ago. The Charter of Sepulchres grants the bank exclusive licence both to practise necromancy and to punish its mis-use. I'm not very good at being threatening, but as an accountant, I can assure you that thoughtlessly provoking a conflict with my em-ployers will prove extremely costly for the Myrmidons."

Second Augur Lawson made a sound somewhere between a sigh and a groan. "I was just coming off duty. I bought a pie from Cord-wangle's Superior Pie Emporium and was really looking forward to eating it. I really do not need any of this right now." He turned to the somewhat bemused-looking officers. "Clear off, the lot of you. Augur Extraordinary Standfast is out of bounds and anybody who backs her up will be up on disciplinaries faster than you can say 'Sorry we inter-rupted your dinner, Second Augur Lawson.'"

I could not help but note that the Augur Extraordinary waited until the uniformed Myrmidons had departed, which they did with great alacrity and a palpable sense of relief, before rounding upon her colleague. "You will regret this, Lawson."

"Already do. Now let these people go."

Ms. Haas, who had watched the altercation with obvious plea-sure, chose this moment to interject. "You heard the man. Put your little pistol back in your trousers and go back to flogging yourself and crying or however else you spend your evenings."

Needless to say, this did not inspire the Augur Extraordinary to lower her weapon. "I'm taking the sorceress."

"You know what?" Second Augur Lawson spread his hands in an

expansive gesture of apathy. "Fine. You can have her. She's more trouble than she's worth."

Ms. Haas shot Lawson a familiar smile. "And there I was thinking you didn't like me."

She then permitted herself, with an uncharacteristic lack of protest but a characteristic air of superiority, to be led from the building by the Augur Extraordinary. Mr. Donne, for his part, apologised several times, thus somewhat undercutting his effort to portray himself as the untouchable representative of his order, and thanked me rather abashedly for the small part I had played in preserving his life during the evening's events. Then, with a rather regretful look in my direction, he quit the hall. This left me alone amongst the glittering wreckage with the Second Augur.

"If I were you," he said, "I'd go home and forget this ever happened. And maybe in future try to avoid standing between two angry wizards."

"Thank you for the advice, but I hope I shall never sit idle in times of trouble."

Sentiments such as those I had just expressed seldom drew approval in Khelathra-Ven and, on this occasion, earned me a hard stare from the Second Augur. "In my experience, people who sit idle live much longer lives."

"I was raised to believe that longevity has little value without purpose. And surely," I added, rather more boldly than our acquaintance warranted, "a public servant cannot be so cynical?"

"Have you met the public?"

"Well"—I blinked—"not all of them. But, then, I rather think that would be impossible."

The Second Augur narrowed his eyes. "Is that what passes for a joke in Ey?"

"Oh no. The only joke we're allowed to tell in Ey is: How many unbelievers does it take to replace a gas lamp? None. They're too busy wasting their time on frivolities."

There was a long silence.

"We are also permitted," I continued, not entirely certain what had come over me: "Your mother is so impious her immortal soul is in serious peril."

At this, Second Augur Lawson laughed, a reaction from which I derived considerable satisfaction, for it was not one I was accustomed to engendering. "You're a surprising fellow, Mr. . . ."

"Wyndham, sir. John Wyndham."

"Well then, John Wyndham." He was still smiling faintly. "I should wish you a good night and a safe journey home."

"I thank you for your concern, but I fear I must detain you a moment longer."

"Must you, now?" I could not quite read his tone and hoped that I had not inadvertently made myself a suspect.

"I would like to know what has become of my housemate."

After a slight pause, the Second Augur said rather warily, "You're living with Shaharazad Haas?"

"Yes. For some weeks now."

"Oh, dear me. She is going to eat you alive."

"In my experience, she dines rather modestly."

I was dismayed to observe that the Second Augur's manner towards me had altered perceptively. "I'm serious, Mr. Wyndham. Chaos follows her around like orphans after a pie seller."

"You seem to have pies rather on your mind, sir."

"I'm hungry, but I'm trying to help you here."

"What would help me," I insisted, "is knowing how I might facilitate my companion's release from custody."

This made him laugh again, although in a far less pleasant way than he had the first time. "There's nothing you can do and there's nothing you have to do. Shaharazad Haas never cleans up her own mess." He did not say "mess."

"Even so, I cannot countenance abandoning my friend in her hour of need."

"She's not your friend and she's not in an hour of need. She's in an hour of deciding to mess with the Myrmidons." Once more, he did not say "mess."

I thought it quite impossibly presumptuous that the Second Augur would believe he knew more about my relationship with Ms. Haas than I did myself. It was true she never did her own laundry or tidied away her own teacups, and that she left me to scrub suspicious bloodstains out of the floor of the kitchen, had once vomited in my hat, on a separate occasion prevailed upon me to move her hand from her waist to her forehead because she lacked the energy to lift it herself, and, on this very evening, had thrown a chandelier at my head, but I remained convinced that she was, deep down, a good and honourable person.

As I was opening my mouth to defend her, the Second Augur interrupted. "Look. Just go home. You'll probably find she's already there. She's far too good at taking care of herself."

Not wanting to seem obstreperous or ungrateful, and persuaded that I would be better able to aid Ms. Haas with the resources available to me at 221b Martyrs Walk, I followed the Second Augur's advice. And, to my very mild chagrin, found that he had been entirely correct.

CHAPTER SIXTEEN

❧

An Interlude

Ms. Haas was stretched out on the chaise longue, still clad in her tattered and bloodstained silks. The air was filled with the now-familiar scent of Valentino's Good Rough Shag.

"Ah. Wyndham." She attempted to prop herself on her elbows and seemed to immediately regret it. "What kept you?"

"I was endeavouring to see if there were any means by which I could secure your release."

"How very silly of you. Surely you recalled Mr. Donne's assertion that the entire matter fell beneath the auspices of the Ossuary Bank? I may have hinted to the Myrmidons that the necromancers would, even as we spoke, be conjuring a phalanx of vengeful phantoms to destroy me and anything that stood in their way. After that, they were quite keen to let me go."

"But was that true?"

"Not in the prosaic sense." Reaching down, she scrabbled amongst the discarded syringes on the floor for one of her many phials of intoxicants but, in this case, the search proved fruitless. "Still, they'll probably have a go at killing me sooner or later. Most people do."

I was pleased that my companion appeared to have been neither incarcerated nor assassinated but, having some medical experience from both my work at the hospital and my time in the Company of

Strangers, I noted also that she still had a bullet lodged in her shoulder, alongside sundry other flesh wounds.

"If you will forgive my bluntness," I said, "you should let somebody look at your injuries."

She managed an imperious sneer. "I'm perfectly well, Captain. I require only a good night's sleep and enough opium to kill a small child."

"You require a number of sutures and the removal of a lead slug that is currently embedded somewhere in the vicinity of your left clavicle."

"I shall make a bargain with you. Bring me a glass of laudanum and you may poke me with whatever needles you wish."

I was not entirely aware that I had been attempting to strike a bargain, but I was also fast coming to the realisation that Ms. Haas would only be willing to accept my assistance if I allowed her to pretend she was doing me a favour. Repairing to my bedroom, I retrieved what medical supplies I still possessed from my time in the company and prepared for Ms. Haas the narcotic she requested, combining the drug with its solvent in a rather less dangerous ratio than was my companion's common practice.

On my return to the sitting room, I found that the lady had managed to manoeuvre herself into an upright position and she took the glass of laudanum from me with neither thanks nor complaint, which I took as a net victory. Practical necessity taking precedence over regular propriety, I peeled away those areas of Ms. Haas's clothing that were obscuring her injuries. The process was doubtless rather painful for her, but she seemed at least to derive some pleasure from my evident discomfort at the intimacy. Employing a long disused pair of forceps I was able, with some effort, to locate and retrieve the bullet. For want of a more conventional or appropriate receptacle, I dropped it into a half-empty teacup, where, I seem to recall, it remained for the best part of a week.

At the clink of lead on china, Ms. Haas opened heavy-lidded eyes. "Deftly done, Captain. I shall bear you in mind the next time I get myself shot."

"Perhaps," I suggested, "you could instead endeavour not to be."

"Given what you know of me, Mr. Wyndham, do you think that is at all probable?"

I did not. As fresh blood was now welling from Ms. Haas's shoulder, a circumstance that caused me rather more distress than it caused her, I cleaned the area as best I could and began to stitch the wound closed. In my childhood, my father had strongly encouraged me to develop those skills he deemed appropriate and, while I have found little use for most of them, I have always found sewing to be of eminent practical value. It is a skill the acquisition of which I would recommend to anybody, for it stood me in good stead as a student, as a soldier, and throughout my adventures with Ms. Haas, around whom things tended to need fixing with disturbing regularity.

Whether as a consequence of the day's exertions or the laudanum or whatever she had managed to take before I arrived home, Ms. Haas remained unusually quiet throughout the whole process. As I was tending the gash on her ribs, however, she patted me absentmindedly on the head and observed in the dreamlike tones of one who has consumed far too many sedatives, "You know, you're a terribly convenient young man to have around."

"Thank you." Although I was aware that she was not, perhaps, speaking as she would have done were she entirely in command of her faculties, I could not help but feel gratified, for I have ever aspired to be of service to others.

I was loath to take advantage of my companion's disorientated state, but there had been a number of questions troubling me since the start of the evening and I suspected that if I did not ask them now I would not have another opportunity. "If I might," I went on, "why did you destroy Mr. Donne's servant?"

"Former lover." She flopped back against the cushions and stared at the ceiling. "We hadn't been close in a decade, but it was the principle of the thing."

"Meaning no disrespect," I replied, "I had not thought you to be strongly motivated by principle."

"Aha." She gave a hoarse laugh and wagged one finger in what I believe she thought was my face but which was actually a space some inches to the left of it. "That is where I have you fooled. I am, in fact, a woman of deep, abiding principles. And the most personal and most sacred of them is this: nobody touches my things."

I was not, in candour, convinced that this constituted a "principle" in the generally accepted sense. "Is that also why you sent me to interfere in Miss Viola's personal life?"

Her hands twitched in what appeared to be the most expressive gesture she could currently manage. "Well, there was some chance that I might have discovered a promising suspect amongst Miss Beck's associates. But I confess it was always slim."

"Was that reason enough to risk the happiness of two blameless young women?"

"Firstly, Eirene has never been blameless. Secondly, even a remote possibility of finding useful information is always worth pursuing. And, finally"—here the corners of her lips turned up rather cynically—"I was very, very curious to see the woman who would tame Eirene Viola."

With the last of Ms. Haas's injuries dressed, I began to clean and store my apparatus. "Well, I personally found her very charming and thought they made a most handsome and affectionate couple. I am sure they shall be very happy together."

"Is that what you think?"

"Indeed I do," I exclaimed. "It seems plain that they love each other very much."

"Oh, I've no doubt that they love each other. And that is exactly why they will make each other miserable."

"That seems a perverse line of reasoning."

"Come now, Mr. Wyndham. The only people in this world who can hurt us more than those we love are those who love us in return."

I felt moved to protest at this but, reflecting on the circumstances of my childhood, I found myself unable to. Thankfully I was spared the need to formulate a response of any kind because my companion had closed her eyes and lapsed, with typical abruptness, into unconsciousness.

CHAPTER SEVENTEEN

The Docks at Shattered Point

Following that night's misadventures, Ms. Haas retired to her chambers, whence she did not emerge for several days. When she at last reappeared, bursting into my bedroom still in the tattered remnants of the outfit she had been wearing during our previous excursion, I was perturbed to note that her eyelashes were caked in blood and her forearms adorned with myriad injuries that appeared to be tiny bite marks.

"Come, Wyndham," she said. "To Ven."

I was not, at this stage, so accustomed to my companion's violent changes in mood as I would later become and was, therefore, unprepared both emotionally and logistically for this unexpected call to action. The hour was already uncomfortably late and, having completed my logs of the day's dispensations at the hospital, I had undressed to my shirtsleeves and was making ready to retire. "Is now really the best time?"

"Now is always the best time."

"It is after midnight and you appear to be injured."

She glanced at her arms with mild curiosity. "My, my, they were voracious this time, weren't they?"

"They?" I blinked. "And also . . . this time?"

"Really, Captain. If you are going to insist that I explain myself every time an otherworldly being assaults my psyche and attempts to devour me, our conversations are liable to become both repetitious and disruptive."

"It has been my experience that one's comrades being devoured is generally rather more disruptive."

Sighing, she scraped the blood from her eyes with the edge of a fingernail. "Do be sensible. If an entity attempts to destroy me and fails, it will impact your plans only minimally. If it succeeds, I will be quite incapable of describing its nature to you afterwards."

"You could always warn me in advance, and thus engage my assistance against whatever forces assail you."

"I told you that I was not entirely lying when I said that the Ossuary Bank would pursue redress against me for my insult to Mr. Donne. That you, despite this knowledge, left me to spend two days being assaulted by their invisible enforcers and I, despite your absence, was able to overcome the attack suggests that our current arrangement is perfectly serviceable. You can be of most assistance by protecting me from tedious distractions and minding your own affairs. Tasks that you have, hitherto, accomplished admirably."

I conceded the point.

"Now then, if you've finished trying to coddle me"—Ms. Haas strode across the room and flung open my wardrobe—"I suggest that you change. You are about to become very, very wet indeed."

From my companion's promise of incipient saturation, it was clear that she had decided—for whatever reason—that now was the most opportune moment for us to interview Mr. Enoch Reef, the Vennish information broker with whom Miss Viola had worked some years previously. Not wishing to delay our endeavour (for I had been conscious for much of the past week that Miss Viola's time could easily be running out), I hastily donned a set of striped waterproof undergarments over which I fastened my most expendable doublet and breeches. For her part, Ms. Haas had selected a deep blue bathing dress of a type that had been modish some six years before and an oiled greatcoat that sported no fewer than six bullet holes and a long rent down one side that, by my judgement, had been made by one of the serrated weapons commonly used by the sky-pirates of the Blackcrest Mountains. A bandolier holding several harpoons, and a harpoon gun barely concealed beneath the greatcoat, completed the ensemble.

Satisfied with her attire, and with my own, she hailed us a hansom and, within the hour, we were standing upon the docks at Shattered Point. For those amongst my readership who have not journeyed to Khelathra-Ven I should explain that the sunken city of Ven is accessible from various locales via public submersible and that the docks at Shattered Point are the most frequented and most convenient of these points of ingress. I should perhaps further explain that, although the city of Ven is wholly underwater, the strange magics of its eternal overlords, in combination with the industrial ingenuity of Khelathran entrepreneurs, allow some districts to retain a breathable environment into which surface dwellers can safely venture. It was in just such a district that I had lived during my years at university. It was not to such a district that we were currently journeying. This meant that we would require the services of a reputable wormerer and a disreputable pilot.

The wormerer Ms. Haas located stood at the end of a rickety jetty halfway along the dock. His wares writhed in a barrel beside him, their strange keening song barely perceptible at the edge of hearing.

Ms. Haas prodded the barrel with the tip of her harpoon gun and then peered into the murky waters. Apparently, whatever she witnessed within was satisfying to her.

"Two, please," she said.

The wormerer had the webbed digits and needle-like teeth common amongst the inhabitants of certain parts of Ven. Both features were displayed to advantage as he held up four fingers and grinned. "Four rials."

"You, sir, are having a laugh."

"Folks as buy cheap worms tend to get their brains ate."

"What a coincidence. The same thing happens to people who mistake me for a tourist."

He made an odd burbling noise, the emotional timbre of which I was unable to discern. "I can go to three, what with you being a pair and all."

"I will give you two rials, which you know is more than these beasts are worth, and I shall select them myself. This is my final offer."

"Moonlight robbery is what it is, but I'll take it."

Ms. Haas handed the gentleman his payment and, in return, he gave her the two small grey tablets that we would need to take in order to destroy the worms before they took control of our minds entirely. Then she spent some time considering, and poking at, the contents of the barrel before plucking out two of the slick, eel-like creatures and transferring them into an oilskin bag.

Our next order of business was the commissioning of a submersible, a task that would prove somewhat more straightforward, as Ms. Haas appeared to be on quite familiar terms with the captain whose services we eventually engaged. The gentleman in question went by the unlikely name of Saltpetre, and his dress and manner were no less outlandish than his moniker. He was clad in rough and dusty leathers of a design I had never seen before, and his face was concealed partly by a set of aviator's goggles and partly by a pattern of intricately inked tattoos. His vessel was distinctive even amongst the idiosyncratic craft of the submariners in that it appeared to lack a name and several aspects of its design suggested that it had been intended to function amphibiously. Of greater concern was the vehicle's obvious state of disrepair. Its armour was scored and shell-marked, and its hatches—although they appeared watertight—were mottled with altogether too much rust to inspire confidence.

As our pilot set about his preparations for departure, I took the opportunity to draw Ms. Haas aside and convey, with as much discretion as could be managed, the extent of my reservations.

"Your point is well made, Mr. Wyndham," returned Ms. Haas, as she idly checked the action on her harpoon gun. "But our options are limited. Few captains will venture into the deeper reaches of Ven, and fewer still can be trusted."

"You trust this . . . this"—my descriptive powers failed me—"personage, then?"

"Insofar as I would trust anybody in his line of work. We have travelled together before and he has conveniently few ties in the city. Half the pilots on the docks are in the pay of some power or other and while Saltpetre has his own loyalties they are not relevant to our present endeavour."

"If I might ask, to what are they relevant?"

"To a conflict that shall not take place for approximately eighty-four thousand years."

And, with that, she climbed nimbly up the side of the submersible and disappeared inside. I followed, still uncertain but undeniably curious; a state of mind that, alongside abject terror and absolute bewilderment, would come to characterise a significant fraction of my acquaintance with the sorceress Shaharazad Haas.

A few moments later, we were joined by Mr. Saltpetre, who dropped through the hatch with a certain feral agility and slammed it closed behind him. He elbowed me out of the way and took his place in the one available seat—a tattered chair, surrounded by a disorderly array of dials, switches, levers, and wheels. These he operated in some arcane sequence, causing the whole machine to shudder tumultuously into life. I was conscious of a sensation of motion and we began our descent.

Whatever strange energy animated the vehicle had bathed the interior in a sickly green light that appeared to emanate from a dusty glass jar set into one wall. While I was glad not to be in total darkness, the scene it illuminated was far from prepossessing. Between the metal tubes and the humming boxes and the devices that scribbled undecipherable data onto ever-unspooling rolls of paper there was barely room to think, let alone to stand. There could be no doubt that the vehicle into which we had sealed ourselves was primarily military in function, for I had seen similar machines in my time at the Unending Gate. Some swam, some crawled, and some flew, but all were designed for the same purpose—to ensure that death came sooner to one's enemies than to oneself. In truth, I was not entirely delighted to find myself within one again, although I was able to bear the experience without complaint.

Once the engines had been primed and the course set, Mr. Saltpetre turned to address us. His accent was not one I had heard before, and his voice gruff and throaty, but I have done my best to capture the gist of his speech here.

"Okay, Shaz, Shaz's mate," he said, "we're running low, and as quiet as this bucket of bolts can get. We're going to have to go the long way round the pearl farms, steering clear of the Colossus and the Coral Towers. We'll take a shortcut through the Unremembered Gardens and I should have you in Keeper's Shallows within the hour. When we get there, you'll need to hop into the torpedo tubes, and remember to swallow your worms before you get fired out, or you'll probably drown. If you're not back at the boat by dawn, I'll assume you're dead and leave without you."

He did not say "leave." He used an idiomatic phrase ending with the word "off" that I am certain my gentle readers shall not have heard.

The journey itself was uncomfortable but uneventful, and we passed it mostly in silence. When Mr. Saltpetre indicated that we had arrived at our destination, Ms. Haas passed me one of the creatures that she had purchased earlier in the evening. I had never used a Surfeiting Worm before, as I had always restricted myself to the aerated sectors of Ven, but I was familiar with the principles of their use.

The Surfeiting Worm is, from a scientific perspective, a remarkable entity. The product of millennia of careful breeding and sorcerous manipulation, it enters through the mouth and crawls into the trachea, where it secretes certain chemicals that permit it to interface with the host's lungs, larynx, and central nervous system. A form of mystical hybridisation then occurs, permitting the user to filter life-giving airs from the water, much as a fish or eel would, and also to communicate with other worm-users and subaquatic entities, the creature's tail supplanting some of the functions of the user's own tongue. Regardless of the academically fascinating opportunity before me, I confess that, holding the animal in my hand, long, lithe, and wriggling as it was, I did not relish the prospect of giving it access to my person. Nevertheless it was, for the sake of our client, necessary that I do so.

I shall spare the reader a precise description of how it felt to have the worm squeeze its way down my windpipe and infiltrate itself securely into my bronchial tubes. There was a brief sensation of choking and a strange awareness of alien thoughts impinging gently against my own. Should you ever visit the great city of Khelathra-Ven and feel the need to explore the sunken ruins of Ven you may perhaps have cause to make use of the worm yourself. I would be remiss in my duty as a chronicler of adventures were I not to remind you of the paramount importance of selecting a healthy specimen from an accredited wormerer and of being certain to take the exfiltrating toxin as soon as your work under the sea is concluded, lest the creature solidify its hold on your nervous system and suborn your brain for its own inscrutable purposes.

I hunkered down into the torpedo tube and waited for Mr. Saltpetre to fire.

CHAPTER EIGHTEEN

The Eternal Empire of Ven

Before I proceed with the central thrust of my narrative, it behooves me to ensure that the reader has an adequate understanding of the history behind the lost and marvellous place to which we now journeyed. My editor is not in agreement with me on this matter and has requested on several occasions that I excise these elucidating passages in favour of scenes of a more sensational or salacious nature. For those amongst you who share my editor's predilections, please rest assured that following this necessary digression there shall be a sequence in which we fight a shark, another in which we are suspected of murder, and a third in which we are drawn into intercourse with several members of the city's vile criminal underworld.

Any exegesis on the history of Ven must inevitably begin with an acknowledgement that the vast gulf of history between the collapse of its empire and the present day, combined with the extratemporal nature of both that realm and the enemy which ultimately destroyed it, makes all historical speculation circumspect. Much has been written on the subject, and very little agreed. My somewhat biased opinion is that the most reliable authority on the matter is Professor J. R. Donahue-Kishen, with whom I was acquainted at university, who has made this subject zir life's work, and of whose researches I have made liberal use in the following passages.

For those who would prefer to "skip straight to the action," as my editor puts it, you need only know the following: that Ven was once the heart of a mighty empire that stretched across time and space, that the empire was destroyed by a terrible enemy, and that it has since sunk beneath the waves. You may now turn to the beginning of the next chapter, in which Ms. Haas and I fight a shark, although if you are reading this in the serialised edition you shall be forced to wait until next month's instalment of *The Strait* magazine to hear of this diverting incident. For the remainder of my readers, I present my inadequate summary of the decline and fall of the Eternal Empire of Ven. Should you wish to read more on this subject, I direct you to Professor Donahue-Kishen's excellent treatise *The Eternal Empire of Ven: An Analysis of Its Origins, Descent, Dominion, and Destruction*, presented in detail, and illustrated with woodcarvings by Lady Quinella Thrumpmusket.

The Eternal Empire of Ven was so named because its provinces and colonies extended not only across the known world but to distant stars, distant galaxies, distant realities, and even distant times. At the height of its power, a Vennish Lord could reach out his, her, their, or zir hand and pluck fruit from the crystal trees that grew on the mountains of burning wax at the dawn of all creation and then cast the pit into the great and sucking void that shall swallow the cosmos at the end of all things.

During their ascendancy there existed no army, no nation, no world, and no god that could challenge the Eternal Lords of Ven and this fact may, at the end, have proved their undoing. Having achieved dominion over everything that was, they turned their attention to that which was not. To the uncountable infinities encompassed by the anti-worlds and unlands ruled over by the Empress of Nothing, that terrible mistress of all that never was, nor would never be.

Where the real had bent easily to their arcane technologies and limitless magics, the unreal legions of the Empress of Nothing were an enemy beyond reckoning. They unmade the patterns that bound the empire together, unmooring the Eternal Lords of Ven from time itself and consuming their works in water or fire or oblivion. The great nexus city itself crashed beneath the waves and was drowned, its masters imprisoned within their towers, where they remain, their once boundless power folded in upon itself into a fragile, local omnipotence. As the millennia passed, the seas changed them, and they the seas.

Over time other creatures from the fathomless depths of the oceans have crawled or swum or slunk into the ruins of Ven, and scholars are divided as to whether these beings are intruders who the Eternal Lords tolerate or if, from within their Coral Towers, the once-mighty sorcerers have reached out and gathered about themselves new subjects and new servants. A tiny datum in support of the latter interpretation is that when the Eternal Lords made their overtures to the Council of Interested Parties during the secession of Khelathra from the Uthmani Sultanate their interests were represented by one of the piscine hybrids now native to the strait.

Today surfacers venture into Ven to view its unique sights, to indulge in certain vices that I shall not name, to trade in pearls and other, more esoteric materials, and to access some of the remote pathways that connect the underwater city to distant realities. Occasionally somebody from the upper city will be permitted audience with one of the Eternal Lords and will often take this opportunity to negotiate for access to or even the creation of a specific gateway. Such encounters abound with both opportunity and danger, for while the masters of Ven are not easily stirred to action, once roused, their capacity to offer aid or injury to those who catch their eye is near limitless.

Persistent rumour holds that an emissary from one of the Ubiquitous Companies once slighted a Vennish Lord by the name of Nine Opals. The individual in question worked for the Ubiquitous Company of Skrive Makers. That nobody now knows what a skrive is, or what any such thing may ever have been, or what purpose manufacturers of such things may have had in negotiating with an Eternal Lord, but everybody nonetheless agrees that this was, indeed, the name of the company may serve to illustrate quite how absolute is the peril one faces when trifling with matters Vennish.

❦

CHAPTER NINETEEN

Keeper's Shallows

I emerged from the torpedo tube with such velocity that I did not notice the shark until we had already collided. It was a large specimen, of *Carcharodon marvosi*, a terrible and justly reviled predator once native to the planet Marvos before the industrial excesses of that world's people drained its oceans and scoured its lands into a red desert.

Underwater combat had not formed part of my training with the Company of Strangers, but I had, on occasion, been called upon to defend myself in environments that lacked air or gravity and so I was not entirely without resources when the voracious beast rounded upon me, its mouth wide and displaying countless rows of razor-like teeth. In such a circumstance the instinct to flee can prove both overwhelming and fatal. Large hunting animals will naturally pursue anything that attempts to evade them. I did my best, therefore, to remain calm and resolved, where possible, to answer aggression with aggression. I did my best to strike it a forceful blow upon the nose as I often read of people doing in adventure stories, but the drag of the water, combined with the infelicitous angle, meant that I did little but graze my knuckles on the edge of its snout. If I wished to put the monster to flight, I would need more precisely to target its areas of vulnerability.

I was, in this respect, fortunate to be so close to the beast, since its bulk—roughly equivalent to that of a locomotive carriage—was such that it had difficulty manoeuvring round in order to bring its jaws to bear. Thus, I was afforded the opportunity to dig my fingers into its gill slits as it passed, my twofold aim being to discommode the creature enough that it might retreat and, failing that, to give myself some purchase whereby I might hold my body out of its reach. I soon learned, to my dismay, that the skin of a Great Marvosi Shark has more in common with scree or shale than with the soft epidermis of more wholesome animals, and I fear I cut my palms rather badly.

My stratagem nevertheless proved partially successful in that I was most certainly able to excite the shark, and was momentarily able to keep it from either devouring or dismembering me. Regrettably, the creature soon pulled itself free of my grip, taking more skin from my fingertips with it, my blood curling through the water in dark red wisps. As I sought in vain for some form of shelter, the dreadful fish circled around for a second attack. I was, in this moment, conscious that I might very shortly die and was, in all candour, quite sanguine about the fact. My encounter in the Mocking Realm had haunted and disturbed me, for it represented something quite beyond my prior experience. A mere gargantuan killing machine, by contrast, was an eminently comprehensible danger and my time at the Unending Gate had quite inured me to the risk of impending annihilation.

It was some comfort to me that the shark seemed at least a little cautious about coming for me again. I had, if nothing else, given it something to think about. And this hesitation perhaps saved my life, for it allowed my companion, the sorceress Shaharazad Haas, to swim into a position of vantage, take aim, and loose her harpoon into the creature's left eye. I am relatively certain that sharks are, under normal circumstances, silent, but, owing to my peculiar, and hopefully temporary, symbiosis with the Surfeiting Worm I distinctly heard what sounded like a scream of pain as my erstwhile attacker thrashed about in an ever-growing cloud of its own blood and humours.

Perhaps deciding that easier prey lay elsewhere, the shark turned away and slunk off through the murky depths. I watched it depart with a sense of mingled relief and wonder. Now that it was no longer attempting to do me harm I was able, briefly, to appreciate it for the marvellous specimen that it was—a study in grace and ferocity that seemed to embody the indomitable spirit of Marvos.

Ms. Haas, meanwhile, reached into her bandolier and reloaded her weapon. "Well handled, Mr. Wyndham. I have had several companions eaten by sharks in similar circumstances, and I'm sure at least three of them would be alive today had they shown your wherewithal."

I was somewhat at a loss as to how to reply to this. While it was always gratifying to have one's competencies acknowledged, I could not help but wonder about the fates of those other unfortunates. I settled on, "Thank you, Ms. Haas."

"Now come along." She executed a flawless subaquatic somersault and began swimming downwards.

Our ultimate destination was an overgrown ruin, a once-splendid quarter of Ven fallen long ago to rubble and rebuilt in the intervening years into a haphazard, many-tiered shanty. I trusted that my companion had at least some inkling of the location of our quarry as we made our way through twisting corridors of ancient stone and rotting driftwood, past the tarnished hulls of steamships and starships, and deeper still into tunnels with walls neither concave nor convex, and slick with luminescent algae.

My companion paused by a primitive statue of some bloated, blasphemous deity. "You know, I really should have written down his address. Non-euclidean street maps can be so difficult to navigate."

"Forgive me for asking, but are we lost?"

"A sorceress is never lost. However, on occasion, her path will show her vistas unfamiliar to her conscious mind."

"How is that different?"

"I assure you, my dear, it's much more fun."

One of Ven's hulking, ichthyoid denizens emerged from a passageway I was certain had not been there a moment before. "Look," I said, "why don't we ask that gentlebeing for directions?"

"I do not need directions. I know precisely where we are not."

"Excuse me, siram." I paddled over towards the stranger, employing the formal neutral address that exists in Khelish but not Eyan or Athran, and which my limited knowledge of the inhabitants of Ven suggested was most suitable for such a creature. My understanding of the species' reproductive biology was minimal (Ms. Haas once lent me a book on the subject, which I left in my room for some days and surreptitiously returned unread), but I was aware that their culture lacked a concept of gender.

It peered at me with its bulbous, unblinking eyes. When it spoke I was aware that the words I heard in my mind were not the sounds it was, in fact, making, but rather an illusion projected by the Surfeiting Worm. "Yeah? What?"

"We are looking for a person by the name of Enoch Reef, who I believe has lodgings in this area. Might you possibly be able to assist us?"

"Aw, mate." It made a frankly alien gesture with its claws which, in context, I took to signal the particular blend of sympathy and frustration that one reserves for a well-meaning stranger who has naively asked one for assistance with a task whose magnitude they have greatly underestimated. "You're well out your way. What you want to do is go back up the Tunnel of Lost Souls, take a left round where the Temple of S'uh'faxla'hca used to be 'til it got closed down and they put one of them fancy pubs that do the posh food over it, then that got closed down on account of health code violations. Then you want to take another left, second right, third down, straight ahead, and if you get to a yawning abyss where the mutilated corpses of drowned sailors swirl in a dance of endless torment you've gone too far."

"Thank you. You've been most helpful."

"No scales off my snout." It kicked its powerful hind flippers and swam off with an alacrity that belied its bulk.

Ms. Haas was bobbing with her arms folded. "It would have been the work of moments to determine that information for myself. But I can't believe the Temple of S'uh'faxla'hca has closed down. They had the most incredible unholy fornications every ninth new moon."

With what seemed to be a genuinely wistful air, she reversed course and led me onwards. As I became accustomed to the gloom and the peculiarities of the architecture, I was able to discern more of my surroundings. What appeared from the outside little more than the desolate remains of a fallen civilisation was, in fact, a hive of industry. Much of the industry in question was obviously of a dubious nature, but here and there we saw signs that this otherwise benighted region was beginning to attract the kind of fashionable attention that so often lighted, however briefly, upon such places. Thus a ruined temple filled with worm-addled beggars would sit alongside a bijou kiosk selling hand-curated whelks to gullible visitors in search of an authentically Vennish experience.

Our journey naturally led us to the darker recesses of the district, in both the figurative and the literal senses of that term. So it was that Ms. Haas and I swam through a narrow crack in the side of a great cyclopean stone and found ourselves floating a few short feet from the impaled corpse of a well-dressed young gentleman.

Between a childhood lived under the thrall of a sadistic sorcerer king, an adolescence against the backdrop of bloody revolution, and an early adulthood spent waging ceaseless war against the Empress of Nothing I had seen much of death. As such, I was surprised but not shocked to find a gruesomely skewered cadaver drifting past my nose. Perhaps the fact that I had arrived at my present location as a consequence of following the directions of a talking fish monster and was able to survive only due to the presence of an alien symbiote in several of my more vital passages also contributed to my perhaps callous-seeming equanimity.

"Oh, dear," I observed. "How regrettable for the poor fellow. I wonder who he might be and what might have brought him to this unhappy end."

Ms. Haas would have been tapping her foot had she been standing on a solid surface. As it was, it became an odd sort of waggle. "Really, Wyndham. Do you pay no attention? This gentleman was clearly a student of the University of Khel who was ambushed en route to a meeting with the very Mr. Reef we ourselves are seeking by some third party wishing either him or Mr. Reef harm. He was local, of Athran stock, from a good family whose means have recently diminished. He smoked Professor Lipquist's filterless cigarillos, was frightened of bees, and kept an Ulveshi shape-shifting parakeet."

"Surely you jest, Ms. Haas."

"Not at all. Everything is plain to the trained observer. You said yourself that it was common even in your day for students of the university to sell snippets of gossip to Mr. Reef and his ilk. The man is clearly Athran by his complexion and attire, which would at one point have been the height of fashion but, since his wardrobe has not kept pace with current trends, and since the soles of his shoes are worn nearly through, when any self-respecting gadabout would have replaced them long ago, we can deduce quite simply that he once had means but has access to them no longer. His youth makes it yet more likely he is a student and his presence so close to the lair of an information broker is further evidence that he had need of money. I would therefore stake the reputation I do not, in fact, possess on both conclusions."

"This is remarkable," I exclaimed. "But what of the cigarillos, the bees, and the parakeet?"

"The ash from his frankly odious brand of tobacco leaves a distinctive stain that I noticed at once on his lapel. Remember, I remarked that he was wearing an old suit. The Ulveshi shape-shifting parakeet is a popular exotic pet, often purchased by young ignorants who do not understand the best way to care for it and come off the worst as a result. You can see the man's right hand bears a number of scratches, all of which appear to have been made by a different creature. Either he keeps a tiny but extraordinarily diverse menagerie or, like many of his sort, he owns an Ulveshi shape-shifting parakeet. As for his fear of bees, on that detail I was just playing with you."

She did not use the word "playing." She employed a different phrase, one with connotations of intimate relations. Having long grown accustomed to such ribbing, I gently redirected Ms. Haas's attention to the matter of the deceased gentleman. "You also said that he had been ambushed by somebody wishing harm to either him or Mr. Reef?"

"Now I *am* disappointed. You are a military man, Captain. What do you see?"

I considered the corpse as directed. The spike of a harpoon projected from his chest, but I could see no other signs of injury or struggle. "He was pierced through the back," I said. "Had this been merely a case of robbery gone wrong his attacker would have been facing him and would have resorted to violence only if there was no way to relieve our unfortunate friend of his valuables. This shot was aimed to kill and clearly came without warning. Thus, it was deliberate murder. Thus, the attacker was motivated by either personal animus against our unknown victim or by enmity, either professional or personal, against the man to whom we presume he was about to sell information."

"Very good. We shall make something of you yet." She began to pace, or as close as one could come to pacing underwater, which meant sculling back and forth. "And since it seems improbable that the sort of person who would want to murder a student of little consequence would choose to do so directly on the doorstep of a hardened criminal it is more likely that Mr. Reef was the true target in this case.

Which suggests further that we have swum into the middle of an underworld power struggle. Well, bother."

She did not say "bother." She used a phrase bearing a striking similarity to that which she had used earlier. We cast about for possible routes of egress but, as fate would have it, we had stumbled upon this scene at the least opportune moment. No sooner had we resolved to depart than a band of evident ruffians slithered through a large fissure in the masonry. They were five in total, two probably human, three probably not, all of them equipped with a variety of spears, javelins, and other armaments appropriate to the environment. They moved to encircle us with a precision that, while not military, nonetheless spoke of some familiarity with the business of violence.

Their leader, a tall, loose-limbed lady, whose webbed fingers and silver, piscine eyes spoke of centuries of interbreeding between the natives of this realm and its human visitors, glided forward, pointing a hydraulic dart gun at my companion. "Drop 'em."

I was briefly uncertain what the "'em" was that we were supposed to drop but then recalled that Ms. Haas still sported her compact harpoon launcher. Considering compliance the most likely path to survival, I raised my hands to demonstrate my good faith. On the basis of her prior behaviour, I laid odds at somewhat less than 50 percent that my companion would do likewise.

She did not do likewise.

"I," she said, "am the sorceress Shaharazad Haas. I have travelled to the deepest vaults of N'ruh, I have walked alone in the Writhing Halls, and I have whispered to the Gods Who Slumber. I am an anointed priestess of Thagn and Iqthelduroth. I have uttered the Dread Curse of Velrashtoa. Please don't think I need a pointy stick to kill you."

Our adversary said nothing. Instead she shot Ms. Haas in the chest.

My hand went instinctively to a weapon I was not, in fact, carrying. Then I watched in horror as my companion slumped, blood streaming into the surrounding water.

The ruffianess turned her attention to me. "I take it you're going to be more sensible."

Honour suggested that, my comrade having chosen to fight, I should stand by her to the last. Good sense dictated otherwise. And while I have always prided myself on my good sense, it was not in me to abandon a friend. "I fear I may not be."

She slotted another barb into her dart gun and trained it upon me. "Tell me who sent you."

"Dear lady, you have as good as murdered my companion in front of me. You find me in no mood to be compliant."

From nearby, I heard a low but disquieting murmur. The blood that still seeped from Ms. Haas's wound flowed black, then green-black, and a similarly hued ichor began to ooze from the walls. When my companion raised her head, I saw that yet more of the vile fluid flowed forth from her mouth and eyes, coalescing into blasphemous tentacles. Observing the same, the band of ne'er-do-wells turned upon their heels, or appendages that passed therefor, and fled into the darkness. Their leader, however, swiftly found herself ensnared by the loathsome members that my companion had conjured from what recesses I dared not speculate.

"Your loyalty is touching, Captain." Ms. Haas's voice was full of echoes and whispers. "But believe me, when I am murdered it shall be spectacular."

She was, in retrospect, partially correct on that account.

With a twist of her fingers, she dragged her captive across the chamber and spun her to face us. "Now, who are you and who do you think we are?"

"I have no interest in cooperating with you," retorted the prisoner, struggling vainly against her tenebrous bonds. I should also mention at this juncture that the word "you" was preceded not by the phrase "I have no interest in cooperating with" but by a single word whose connotations we have already discussed at length.

Ms. Haas rolled her eyes. "Yes, yes, you're being terribly defiant. But now I'm bored. You will answer my questions or I will rend your body asunder and gift your soul as a plaything to Iqthelduroth the Lurking Effulgence, whose unspeakable depredations will prove really quite unpleasant for you."

There was a reflective pause. Then, "Name's Asenath Reef. And the way I see it, you've just shot one of Enoch's informers."

"Ah." My companion cast me a look of significant self-satisfaction. "You see, Mr. Wyndham, I was correct in every particular. We have, indeed, become entangled in an underworld conflict, and young Asenath has clearly mistaken us for agents of their enemy. Wilde, perhaps. Or the Throat-Slitters' Consortium. Possibly even the Unquenchable Flame. I understand they're getting rather big in these parts."

Miss Reef gave a largely tokenistic tug at the bands of living darkness that still enwrapped her. "Seeing as how you're so well-informed, doesn't seem like you've got much use for me."

"In your position," returned Ms. Haas, sharply, "I'd be very careful about making myself sound dispensable."

"Enoch won't be too happy if I wind up dead."

"Do you really think a Vennish gossip peddler is remotely capable of harming me? Judging from your example, his minions pose me no danger and I have no fear of scandal."

"My brother deals in more than scandals." A flash of too-pointed teeth. "A sorceress lives or dies by her secrets."

"I'm not sure I respond kindly to blackmail."

"I'm not sure I've seen you respond kindly to anything."

Ms. Haas seemed genuinely wounded. "You shot me. In the circumstances, I feel I took it rather well."

I cleared my throat, or attempted to, realising too late that the orifice in question was still occupied by a symbiotic worm. "If I might, we're becoming a little distracted."

"Quite right. Where was I?" My companion subjected Miss Reef to her steeliest gaze. "We have business with Enoch. You will take us to him. That is the end of it."

She did. But it was not.

CHAPTER TWENTY

An Impediment

Miss Reef brought us, by a labyrinthine path, to a building that may once have served some unholy and unknowable purpose but which now seemed to function primarily as a warehouse. It was here, Miss Reef informed us, that her brother held his ramshackle court. We entered, although Ms. Haas insisted that Miss Reef remain a few paces ahead of us, far enough forward that she would be first to trigger any booby traps, but not so far that she could easily flee into a den filled with her compatriots.

As we made our way through stacks of barrels packed with I knew not what illicit merchandise, it became increasingly apparent that something was very wrong. We found the first body, bloated and distended, knocking lightly against the ceiling. Miss Reef covered her mouth with her webbed fingers, recoiling in obvious horror.

"Interesting," murmured Ms. Haas.

The next two corpses lay withered near the floor, their limbs twisted at grotesque angles.

My companion prodded one gently with the tip of her harpoon gun. "Most interesting. What do you make of this, Mr. Wyndham?"

Had my past been other than it was, I am sure I would have had no idea what could have reduced these people to such detritus. Unfortunately, I knew all too well the kinds of sorcery that desiccated the flesh and rotted the viscera. "Did I not know better, I would suspect the dread servants of the Witch King. Since he is dead and they are ashes, I presume our culprits are unrelated practitioners of similar necromancies."

"It does seem that way, does it not."

Miss Reef's already wide eyes widened. "It's the bank. It's got to be. They've had it in for Enoch for years."

"Take heart, dear lady." Despite her recent attempt to murder us, I felt for Miss Reef in that moment. It is a difficult thing to lose one's family. "Your brother may yet be well."

"Come, Captain," said Ms. Haas, with the merest trace of a sneer. "Do you really think the Ossuary Bank would send a team of mystically empowered assassins into the depths of Ven specifically to kill one person, and then let that one person get away?"

"There is always hope, Ms. Haas."

"I have met Hope. It is a terrifying entity with altogether too many eyes."

We progressed deeper into the warehouse, finding yet more bodies in similar states of distress, and coming at last to a small private office, where one last corpse floated forlornly behind a desk littered with meticulously inscribed wax tablets. Judging by our escort's visible distress, this must have been the man we were seeking, Mr. Enoch Reef.

"Well." Ms. Haas nudged her captive farther into the room. "I daresay that this piece of theatre has been more diverting than the last we attended. But if you do not cease playing games and tell us where your brother really is, then I shall stop being bored and start being angry."

Miss Reef twisted her fingers agitatedly through her hair. "What are you talking about? He's there. Poor Enoch. They've finally got him."

"Word of advice: stick to shooting people. You're a terrible actress."

I glanced between the corpse, Miss Reef, and Ms. Haas. "I fear I'm quite at sea."

There was an uncomfortable silence.

"Mr. Wyndham," said my companion at last. "If that pun was intentional, you are a villain. If it was not, you are a fool."

"I would probably rather be a fool than a villain, but I don't understand why you are so convinced of this lady's insincerity."

Ms. Haas drifted over the desk and began sifting through the documents that lay upon it. "Various reasons. Firstly and most simply, it would be an extraordinary coincidence that Mr. Reef would happen to be murdered by a disinterested third party at the precise moment that we were visiting *and* that a rival criminal power, unrelated either to us or to the individuals who purportedly carried out this crime, was launching an attack against him. That we would stumble into an underworld conflict is possible. That we and the Ossuary Bank would stumble into the same underworld conflict simultaneously without crossing one another's paths is manifestly implausible."

I turned to Miss Reef, to gauge her reaction to these observations, and found her curiously impassive.

"Secondly, as you observed, our companion exhibited obvious shock on discovering the bodies of her former associates. She, however, is clearly of the blood of the deep places and her kind are not like ours. They are slow to take fright and slow to anger, which suggests that this pantomime was entirely for our benefit." My companion caught Mr. Reef's body, drew it closer, and began a thorough inspection. "Thirdly, a direct frontal assault is not the modus operandi of the Ossuary Bank. After all, we are here because the last time that group quarrelled with dear Enoch they responded by bribing one of his associates to betray him. While they made a token effort to kill me, I don't think their heart was really in it and I had just beaten one of their members in a magical duel. Their policy is normally to repay like with like, and while they could send an army of undead monstrosities to suck the life force from any who stood in their way, we must remember that they are, ultimately, a pack of bean counters in silly costumes. And, finally, why don't you take a look at this body, Mr. Wyndham? While I"—she readied her harpoon gun—"ensure that Miss Reef doesn't try anything silly."

I swam over to the desk. Ms. Haas had disordered the unfortunate gentleman's garments in such a way that more of his skin was visible, which meant I saw at once that his flesh bore the unmistakable signs of having been nibbled at by fish and then, after some days or weeks, hastily treated with a concoction of alchemical preservatives such as might cause the desiccation of tissue and distortion of limb we had observed in the previous victims. Upon still closer scrutiny, I recognised the telltale discolouration that would be caused by tinctures of ambric green, lethocite, and other salts.

"Why," I exclaimed, "this man was not killed by necromantic sorcery at all. He appears to have died of natural causes."

Ms. Haas gave a sharp nod. "Quite so. Which leads us to the inevitable conclusion that this entire tableau is a sham. Not, of course, constructed for us, but to deceive the enemy for whom I suspect Asenath here still erroneously believes that we work. Now"—she raised the harpoon to aim it squarely at Miss Reef's head—"I will not ask you again. Where is your brother?"

From her reaction, or rather lack thereof, it did not seem that the lady was inclined to be cooperative.

"I assure you," I said, "despite everything that has happened between us, we have no wish to harm your Mr. Reef. We simply need to speak to him on the matter of his relationship with Miss Eirene Viola. Once we have the information we need, we shall not bother him again. We just need to know where we can find him."

Miss Reef seemed to relax a little. "It's not a where. It's a when."

❧

CHAPTER TWENTY-ONE

Twenty Years Hence

With only mild additional coercion, Miss Reef revealed to us the location of her brother's hiding place. I have intimated before that Ven is a strange city. A peculiar legacy of its history is that its streets and alleys are riddled with chinks and chasms that lead to what once would have been the distant recesses of the Vennish Empire. Only the Eternal Lords know for certain how many such lacunae there are in the city, although the largest and most stable see regular use for commercial purposes. It is these, for want of a less inaccurate term, portals that allow the great city of Khelathra-Ven to trade so prosperously with such distant worlds as Marvos, Carcosa, and the Dread Wastes of Bai. More unusual are those gateways that lead not to distant worlds but to other times. These paths are more jealously watched by the Eternal Lords, for their misuse could prove not merely disastrous but retrospectively disastrous. An ill-fated expedition to the court of the Cataclysmic Sultan could annihilate the city and everything in it, but a mistimed journey to the distant past could make it such that the city had never been. It is this outcome that the Eternal Lords seek to avoid at all costs.

There are nevertheless some individuals, guilds, factions, companies, and corporations that are permitted to traverse the timestreams within certain negotiated parameters in order that all might benefit from the infinite bounties of past and future. Further, there are some, such as Mr. Saltpetre, the submersible pilot who had brought us to Ven, who choose, either from necessity or greed, to run the timeways without official sanction. An unintuitive feature of the rules by which the Eternal Lords permit travel up and down the corridors of history is that the most oft-traversed paths are those that lead the furthest. If one journeys back ten thousand or even a million years, one finds oneself sufficiently detached from anything resembling one's present world that it is difficult for one to engage in deliberate mischief. A journey to a time such as that from which Mr. Saltpetre hails, some eighty-four millennia hence, can be little distinguished from a journey to a distant land or alien world, so unrecognisable is it to anybody setting out from present-day Khelathra-Ven. Far smaller, more dangerous, and more closely guarded are those rifts that lead only years or decades into past or future.

It was through one of these, located in a tiny, kelp-covered crevice in a forgotten pit in the depths of Keeper's Shallows, that Mr. Reef had fled, taking up residence in an instance of the very building in which we had just sought him, safely sequestered away from his enemies by the distance of some twenty years.

On squeezing through it, we emerged exactly where we had started, and I was briefly disappointed at the thought that we had gone through all that wriggling in order to go absolutely nowhere. Soon, however, I began to notice differences—small indications that while we remained in the same place geographically, we had clearly been translated temporally. The pit seemed still to have been forgotten, though the detritus that filled it was of a subtly different character, and the streets, although no more or less crowded than the ones we had left, seemed to contain more upworlders and fewer Vennish natives. The vast slabs of alien rock that formed the foundation of the city remained unchanged as I was certain they had for millennia, but the gangplanks and hoardings that had made up the more temporary structures had either moved elsewhere or disappeared entirely. In their place stood a number of sturdier-seeming constructions, still less implacable than the antediluvian stones around them, but clearly erected out of purposeful design rather than desperation. As we swam back towards the warehouse, I noticed several commercial ventures which appeared to be doing brisk trade, including another, somewhat larger curated whelk stall, a shop selling delightfully handcrafted but otherwise utterly blasphemous figurines, and a restaurant by the name of Squamous Fine Dining, in which guests were invited to catch and devour the live fish that swam throughout the building.

On arriving at our destination, we found that the warehouse, once filled with nothing but crates and corpses, had since been repurposed as an establishment specialising in the provision of certain services to surface dwellers with a predilection for such things. It appeared now to be operating under the rather vulgar moniker of "the Erotic Order of Dagon." We made our way through the institution, declining the several offers we received from beings wishing to subject us to depravities beyond imagining.

My companion made a noise that, in an aerated environment, would probably have come out as a weary sigh. "Honestly, I remember a time when being violated by a monstrosity from the abysmal darkness was something you really had to work at. Young people today have no idea, do they?" She paused. "That is to say, young people twenty years from the time we've just departed will have no idea, will they?"

"Tell me about it." Miss Reef flicked her tail disdainfully.

We were led at last into the same back office wherein we had previously found the withered corpse that had not, in fact, been Mr. Reef. Apart from the absence of cadavers, it was much the same, a large desk hewn from some otherworldly stone, piled high with meticulously kept records on wax tablets. From behind it, Mr. Reef glared at us, producing as he did so a hydraulic pistol from some secret compartment.

"Oh, not again," grumbled Ms. Haas. "Asenath, if you would kindly explain to your brother that he will be in danger from us only if he fails to put his weapon down, I would be very much obliged."

One of Mr. Reef's bulbous eyes swivelled independently to glance at his sister. "You all right?"

"Yeah." She gave a loose-jointed shrug. "They're weird, but not with Wilde. And there's no point shooting her because it doesn't take."

After a moment's consideration, Mr. Reef put his pistol down. He was older than his sister but bore the same marks of their inhuman heritage. His limbs were thin, his cheekbones sharp, and his manner suggestive of one with a significant facility for longevity. Steepling his webbed and bony fingers, he said, "This isn't something I usually have to ask in my line of work, but what is it exactly that you want?"

"Information." Ms. Haas finally lowered her harpoon gun. "But not of the sort you normally supply, for it concerns you personally."

"And what makes you think I'd just give that to you?"

"Expediency, Mr. Reef. You're a suspect in a case of blackmail, not a tenable position for a person in your industry."

He betrayed no visible sign of emotion, but his tone grew colder even by the standards of our frigid surroundings. "I'm a lot of things, but I'm no blackmailer."

"Some years ago," began Ms. Haas, "as measured relative to the temporal reference point from which we all originate rather than the one we presently occupy, you employed a woman by the name of Eirene Viola. After serving you as faithfully as is within her capacity, she was subverted by the Ossuary Bank, who prevailed upon her to steal from you the list of their clientele that you had recently acquired."

"And?" Mr. Reef gave a slow and, given our environment, wholly unnecessary blink.

"And so far, you haven't done anything about it. Which strikes me as odd."

"I'm not human, Miss . . ." He looked briefly like somebody correlating the contents of his mind. "It's Shaharazad Haas, isn't it? I might've known. Anyway, my kind don't get angry and we live long enough that it's stupid for us to hold grudges. Eirene took a chance and got one over on me. Can't say I wouldn't have done the same."

"A commendable attitude, I'm sure, but I would have thought you might want to, as it were, set an example."

"My entire business relies on people who don't know me very well trusting me enough to tell me things for money. It does me no favours if my associates start showing up dead."

Ms. Haas drifted idly on a passing current. "And you're honestly telling me that even if the opportunity to revenge yourself on Miss Viola fell accidentally into your lap you wouldn't take it?"

"One"—he counted off on his fingers—"I'm busy fighting a turf war with a bloodthirsty barbarian from another planet. Two: when things fall into my lap I work out how to sell them. Now as it happens, I did find out that dear old Eirene was settling down with a member of the Ubiquitous Company of Fishers. And should any of Miss Cora Beck's friends or enemies come to me asking if I should happen to know of anything that might be helpful to them, then I may, indeed, divulge that her good lady wife, or wife-to-be, depending on when I get that visit, has the kind of past that doesn't go down so well in respectable circles. But why would I give that up for free?"

My companion gave the matter some thought. "Thank you, Mr. Reef. You've been most helpful. Come, Wyndham."

The abruptness of this concession rather startled me. "Are we leaving?"

"Unless you wish to sample the whelks or be violated by reticulated monstrosities from the fathomless depths, either of which, incidentally, I'd be more than happy to make time for."

"But what of the case against Mr. Reef?"

The comment was, in retrospect, somewhat inopportune. "Hey"—Mr. Reef spread his webbed fingers—"I'm right here."

"Forgive my companion," said Ms. Haas, who throughout our acquaintance would prove far more willing to apologise for my behaviour than for her own. "He's new. It helps if you try to find it endearing."

I was not certain how to take this. "I simply fear that we have come a long way for little information."

"A fear I will happily assuage. Would you like me to do so now, in front of the gentleman in question, or at home in private when our brains are no longer being slowly eaten by psychic invertebrates?"

Mr. Reef leaned forward with a rather hungry expression. "Don't hold back on my account."

Even without Mr. Reef's comment I would have found my companion's position compelling, and now that my attention had been drawn to it, I was concerned that the worm might be taking active steps to persuade me against its removal. "Meaning no disrespect or ingratitude," I told Mr. Reef, "I am suddenly convinced that we should return to the surface as quickly as possible."

"Are you sure, Mr. Wyndham?" asked my companion. "You wouldn't rather bob about down here for a few more hours asking silly questions?"

I thought that was a trifle harsh. "Your point is well made, madam."

Bidding a rather more formal farewell to Mr. Reef than was perhaps necessary I followed Ms. Haas out of the premises, paying as little attention as possible to the events occurring within them, and back to our own time.

CHAPTER TWENTY-TWO

A Respite

We rendezvoused with Mr. Saltpetre at the prearranged location, a stretch of open water slightly above a nearby kelp forest in our native timeline. He returned us forthwith to the shore, whereupon Ms. Haas and I swiftly partook of the exfiltration tablets. The worm's influence on my nervous system was already such that I was conscious of a mild reluctance to ingest the poison, but I steeled myself to do so and, once the nausea, retching, and bleeding from the throat had passed, experienced no further regrets.

Our sojourn in the ocean had started sufficiently late and lasted sufficiently long that the predawn light was beginning to wash over the slums and spires of Athra. In these transitional hours, the criminal classes turn at last towards their beds, while servile and mercantile persons shift from slumber to the contemplation of their forthcoming day's labour. All of which meant that a gentleman roaming the streets in his bathing attire ran an unacceptable risk of drawing the attention of respectable individuals. Therefore, we hailed a passing hansom and returned posthaste to 221b Martyrs Walk.

Mrs. Hive was not best pleased with us upon our arrival, for we were dripping wet, we bore with us the deep-sea scent of dead fish and mad gods, and my companion was still bleeding an oily black ichor, traces of which remain upon the hall carpet to this day. Ms. Haas defused the situation with a variety of vague promises that Mrs. Hive received with a sceptical buzzing before shuffling the increasingly deliquescent corpse of the stevedore back upstairs to her lodgings.

"Be a good fellow and make up the fire." Ms. Haas swept past me into the sitting room and cast herself across the chaise longue. "I find myself unaccountably fatigued."

Given the night's events I also found myself a little weary, but nevertheless endeavoured to see to the comfort of both of us. Having tended to the grate, I retired to my room and, realising I would soon need to leave for the hospital, changed into my normal attire. Suspecting a little light refreshment would be of benefit, I then prepared a pot of tea and a little toast, which I carried back into the sitting room.

I was greeted by the unmistakable perfume of Valentino's Good Rough Shag. My companion was supine, steaming lightly and smoking heavily.

"I'd thought Mr. Reef such a likely prospect," she muttered. "It was most impertinent of him to be innocent."

I poured the tea and put a cup and saucer down within easy reach of her trailing hand. "Are you quite certain he was being truthful?"

"It is possible that everything we observed in Ven had been carefully stage-managed in an elaborate effort to fool us, but while my reputation has sometimes caused my quarries to go to quite absurd lengths to throw me off their trail, Mr. Reef did not appear to be expecting me specifically and would scarcely have orchestrated such an outlandish charade merely to provide himself with an alibi in a petty case of blackmail." She brought her pipe to her lips and inhaled deeply. "After all, to believe that he has deceived us is to believe not only that he faked his own death at the hands of the Ossuary Bank, which he most certainly did, but that he also faked the conflict whose existence necessitated that fabrication. Frankly, if he implemented such a needlessly circuitous plan to cover such a trivial offence he *deserves* to get away with it."

"And of course," I added, "as he himself observed, personal vengeance is not ordinarily a preoccupation of his people."

"For someone in that line of work, revenge is a complicated value proposition. Even if Mr. Reef would not experience emotional satisfaction from seeing Eirene suffer he could still easily have concluded that a demonstration of power would have been in his professional interests. But given the circumstances in which we found him, I'm sure his priorities currently lie elsewhere. From everything I've heard, Ann Wilde is an adversary who demands one's whole attention."

Ms. Haas continued her exegesis for quite some time although I confess, having settled into the wingback chair, I allowed the night's exertions to overcome me and drifted off to sleep. I was aroused, some indeterminate period later, by a vigorous rapping upon the front door.

My companion, who appeared to have continued her discourse quite undeterred by my incapacity, paused a moment. "Do go see to that, will you?"

Stirring myself, I went to investigate and found Miss Viola in a state of some consternation, her hair unbound, and a piece of paper clutched in an ungloved hand. She pushed past me and I followed her back to the sitting room.

"Hello, my dear," purred Ms. Haas, without moving from the chaise or, indeed, opening her eyes. "I take it you've had another note."

Miss Viola attempted to supply her with the offending document, but Ms. Haas waved it away. So I stepped forward and took it instead.

❧

CHAPTER TWENTY-THREE

The Second Letter

To the Lady Eirene Viola Delhali, daughter of the late Count of Hyades,

I told you not to test me.

I have been reasonable so far, but if you do not break off your engagement to Miss Cora Beck immediately I will be forced to take action on your behalf.

Be assured my knowledge of your affairs is intimate. I know, for example, that two days ago you took Miss Beck to the Lake of Stars in Little Carcosa. You put your arms around her and showed her your favourite constellations in the dim waters.

This is your final warning.

I hold your future in my hands.

"Tell me you didn't." Ms. Haas draped her wrist despairingly across her brow. "I've never heard anything so cloyingly sentimental."

Miss Viola snatched up the untouched cup of tea from the foot of the chaise and upended its contents over Ms. Haas's head. She then emphasised her displeasure by flinging the now empty receptacle into the fireplace. "Just because you have never cared for anything or any-body, that doesn't mean you—oh, what's the use."

"If this is what caring leads to"—Ms. Haas settled herself more comfortably as the beverage soaked gradually into the chaise—"I want no part of it. What happened to you, Eirene? We used to do such extraordinary, remarkable, terrible things together. And now you're canoodling with a fishmonger in front of a magic pond moping about your lost homeland."

"Because it's so much more glamorous to live in a dingy set of rooms you rent from a swarm of sentient insects and share with a complete stranger because nobody who has known you for more than six months can stand your company, and to spend your days drugged out of your mind on a dirty sofa because you can't bear to be alone with the cacophony of demons you call your thoughts?"

A smile curled the corners of Ms. Haas's lips. "I'm starting to remember why I liked you."

"Should we," I suggested, "perhaps turn our attention to what we may deduce from the contents of this latest communication?"

Miss Viola subsided into one of the wingbacks. "I hate the idea that someone's watching me."

"On the contrary"—Ms. Haas at last deigned to sit to upright—"I believe you can take enormous comfort in it. Our previous difficulty has been that your enemy gave us scant indication of his, her, their, zir, or its methodology or capabilities. But the means by which an entity observes another entity can be most revealing."

"How do you mean?" I asked.

"We have three suspects remaining. One is a mortal woman from the professional classes, one a vampire, and the last a former aristocrat turned party loyalist in a shadow-haunted otherworld. While any one of them might employ anonymous notes as a means of coercion, the resources and strategies that they would have available for the undertaking of surveillance are quite different. Eirene, have you happened to observe anything suspicious of late?"

The sound Miss Viola uttered at that juncture was perilously close to a snort. "I know you think I've lost my touch, but I would have noticed if I had a byakhee following me while I go shopping for hats."

"Gods," sighed Ms. Haas, "your life has become so bourgeois. Of course, the absence of cadaverous, bat-winged, mole-faced vulture-beasts doesn't rule out a Carcosan connection entirely. I'm sure your former fiancé has the resources to hire mortal agents as he wishes. But what of—?"

"No, I haven't seen any wolves, bats, ravens, or mysterious and unseasonable mist trailing after me either."

"Still, I assume the Contessa has tasted your blood. Then again, haven't we all?"

Miss Viola lifted a brown glass bottle, mostly denuded of laudanum, from the side table but appeared to think better of throwing it. "Your point being?"

"That such connections can be used to spy upon a person's thoughts and may, depending on the Contessa's precise nature, provide her with sufficient power over you as to thwart even the protections of the Mocking Realm. Have you experienced any strange presences in your dreams or an unaccountable sense of being spied upon?"

"I'm Carcosan. There are always strange presences in my dreams."

"Not helpful." Ms. Haas began refilling her pipe. "Which means we shall simply have to continue as planned."

"You mean I'm just supposed to sit here and hope whoever this is doesn't ruin my life while you're *continuing as planned*."

"Eirene, my dear, when you brought this case to me I developed a stratagem. This new information has not allowed me to formulate a superior alternative. Therefore, I shall carry on exactly as I am."

Miss Viola rolled her eyes. "We'll carve that on your tombstone. But what am *I* to do?"

"If you must do something, then I suggest you take Miss Beck away for a while. Removing yourself from your usual haunts may make it harder for this blackmailer to follow you."

It seemed an eminently sensible suggestion to me, but Miss Viola did not look reassured. "You're using me as bait again, aren't you?"

"Amongst other things." Ms. Haas issued forth a stream of smoke. "A change of scenery would clearly do you good and if your nemesis proves able to track you no matter where you go that will tell us more about their capabilities. You should also have ample opportunity to indulge your new fondness for holding hands in twee environments. It's a win-win."

"Cora's going to Aturvash on business next week. I suppose I could go with her."

Ms. Haas curled her lip contemptuously. "Charming though I find the idea of you taking a walking tour of a salt mine, I think you'd be better off if you were both somewhere less expected. With a little more time, I'm sure we'll find whoever is sending these letters, but blackmailers are fundamentally cowardly creatures. And if this person fears exposure, they may decide to intervene with Miss Beck directly, in which case it would be awfully convenient if she was hard to contact."

"Shaharazad," protested Miss Viola, "I can't just yank my fiancée away from her duties until this all gets sorted out."

"Well, you could tell her the truth instead, but I thought the whole point of this exercise was to avoid that."

"And of course she won't get at all suspicious if I turn up tomorrow saying, 'Darling, I've had a wonderful idea, let's take a spontaneous holiday of indefinite duration and not tell anybody where we're going.'"

"Eirene, my dear, I have absolute faith in your talent for duplicity." Ms. Haas flicked ash casually over the back of the chaise longue. "Now go take the fishmonger somewhere fun. I hear the City of Blood and Glass is wonderful during the current astrological configuration."

Miss Viola departed soon after and I, leaving my companion fully insensible in the sitting room, was obliged to make my way rather unsteadily in to work. It was not my finest eight hours of labour, since not only had I scarcely slept the night before but my mind was abuzz with the new and mysterious possibilities laid out before us in the latest missive. And indeed in my fatigued state I indulged in several rather fanciful speculations about the blackmailer's possible identity, although as it transpired not even my wildest imaginings came close to the remarkable truth of the situation.

CHAPTER TWENTY-FOUR

Mr. Percy Lutrell

The next few days passed quietly. I ran the same tests on the second letter as I had run on the first and came to the same conclusions: that it had been touched by nobody save Miss Viola and myself, Ms. Haas on this occasion having avoided contact with it entirely. The paper and ink were of the same stock as those used previously and still offered no insight into the nature or origins of the writer. Now that the excitement of our recent adventures had subsided, I became conscious of some doubt regarding our ability to bring this matter to a swift and satisfactory conclusion. Ms. Haas, for her part, spent the time engaged in sundry activities, many of which did not seem directly applicable to the task at hand, but which also included researches into the life and habits of our next suspect, Mrs. Yasmine Benamara.

In the years since her *affaire de coeur* with Miss Viola, Mrs. Benamara had achieved some notability as a poet in her own right. Her first volume, *Two Parts of the Moon*, was well received amongst the literary set in Khel and Athra, or as well received as any such work can be, which is to say it was condemned as reactionary by progressives and as immoral by traditionalists. She was also in the habit of hosting regular literary salons to which she would invite that particular class of intellectual neither too high born nor too high minded to attend upon a barrister's wife. Unusually, this was a social circle to which I, as a varsity man from no especially exalted background, had greater access than Ms. Haas, who had no time whatsoever for the lives and interests of ordinary people. I was in the process of reaching out to see if any of my university friends might have crossed paths with Mrs. Benamara when Ms. Haas, never overendowed with patience, elected to expedite the situation.

My first inkling as to her preferred methodology came when I arrived home one evening to discover a strange gentleman in the sitting room. He was a little taller than I, thin lipped and white haired, with a faint hunch to his shoulders. His demeanour managed at once to be unprepossessing and judgemental.

I eyed the stranger in some consternation. "I beg your pardon. Are you waiting for Ms. Haas?"

"On the contrary," he returned, in a voice that aspired to both aristocracy and authority, achieving neither, "I am waiting for you. We have secured an invitation to Mrs. Benamara's salon and you are to change and come with me directly."

"I'm afraid you have the advantage of me, sir."

"My name is Percy Lutrell. I am the literary critic for *The Esoteric Review*."

"That doesn't explain what you're doing here or why you're waiting for me personally."

Mr. Lutrell raised a meagre crescent moon of an eyebrow. "You appear to be an intelligent man, Mr. Wyndham. Surely you can work that out for yourself."

Ordinarily, I would have had no inclination to play such a game with a total stranger who had appeared out of nowhere in my sitting room. But my brief acquaintance with the sorceress Shaharazad Haas had somewhat eroded my sense of normalcy. "I am certain I have no idea. I can think of no reason that a celebrated literary critic in the employ of a respectable periodical would have any connection with myself or Ms. Haas."

"Then begin from there."

"I'm not sure I follow you."

"You have said yourself that it seems highly improbable that a celebrated literary critic in the employ of a respectable periodical would have any connection with you or Ms. Haas. Yet here I stand. What may you conclude from that?"

I considered it a moment. "That something very improbable has occurred or that you are not, in fact, a celebrated literary critic in the employ of a respectable periodical."

"Bravo, Captain." Mr. Lutrell disposed himself with disconcerting languor upon the chaise longue. "So who am I?"

"I haven't the faintest—"

The interloper raised an impatient finger. "None of that, if you please."

It was becoming rapidly apparent to me that I was being toyed with, which was, in itself, something of a giveaway. "Madam," I said, "this is most inappropriate. Personating others by sorcery is monumentally illegal for a variety of very good reasons."

Mr. Lutrell's image shimmered in a fashion familiar from my misadventure at Mise en Abyme, and when I was able to focus again I saw Ms. Haas's laughing face before me. "Come now. If we didn't do things simply because they were illegal we'd get nothing done whatsoever."

I am afraid I responded to that suggestion a little sharply. "I have managed quite well these past seven and twenty years."

"Not the best example, Mr. Wyndham. You were a child for half of them, which hardly counts. And, as for the rest, they were spent severally under the reign of a charming but, even I will admit, tyrannical sorcerer king, then under the more evenhanded but no less draconian rule of the Lord Protector of Ey, and, of course, most recently you have been in a lightless nonspace beyond reality where the very concept of a functioning legal system is just one of the many abstractions that the Empress of Nothing seeks daily to devour into unmaking. Bless her."

Over the entire course of our acquaintance I can recall two and a half occasions on which Ms. Haas allowed another person to have the last word in an argument. This was not one of them and I conceded the point as gracefully as I was able. In truth she had reminded me that these matters were more complex than I am entirely comfortable to own. Although in Khelathra-Ven I have endeavoured always to conduct myself in accordance with the ordinances of the city, the fact remains that there are parts of this world in which the laws of the land are not acceptable to me, and I not acceptable to them.

"Are you absolutely certain," I asked, "that this is the most effective way to proceed?"

Ms. Haas stifled a yawn behind her hand. "It's the least tedious way to proceed. And also the one that gives Mrs. Benamara the least room for evasion or deception."

"And the risk of being arrested and hanged?"

"That's precisely what makes it so much less tedious than the other options."

I was, by now, beginning to understand a little of my companion's manner and was able to discern with some reliability when she was being sincere, when she was amusing herself, and when she was merely intending to provoke a reaction. In this case, her remark fell somewhere between the second and third categories. As such, I saw little purpose in pressing the issue. "Do we have an actual plan?"

"Certainly." She sounded faintly affronted. "We shall attend the salon in the guise of Mr. Lutrell and his faithful secretary. That's you. Then I'll draw the suspect aside in order to ask her some questions about her latest work and use my art, guile, and intense personal charisma to lead her into confessing any role she might have had in the blackmailing of Eirene."

"That doesn't sound like a plan, so much as a sequence of conversations with tremendous scope to go wrong."

She rose imperiously from the chaise. "I am the sorceress Shaharazad Haas. I never go wrong. I merely achieve things in a manner I had not intended."

And so it was that Ms. Haas, glamoured into the appearance of Mr. Lutrell, and I, not glamoured into anything, made our way to the docks.

CHAPTER TWENTY-FIVE

The Khelathran Strait

The Benamaras, who it appeared had remained married despite the unfortunate incident involving Mrs. Benamara and Miss Viola, lived in a fishing village turned suburb named Ecet's Cove. As the great city of Khelathra-Ven had expanded over the years, it had swallowed a variety of such settlements, incorporating them in a manner that it would be falsehood to describe as seamless into its ever-growing conurbation. Although the coastal suburbs could be accessed by road from the centre of Khel and would make for a pleasant carriage journey, they were most conveniently accessed through use of one of the many barges that plied the waters of the Khelathran Strait. I had lived in such an area for six months during my time at university, when I stayed in a cellar room in a house that I shared with four other students. It was swelteringly hot in summer and freezing in winter, and the kitchen was invariably a nightmare of used crockery and absent cutlery. Nevertheless, the beauty of the location made up for the privations of the accommodations and the impracticality of the commute.

The vessel we boarded on this occasion was operated by an extravagantly dressed woman with mechanical eyes and towed by some mysterious leviathan discernible only by the occasional glimpse of a many-hued fin breaking the water's surface. Our journey took us eastwards, away from the Rose Gold Bridge and beneath the steel skeleton of the half-constructed railway line that enterprising Athran industrialists hoped would one day allow passengers to travel between the northern and southern cities in a matter of minutes, weather and labour disputes permitting. Given the history of similar projects I was not myself optimistic. A short while later we passed the Isle of the Dead, that ancient necropolis where once the god-kings of Khel had been interred under the watchful eye of Anu, Lord of the Underworld, and which was now home to the headquarters of the Ossuary Bank, reputed to be the most influential financial organisation in six worlds. The countinghouse itself sat atop the great cliff that occupied much of the island and, in the last rays of sunlight, one could just about make out the vast effigies of Anu and Amn carved into the unforgiving rock by hands long stilled and forgotten.

I turned to my companion, only momentarily disconcerted to discover that she was Percy Lutrell. "It's a pity, is it not," I remarked, "that so sacred a monument is now the abode of commerce, necromancy, and usury?"

"To me it seems rather appropriate. The old gods were always transactional beings. You give this sacrifice for that favour. Make these offerings for those blessings. At least the bankers are honest about it."

"But is there not value in the things we create in honour of something greater than ourselves?"

Mr. Lutrell stroked his chin pensively. "My good man, in all the universe there are two sorts of gods: those that are like us and those that are not. Those that are like us are no better than we are. And those that are not are infinitely worse."

"It's not the gods themselves, Ms. Ha— Mr. Lutrell. It's the ideals they stand for."

"In my experience, the only principles a god stands for are deflowering virgins and burning people."

"That's an oversimplification," I protested.

"Yes." He smirked. "Religion tends to be."

I thought it best to let the matter go, and the monument that had precipitated the conversation gradually faded into the gloaming. As night drew in, gas lamps and arc lights crackled into life in both cities. On the hills of Athra, the windows of the Winter Palace glowed as brightly as they must have done in the days when the kings of Leonysse still sojourned there, though now they represented not the gaieties of the royal court but the industry of municipal clerks, labouring tirelessly over their minutes and memoranda. In the skies above Khel heatless alchemical flames burned along the edges of the mechanical platform that transferred scholars between street level and the entryway of the famous flying library, known colloquially as the Fata Morgana. Though they were not all visible, I knew also that a million smaller lights illuminated public streets and private homes, and I was struck for a moment by the bewildering immensity of things.

CHAPTER TWENTY-SIX

The Salon of Mrs. Yasmine Benamara

Some thirty minutes later, we disembarked at a small, suburban dock.

"She'd better be guilty," opined Mr. Lutrell. "If I find that we've come to this godsforsaken place for nothing I shall be most put out."

I looked around me at the tidy cobbled streets lined with brightly painted houses and sweet-smelling trees and was hard-pressed to observe anything to which any reasonable person might object. Although, given what I was fast learning about my companion, that was probably the exact issue.

I placed a consoling hand on his shoulder. "Fear not, Mr. Lutrell. We may yet be attacked by a beast from another dimension or an assassin hell-bent on halting our investigation."

"That's very kind of you, but I fear the most deadly weapon we're likely to be confronted with in a place like this is a sternly worded letter from the borough council. Besides, I've been to this sort of salon before. Nothing interesting ever happens at them."

This, it transpired, would be one of the few occasions on which my companion was wrong. Although she would, when later confronted, refuse to admit it.

It was a short walk up the hillside to the Benamara residence, an eminently respectable detached property commanding a fine view of the strait. On Mr. Lutrell's presentation of his invitation (to this day, I know not where he acquired it) we were ushered inside by a demure maidservant. We followed her into a tastefully appointed chamber, decorated in modern Khelish fashion, which leaned towards geometric designs, bold colours, and abstract patterns. The guests, who were mostly lounging on divans and floor cushions, ran a terribly specific gamut, from the controversial end of bourgeois to the bourgeois end of controversial; which is to say I recognised one or two unorthodox theologians but no outright heretics, a number of famous beauties but no actual courtesans, and a group of celebrated reformers who nevertheless drew the line at revolution.

At the sight of my companion, a louche, long-haired Khelish gentleman, dressed flamboyantly in a somewhat outmoded Athran style of slashed sleeves and half hose, rose from where he had been reclining. "Mr. Lutrell," he cried. "How dare you show your face in this company? Your review of my *Sigurd and Ivan* was the most ill-articulated, venomous, petty-minded, plebeian agglomeration of sputum that has ever disgraced print."

Mr. Lutrell's pale eyes glinted. "Lord Bahrami—"

Unfortunately, I cannot reproduce for my readers the remainder of his response. Suffice to say, it was short, to the point, and quite spectacularly vulgar, recommending as it did a course of action quite beneath his lordship's dignity, not to mention his physical capacity. It also garnered a reaction from the room that I, having grown accustomed to moving in circles with no regard whatsoever for social mores, found quite unsettlingly appropriate.

"You"—Lord Bahrami subjected my companion to a look of rather magnificent contempt—"are no gentleman. And, worse, you are no wit."

Although, of course, I had the utmost respect for Ms. Haas's abilities in many areas I was becoming concerned that in the art of subterfuge her extraordinary talents were somewhat at odds with her mercurial nature and fondness for the dramatic. Indeed, I was not entirely certain that she was, in this exact moment, cognisant of the fact that she was meant to be playing a part.

"Come now, *Mr. Lutrell*," I whispered. "We should avoid making a scene."

"Ah. Quite right." He closed his mouth with a snap. "And you are most correct, Lord Bahrami. I am no gentleman, nor no wit. Nor any person of value or consequence. And certainly not possessed of any remarkable gifts of will, intellect, or capacity to command—"

I thought it best to prevent Mr. Lutrell from further disquisition. "Well said, sir. You are, after all, merely a literary critic."

"You didn't have to interrupt me, Captain. That's exactly what I was saying."

"Believe me, Lutrell, nobody cares what you are saying." Lord Bahrami turned and, moving with the slightest of limps, vanished through an archway into the perfumed garden beyond.

Unfamiliar as I was with this variety of artistic gathering, I was at a loss as to whether the disruption caused by our arrival was an unforgivable social transgression or an expected element of the evening's entertainment. This uncertainty, I fear, left me somewhat discombobulated. My companion, however, suffered no such affliction, making directly for a tray of baklava and helping himself with indelicate gusto.

Across the room, a lady extricated herself from a small crowd of guests and came towards us. She looked to be in her late twenties or early thirties, with a grace of bearing and neatness of person I found rather charming. As she walked, her tastefully embroidered abaya fluttered gently in the breeze from the open windows.

"Mr. Lutrell?" she asked.

He paused in his assault on the refreshments. "Yes?"

"I'm so sorry about Bahrami. You know how geniuses are."

"I can quite confidently say that I do."

"I'm very glad you could make it to my little gathering. I would love to introduce you to some of my guests."

With that, the lady—who I presumed to be Mrs. Benamara—took my companion by the arm and drew him firmly away from the pastries. I trailed after them, content to observe and place my possibly misguided faith in Ms. Haas's judgement and subtlety. We moved first to an eclectic cluster of persons, engaged in an animated discussion of Ilari love poetry.

". . . fully aware of the cultural and historical context," a pallid gentleman was saying in an accent I couldn't quite place. "But the verses themselves are vilely insipid."

His interlocutor, a dark-skinnned Khelite in the silk-trimmed robes traditionally worn by fellows of the university, subjected him to a withering glare. "The mere thought that an educated person could hold such an opinion—"

They paused, as if the notion was genuinely too dreadful to countenance, and were immediately interrupted.

"Vasile is not an educated person," murmured the third guest from behind an elaborate and grotesque carnival mask. "He's from Pesh."

Vasile, as the pale gentleman was apparently known, flushed a sickly shade of pink. "As one exile to another, I'd thank you not to use my homeland against me."

"Darling, you wrote an entire cantata about your people's hostility to original thought."

"That is precisely my objection to Farah's tedious obsession with the Ilari." He paused, coughing into a slightly bloodstained handkerchief. "There is neither originality nor value in devoting one's life to fellating an extinct civilisation."

The scholar sighed. "Oh, Vasile. It is comments like that which ensure your works will ever be the sensation of the moment; a child's tantrum that draws brief notice, fast grows wearisome, and is soon forgotten."

To my relief our hostess chose this juncture to formally introduce Mr. Lutrell. Of our present company, I learned the following. The consumptive gentleman, Mr. Vasile Kovac, was a recent arrival from the Hagiocracy of Pesh, a composer of revolutionary bent and atheistic leanings. The academic I already knew by reputation; they went by the mononym Farah and were one of the foremost authorities on Ilari poetry. The second gentleman in the group, who had not thus far spoken, was Iacomo Van der Berg, an Athran poet of the jobbing sort, who had spent the last fifty years producing unexceptionable verses on such subjects as society weddings, military victories, significant deaths, and civic festivals.

This just left the masked lady and her companion. The former went by Ambrosia de Luca and, as I might easily have concluded from her attire and the peculiar lambency of her eyes, was of Carcosan stock. Apparently she was an up-and-coming playwright, whose works to date had focused primarily on adapting traditional Carcosan folk narratives such that they could be enjoyed by a Khelathran audience without too great a risk of the terrible truths contained within them, driving said audience irreversibly to madness. Her partner, who had apparently come to the salon out of duty and affection and did not appear to be enjoying a moment of it, was a Marvosi force captain by the name of Domitia.

For those who are unfamiliar with that people or their homeland, the world of Marvos is a vast red desert orbiting an unremarkable yellow star at the edge of a distant galaxy. The Marvosi themselves are tall, green skinned, and warlike, their conquests driven by an unending need for two resources: water and labour. They make fine soldiers but terrible dinner guests. At mention of my name, the force captain looked down at me with slightly more interest than she had hitherto displayed. "John Wyndham? Captain John Wyndham who held the pass at the Senescent Void?"

Preferring not to discuss such matters, I replied only by a slight inclination of my head.

"Impressive." She paused. "For a human."

Miss de Luca batted playfully at her lover. "Try not to be such a stereotype, darling."

"It was a compliment. Most humans are weak and cowardly."

"You do remember that I'm a human, as is everyone else in this room."

"Yes." Force Captain Domitia blinked slowly. "And the majority of you are weak and cowardly. I fail to see how the comment was relevant."

That Mr. Lutrell had remained silent until this point had engendered in me an overly optimistic complacency. He now entered the discussion. "We're not all weak and cowardly," he observed. "Some of us are arrogant and undisciplined."

"That is worse."

"I wonder"—Mrs. Benamara placed a hand gently on Mr. Lutrell's shoulder, making a none-too-subtle attempt to steer the conversation in a more productive direction—"have you yet had the opportunity to attend Mr. Kovac's latest opera?"

Mr. Lutrell started, an expression of visible horror on his face. "Gods, no. Why would I do such a thing?"

"Because," I suggested, "you're a literary critic, sir."

"Oh, opera. I'm so sorry. I thought you said ritual disembowelling of a sacrificial heifer."

There was a brief pause, and then Mr. Kovac said, "It is called *The Pyres of Autumn*. It takes its inspiration from the revolution in the Kingdom of Ey. A group of villagers become convinced that the spirit of the Witch King is influencing members of their community and turn upon one another in a futile outpouring of hostility and fear. It is a sad but necessary commentary on the corrosive effect of religious superstition on the minds of simple people."

While I was aware that the regime in Ey was not without its failings, I was not wholly pleased with the way Mr. Kovac appeared to be representing my country. I cleared my throat. "Might I ask why you did not choose to locate this narrative in Pesh?"

Mr. Kovac crushed his handkerchief in his fist. "I am under no obligation to justify to a theocrat the manner in which I choose to write on the subject of theocracy."

"With respect," I demurred, "Ey is not a theocracy. It is a parliamentary republic."

"A republic governed in accordance with the tenets of a cult that worships a deity who is nothing more than a mindless ball of degenerate nuclear matter."

At this, Mr. Van der Berg broke his silence. "Come now, Vasile. Art's all well and good, but the Creator is a god and worthy of respect."

"Pay him no mind, Iacomo." Our hostess shook her head indulgently. "You know what Vasile's like."

The unpleasantness might here have dissipated. I was no more content than I had been at the start of the exchange, but I would have let the matter go for the sake of civility, to say nothing of the mission from which it appeared we were becoming increasingly distracted.

Mr. Kovac, however, suffered no such scruples. He turned upon me, with a look of disquieting resentment. "Of course, the great irony is that you stand here piously bleating about the unforgivable slander my opera perpetuates against your people, when your people will be unable to view it because your own Lord Protector has banned all forms of theatrical performance. Thus those most in need of my insight are the ones least able to access it."

"It was not my intent to make you angry, Mr. Kovac." I did not appreciate his tone, but I felt it was important to moderate mine. "I simply wished to know why you would choose to set this story in my country, rather than in your own."

He stifled a fresh bout of coughing. "I cannot write about Pesh without bringing with me the knowledge of the hundred years that my people have been ruled by the Assembly of Hagiarchs. There is too much history. Too much suffering. Too much everything. Writing about a distant land gives me the freedom to do what I otherwise could not."

"That seems rather unfair on the Eyans," remarked Mr. Lutrell, somewhat to my surprise.

"The Eyans are not my concern."

"Did you not just claim that they were the ones most in need of your insight?" Mr. Lutrell grabbed a stuffed vine leaf from a nearby tray. "I'm sure Mr. Wyndham understands that you don't want to reduce the history and culture of your nation to a simple parable about religious intolerance. But at least do him the courtesy of admitting that your creative choices were made for your benefit, not his."

Mr. Kovac curled his lip in open contempt. "Go back to your magazine, old man. You know nothing."

At which juncture, Mrs. Benamara caught him firmly by the arm. "Oh, look, dear Vasile, Ifunanya Liu has just arrived." The lady did a remarkable job of remaining calm and measured, as though it truly were a mere happy coincidence that an appropriate distraction had arisen just as the conversation was becoming awkward. "She was telling me just the other day how greatly she admires your work. Do be sweet and go bother her instead of these people."

"You are all philistines and lackeys," he retorted, although with less venom than he had previously employed, "and I do not know why I associate with you."

"I always thought you only came for the food, Vasile." Mr. Van der Berg sauntered, chuckling, in the direction of the buffet.

Although I was rather ashamed to have precipitated it, the dissolution of the discussion group came as no small relief to me. I was equally conflicted on the matter of Mr. Lutrell's intervention, for while it comforted me to know that my companion would come to my defence, in truth I felt for Mr. Kovac and would not, if left to my own devices, have spoken so harshly to him. It is a hard thing to know that your homeland rejects you and I begrudge nobody the strategies that enable them to bear it.

Mr. Lutrell took the opportunity to pursue the playwright and her consort, the force captain, who had retired together to a more intimate nook. They did not look entirely pleased by the intrusion.

As we approached, the force captain narrowed her violet eyes and uttered a low growl. "Begone. You are not wanted."

"Which part of 'influential literary critic' do you not understand?" returned Mr. Lutrell.

"The part that would stop me breaking your spine like the leg of desert spider."

"Darling"—Miss de Luca put a restraining hand upon the Marvosi's muscular thigh—"we've spoken about this. In our part of the cosmos, threats of physical violence are not considered a sign of respect."

Mr. Lutrell smirked in a manner that, momentarily at least, made him look a lot more like a sorcerer and a lot less like a journalist. "Believe me, as physical threats go, that was pathetic."

There was a brief, uncomfortable silence.

"Ambrosia"—Domitia reached slowly for her gladius—"this man is annoying me. Let me kill him. It will save a lot of time and energy."

I was, at this point, in no especial fear for Mr. Lutrell's safety. I had seen only a fraction of my companion's sorcerous powers but was confident that she would be in no danger from anything so prosaic as a sword, even one wielded by a Marvosi force captain. Still, I was keen that this altercation not escalate, as it would likely lead to our expulsion from the party and unnecessarily impede our investigation.

Placing myself between Mr. Lutrell and Domitia, I stood as firmly as I was able and spoke as follows. "Force Captain, you are armed and we are not. You will draw your sword and kill us now, or you will be silent."

This was, I will admit, a gambit not wholly without risk. During my time with the Company of Strangers I had, on occasion, needed to face down angry Marvosi and had always found they responded best if you spoke plainly and stood your ground. I had been stabbed twice and suffered a broken jaw attempting such a strategy in the past, but those outcomes had always been preferable to the alternative.

After appearing to seriously contemplate both options, Force Captain Domitia loosened her grip on her weapon and nodded sharply.

"So, Mr. Lutrell," said Miss de Luca, barely missing a beat, "what can I do for you? You've already made your feelings on *The Inhabitant* quite clear."

"Remind me again what I said?"

Miss de Luca's very red lips twisted into a mocking smile. "You said it was unthinkingly decadent and blindly amoral, without the subtlety of observation or originality of expression that might make such shortcomings forgivable."

"Dear me. I do sound like an utter prig, don't I?" Mr. Lutrell did not, in fact, say "prig"—although I hope I have preserved his sentiment if not his precise vocabulary.

"Yes, darling, yes, you do." Miss de Luca's tone left me in little doubt as to her opinion of Mr. Lutrell.

"If you don't mind my asking," he went on, "you must have been very young when the revolution came to Carcosa. Doesn't that make it rather challenging to write about?"

"My father made certain that I remembered my heritage." Miss de

Luca was hard to read behind the mask, but I fancied I heard sorrow in her voice. "My mother was taken when they purged the Repairers."

"That must have been difficult."

This was an understatement. If Miss de Luca's mother had indeed been a Repairer of Reputations, a member of the rightly feared secret police that once served the kings of Carcosa and now worked for the party, then the Carcosan state would have gone to great lengths to capture and reeducate her entire family. Either Miss de Luca was immensely fortunate or she was a spy.

She shrugged. "It's one such tale amongst many, and you may find its like in poems and playbills across reality. Even dear Iacomo has his *In Memory Of*—seven hundred and twenty-three verses on the theme of how sad it is when your friends die. Grief, we are given to understand, is universal. But how do you grieve for a nation? For a life you never knew? For a world that was stolen from you?"

"Well, personally I wouldn't." Mr. Lutrell lowered himself in a somewhat ungainly fashion onto a cushion. "Who we were is so much less interesting than who we are."

"We are the stories we tell about ourselves. And I would rather be Cassilda on the shores of Lake Hali or a stranger in a pallid mask than a foreign girl with a dead mother."

"And what of our hostess?"

Miss de Luca inclined her head very slightly in Mr. Lutrell's direction. "What of her?"

"She seems rather fascinated by things Carcosan herself, if her reputation is to be believed."

"Oh, darling, that was years ago. And her interest in me has been purely artistic."

"Had it not been," put in Domitia, "I would have killed her."

Catching her paramour's hand, Miss de Luca kissed it playfully. "I find your ferocity terribly attractive, dear one, but do stop threatening to murder people."

"I tolerate this only because I enjoy your company." The force captain did not say "company." She made a rather more specific reference.

Mr. Lutrell coughed as politely as he was able to manage. "What actually did happen back then? With the scandal, I mean."

"I didn't realise," replied Miss de Luca, somewhat coldly, "that *The Esoteric Review* had diversified into gossipmongering."

"On the contrary, in this matter I'm merely an amateur enthusiast."

"Perhaps you should restrict your attentions to Yasmine's poetry rather than her personal life. Have you even read her latest collection?"

I was, by now, familiar enough with Ms. Haas's temperament to know that she did not respond well to either setbacks or criticism. Thankfully, Mr. Lutrell just looked peeved. "Unfortunately an advance copy has not yet arrived at our offices. Perhaps it was devoured by wild dogs en route."

"Well"—Miss de Luca plucked a slim volume from a nearby table—"allow me to supply you with a copy in order that you will not embarrass yourself further."

Mr. Lutrell accepted the proffered chapbook with ill grace. Regaining his feet, he gave a curt bow, and we left Miss de Luca and the force captain to their private discourses.

"Dash it all," muttered my companion, once we were more or less out of earshot. "I hadn't reckoned on her actually liking the Benamara woman. That was less informative than it could have been. Surely the entire purpose of these gatherings is to trade salacious details of the lives of one's peers?"

Personally, I had respected Miss de Luca the better for her circumspection, but it was true that it had proven something of a hindrance to our cause. "What are we to do now?" I asked.

"The time may have come, Wyndham, for a little skulduggery. I suggest I cause a distraction here while you slip away and search the rest of the house for something useful."

"Is that not technically theft?"

"Not if it is in the pursuit of a higher cause."

This brought me little comfort. "I don't believe the law works that way."

"That is a limitation of your beliefs, not of my strategy. Now go look for incriminating letters and, for pity's sake, don't forget to check the letter rack."

I wanted to continue my protestations. While I was willing to face physical and supernatural danger in pursuit of a solution to this mystery, I quite drew the line at burglarising the home of a well-regarded poetess who had so far given no indication that she had done anything more sinister than host a salon for an assortment of guests of whom my companion and I were by far the most dubious.

Fortunately, or perhaps unfortunately, my commitment to my principles in this matter was never tested, as we were interrupted by a roar of greeting from an enormous bearded gentleman, whose curling locks tumbled from beneath a tricornered hat.

"Percy bloody Lutrell. What the deuce are you doing here?" He did not say "deuce." "Aren't you covering the Festival of Metaphysical Theatre in El'avarah?"

Mr. Lutrell didn't even blink. "Clearly not. I'm here."

"You decided to skip one of the most prestigious events of the entire calendar to come to a bourgeois shindig with a shower of buffoons?"

The shower of buffoons seemed unhappy with this characterisation, but none saw fit, as yet, to challenge it.

"I wouldn't call them that," replied Mr. Lutrell, with a pious look.

"But you *did* call them that. Only last week. You said to me at the Sea-god's Nipple: 'Yasmine Benamara's got another book of her bloody awful poems out and she's asking me to come to one of her terrible parties with that shower of buffoons who obviously hate her and her prissy verses.'"

"Sir"—Mr. Lutrell stiffened, adopting an expression of the utmost sanctimony—"you insult me, and you insult our host."

"Percy, you haven't called me 'sir' in the twenty years we've known each other. What the pish is wrong with you?" He did not say "pish."

Mr. Lutrell was looking mildly harried. "I . . . I must be feeling a little out of sorts. Perhaps it's the baklava."

"What are you saying, man? You hate Khelish food. You once told me that putting pistachio on a pastry was the culinary equivalent of perfume on a prostitute: cheap, excessive, and fooling nobody."

"Honestly." Mr. Lutrell put a limp wrist to his forehead. "The more I learn about myself, the less I think of me."

The piratical gentleman set his hands on his hips. "All right. Who the devil are you? And why in the name of whatever gods you believe in have you chosen to impersonate Percy Lutrell? I mean, I'm his best friend, and even I think he's a complete cat's rectum." He did, in fact, on this occasion say "rectum." I have considered the matter and believe the word sufficiently technical that I may use it here without causing offence.

At this juncture it may perhaps have still been possible for us to salvage the deception. Our interlocutor had, after all, provided no direct proof that my companion was not who he claimed to be. Any hope I might have had in this direction, however, would have relied upon Ms. Haas's being the sort of person who valued subtlety over spectacle.

"Who am I?" repeated Mr. Lutrell, his image shifting momentarily out of focus and then resolving itself into that of my companion, who, despite her avowed intent to attend this function incognito had nonetheless chosen to attire herself in an evening gown of sea-green satin. "I am the sorceress Shaharazad Haas. I trust you've heard of me."

CHAPTER TWENTY-SEVEN

An Arrest

Ms. Haas's revelation of her identity inspired less chaos than I had feared and, I suspect, than she had hoped. Mr. Van der Berg muttered something to a servant while Lord Bahrami opined loudly from the back of the room that he had known the whole time, somewhat to the derision of his peers. Mrs. Benamara rose from where she was sitting and approached us with an air of composure that I felt did her genuine credit.

"Your reputation does, in fact, precede you," she said. "But I can think of no reason that you would wish to infiltrate one of my gatherings, much less go to such lengths to do so."

"My dear lady, I went to no lengths at all." There was a brief pause, one I took correctly to indicate that Ms. Haas was, in fact, about to provide us with a soliloquy which would leave the assembly in no doubt whatsoever as to her remarkable talents, unnatural powers, and single-minded devotion to her goals. "I merely ascertained from one of several sources, whose names I shall not disclose, the identity of an individual you were likely to have invited to this scriveners' tea party and who would be likely to have spurned that invitation. It was then just a matter of employing certain gifts that I have been granted in exchange for certain bargains and sacrifices I made in years long past to take on the appropriate likeness."

"That still doesn't explain what you're doing in my house."

Stretching out a languid hand, Ms. Haas plucked a vine leaf from the buffet. "Right now, I'm sampling your canapés. Which, I must admit, are excellent. But if you mean my purpose in coming here, I wish to speak to you about Eirene Viola."

"I don't think," returned Mrs. Benamara icily, "I'm inclined to talk to you, on that or any subject."

Ms. Haas sighed with her usual air of exasperation at the world in general. "I assure you, matters will be resolved far more swiftly and far more to your satisfaction if you change your mind. I can be really quite irritating, and this is a very charming neighbourhood. It would be such a shame were something eschatological to happen to it."

Despite our long acquaintance I would never learn entirely to be at ease with the alacrity with which Ms. Haas moved to threats of supernatural annihilation, although honesty compels me to observe that this approach was efficacious on more occasions than it was not. In this case, however, we were denied the opportunity of seeing whether Mrs. Benamara would have responded favourably, since we were interrupted by Mr. Van der Berg.

"You look here," he blustered. "Maybe you can get away with this nonsense in a rookery in Athra or the back alleys of Ven, but we don't stand for your sort around here. I've sent the girl for the Myrmidons and unless you want to get what's coming to you I suggest you clear out sharpish and leave this good woman alone."

My companion gazed at him with devastating pity. "Oh, where to begin? Firstly, what's coming to me is something infinitely more terrible than any mortal agency could devise. Secondly, I do not have a sort. I am unique and you may thank your stars for it. Thirdly . . ." And here, once again, I am obliged to censor Ms. Haas. But I am certain that readers familiar with such terminology as she employs—or rather, employed while yet she lived—should by now have sufficient familiarity with her patterns of speech to make good the omission.

"Enough, Iacomo." Mrs. Benamara cast him a severe look. "There's no call to answer discourtesy with discourtesy. As for you, Ms. Haas, you have not only behaved in an exceptionally rude manner, you have also flagrantly engaged in criminal trespass abetted by sorcery. Threats aside, I see no reason why I should speak to you in these circumstances."

Ms. Haas took a step across the room, her shadow moving strangely in the lamplight. "Are you really going to risk the wrath of one of the most accomplished magical practitioners still at liberty?"

"Are you really going to murder me in my own house?" Once again, I found myself silently commending Mrs. Benamara for her fortitude, but I could not help noticing the way her hands trembled, and I do not consider this confrontation one of Ms. Haas's finest moments.

"Well, obviously not," she grumbled. "But it would be so much easier if you were to behave as if I would. Look, I'd hoped that this evening would be at least momentarily diverting, but now I'm very, very bored."

Tucking the book of Mrs. Benamara's poetry under her arm, she drew up the many layers of her skirts and petticoats, a gesture that would have been utterly shocking to me two months before and was now merely disconcerting. Tucked into an unmentionable item of hosiery, she appeared to be keeping various small objects, including a wickedly sharp stiletto, a thin rod of bone that I assumed had arcane significance, and her card case. "Here's my calling card. I will get to the bottom of this matter one way or the other, and it will go much better for both of us if we can do so in a mature and civilised fashion. Come, Wyndham. We're leaving."

This, it transpired, was true. But not for the reasons Ms. Haas expected. We made it only as far as the front door before we were confronted by a band of grey-uniformed Myrmidons. They were led by the same gentleman who had intervened in the unfortunate business with Mr. Donne.

"Oh no, not you again," he and Ms. Haas groaned in unison.

Ms. Haas was the first to recover from her dismay. "Well, Mr. Wyndham, it seems I am once more about to be arrested. Unless, of course, Second Augur Lawson will listen to reason when I endeavour to explain that I am in pursuit of a matter most delicate and quite beyond the wit of the imbecilic constabulary employed by the council."

"You flatter us, Ms. Haas. And what is it this time? An engineer with a missing thumb? Somebody who's broke their beryl coronet? A goose what's swallowed a priceless jewel?"

"It's a case of blackmail, Lawson. And you know how I despise blackmailers."

"And this is criminal trespass with allegations of sorcery and, as I have told you many times, Ms. Haas, you are not allowed to break the law. And I know, as you have told *me* many times, that you could turn my bones to sand and my blood to living fire, but I'm still taking you in."

"You know I only allow this because I feel sorry for you." Ms. Haas presented her wrists with theatrical contempt, and a nervous young Myrmidon came forward to put her in irons.

Second Augur Lawson then turned to me. "You as well, I'm afraid. Though I suspect you were not the primary instigator of the affray."

I own that my feelings, on being placed for the first time in chains by a member of the official force—especially one with whom I was already acquainted and who had been so civil to me at our first meeting—strayed perilously close to mortification and I found myself utterly unable to meet the Second Augur's gaze.

"For pity's sake." Ms. Haas did not say "pity" and, in light of our circumstances, I dearly wished she had. "You may play your little games with me all you like, but let Mr. Wyndham go. As I told your colleague not last week, he's plainly harmless and would do nothing exciting whatsoever without my setting him a bad example."

The Second Augur closed his metallic fingers around my companion's silk-gloved forearm and began leading her away. "Well, maybe you should think about that the next time you get him to do something illegal."

"On your head be it, Second Augur."

And with that we were transferred into a black carriage drawn by a mechanical bull. So incarcerated, we were taken through the city at none too urgent a pace towards New Arcadia Yard.

My upbringing had taught me very strictly that when one has transgressed one must bear whatever punishment is deemed suitable with grace and stoicism. In this particular circumstance, that was proving more than usually difficult. I had, of course, undertaken my role in the evening's proceedings by choice and could, in theory, have walked away the moment the notion of infiltrating a respectable woman's home by sorcery was suggested, but Ms. Haas's force of personality and bullish assumption that any course of action she suggested would automatically be undertaken by those to whom she suggested it had carried me along despite my better judgement. This does not, of course, excuse my behaviour and nor does it excuse the unbecoming sense of resentment that I felt towards my companion in the moments following our arrest, although it does go some way towards explaining them both.

Ms. Haas, who possessed the uncannily cat-like ability to make herself comfortable in the most precarious of positions, had sprawled out across one of the rough wooden benches that were bolted to the walls of the carriage. By the uncertain light that filtered in through the windows she was leafing idly through the volume of Mrs. Benamara's poetry she had been given at the salon. The activity was hampered slightly by the fact that her hands were manacled together at the wrists, but she negotiated the impediment with a facility suggestive of familiarity.

After a while, she looked up. "I am capable of many things, Mr. Wyndham. But change is not amongst them."

I was not certain what had prompted my companion to offer this seemingly non sequitous observation. Not trusting myself to respond appropriately, I waited to see what would follow.

"I am aware," she continued, "that I often speak of such things lightly, but you should understand that of the very small number of people I have genuinely considered friends almost all have come to bad ends. I cannot live in the world that people such as yourself find comfortable, and the world in which I live is perilous to visit, worse to inhabit."

I was growing accustomed to Ms. Haas's moods and there had been evenings over the past month during which her conversation had taken a decidedly melancholy tone, but this was the first time, and it was close to being the last, that she spoke to me with quite this level of candour. "I'm not sure I follow you."

"I simply mean that I know my actions tonight have"—she frowned—"inconvenienced you. But you should understand I do not have it in me to regret taking them. Should you persist in keeping my company, this is far from the most"—another pause—"inconvenient thing that will happen to you."

All of these predictions proved typically prescient. Although I flatter myself that Ms. Haas's long acquaintance with me did not leave her totally uninfluenced, she retained her capricious will, her merciless intellect, and her tendency to reduce the world, and everyone in it, to either a game to be played or a problem to be solved. Even so, I have never regretted the years we spent together and, as astute readers may no doubt deduce from the existence of this document, her disregard for my comfort was never so absolute as to prove fatal.

Looking back at what was to prove the first of many incarcerations, I believe I made a decision in that moment. Over the then-short duration of our relationship, Ms. Haas had always accepted me for who I was without question or hesitation and it seemed only fitting that I should extend her the same courtesy.

CHAPTER TWENTY-EIGHT

❦

New Arcadia Yard

Our carriage arrived at New Arcadia Yard, a custom-built facility to which the organisation had recently moved, and the Myrmidons assisted us with a kind of rough courtesy from the back of the vehicle into the main building, down a warren of discreet side passages, and into separate cells. I found myself in a small room, containing one chair, one item of furniture that may have passed for a bed, and another the function and purpose of which I shall not describe in detail. The window was, of course, barred and the door likewise, but the walls were of whitewashed brick, meaning that I had no sense of my location within the complex or of where Ms. Haas might be. While my situation clearly left a great deal to be desired, I was at least grateful that I had not been thrown into company with some genuine hoodlum, against whom I might have been required to defend myself.

The Myrmidons having confiscated my pocket watch, I was not at all certain how much time had elapsed between my confinement and my eventual summons to a nearby interview room. Like my cell, it was sparse and functional. Second Augur Lawson awaited me behind a plain wooden table, upon which rested a wax cylinder recorder. This he turned on with a click and hiss once I had taken my place in the other available chair.

He leaned forward, propping himself on his elbows. "Fifth day, seventh month, third year, Twenty-first Council. Interview commencing ten fourteen p.m., Second Augur Lawson conducting. The suspect was apprehended in Ecet's Cove outside the home of Mr. Jamal and Mrs. Yasmine Benamara on suspicion of aiding and abetting housebreaking by sorcery. Please state your name for the record."

I had never been less certain what to do in my life, so I turned my head to speak into the recording trumpet, which had the fortunate side effect of sparing me the embarrassment of having to look directly at the Second Augur. Perhaps I was merely self-conscious owing to the inauspicious circumstances surrounding our interaction, but there was something almost amused in his otherwise stern countenance, and I could not shake the conviction that his mirth was at my expense.

"John Wyndham," I said, as clearly as I could.

"And what were you doing in the home of Mr. and Mrs. Benamara?"

It occurred to me many years after the fact that I could simply have remained silent, or requested the services of a lawyer-priest of Estra (a notable irony since Mrs. Benamara's husband was, to the best of my knowledge, still an anointed member of that ministry), but the thought of being anything other than cooperative simply did not cross my mind. "I had been invited to a literary soiree as the guest of Mr. Percy Lutrell."

"And Mr. Percy Lutrell was, in fact, the sorceress Shaharazad Haas, disguised by means of illusion?"

"Yes."

"And you were aware of this at the point of your entry into the building?"

"I was."

Second Augur Lawson regarded me with an expression that could have been anything from admiration to incredulity. "It's not looking good for you, is it, son?"

"It does not seem so."

"What is the nature of your relationship with the sorceress Shaharazad Haas?"

"She is my co-tenant."

"And"—he scratched the side of his jaw thoughtfully with his metal hand—"do you always go around committing crimes with your co-tenants?"

"I'm afraid I must admit that during my university days my roommate and I once broke into the Hall of the Learned and decorated each of the statues with a comical hat. The university never got to the bottom of the matter, and it has sat ill with me ever since."

"To your great good fortune, we do not have authority on varsity grounds, so this most heinous crime will forever go unpunished."

At last I directed my gaze to his. "Are you making sport of me, sir?"

"Certainly not." His mouth twitched in a fashion that belied the gravity of his tone. "That would be most inappropriate. Now, at the time you agreed to accompany the sorceress Shaharazad Haas on this escapade were you aware that you were under any manner of enchantment, ensorcellment, bewitchment, or hex?"

"I don't believe so."

"Is it possible?"

"Where witchcraft is concerned, I would have thought anything is possible."

At this, he turned off the recording device abruptly. "You're not helping yourself, Mr. Wyndham."

"I was not aware that I was supposed to be."

"You've been arrested. Who else are you supposed to be helping?"

"I rather thought I was supposed to be helping you." I straightened my cuffs. "The law, as I understand it, is meant to be applied to everybody equally. It is your job to decide which persons should progress to the next stage of the judicial system and, in order to do that effectively, it is helpful if you have the most accurate and correct information available. If, once I have told you what happened to the best of my recollection, it is your judgement that I should be tried in the temple-courts before a hierophant-judge then I am willing to accept that. I trust you to do your duty with honour."

Second Augur Lawson stared at me for a long moment and then covered his face with his palm. "How are you not dead yet?"

"It is a question I often ask myself. I sometimes take it as a sign of the Creator's mercy, but since He allowed so many of my friends and comrades to perish beyond the Unending Gate the explanation has never wholly satisfied me."

"Oh, for— Look." He returned his hand to the table and subjected me, once again, to his scrutiny. "You've confessed on record to aiding and abetting housebreaking with sorcery. If you'd said you were under a spell, or you didn't know what was going on, I might have been able to let you go. But you didn't, so I can't."

"Well, of course I didn't. Not only would it be a lie, it would be deeply unfair to Ms. Haas, who has always been most kind to me."

Seemingly without conscious volition, his arm came up once again, and he briefly made the gesture I have come to associate with the response of Khelathrans to my Eyan idiosyncrasies. "All right, I can't stop this going to court, but I'll tell you this for free. Stay the ——" And here he used a word most unbecoming of his rank, position, and uniform. ". . . away from Shaharazad Haas."

"I am not sure it is your place to advise me on such matters."

"Clearly somebody's got to." He leaned back in his chair. "She already nearly got you killed. Now she's got you arrested. This will keep happening until you sharpen up and realise she is a bad person."

On one level I could appreciate that Second Augur Lawson's intentions in giving me this warning were kind, a facet of his personality I would recognise on several occasions, although he would always do his best to hide it. On another, however, I felt something that I would almost describe as being close to insulted by his insinuation that my judgement was not to be trusted and I could not look after myself. This aspect of the Second Augur's temperament I would also observe on future occasions, although he would eventually learn to curtail it and I to forgive it. "My thanks," I said. "That is most solicitous of you."

He gave me a look that suggested he did not like my response any more than I had liked his initial comment. Moving his chair forward, he turned the recording device back on. "Thank you, Mr. Wyndham. Interview concluded at—"

As it transpired, the interview could not be officially concluded, interrupted as we were by the crash of the interview room door being flung open behind me. So intemperate was the entrance that I fleetingly entertained the notion that it could be none other than Ms. Haas engaged in some well-intentioned but perhaps ill-advised jailbreak.

This did not prove to be the case.

CHAPTER TWENTY-NINE

Augur Extraordinary Joy-in-Sorrow Standfast

Turning in my chair I beheld, to my dismay, Augur Extraordinary Standfast, the lady who had recently been so very enthusiastic about the idea of arresting me, shooting Ms. Haas, and starting a war with the Ossuary Bank.

The Second Augur did not seem best pleased to see her either. "What do you want, Standfast? As you can see, I am in the middle of interviewing this suspect."

"He's not your suspect anymore," returned the Augur Extraordinary, a statement which, when combined with her manner, bearing, and prior behaviour, did little for my confidence.

"It was my team picked him up."

"The crime includes a charge of witchcraft. You know as well as I do that means it falls under the jurisdiction of the Sorcerous Crimes Unit."

"And you know as well as I do," said the Second Augur, folding his arms, "that the final decision on what matters get passed over to the SCU lies with First Augur Mehdiyeva."

"I spoke to her twelve minutes ago. This case is ours."

"It's just someone gate-crashing a party."

The Augur Extraordinary scowled. "It is not his first association with a magical offence and he clearly keeps company with a notorious sorceress. Witchcraft is a contagion. Unless purged, it spreads and it flourishes."

"Remember you're in Khelathra-Ven, not the Commonwealth. We're here to solve crimes, not burn people."

It had been a trying evening and one that had contained rather more unflattering generalisations about my country than I could remain sanguine about. "If I might," I interjected, "the witch hunters of Ey seldom condemn anybody to the pyres. They are very much seen as a tool of last resort and are employed only when the individual in question has rejected all opportunities for penance."

This comment endeared me to neither party, earning me a look of exasperation from Lawson and one of outright contempt from the Augur Extraordinary.

"Look"—the Second Augur stood up and began squaring away his notes—"we've got his statement. He's copped to aiding and abetting. He's clearly not a wizard. You can interview him if you like, but you'd be wasting your time and his. Go talk to Haas. She's the actual sorcerer."

"Your advice is noted. I'll take it from here."

Second Augur Lawson collected his papers and the wax cylinder, shot me one last look, which I could not entirely read but elected to interpret as sympathetic, and exited, leaving me alone with Augur Extraordinary Standfast.

We were silent for some minutes. During this period, she did not sit down, preferring instead to prowl the room behind me, her boot heels clicking ominously against the flagstones. I presumed that this behaviour was intended to intimidate me, and in this regard, I feel it was only partially successful. There was certainly something disquieting about it, and I did not enjoy having a person in the guise of an Eyan witch hunter constantly flitting in and out of my peripheral vision. Nonetheless I had faith in the city's system of criminal justice and was certain that, however unpleasant the Augur Extraordinary may be in her manner, the harm that she could do to me was strictly limited by the laws of the land.

At last she circled round in front of me and leaned over the desk, bracing herself on her red-gloved hands. "State your name."

"John Wyndham."

"Is that your real name?"

"Yes."

"The name you were born with?"

"As you are no doubt aware, I was born in Ey. And since I am clearly not a child, you must also recognise that I was born prior to the revolution and that, therefore, any record of my birth would have been kept by the local Tallyman and destroyed in the revolution."

Her mouth thinned in evident frustration. "What did your parents call you?"

"My mother calls me John. My father and I have not spoken in many years."

"Why have you been so remiss in your duty to your father?"

This stung a little, as I am sure it was meant to. "I do not believe this line of questioning is relevant to the accusations against me."

"I decide what's relevant."

"Then, if you insist upon it, my father does not approve of me. As I'm sure yours does not of you."

This last comment, I think, struck a reciprocal chord, and it is somewhat shamefacedly that I admit the effect was intentional. She pushed herself upright, regarding me with an expression that had progressed beyond contempt and was fast approaching the territory of hatred. "Do not pretend that you know me."

"With respect, Augur Extraordinary, I know enough." I folded my still-manacled hands. "By your speech and manner I can see that you are a devoted adherent of the Church of the Creator. By your dress it is clear that you at least style yourself after the witch hunters, who protect the people of our homeland from those of the Witch King's servants who yet remain at large and those weak-willed individuals who may fall under his sway. That you have chosen to travel nearly a thousand miles to a foreign city quite unsuited to your values and beliefs merely in order that you might pursue a career analogous to the one denied you in Ey suggests, paradoxically, a devotion to your faith so strong that it would cause you to disregard some of the most basic precepts of the society in which you learned that faith."

I should, perhaps, have stopped here. But I confess that between my particular discomfort at the line of questioning the Augur Extraordinary had chosen to take and the strange exhilaration that came from giving myself licence to speak freely when I ordinarily would have done no such thing I became unforgivably indiscreet.

"Your name," I continued, "Joy-in-Sorrow, signifies that your mother died bearing you and must, therefore, have been given to you by your father. A man who would bestow such a name upon his child is clearly a pious and, more importantly, orthodox adherent of the church's teachings. This is not the sort of person who could be anything but ashamed to see his daughter running around the south dressed in men's clothing and pursuing a calling that is explicitly forbidden to her sex."

At this, she struck me. And, while I have spent much of the latter part of my career advocating for more structured regulation of the techniques employed by the Myrmidons during interrogations, I do, in retrospect, understand, if not entirely forgive, her reaction.

She brought her face very close to mine and spoke in a voice barely above a whisper. "I am an Augur Extraordinary of the Sorcerous Crimes Unit. You are a suspect. Take that tone with me again and I will have you up on charges of attempting to subvert a Myrmidon by witchcraft."

My emotions in that moment were sufficiently complex that I am finding them, even so many years after the fact, difficult to articulate.

Having been attacked by this woman both verbally and now physically my instincts quite naturally ran to the defensive, but I was not quite so lacking in compassion as to be unaware that my remarks had, in fact, gone rather too far and been rather too personal. I was, of course, also still mortified at having been arrested in the first place and increasingly uncertain about what the future would hold, since the charges against me appeared to be mounting in severity.

The truth is, I was somewhat loath to back down, since I have never in my life found it pays to submit in the face of aggression. However, I had, in this instance, genuinely wronged the lady, albeit in response to her own discourteous behaviour. I decided it would be best to apologise.

"I am sorry, Augur Extraordinary," I said. "I spoke injudiciously and of matters on which it was not my place to speak."

This did not, however, have the desired mollifying effect. "I don't want an apology. I want you to answer my questions. Now, what is your relationship with the sorceress Shaharazad Haas?"

I opened my mouth to reply but was, once again, interrupted by the crash of the interview room door being flung open behind me.

"He's my companion," announced Ms. Haas, for on this occasion it was, in fact, she. "But not in a sexual way."

I was a little bemused that she felt the need to clarify that point, but very glad to see her.

Augur Extraordinary Standfast, needless to say, was not. "You have no right to be here. Return to your cell or I will take you there by force."

"I think Commander Pennyfeather might have something to say about that." Ms. Haas flourished an official-looking letter bearing the seal of the leader of the Myrmidons.

"How do I know this isn't a trick?"

Ms. Haas appeared to give the matter some thought. "Well, you could ask him yourself, but he's just gone back to bed so I doubt he'd appreciate the disturbance. Alternatively you could simply rely on the fact that if I ever did choose to leave your custody illicitly everybody in this city knows that I live at 221b Martyrs Walk, so you could send a cart to collect me in the morning. Now come, Wyndham. It is getting late and we have much to discuss."

Since the Augur Extraordinary did not seem disposed to prevent me, I rose gratefully to my feet. My hands, of course, were still in shackles, a detail that did not appear to concern Ms. Haas. She set her fingers lightly over the locks and whispered a soft invocation, causing the mechanisms to spring merrily open.

Catching the chains as they fell, she tossed them across the room to Augur Extraordinary Standfast. "I believe these are yours."

The Augur Extraordinary left her arms pointedly folded and the manacles clattered to the floor beside her. "Get out."

We obliged.

CHAPTER THIRTY

Some Poetry

I confess I was quite relieved to collect my personal effects from the front desk and depart New Arcadia Yard. My encounter with the Augur Extraordinary had been unpleasant in ways to which I had grown unaccustomed since leaving Ey and had left me a little shaken. On our relatively short journey by hansom to 221b Martyrs Walk, I endeavoured to distract myself by asking Ms. Haas how in the world she had contrived to secure our release from the custody of the Myrmidons.

"Commander Pennyfeather," she explained, "is an odious little twerp, but his ambition makes him biddable. A truly staggering number of influential people throughout Khel, Athra, Ven, and beyond have reason to be grateful to me for various services I have rendered them, and the merest implication that one of them might be displeased by my arrest has generally proved enough to bring the man abjectly to heel. If that fails, I can also remind him of the innumerable high-profile cases that my assistance has been instrumental in solving, and that his reputation as a firm-handed, fair-minded, and above all efficacious commander of Myrmidons may at any point depend on his ability to call once more on my assistance."

I was somewhat troubled by this revelation, although I was somewhat more troubled by the realisation that I had quite deliberately waited until I was safely out of the hands of the Myrmidons before eliciting it. "I'm not sure being well connected or having been of assistance to the commander in the past should allow one to disregard the law."

"Oh, I quite agree. I believe the right to disregard the law is intrinsic and inalienable."

"That's not quite what I meant."

"I shall tell you a liberating but terrifying truth, Mr. Wyndham." Ms. Haas hitched up her skirts and produced from her other intimate garment a book of matches and a packet of Valentino's Good Rough Shag. "This cosmos which we inhabit is vast and indifferent. Every law, every teaching, and every tenet by which you might choose to live your life is a fiction that exists only so long as those around you agree upon it. In reality, you are entitled only to what you can take, duty bound to do only what you cannot avoid doing, and protected only by what power is in you to protect yourself."

"Perhaps you are right, Ms. Haas. I am, after all, well aware that the Creator Himself is believed by experimental theologians to be nothing but a seething mass of mindless energy. But it seems to me there are certain things which, even though they may not be the case, our lives are improved if we behave as though they were."

She put her pipe to her lips and lit it. "That, Captain, is why I got us out of prison while you have spent your life in one."

"I should perhaps point out," I pointed out, "that you also got us into prison."

"Which"—Ms. Haas grinned unrepentantly—"was still more interesting than anything else you could have planned for the evening."

"Was the point of this excursion not to determine whether Mrs. Benamara was the source of the threatening letters that Miss Viola has been receiving? A criterion by which it must be judged to have failed spectacularly."

"On the contrary, much as I predicted, it has succeeded perfectly well. Just not by the mechanism I originally intended."

"But," I protested, "we have come no closer to either eliminating or confirming Mrs. Benamara as a suspect."

Ms. Haas cast me a mocking look out of the corner of her eye. "Well, of course we have. It couldn't possibly have been her."

To the best of my recollection, Ms. Haas and I had seen all of the same things, spoken to all of the same people, and heard all of the same comments, and I could not for the life of me think of anything that even a mind as remarkable as hers could have pieced together into an irrefutable case for either guilt or innocence. Unless, of course . . . "Was there something in the poems?"

"Well deduced, Mr. Wyndham. Yes, our dear Yasmine's latest volume, which goes by the rather obvious title of *Bitter Fruit*, is a terribly emotional and, I am sure, adequately moving sequence of verses on the various passions, heartaches, tribulations, and disappointments that have characterised the last few years of Mrs. Benamara's romantic life. The eponymous poem is quite explicitly about Eirene, as are several of the others."

"That surely doesn't mean anything by itself."

She inhaled deeply from her pipe. "Not by itself. But several of the other verses speak quite eloquently of the long and difficult process by which she rebuilt her relationship with her husband. And it would seem odd to put such effort into repairing a marriage only to imperil it by stooping to so petty and provable a crime as blackmail, especially when one is married to a lawyer. On top of that, several of the poems that do concern Eirene reveal quite specific details of their relationship that, were I attempting to blackmail somebody, I would withhold specifically for use as a threat. It is, of course, possible that a blackmailer might also choose to publish some of her blackmail material in a widely circulated volume of popular verse, but it seems terribly, terribly improbable."

"And also," I added, "Mrs. Benamara seemed a very gentle and respectable lady, and I find it hard to believe that she could possibly be involved in anything as sordid as this."

Ms. Haas answered this very reasonable observation with a groan. "Oh, Wyndham. What are we to do with you?"

"Perhaps you could try getting me arrested again. You seem to consider that improving."

"Well, without that little distraction, the evening would have been a complete wash."

It was not becoming, but I saw here the opportunity to score at least a small victory over my companion. "You will admit, then," I remarked, "that you were wrong to claim that nothing interesting would happen at the gathering we attended?"

She gave a throaty chuckle. "I own no such thing. We went to a tedious party, with tedious people, and were then arrested by a tedious man who put us in tedious cells and then you, on top of that, had the added tedium of being interrogated by a tedious woman from your tedious country. It was the dullest evening I've spent outside my own home in the past five years. And five years ago, I was stranded in a featureless desert."

My interview with the Augur Extraordinary had been anything but tedious, but I resolved to put the experience out of mind and to move the conversation in another direction. "You just said"—my voice rose slightly—"our arrest provided a distraction that salvaged the evening."

"Do stop being tiresome, Wyndham."

Her chuckling became laughter and, with New Arcadia Yard already vanished into the night, I did my best to smile with her.

CHAPTER THIRTY-ONE

The Manor at Quatreface,
Part the First

Despite the excitement of the previous evening we were actually able to arrive home at a comparatively sensible hour, and I was able to get in a good night's sleep and respectable day's work before Ms. Haas whisked me away on the next adventure.

I entered the sitting room to find her—I would say waiting but perhaps it would be better to say occupying the time of my absence—sprawled on the chaise, smoking and reading the latest edition of the *Times*. She was dressed in a gentleman's black evening suit of an extremely modern cut that highlighted her figure in a manner that, even accounting for my Eyan sensibilities, seemed to border on the indelicate.

"Ah, Wyndham." She glanced up from the paper. "What do you make of this matter of the Emir of Bahl's missing amulet?"

"A most perplexing crime. I understand that the Myrmidons are quite dumbfounded."

"Of course they are. Because they, like you, have made the mistake of assuming that a crime has been committed. The item in question went missing from a room whose doors and windows were all locked and bolted while the emir was visiting the mistress of the Ubiquitous Company of Printers and Typesetters, Ms. Mia Toksvig, with whom he was negotiating the price of ink. If you will refer to that issue"—she pointed imperiously at a carefully discarded magazine—"of the *Ladies' Aspirational Repository*, you will note also that Ms. Toksvig recently journeyed to the Kingdom of Utu, from which she returned with a small, and poorly trained, pet monkey. That exact species of primate is renowned for its inquisitive nature and attraction to shiny objects. There were no means by which a human could have entered the room in which the theft took place, but I have been to the guild house of the Ubiquitous Company of Printers and Typesetters and I know for a fact that most of the rooms have small apertures built into the walls for the purposes of ventilation. Through such an opening, a small animal could crawl easily. I have no doubt that the monkey keeps a veritable hoard of stolen treasures in some out-of-the-way place, likely amongst the rafters of that, as I recall, rather old-fashioned building."

"Good gracious," I exclaimed. "If there is even the smallest chance of your conclusions being correct we must tell the authorities at once."

She stretched theatrically and made a great show of stifling a yawn. "I've already penned a letter to Commander Pennyfeather. Assuming my summary of events is accurate, and I am certain it is, I will, once again, have demonstrated to him the advantages of my being kept at liberty. Undoubtedly, my intervention will irritate the likes of Second Augur Lawson, but that is very much their fault for being terrible at their jobs."

I should reiterate that I reproduce Ms. Haas's deprecating comments about the Myrmidons in the interests of maintaining an accurate record and do not intend for them to be interpreted as representative of my own opinions, or indeed a reflection on the fine employees of that institution, who I have always found to be excellent public servants.

Before I could reply she cast the paper aside and leapt to her feet with a cry of "Come, Wyndham. Our quarry awaits."

"Would that be our quarry the vampiress?"

Readers who are following this narrative in its serialised edition may have forgotten in the months between the publication of the first instalment and the present that our suspects were as follows: Mr. Charles du Maurier, impresario of the theatrical experience known as Mise en Abyme (whom we eliminated from our enquiries in the light of the shrewd character of his current protégé), Mr. Enoch Reef (who, it transpired, had been engaged in an underworld conflict that would have made it quite impractical for him to waste resources blackmailing civilians), Mrs. Yasmine Benamara (our encounter with whom was detailed in last month's edition), the Contessa Ilona of Mircalla (a vampire, whom we have yet to meet), and Citizen Icarius Castaigne of the People's Republic of Carcosa (who will appear in a future escapade).

To return our focus to the matter at hand, I had asked Ms. Haas to clarify the nature of our next suspect for the simple reason that I was deeply (and, as it turned out, accurately) concerned about the dangers that may await us were we to bait a vampiress in her lair during the hours of darkness. Once Ms. Haas had confirmed that the Contessa was, indeed, our subject and I had articulated these very reservations to her she assuaged my fears in her usual fashion.

"Oh, don't be such a wet blanket, Captain. If it reassures you, bring one of the pistols. I believe there are a half dozen silver bullets in that slipper over there. And in one of the decanters you will find water consecrated in the name of several solar deities, including your own peculiar nuclear god." She paused thoughtfully. "Unless I drank it. I was a little low on mixers the other day."

I fetched my cane against the possibility that my wound would inconveniently resurface and availed myself of the offered pistol and ammunition. I would not normally go armed into a respectable part of the city, but when one's destination is haunted by the living dead one reconsiders the relative merits of propriety and security. Ms. Haas had not, as it happened, consumed the holy water or, at least, I found that one of the decanters contained a liquid that appeared to be water, and which I assumed, therefore, was the reagent to which she had referred. Although, given its proximity to the whiskey, it may have been soda, and, given the overall disarrangement of Ms. Haas's drinks cabinet and alchemical apparatus, it could also have been a solution of brine, the collected tears of a thousand virgins, or an extremely dilute medical sample. Nevertheless, I decanted it into a hip flask, hoping that, in extremis, I might at least be able to distract or discommode an adversary.

While I had been thus engaged, Ms. Haas had completed her ensemble with the addition of an opera cloak lined in red silk, a collapsible top hat, and a gold-rimmed monocle.

"Madam," I exclaimed, "you surely cannot be intending to confront an unliving tyrant in such impractical garments."

She gave me one of her mocking looks. "In case it escaped your attention during our last escapade, I am gifted with the capacity to alter my appearance at will. I can be anyone I wish whenever I wish, one of the perks of which is that I can wear whatever the ——" And here she employed one of the words I prefer not to set before my audience. ". . . I please."

It was a fair point, although since she did not, in fact, often change her appearance in order to conceal her inappropriate sartorial choices it sounds, in retrospect, rather like an excuse.

We bade farewell to Mrs. Hive, whose present body had lost an arm and most of its face, meaning she would soon be obliged to purchase another, and hailed a cab from the end of Martyrs Walk. As we rattled through the cobbled streets of Athra, I enquired further into our strategy.

"Are you absolutely certain," I asked, "that this is the best time of day to be going to the home of a vampire?"

She put a finger pensively to her lips. "It's what you might call a compromise. If our intent was definitely to slay the Contessa in her sleep we would attempt to come upon her just after dawn or close to noon, when the sunlight would render her weak. By extension of this reasoning, however, if one wishes to visit socially, arriving before sunset is considered spectacularly rude. It's approximately equivalent to trying to call upon a human while they're in the bath and you are dressed in a suit of Marvosi body armour and carrying a rifle. Which is to say, rather gauche."

"I do follow your reasoning, but what if, for example, she tries to slay us?"

"Well, that is why we're not visiting at midnight. And besides"—she patted me on the knee—"I rather hope it won't come to that. Vampires are rather tricky creatures. On the one hand, they're immortal, and immortal beings have far less cause to behave rashly than mortal ones. But on the other, they're also creatures of overwhelming and unbearable passion, a quality that makes them a great deal of fun in some contexts but terrible bores in others."

I asked one more question. It was a question I would ask many times over the course of my long acquaintance with the sorceress Shaharazad Haas, never receiving an entirely satisfactory answer. "Is there a plan?"

"Of course there's a plan. We go to her house, we have a conversation, we see how things develop from there."

"Wasn't that the plan last time?"

Ms. Haas brightened. "Yes, and everything worked out wonderfully."

We disembarked outside the high stone wall of the Contessa's estate. The gates were closed but not locked, although rust and decay made them difficult to push open, and the grounds beyond were overgrown and ill lit. Perversely, for we were not a hundred yards from the road, I could have sworn I heard the howling of wolves in the distance. The house itself was just visible, its turrets and spires casting ominous shadows in the fading sunlight.

Ms. Haas pressed her fingers to her temples. "Vampires," she declared, "are the worst. For the price of this pile of weeds and rubble she could live basically anywhere. But, no, no, it has to be a crumbling manse in an obviously haunted wood. I mean, where did she even *get* barghests?"

I did not quite share my companion's jaded attitude to our circumstances. But the chill in the air, the beasts prowling the night, and the threat of some unhallowed abomination descending upon us without warning put me uncannily in mind of my early childhood. Much has improved since those days but, even now, there are still forests in Ey where one does not walk if one wishes to emerge with one's mind and one's soul intact.

We pressed on towards the castle, which took some while for the grounds were extensive and not easily traversed. I was glad of my cane, for my old wound had been playing up lately, and the rough terrain would likely have further aggravated it.

When at last we arrived, we found the windows lightless; indeed, there was no sign whatsoever of habitation save a scattering of bats circling one of the towers. The front door, which was heavy oak, its knocker gripped in the mouth of some leering imp, swung open soundlessly as we approached.

"Perhaps," I remarked, "I'm being overcautious. But does that not look to you rather a lot like a trap?"

My companion nodded. "Yes, were she observing tradition, and, from the look of this place, the Contessa is nothing if not a traditionalist, she would have met us at the door to give us some assurance of our safety. The fact that she has not implies either that she is not at home or that we are being encouraged to trespass and, thereby, invite reprisals."

"How then should we proceed?" In all honesty, and this may have been my upbringing or my military experience speaking, I was edging towards the opinion that the most practical course of action would be to set the building on fire and run. Unfortunately, this would be unlikely to provide us with the information we required.

"I suspect you will dislike this suggestion"—Ms. Haas peered into the darkness beyond the doorway—"but I think it might be best if I were to go through the main entrance in order to draw the attention of whoever or whatever might be lurking inside, while you skirt the boundaries and seek an alternate route."

Contrary as it ran to my instincts, I was forced to concede that Ms. Haas's strategy had a great deal to recommend it. If the main entryway was indeed a trap, Ms. Haas was more likely to survive it than I and if one intended to bait out an ambush one did not do so by committing one's whole force. I nodded my assent.

Needing no further encouragement, my companion swept into the mansion, her cloak billowing about her. The moment she was across the threshold, the doors slammed shut, which rather confirmed our suspicions of skulduggery. In a situation like this, my natural impulse would always be to go immediately to the aid of my friend, but in the face of real danger such kindnesses can prove fatal. I have learned from bitter experience that the success of an operation and the survival of those engaged in it are best served by adherence to the agreed plan, rather than impulsive acts of private compassion. So, I trusted that Ms. Haas's abilities would prove equal to whatever she faced and turned my attention to the task she had laid before me.

Taking a firm hold of my cane in one hand, and the pistol in the other, I swept the perimeter, proceeding clockwise from the door and keeping a weather eye out for ghosts, ghouls, and barghests. The most obvious points of access were the open and unguarded windows high in the tower. While I believed myself capable of scaling its rough walls with relative safety, I had no wish to be caught thirty feet above the ground with no free hand when attack by a flying enemy was possible at any moment. Further, my time beyond the Unending Gate had taught me that one must never underestimate the physical strain a long, vertical ascent would place upon one's body or the severe detriment of such fatigue on one's capabilities afterwards. I resolved, therefore, to assault the tower only as a last resort.

I completed my circuit and found no other suitable entryways at ground level. I had hoped to identify some manner of storm cellar or servants' entrance, but every door was firmly sealed, and I discovered no hatches or trapdoors of any kind. Looking again at the building, I noted that it was a mix of architectural styles, having clearly been added to over the span of many years, but that the oldest parts seemed to date back centuries. Reasoning that such buildings often contained crypts, catacombs, or even dungeons that extended well beyond their walls, I concluded that, before ascending the tower, it would be prudent to scout the grounds to see if they afforded a more convenient point of ingress.

I began to spiral my path outwards, acutely aware as I did so that night was fast closing in around me and that, being alone, I had nobody to watch my back. Having completed three or four ever-widening circuits of the house I caught sight of another structure in the distance; a half-ruined stone building that might once have been a chapel sat beside a weed-choked lake that might once have been ornamental. It seemed that this would be the most likely place to contain a hidden entrance to the mansion proper and, tightening my grip on my pistol, I made straight for it.

The sun having set, the high wall blocking out the streetlights, and the trees obscuring the stars, the darkness was near total. Worse still, the howling of the wolves had stilled, replaced by the more imminently threatening sound of large beasts dragging themselves through undergrowth.

I should caution readers that the scenes I am about to describe may prove shocking to many, involving as they do encounters with beings both savagely violent and unnaturally lascivious. Be advised also that the tunnels to which I was indeed able to gain access were, to the best of my understanding, part of the crypts once attached to an abbey consecrated in the name of the Insular Church. I argued with my editor for some days over the tastefulness of including in this text scenes of a lurid nature that occur within a location sanctified for the burial of the dead. Ultimately, however, he convinced me that the inclusion of these sequences was utterly necessary to the reader's understanding of events as they unfolded and I have, as a consequence, left them intact in spite of my personal misgivings.

Thus I am compelled to narrate that it was at this moment that the barghest sprang from my two o'clock position. It was a repulsive being, dog-like in aspect but rancid to the point of deliquescence and weeping vile humours not only from its jaws but from the innumerable lesions that dotted its skin. Before I could bring the pistol to bear, the full weight of the slavering thing was upon me, knocking me to the ground. Thanks either to my ill fortune or its malign intelligence, one of its heavy forepaws came down upon my wrist, preventing me from raising the gun again. It was only the fact that I had managed to raise my knees as I fell that prevented the creature from instantly tearing my throat out. For a few unpleasant moments my world was nothing but fangs and fur and the corpse-cold secretions that dripped from its muzzle.

I did not have the strength to force the beast away but, braced as it was astride me, I twisted my left arm around its right foreleg, removing its primary support and bringing it tumbling to the dirt. At the same time, I pushed sideways with my legs, for the monster would surely have crushed me had its whole weight fallen straight upon me. I scrambled to my feet faster than it was able to, and as it thrashed and snarled in its confusion at my unexpected resistance, I shot it in the head. I thought it best to shoot it again once I had composed myself, since I was not wholly certain that a single bullet could be relied upon to overcome whatever dark animus gave the creature its semblance of life.

I was, of course, conscious that I had just fired off several rounds from a large-calibre handgun in the grounds of a private residence not so very far from a public thoroughfare in Athra. Still, if luck was with me (as I would later discover, it was not), the neighbours would be accustomed to strange sounds emanating from the Contessa's residence.

Reloading my pistol, I listened intently in case the creature had a mate or a pack, but I heard nothing. Perhaps the noise had scared the others away or perhaps these creatures were so debased as to take delight in one another's destruction. Regardless, I reached the chapel without further molestation. Little of its original architecture remained, although I could see, within, the remnants of the gaudy trappings of the Insular Church. The gilt had flaked away from the statues of saints and angels and the jewels had long been stripped from the tabernacle, although the image of the Saviour, Yohannah, broken upon the wheel still dominated the apse.

I had been raised to be suspicious of such icons and to hold their veneration as tantamount to idolatry, but I have always taken comfort in the presence of sacred things, especially in dark places. Behind the altar, I found displaced flagstones and a narrow staircase leading downwards. Not for the first time that night, I was struck by the monumental folly of trespassing in the abode of an unknown vampire protected only by a pistol, a walking stick, and some water of unsubstantiated holiness. Nevertheless, I would not leave Ms. Haas to face this place alone, nor leave Miss Viola with her questions unanswered and her engagement in peril.

It is the convention in my faith for the wheel always to be displayed unoccupied. The Reformed Church of the Creator teaches that, since the Saviour ascended from the wheel into a body of pure fire and spirit, the symbol should be presented in a context that emphasises Her triumph rather than Her suffering. In that moment, however, I was glad to be reminded that She was watching over me. Her serene gaze, despite the mortifications of Her flesh, strengthened my resolve as I began my descent.

❧

CHAPTER THIRTY-TWO

The Manor at Quatreface, Part the Second

Leaving the light of the chapel, I was enveloped in perfect blackness. My first concern was, of course, that I was at real risk of attracting grues, those strange, invisible, extradimensional predators that are drawn inexorably to lone wanderers in dark places. I was not overjoyed at the necessity of disarming, but circumstance forced me to return my pistol to my jacket pocket in exchange for a book of matches. I struck one and was relieved to see that a torch rested in a bracket on the wall. Lighting it quickly, I lifted it free and pressed on through the gloom.

The catacombs were extensive and, out of deference to the dignity of their occupants, I shall describe only the five tombs which, by virtue of their occupants (or, more correctly, lack thereof), are pertinent to this narrative.

The first three came as a set, a triptych of stone sarcophagi, all open and containing plain pine coffins filled with soil. Their discovery made me immediately uneasy, for I had heard enough rumours of vampires to know that the strong amongst them sometimes collected about themselves perverse families or dark harems of their weaker kin. All of which meant that this house was perhaps not the lair of a vampire but the lair of a nest of vampires. While I had been apprehensive about the possibility of confronting the Contessa, I had taken some small consolation from the fact that there were, at least, two of us and one of her. That I now had to add numbers to the already long list of advantages she had over us was unfortunate.

The fourth tomb did, undoubtedly, belong to the Contessa, being richly appointed and inscribed with not only her name but the names of her ancestors. There were fewer of these than one might expect for, although her lineage stretched back centuries, so did she. The sarcophagus was topped by an effigy that I took to be a representation of the Contessa herself, although, in honesty, it looked much like every other graven image on a burial marker I have ever seen—eyes gently closed, hands pressed together in prayer, hair unbound and flowing in waves both flattering and easy to carve, a face with neither blemishes nor idiosyncrasies.

Like the other sarcophagi, the lid had been pushed aside, but, unlike the others, it contained no coffin, although there was a scattering of earth left within. This was at once reassuring and disconcerting. On the one hand, the absence of the coffin suggested that the Contessa had, for now, quit her residency at the manor, which marginally increased our immediate physical safety. It also, however, suggested that she had reason to leave abruptly and the fact that her departure appeared to coincide exactly with our investigation was especially troubling.

More troubling still, however, was the fifth tomb. Detailed in silver, built of white marble, and strewn about with rose petals, it far more resembled a bridal bed than a place of rest. And by the light of the hundred or so candles that had been lovingly arranged around it I could make out the name and likeness of Miss Eirene Viola. It would be untrue to say that this discovery reassured me as to the surmountability of Miss Viola's present difficulties. I had no wish to linger long in that chamber, seeing no means by which my doing so could be beneficial to Miss Viola, Ms. Haas, or myself.

I pressed on through the tunnels until I found, at last, another staircase leading upwards into what I hoped was the main house. This led me into a long and echoing corridor which ended abruptly in a smooth wooden barrier. I was momentarily perplexed by this imped-iment, but a brief inspection of my surroundings revealed a lever set into the wall. While I was naturally wary of activating a wholly un-known mechanism in a hostile castle, I could see no purpose to in-stalling within one's home a lever that had no function but to cause harm to one who threw it. Placing my faith in the rationality of an undead aristocrat who had constructed a nuptial tomb for a woman who had recently announced her engagement to another person en-tirely, I pulled. There was a brief scraping, as of metal moving against metal, and I was, to my satisfaction, not dropped immediately into a pit of crocodiles. Rather, the obstruction before me pivoted about its centre, allowing me to walk past it into the room beyond.

To my consternation, I now found myself standing in a lushly ap-pointed and well-stocked library. Glancing at the embers falling from my torch and singing the carpet upon which I stood, I hastily returned to the tunnels and deposited the offending item in a convenient wall sconce. This, unfortunately, left me once again quite literally in the dark.

I groped my way across the room and threw open the velvet cur-tains, admitting just enough moonlight to enable me to locate a gas lamp, which I gratefully ignited. Feeling strongly that my first order of duty should be to locate Ms. Haas, I left the library and navigated my way back to the entrance hall, lighting the rooms as I went. This would, of course, have advertised my presence to anyone else in the building, but I strongly suspected that whatever denizens lurked there required no assistance locating interlopers in their domain, and I was certain that, should it come to a confrontation, the darkness would incommode me more than it did them.

I had not expected to find Ms. Haas where I had left her; a specific application of a general principle. But the hall through which she must have passed appeared to have been the site of an outright brawl. The paintings, which were mostly cold-eyed Mircallan aristocracy, had been torn from the walls and flung across the room, with sufficient force to crack the frames and gouge chunks out of the floor. Several statues, in the classical style of ancient Khel, lay shattered at the foot of the grand staircase, marble dust and splinters of stone strewn amongst the brass and crystal wreckage of a fallen chandelier. I could see, however, no sign of either participant, but I was reassured to find no blood on any of the many hazards.

Ascending the first flight of the staircase, taking care not to injure myself on the broken glass, my attention was drawn to a large and curiously intact grandfather clock. As I approached, its hands whirled with a peculiarly malignant energy, and then stopped dead on midnight, its sonorous chimes somehow striking an accusatory tone. Curiosity overcoming caution, I looked more closely at the device and saw fresh scratches on its door. At first I took them to be collateral damage from the altercation that had taken place around it, but their design was too symmetrical and too ordered. They had the character of the mystical signs I had seen Ms. Haas utilise in her various rituals at home and, indeed, seemed oddly reminiscent of the set of sigils she had carved into our hatstand and, more recently, into her own chest. As if in response to my attention, the clock face began to ooze ectoplasmic fluid, and I thought it best to move away quickly.

From there I proceeded to search the various rooms and floors of the manor in the most systematic fashion practical. Overgrown and weather-beaten as it had been, the exterior of the building spoke of utter desolation, but its interior spoke more of simple underoccupancy. There being no sign of servants, it was likely that the Contessa lived alone, apart from whatever vile minions haunted her grounds and patrolled her halls, and could, therefore, have had neither the capacity nor the necessity to make good use of the whole estate. Thus, the library and one sitting room were well-kept and well-appointed while the kitchen, for which she can have had no purpose, was in a state of veritable ruin, although it showed signs that somebody had attempted to use it recently, albeit not wholly successfully.

Of the bedrooms, only one seemed habitable. I should hope that, by now, the reader will understand without my expostulation that I would never have ventured into another person's private chamber un-invited (or, indeed, invited, under most circumstances), but in the bat-tle against supernatural evil one must occasionally do unseemly things. This boudoir appeared to have been set aside for the use of guests, and I was disturbed (if not entirely surprised) to note that its door sup-ported a heavy and secure lock and could be bolted from the outside. What did surprise me was that I found indications of occupation.

There were several suitcases, unpacked and bearing the name of a Mr. J. Wangenheim. From the quality of his luggage, and of the change of clothes that lay neatly folded on the room's only chair, I took him to be a professional gentleman of the more common sort, perhaps a clerk or a newspaperman. By one window there stood a writing desk, on which lay an ominously unsent letter. Once again, please be assured that I am not in the habit of prying into the personal correspondence of strangers, but it was imperative I take any and all opportunities to discover information that would prove of value to Miss Viola. The letter read as follows.

> My darling Greta,
>   Wonderful news! I have almost finished the work for which the Contessa hired me and should soon be able to leave this dreary place. I am sorry I have been unable to visit, but the Contessa is most particular and has instructed me, under pain of severe personal and professional consequences, that I am not to stray from beneath her roof until my task is complete.
> Thankfully that day is nearly here and, with the generous remuneration the Contessa has promised, our future shall be well

provided for. I will at last be able to ask Mr. Bigglesthwaite for a partnership or perhaps, if my calculations are correct and the Contessa is as generous as she has assured me she will be, begin my own firm. We should even have enough set aside to make a down payment on that beautiful little house by the river you so admired.

I must say, Greta, this has been the queerest of assignments. Why would a Mircallan noblewoman be so interested in researching the history and habits of a minor warden of the Ubiquitous Company of Fishers? Why does this house appear to have no servants? Why, when I woke last night and tried the handle of my door, did I find it so securely locked? I shall be glad when this whole affair is over, for, in truth, I am not entirely certain that the Contessa is an honourable woman and I begin to fear that she will put the information I have compiled for her to some ill purpose. Still, one must endeavour to see the good in any situation and I am thankful that this brief exposure to the darker and more sinister side of life has allowed me to appreciate more fully the brightness and joy you bring into my world. I am more determined than ever that we shall be married the instant I return to you.

I remain forever,
Your loving Jonathan

CHAPTER THIRTY-THREE

The Manor at Quatreface, Part the Third

I replaced the letter and left the room hurriedly. I did not like to speculate as to the fate of its occupant but, given that we found the house in darkness on arrival and that his missive was dated two days earlier and had still not been sent, it seemed to me likely that he had either escaped, perished, or met some worse fate. I sent a silent prayer that it would prove to be the former, then endeavoured to put the matter out of mind.

The only section of the house I had thus far failed to search was the tower, and so it was towards this that I now proceeded. That I had yet to cross paths with Ms. Haas concerned me a little, but I took consolation in the knowledge that she was more than the equal of anything she might encounter, and further consolation in the fact that I had come thus far without falling prey to any of the building's supernatural inhabitants.

The rooms in the tower seemed better maintained on average than those in the main house. Even those primarily dedicated to storage were neatly arranged in a manner that spoke of regular use. One of them was dedicated entirely to clothing of the feminine variety. Although this was very much not my area of expertise, I noted that the garments therein were divided into two distinct collections that differed from each other in style, cut, and size. The more extensive of them consisted of a great many sombre gowns in tones of black, red, and silver and represented a bewildering range of fashions stretching back at least four hundred years. The others, by contrast, seemed to belong to no era with which I was familiar. Many of them, frankly, more closely resembled nightwear (and inadequate nightwear at that). These items, from what I could tell by brief examination of their gauzy fabric, had been designed for a person whose stature much resembled Miss Viola's.

I climbed another flight of stairs and found myself in a study, the second most notable feature of which was the large array of journals, codices, papers, and memoranda that were piled upon its shelves and scattered across its floor. Its most notable feature, however, was the corpse. He lay pallid and lifeless upon the sofa, his clothing dishevelled and his throat, wrists, and chest marked with puncture wounds. Doubtless, this was the unfortunate Mr. Wangenheim, and though I was sorry for his fate, I had no wish to share it. I drew my pistol.

Out of nowhere, fingers closed upon my wrist, holding me with a gentleness that belied their unnatural strength. I turned my head and beheld a golden-haired gentleman with penetrating sapphire eyes and red, voluptuous lips.

"You will not need that here," he said, his voice soft and touched with a Mircallan accent.

Some distant part of my mind felt strongly that I did, in fact, very much need my firearm. But, even so, my fingers opened, and the weapon fell unheeded to the ground. The blond gentleman smiled approvingly, though his teeth were too white and too sharp.

"Come, my brothers." He drew my now empty hand to his mouth and subjected it to several liberties that, even these decades later, I blush to relate. "We have a new guest to entertain us."

There was a flicker of movement by the window and I saw two more gentlemen, like the first, dark where he was fair but possessed of the same terrible lasciviousness. They lingered in the moonlight, their shirts unfastened to the sternum and their pale skin gleaming wantonly.

I hesitate to describe the perilous delights to which the vampiric gentlemen enticed me, but honesty forces me to disclose to my readers that the temptation towards acquiescence was considerable and exposed me to dangers both physical and spiritual. The blond gentleman, having initiated matters, drew me fully—and, I confess, unresistingly—into his embrace, though the nature of my attire, which accorded with my homeland's strict standards of modesty, delayed his more intimate advances.

His brothers, if brothers they were, and I sincerely hoped they were not, for the attentions they paid one another went somewhat beyond the fraternal, insinuated themselves also about my person, one of them removing my collar with delicate fingers, the other caressing me in a manner utterly impossible to commit to print. As the four of us sank entwined to the carpet, and my world became nothing but soft kisses and cruel fangs, I felt very certain that I would die. But, under the seductive influence of the vampires, so darkly pleasurable was the notion that I welcomed it. Indeed, I encouraged it.

I was on the verge of losing consciousness entirely when the three gentlemen sprang away from me, hissing. Looking up blearily I beheld the unmistakable figure of the sorceress Shaharazad Haas. Her eyes seethed with white fire and, as I listened in horror, she spoke aloud the dread syllables of the private name of the Creator. My culture has many taboos, but there are few as absolute as that against the words Ms. Haas now uttered. Outsiders may presume that our habit of referring to the deity only indirectly and euphemistically is a simple matter of respect but, in actuality, invoking the Creator explicitly is not merely presumptuous but foolhardy. His power, if called upon correctly, sears body and soul alike and can easily overwhelm one who calls upon it with devastating consequence. To my relief, Ms. Haas stopped short of incanting the final syllable, which is known to only a few and unleashes the full curse of the Creator's might. But even this fraction of His power had been sufficient to drive my erstwhile attackers cowering to the darkest corners of the room, their skin blackening and blistering.

"Why have you come?" snarled the fairer of the three. "There is nothing for you here."

"I am the sorceress Shaharazad Haas. There is something for me everywhere." My companion sauntered over to the sofa and took a seat beside the late Mr. Wangenheim. "For example, I have a personal interest in this gentleman you recently killed, that gentleman you were about to kill, and those papers—which I hope you haven't disturbed too badly. Now do be good boys and slink back to your coffins."

If they were inclined to protest, they thought better of it, scuttling from the study like beetles from an overturned log. I rose gradually, and somewhat abashedly, to my feet, acutely aware of the disordered state of my garments.

"Thank you," I said. "I . . . That is to say . . . I . . ."

Ms. Haas cast me an amused look. "Mr. Wyndham, if you are really so keen to be brought to the unholy precipice of ecstatic oblivion by the comely spawn of primal darkness, I can direct you to at least a dozen highly regarded specialists who can arrange it for you in a safe, sane, and consensual manner."

"Madam, I assure you I am not in the habit of consorting with such beings."

"You should be." Her gaze alighted on my loosened doublet. "It looks terribly good on you."

"You have very much misunderstood my tastes. But this is not the time. The corpse, Ms. Haas, the corpse."

"Well, he's hardly going anywhere, is he?"

"It is a matter of respect for the dead."

Her lips curled into a wicked smile. "My dear man, you were

about to *consort* with the dead." She did not say "consort." "I'm not sure you're in any position to be lecturing."

"They were monsters driven by abominable lusts. He was a clerk."

"Ah, so you respect the dead only if they are dreary."

"I respect the dead when they are not actively attempting to seduce and murder me."

"How ironic." Ms. Haas arched an eyebrow. "I respect them only if they are. But you are correct. Entertaining as your amorous interlude may have been, we should return to the task at hand."

"How should we proceed?" I asked.

She rose from the sofa, collapsed her hat, and set it gently in the space she had just vacated. "You take the papers, I'll take the books, and we'll see if we can work out what the deuce this poor fellow was up to."

I did as instructed and took a seat at the desk, upon which I was relieved to find a brown folder containing a series of notes in handwriting that I recognised from Mr. Wangenheim's ill-fated letter. They turned out to comprise a summary, presumably for the Contessa's benefit, of the habits, associates, and likely movements of Miss Cora Beck gleaned from the clerk's close study and correlation of the municipal, company, and travel records that the Contessa had procured for him. He had been diligent in his work and the materials he had produced were at once concise and comprehensive. I passed them to Ms. Haas, who perused the contents with interest.

"This," she said, "is unfortunate. One never wants to draw the close attention of a vampire. If I'm any judge, and, let us be very clear, I am, these are the sorts of documents you would order compiled if your intent were to murder their subject as discreetly as possible."

I glanced towards the late Mr. Wangenheim. "Do you really think discretion has any value to a woman who wantonly murders her house guests?"

"Come now, Captain. *She* did not murder her house guest. A

guest was murdered *in* her house. It's a very different thing. And while vampires are creatures of unbridled arrogance and do not always reason as mortals do, I think even the Contessa would understand that butchering someone's fiancée in front of them is not the most effective way to say you want to get back together. Far more convenient, from her perspective, would be if the lovely Miss Beck were to embark on, say"—Ms. Haas flipped over a few pages in Mr. Wangenheim's dossier, as if looking for something specific—"this business trip to the salt mines of Aturvash and never return."

"Why are you so sure she would choose that journey specifically?" I indicated two other entries in the notes. "There's one here to Tanispont and one to El'avarah."

Ms. Haas drummed her fingers impatiently against the desk. "I'm not going to explain something you can perfectly well work out for yourself. Now, why do you think a vampire would not pursue her quarry to Tanispont?"

"Tanispont is a port," I answered after a moment of thought, "and best reached by sea. If my understanding is correct, the undead have difficulty crossing running water."

She offered me a smile which, unusually, seemed to contain no mockery. "You are, indeed, correct in your understanding. What of El'avarah?"

This took me a little longer, for it required me to consider the matter from a perspective I found frankly distasteful. "I suppose," I began, "if I were intent upon murder, and keen not to be discovered, I would want to choose an occasion when my victim was isolated. But whatever business the Ubiquitous Company of Fishers has in El'avarah is likely to be prestigious and, therefore, to involve a large deputation, of which Miss Beck would only be part. Therefore, unless I had significant knowledge of that city or the routes to it, which I suspect that the Contessa does not, being native to a wholly different continent, I would struggle to find an appropriate opportunity for malfeasance."

"Well done, Mr. Wyndham. It reassures me to know that, should you ever be called upon to murder somebody, you will prove at least minimally competent."

As compliments went, it was not one I was entirely happy to receive.

"All of which," continued to my companion, "leaves us with the mines. They are inland, isolated, and not so important that Miss Beck would be travelling as part of a larger entourage."

At that she closed the folder, tossed it back onto the desk, and went to retrieve her hat from where it lay next to the body of Mr. Wangenheim. "Well, I think we're done here."

I blinked in some surprise. "Done? But we have no idea where the Contessa is, or what danger she still might pose to Miss Beck."

"It doesn't matter where the Contessa is. We know that she plans to murder the fishmonger, and since she has been making preparations towards that end for some time she clearly has not also been sending threatening letters to Eirene." Ms. Haas unfolded her hat and set it back on her head, adjusting it to an angle that I considered inappropriately jaunty. "Therefore, she is not our blackmailer. Therefore, we have no further business here. What would you say to dinner out this evening? I find myself peckish."

I had thought my companion had exhausted her capacity to shock me. She had not and, over our long acquaintance, never did. "But . . . but," I protested, "she might murder Miss Beck."

"I daresay she might. What has that to do with us?"

"Ms. Haas!"

"Mr. Wyndham, there were a hundred and twenty-seven recorded cases of murder between Khel, Athra, and Ven in the last year alone." She heaved a martyred sigh. "You can scarcely expect me to directly intervene in all of them."

"That is specious reasoning and you know it. The fact that one cannot do every good thing does not mean that one should do no good things."

"Perhaps not, but I make it a personal policy to do as few good things as possible. They are, after all, so terribly tedious."

I rapped my cane against the edge of the desk. "Madam, I will not stand by and allow an innocent woman to be hunted and slain by a rapacious monstrosity."

"You may do as you like. I'm going to dinner."

"Have you no compassion in your heart?"

"None. I've always felt it would be a dreadful waste."

She attempted to leave but, abandoning all propriety, I interposed myself between her and the door. In the fullness of time, I would become more adept at navigating Ms. Haas's frequently complex motivations. On this occasion, however, it was mostly by good fortune that I was able to find a line of argument that allowed me to bridge the gap between the principles by which ordinary people live and Ms. Haas's whims of the present moment.

"Do you not think," I tried, "that Miss Viola might be somewhat put out if, having secured your assistance in saving her relationship with Miss Beck, you were to choose a course of action that left the engagement intact but rendered the lady herself an exsanguinated cadaver?"

My companion paused thoughtfully. "She has been awfully sentimental lately, hasn't she? And it would be just like her to hold it against me if her fiancée were to be brutally eviscerated." She sighed again, more deeply this time. "Very well, Wyndham. Let us save the fishmonger."

CHAPTER THIRTY-FOUR

Mr. Jonathan Wangenheim

Having persuaded Ms. Haas that our client might prefer that we not permit the murder of her fiancée, we returned to the documents in the hope that they would grant us deeper insight into the Contessa's plan of attack. To my dismay, and to Ms. Haas's mild irritation, the journey to the salt mines of Aturvash had been scheduled to begin on the previous day. More problematically still, we had advised Miss Viola that it would be in her best interests if she were able to persuade Miss Beck to abandon that commitment and, instead, disappear with her to parts unknown. And we had no idea whether she had attempted this, if she had attempted it, whether she had succeeded, and, if she had succeeded, where they had gone. Worse, we had no idea if the Contessa was, or was not, aware of this last-minute change of itinerary, if such a change of itinerary even existed.

"Are you sure," asked Ms. Haas, "you wouldn't rather go to dinner? We seem to be encountering a wearying quantity of variables. Either Miss Beck is in Aturvash or she is not. Either Eirene is in Aturvash or she is not. Either the Contessa is in Aturvash or she is not. Either the Contessa knows Miss Beck's current location or she does not. Those factors alone give us sixteen possible permutations to consider, and they multiply exponentially if we start trying to predict the

Contessa's response to any points of data she might or might not have discovered."

"I assume her response will be to attempt to kill Miss Beck."

Ms. Haas cast a sheaf of papers to the floor in frustration. "Knowing *what* she will attempt does not help us. We must know *where* she will attempt it. And, on that matter, I have no insight." She paused, gazing speculatively at the late Mr. Wangenheim.

"Ms. Haas," I gasped. "I sincerely hope you are not contemplating what I suspect you are contemplating."

"It seems an expedient solution."

"You have made it quite clear that you care little for laws, either municipal or natural, but surely even you would hesitate to further provoke the Ossuary Bank."

She laughed softly. "No, John, I wouldn't."

"But what if this gentleman doesn't want to have his spirit ripped from the afterlife?"

"I find it most vexing that when I was willing to let Miss Beck die because I was more interested in getting dinner you thought I was being terribly selfish. But now you are apparently willing to let her die because you'd rather preserve some silly taboo about disturbing the rest of dead souls. Doesn't that strike you as a little hypocritical?"

"You can't compare the sanctity of the grave to your passing appetites."

"Believe me, Mr. Wyndham, my appetites have done far more for me than your principles will ever do for you. Now help me pull this gentleman onto the floor."

To say I was unhappy at the thought of participating in a necromantic ritual would be something of an understatement, but Mr. Wangenheim's life was over and Miss Beck's was in danger. I am sure there will be many amongst my readership who do not approve of my complicity in this act and to you I will say only that I did what I felt best at the time and, in retrospect, I do not regret it. In the interests of painting a fuller picture of events as they unfolded I have recorded some details of the sorcery Ms. Haas performed on this occasion, but I have consulted with my lawyer, Ms. Gwendolyn Puppinghorn, of Shah, Shah & Puppinghorn, and she assures me that, provided readers could not themselves reconstruct the ritual from the information supplied, its inclusion is in accordance with the proper regulations.

Once we had manoeuvred the unfortunate Mr. Wangenheim into position, Ms. Haas extended one hand above his prostrate body and began walking around him in a series of ever-narrowing circles, incanting as she did an invocation in a language I recognised as ancient Khelish. When the circles had become small enough that she was at risk of stepping on him, she stopped and stood astride the gentleman. Then she knelt across his abdomen and tore open his shirt. Removing her monocle, she activated some mechanism I had not previously noticed, causing a wickedly sharp spike to protrude from the rim. This she drove deep into her palm, smearing the blood that welled up in response to this gesture across Mr. Wangenheim's exposed chest. With one finger she traced an elaborate pattern that stretched from his throat to his solar plexus and then, with a sudden, spasmodic motion, Mr. Wangenheim awoke.

He made a sound that was like screaming, but drier and weaker. Ms. Haas covered his mouth to silence him.

"Less of that," she said. "We don't have long, and I need you to be at least partially coherent."

This last request was perhaps a little optimistic. The perspectives of the dead are very different from those of the living. Dying is a disorientating experience and being summoned back into a cold, potentially decaying body is doubly so. It is for these reasons, as well as a certain ethical distaste, that testimony suborned under necromancy is not acceptable in courts.

Ms. Haas removed her hand, allowing Mr. Wangenheim to speak. He took a ragged breath, presumably out of habit, his glassy eyes shifting restlessly. "You must find Greta. You must tell her to flee. You must tell her the Contessa is a demon."

"My good man," returned Ms. Haas impatiently, "the Contessa has no interest in your silly little fiancée. She's far too busy trying to murder someone else's silly little fiancée. Tell me what you told her about Cora Beck."

"She was angry. She said my information was wrong. That she wasn't going to Aturvash. Said it was ruined. Said I had ruined it."

Had I not been all too sensible of the dangers inherent in wandering a vampire's castle alone, I would have left the room at this stage. Something about Mr. Wangenheim's paralysed expression and thin, inflectionless voice struck me as profoundly disturbing.

"Said she'd boarded a train," he went on. "Said she'd seen her. Gave me the numbers. Told me to tell her where they would go. How she could catch them."

My companion spread her fingers before his face and then tightened them, as if drawing yarn from a spindle. His body twitched, his spine arching with a crack. "Which train?"

"The Austral Express. Athra, Szajnin, Sfantvar, Bagne Loup, Vedunia, Liohtberg." His eyes locked straight ahead. "Athra, Szajnin, Sfantvar, Bagne Loup, Vedunia, Liohtberg. Athra, Szajnin, Sfantvar, Bagne Loup, Vedunia, Liohtberg."

He continued to repeat the list of stations, each recitation more strangled than the last, until, to my immense relief, Ms. Haas spoke the words that broke the spell and, I hope, released Mr. Wangenheim's spirit to its proper resting place.

"Well"—she drew an immaculate handkerchief from her pocket and wiped the blood from her hands—"you have to hand it to Eirene. It requires a certain wonderful nerve to go on the run by taking one's lover on a luxury train through a sequence of the world's most romantic and beautiful cities. I do rather miss her sometimes."

Somewhat the worse for the night's exertions, I lowered myself onto the now mercifully corpse-free sofa. "Is it likely the Contessa will be able to catch up with a locomotive?"

"Ordinarily no. Long-distance travel is not something for which vampires are well equipped. But the Austral Express takes a rather scenic route through the Hundred Kingdoms and has to take a substantial detour around the Blackcrest Mountains. If she follows a more direct path, through the Ensisa Pass, the Contessa should be able to head them off at Vedunia within the week."

"But this is terrible!" I exclaimed. "We must do something."

"Indeed. But, given that the Contessa has at least a couple of days' head start, we shall have to fly if we are to have any chance of reaching the happy couple before they become very unhappy indeed. Fortunately, I know just the person to assist us." She replaced her monocle and strode towards the door. "Quickly, Captain. We must return home and prepare to travel."

As ever, I had many questions. But, as ever, Ms. Haas declined to answer any of them. We descended from the tower into the manor proper and out through the main doors, the grandfather clock shaking angrily at us as we passed. When we entered the grounds, we were greeted by a melancholy howling and, as we approached the gates, by a uniformed Myrmidon, lantern in one hand, truncheon in the other.

"Stop right there."

I stopped right there, dropping my stick and raising my hands.

The young Myrmidon swept a beam of oily yellow light across me. "Who are you, and what's your business here?"

"I'm afraid that's quite complicated. My name is John Wyndham and this is my—" I turned to the space where Ms. Haas had been standing the last time I looked, only to discover I was quite alone. "That is. My name is John Wyndham and I came . . ."

I paused, weighing my options, and decided that, perhaps, on this occasion half the truth was superior to its entirety.

". . . to visit the Contessa Ilona," I finished.

The Myrmidon did not look entirely convinced. "And was it you let the gun off?"

I could not quite bring myself to lie to an officer of the law but, given the urgency of our mission, I permitted myself some attempt at dissembling. "What gun might you be referring to?"

"The one that was discharged in this area at approximately seven forty-five this evening. And which"—the beam of lamplight dipped towards my waist—"might very well be the same gun you are carrying in your jacket pocket."

"Oh, that gun. Yes, you see, I was in the grounds and one of the Contessa's dogs tried to eat me, so I was forced to shoot it."

To say that the Myrmidon's expression was sceptical at this point would be far from overstatement. "In the habit of shooting the pets of people we come to visit, are we, son?"

"Well, as it turned out, the Contessa wasn't quite at home when I expected her to be. So I, um, looked for a way to let myself in. And then I got attacked by the dog and I really think you should know there's a dead body and three vampires in there."

And thus it was I found myself arrested for the second time in two days.

CHAPTER THIRTY-FIVE

Second Augur Gabriel Lawson

"Sixth day, seventh month, third year, Twenty-first Council. Interview commencing nine twenty-three p.m., Second Augur Lawson conducting. The suspect was apprehended outside the Athran residence of the Contessa Ilona of Mircalla on suspicion of trespass, breaking and entering, murder, necromancy, and certain offences under the Mistreatment of Animals Act, Eighth Year, Twelfth Council." Second Augur Lawson sighed deeply. "Please state your name for the record."

I leaned towards the trumpet of the phonograph. "John Wyndham."

"So what happened this time?"

"I hope you know," I said, "that in ordinary circumstances I would cooperate fully with your investigation, but I am presently urgently needed on a skyship to Vedunia."

Second Augur Lawson's heavy gaze settled on me for an uncomfortably long time. "I'd say that you'd be amazed how many people I have in front of me suddenly needing to get on urgent flights to Vedunia but, honestly, they don't normally try that one."

"I assure you, I'm 'trying' nothing but the truth. If I do not get to Vedunia as soon as possible, an innocent woman will die."

"This is one of Shaharazad Haas's little games, isn't it?"

"I'd hardly call a person's life a little game, sir."

"Well, that's the difference between you and your compatriot."

He leaned back, folding his arms. "Nevertheless, I've got a dead body on my hands and you at the scene. I'm not about to release my only witness just because he says he has something better to do. Especially not when he's just told me that the moment he gets out of here, he's bogging straight off to Nivale."

I shifted awkwardly in my chair, my manacles clanking against the table as I moved. "You can't possibly think I had anything to do with the death of poor Mr. Wangenheim."

"I don't believe I mentioned the deceased gentleman's name."

"I read it on a letter in his room."

"The room you illegally entered?"

"It was only ever my intent to call upon the Contessa socially to discuss a matter of mutual interest."

"And finding her not at home you decided, what?" His stern mouth softened very slightly, as though he were trying to repress a smile. "To sneak in the kitchen window?"

"Ah, no. The front door was open, which we took as invitation."

"Very reasonable, if true. And on accessing the property through the open front door, what happened then?"

I blushed. "Um, as it happens, I did not personally enter through the front door. My companion went in alone, and I sought an alternate means of ingress through the catacombs beneath the chapel."

"You went," repeated the Second Augur, his voice as flat as I had ever heard it, "in through the catacombs beneath the chapel?"

"Yes."

The Second Augur reached out and turned off the recording. "Mr. Wyndham, we've had this conversation before. You are not helping your defence."

"I don't understand how being honest can fail to help my defence."

"Because," he said, through gritted teeth, "you are making yourself look guilty."

"Well, I did shoot the dog, and I did enter the house through the catacombs."

"Did it at no point occur to you to *not* do either of those things?"

"With respect, not shooting the dog would have resulted in my death."

He stood up, giving me ample opportunity to appreciate his stature. "Well, if you hadn't been breaking into a vampire's house in the first place, your life wouldn't have been in danger."

"The vampire in question is a suspect in one of Ms. Haas's ongoing investigations."

At this, Second Augur Lawson made several comments that I did not feel were appropriate for an Augur on duty. "Did I not tell you that if you carried on associating with the sorceress Shaharazad Haas, this sort of thing would keep happening? Admittedly, I didn't think they would keep happening quite this quickly. But here we are."

"I'm still not certain that my associations are any business of yours."

He gave me a look that seemed equal parts exasperation and understanding. "They are when they make you break the law."

"And," I told him rather sharply, "I am perfectly willing to face the consequences of any lawbreaking I might have done. Now will you please turn your cylinder back on so that I can explain the circumstances in which I was arrested. And, afterwards, you may decide for yourself whether the public good is best served by continuing to detain me."

He began pacing the confines of the interview room. "I didn't become an Augur to lock up good people who are too pigheaded to either keep out of trouble or get out of trouble."

I was oddly touched at his implied categorisation of me as a good person. And, I confess, I had always secretly wanted to be pigheaded. "That is very commendable, Second Augur Lawson."

After a moment or two, he took his seat again and turned the recording back on. "Please continue, Mr. Wyndham. What happened after you entered the catacombs?"

"Well, before I entered the catacombs I shot the dog."

The Second Augur covered his face with his hands.

"In, I should stress, self-defence."

"Some might say the dog was only defending its mistress's property from intruders."

"Yes, but as it transpired, its mistress's property was a murder scene."

"Ah." He looked up with an almost worryingly hopeful expression. "So you're saying that you"—his voice was very slow and very clear—"entered the property because you believed that somebody within may have been in danger."

I reflected on this. On the one hand, I'd had no inkling of Mr. Wangenheim's existence before I found his bedroom. On the other, I had been searching for an entrance so I could go to the assistance of Ms. Haas, who, although very capable of defending herself, was technically in danger all the while she was there. "Yes," I said carefully. "I did believe someone within was in danger."

"Thank you, Mr. Wyndham. And, for the record, did you murder Mr. Wangenheim?"

"No, sir. I did not."

"Do you have any idea who did?"

"While I was in the house, I encountered three gentlemen"—here I found myself blushing again, rather more deeply than before—"of wholly untrustworthy character. I believe it was they who were responsible."

"And I'm sure," continued the Second Augur, "that it goes without saying that they were also responsible for the necromantic ritual that had been performed upon the body."

"Ah, well, no, actually—"

"As I said. I'm sure that goes *without saying*."

This exchange presented me with a small ethical quandary.

Second Augur Lawson's assertion was faulty and it seemed improper of me not to correct it. However, I was sensible of the need to avoid falling into the hands of Augur Extraordinary Standfast, an eventuality which would surely preclude my leaving New Arcadia Yard in time to be of any help to Miss Viola or her fiancée. Further, while I would not normally want another to face the consequences of a crime they had not committed, the three vampiric gentlemen most certainly had murdered Mr. Wangenheim and had attempted to murder me. In the circumstances I, therefore, felt it defensible to allow the misconception to stand.

"I would not," I offered, "wish to gainsay your professional judgement."

"Very prudent, Mr. Wyndham." Something in the Second Augur's tone suggested that he was not, in fact, complimenting me on my prudence. He began tidying up his notes. "Well. As I see it, we don't have enough evidence to keep you on a charge of murder. And, on the other charges, I believe the discovery of the body mitigates against them in"—and here he gave me a grim look—"*this case only.* But I sincerely hope that, in future, you will stay away from duels between sorcerers, parties to which you're not invited, and houses full of corpses."

"I certainly intend to." But, even then, I was acutely aware of the distinction between intent and expectation.

"Thank you, Mr. Wyndham. Interview concluded at nine fifty-four p.m." There was a click, as the Second Augur turned off the recorder.

"Does this mean," I asked, "I am free to go?"

"As a dicky bird. Although"—he paused a moment, to fasten his eyes directly upon mine—"it might go some way towards showing your goodwill if you were to tell me what this extremely important life-or-death matter that's taking you and Ms. Haas to Vedunia might be. I would also be interested to know what you were looking for at Mrs. Benamara's party and in the house of the Contessa Ilona. And how the ——" His language, once again, became inappropriate. ". . . the two are connected."

I presented my manacled hands in a none-too-subtle fashion. "I'm really not sure why you're asking me about this."

"Because," he said, unlocking the handcuffs, the heat of his fingers lingering strangely against my wrists, "one: if you're aware of a crime, you have a duty to report it. And two: I really don't want to be investigating your murder six weeks from now." He cleared his throat. "It's a lot of paperwork."

"I shall do my best not to increase your administrative workload." This earned me a faint smile, which I also suspected was not entirely paperwork related. "As for duty; while I hold the Myrmidons in the highest regard, I also consider myself bound to respect the wishes of Ms. Haas's client."

"Of course you do." The Second Augur gathered his notes and the recording and left the room.

As I collected my effects, before being escorted from the premises by uniformed officers, I reflected that my visit to New Arcadia Yard had, at least, gone far better than last time.

CHAPTER THIRTY-SIX

The *Clouded Skipper*

Following my release, I returned with haste to 221b Martyrs Walk. There, I found Ms. Haas's monocle embedded in the front door, transfixing upon its hidden awl a note that read: *Hippocrene. The Clouded Skipper. Pack for travel. Come armed.* I removed both items and went inside, hoping I would not have to explain to Mrs. Hive the damage that Ms. Haas had done to the paintwork. I was not so fortunate. To be reprimanded by one's landlady is never pleasant, but when the censure in question is delivered in an atonal buzzing from within a partially skeletonised cadaver, within which a teeming mass of insects swarms and moves with ungodly purpose, it can be quite disheartening. I apologised as profusely as was seemly but, as I found so often to be the case with landlords, landladies, and landpersons of more esoteric character, her displeasure at this most recent infraction called to mind a litany of other transgressions including, but not limited to, the hatstand, the stain on the hall carpet, the bullet holes in the skirting board, the destruction of the watercolour painting that was apparently a great favourite, the bloodstains in the guest bedroom, the fire damage to the rear staircase, and the incident involving the neighbour's cat, the sanctified kris blade, and the spirit of pestilential calamity.

Having, at last, extricated myself from the conversation, I changed from the cooler of my two coats into the warmer of my two coats, assembled an overnight bag, replenished my supplies of ammunition, and set out for the Hippocrene.

The Hippocrene, for those unfamiliar with the present geography or past history of Khelathra-Ven, began its life as a spring and attached stable whereat the erstwhile kings of Leonysse would house the winged horses whose service they would sometimes acquire by means of peculiar virtue, beauty, wit, or skill at arms. Over the years the structure was expanded upon and added to, providing as it did a convenient location for all those wanting to enter the city by air. Eyries and perches were built for the various winged beasts on which foreign dignitaries would arrive and, later, as the arts and sciences governing aerial travel became better understood, great hangars and landing sites were constructed in order to accommodate the enchanted edifices and aeronautical machines that fresh generations of sorcerers, engineers, and sorcerer-engineers would bring into use. So it evolved over time into its modern form, a sprawling expanse covering much of the heath to the northwest of Athra, where one might book passage on a commercial dirigible, charter a wyvern, or, as was the case on this occasion, make contact with an exiled member of the Steel Magi.

My feelings, on ascending a stone tower to a rooftop landing platform and finding Ms. Haas waiting for me, were, to put it indelicately, mixed.

"Hurry up, Wyndham," she called out. "We're almost late."

"You left me to be arrested."

She smiled radiantly. "And look how well it went."

"I could have been indicted for murder."

"Oh, come now. Lawson and his ilk may be bumbling, flat-footed, addlepated, goose-witted, dunderheaded nincompoops"—it may surprise my readers to learn that she did, in fact, use the words "bumbling," "flat-footed," "addlepated," "goose-witted," "dunderheaded," and "nincompoops"—"but even they would be unlikely to conclude that you had pierced a man's flesh repeatedly with your canine teeth and drawn the blood from his veins without leaving any stain or blemish upon your person, and then either found some way to accelerate the cooling and decomposition such that he appeared to have been dead for two days or else returned to the scene of your crime somewhat after the event, despite having already been arrested once in the interim. You were, on balance of probabilities, safe."

My feelings were becoming, frankly, less mixed, and not in the positive sense. "And the necromantic ritual?"

"The secrets of necromancy are well guarded, and it should be abundantly clear to anybody that you are not privy to them."

"You understand that it is also an offence to assist in such an undertaking."

"But you were no help at all." She adjusted the straps on the aviator goggles she had donned during my incarceration. "On the contrary, your tedious moralising is frequently quite the opposite."

"Which you could have told the Augurs if you hadn't abandoned me."

"We were in a hurry. A hurry, I might add, to do something that was your idea. I needed to secure our flight and I had every confidence in your ability to extricate yourself. Confidence that has now proven justified."

In a strange way this did, in fact, reassure me. To a wholly objective observer it would doubtless have appeared that Ms. Haas had signalled a complete failure to understand, or even acknowledge the validity of, any of my concerns with her behaviour. But for one who knew her as I was coming to, there was a sincerity to this overly rational exegesis that was the closest thing she ever came to sentiment. Thus, I allowed myself to be mollified.

Sensing victory, Ms. Haas continued. "In any case, it is good to have you back, Captain. Welcome to the *Clouded Skipper*. Quite magnificent, isn't she?"

I would not myself have chosen so theatrical a word, but it was, in this context, apt. I had seen a number of flying machines in my time, both military craft during my years amongst the Company of Strangers and civilian vessels in my university days, but none of them had quite prepared me for the *Clouded Skipper*. We were to travel inside a sizable cabin fashioned from solid iron, a sturdy structure into which—on closer inspection—doors and portholes had been seamlessly worked. But the great marvel of the vehicle was the vast mechanical butterfly that perched atop the cabin. It was mostly black, fashioned from finely wrought panels of interlocking metal detailed with such meticulous fineness that I could see individual hairs on its legs. Its wings were a still greater marvel: innumerable tiny scales that iridesced eerily in the moonlight, minute variations in their temper and finish creating patterns and eyespots as though it were a living creature. So impossibly delicate was their construction that they seemed almost to tremble in the breeze, as if a stray touch or careless breath might destroy them, but they possessed also the majesty of steel and the unyielding character of iron, which gave them a strength that I felt I could trust implicitly.

"Ms. Haas," I said, somewhat startled. "How did you gain access to one of the creations of the Steel Magi?"

"It's a long story and not entirely mine to tell. All you need to know is that the captain is no longer a magus of the order, and that I once helped him with a personal matter."

I did not wish to press the issue, but my cautious instincts rebelled against the notion of placing myself in the power of a man who had been expelled from a secretive mystical order for crimes of undisclosed magnitude. "If I might ask," I asked, "why precisely is he no longer a magus of the order?"

My companion patted me consolingly on the shoulder. "That is most *certainly* not my story to tell. But you can rest assured that the transgressions for which Blessing was stripped of his status would in no way contravene the rather idiosyncratic grab bag of superstitions you call your principles. If anything, they were foolishly commendable. Or perhaps commendably foolish."

This did not alleviate my concerns.

"Oh, buck up, Mr. Wyndham. I've done far worse myself. Just this week, in fact. I mean, only this evening I left a completely innocent man to be arrested for murder."

"And almost immediately afterwards started making jokes about it."

"You see"—she grinned at me—"I'm simply awful. Yet here I am rushing to the rescue of an innocuous fishmonger who has been unfortunate enough not only to draw the attention of a heartless, ruthless, self-serving fiend but also to be hunted down by a vampire."

I did not think it appropriate for Ms. Haas to be making such intimations about Miss Viola, who appeared to be making a genuine effort to better herself, but I did not get the opportunity to marshal any arguments in her defence for, at that moment, the door of the passenger cabin swung open and a gentleman appeared, who I took for our pilot. He was dark skinned and shaven-headed, dressed in ornate robes fashioned from an inconceivably fine mesh of steel rings.

"You got me out of bed," he began, in tones more resigned than angry, "and told me I had to be ready to leave immediately. Then you made me wait for your friend. And now you are standing around outside my *Skipper* arguing with each other. Please board the vessel or let me go back to sleep."

We boarded the vessel. The furnishings within were sparse but not uncomfortable: low benches bolted to the wall and upholstered with soft fabric designed to be pleasant to sit upon and not too terrible to be hurled against in the event of turbulence. Towards the rear of the chamber a pair of hammocks were available for use on longer journeys, and behind those a discreet door concealed a convenience of personal necessity. Woven steel baskets held supplies of dried fruit for the sustenance of passengers, along with canteens of water secured in pockets of netting. It seemed altogether a terribly civilised means of undertaking a long voyage.

My companion vaulted immediately into one of the hammocks and stretched out, looking every bit as comfortable as she did on the chaise at 221b Martyrs Walk. Having never quite shed the habit of reserving the supine posture exclusively for sleep, I settled myself onto a bench and gave serious consideration to a dried apricot, for while I had taken umbrage at Ms. Haas's willingness to prioritise her dinner over the life of an innocent woman, our commitment to the more moral course of action meant that I had not eaten since luncheon.

Meanwhile, our pilot had taken up a position by the windows at the front of the cabin. "Welcome to the *Clouded Skipper*, the only ship in Khelathra-Ven whose pilot has the misfortune of owing Shaharazad Haas a favour."

At this, she opened an eye. "Not so. A great many aviators owe me favours. There's Klaus Ludendorff, Jacques Pun, Nikolaj Fortescue-Blake, and, of course, Davina Wright, to name but four."

"Davina is currently attempting a solo flight across the Dread Wastes of Bai, Jacques hates you, Fortescue-Blake couldn't fly an or-nithopter across a millpond, and Klaus Ludendorff has been dead for three years."

"Just some of the many reasons that you were my first choice." She gestured languidly in my direction. "By the way, this is Mr. Wynd-ham. It's his fault we're here."

I half choked on my apricot. "I'm pleased to meet you, Mr. . . . um."

"Ngoie," he supplied. "Blessing Ngoie."

"I most sincerely regret that it was necessary to impose upon you at this rather unfortunate hour. A young woman's life is in danger."

He folded his arms. "You know, Shaharazad, if you had men-tioned that earlier I would have argued a lot less about helping you."

"Yet further proof"—Ms. Haas swung smugly in her hammock—
"should any be required, that it is always best to assume I am right
about everything."

"You are impossible."

"I prefer the term 'extraordinary.'"

I was briefly concerned that my companion's weakness for badi-
nage would delay us yet further on our errand of mercy but, to my
great relief, the conversation ended there. Mr. Ngoie lifted his hands
and a cascade of coruscating filaments tumbled down from the ceiling
to entwine him. He closed his eyes and, by some invisible act of will
the secrets of which are, to this day, unknown outside of the Steel
Magi, urged the vessel into the sky.

CHAPTER THIRTY-SEVEN

The Blackcrest Mountains

The flight north from Athra was more comfortable than it had any right to be while still not being, by any stretch of the imagination, at all comfortable. The passage of the *Clouded Skipper* was remarkably smooth, testament to the unrivalled skill of the Steel Magi. But although we were spared the constant shaking, bumping, and droning of engines that so often accompanies aerial travel I was still, in essence, trapped in a chamber approximately the size of our sitting room with a man wired to a giant butterfly and a woman who, when denied a private space in which to indulge her personal vices, retreated into an almost trancelike state of self-absorption.

Having brought a pistol and a change of clothing but no reading material, I had nothing to occupy my mind for the first leg of the journey save unproductive and unanswerable anxieties about the practicability of our current endeavour. The more I reflected on the logistics of the matter, the more convinced I became that we would reach Vedunia too late to be of assistance. I began to imagine that we would arrive to find Miss Beck a corpse and Miss Viola already transformed into the defiled bride of the Contessa. I voiced these concerns to Ms. Haas.

"Mr. Wyndham." She sighed. "You astound me. By some miracle you have managed in one breath to be both tedious and melodramatic.

Besides, if there is anyone who will take well to becoming the debased and lascivious courtesan of a demonic noblewoman, it's Eirene."

With which comment she returned to whatever private reflections I had stirred her from, and I did my best to catch what sleep I could before the sunrise. When I awoke a few hours later I saw through the window that we were approaching the northern edge of the sprawling, thorn-choked forest that covered what had once been Leonysse.

By noon we had reached the foothills of the Blackcrest Mountains and would, if all went well, have passed over them into Lothringar before sundown. Our first indication that all would not, in fact, go well came a few hours later in the form of a sudden, although not wholly unseasonable, darkening of the sky from the northeast. As a consequence of the uncanny smoothness with which the *Clouded Skipper* traversed the skyways it was difficult to be certain when the pilot was making corrections to its course and bearing. But, in this instance, our change of direction was sharp enough to jolt me from my seat and cause Ms. Haas to raise her head blearily.

The metal tendrils that held Mr. Ngoie partially uncoiled, allowing him to drift gently to the ground and turn towards us. His expression was eminently scrutable. "There are pirates coming. I told you there would be pirates coming."

"And I told you," said Ms. Haas, bestirring herself from the hammock, "that we would deal with it."

"And how exactly do you intend to deal with it? The *Skipper* is not a warship. Her defences are limited."

"But mine are not." Ms. Haas strode to the doorway, producing a silver whistle on a long chain from beneath her suede-and-fleece jacket. "I intend to call forth a winged steed from the shores of distant Aldebaran, ride it out into the tempest, locate the chief miscreant, and shoot him, her, or them in the head, thus dispersing both the storm and the pirates. I shall then return the beast to the stars, before it decides to exact payment in blood, and we can proceed to Vedunia, where Mr. Wyndham will get to rescue a lady from a vampire."

I should perhaps take this moment to explain a little more about the nature of the threat we presently faced. Readers will, of course, have heard tell of piracy on the high seas, and many will doubtless have heard also of the sky-pirates of the Blackcrest Mountains, especially since they were made so famous by Ms. Francesca Vandegrift-Osbourne's celebrated novel *Treasure Peak; or, The Mutiny of the* Admiral Newton: *An Adventurous Tale for Young Folks*, illustrated with woodcarvings by Lady Quinella Thrumpmusket. Although many aspects of that most diverting book have been exaggerated or, indeed, fabricated for the purpose of Ms. Vandegrift-Osbourne's narrative, several of its more pertinent details are, at least, broadly accurate. The pirates really do operate out of lairs in the Blackcrest Mountains, whence they prey upon passing ships carrying trade between the world's northerly and southerly powers. The book is also correct in its characterisation of the pirates as travelling primarily by storm, although they will sometimes make use of captured vessels in order to transport goods and cargo. The winds upon which they habitually fly are conjured by a cadre of sorcerer-priests who trace their origins back to the earliest days of the mountain folk, long before the coming of the church.

Much like the highwayman, the gentleman thief, and (in some more recent literary treatments) the vampire, the sky-pirates are often imbued in the popular imagination with a certain romance. It would be convenient to say that this portrayal belies the real cruelty and violence of which they are capable, but this, too, would be an oversimplification. I have, over the course of my adventures, had occasion to interact with the sky-pirates in a variety of different contexts and have found that they, like most people, possess an equal capacity for both good and ill. And while I, of course, condemn the methods by which they sustain themselves, given their circumstances, living in a high and barren place on the fringes of a world that rejects them, it is not clear to me what actions they might reasonably take for their own betterment. Of course, regardless of the complexities that may underpin their lives, my first encounter with the sky-pirates of the Blackcrest Mountains, in which they made a spirited attempt to murder me and everyone I travelled with, did not present them in the most flattering light.

"That," replied Mr. Ngoie, "is a terrible plan."

"Too late. I'm doing it."

Ms. Haas flung open the cabin door, exposing us to a sudden burst of wind that swept several apricots out of their basket, onto the floor, and out into the yawning void beyond. Placing the whistle to her lips, she stepped out also, dropping precipitously from view. While over the years I became increasingly accustomed to Ms. Haas taking such actions, I never quite lost the habit of fearing on every occasion that she had, at last, overreached herself and simply perished. That these fears proved always unfounded may go some way towards explaining why it has taken me so long to accept that my dear friend, the sorceress Shaharazad Haas, is, alas, no more.

I started up and stumbled across the room, bracing myself on a handrail as I scanned the horizon for any sign of either my companion or our enemies. To my considerable relief, it was the former I espied first, astride a strange creature with webbed feet and membranous wings, rising sharply to confront the oncoming storm. The confrontation was swift in coming, for the pirates and the meteorological phenomenon on which they travelled moved quite literally like the wind. There was just time for Mr. Ngoie to become once more enwreathed in the complex harness through which he appeared to control the *Clouded Skipper* and for me to take up a position by the door, my pistol at the ready, and then all was darkness and rain and lightning. It was almost impossible to make out anything in the tumult, just hazy figures swooping and pinwheeling, growing somewhat less hazy as they approached our ship.

At least a dozen of them came at us, descending, and for that matter ascending, from all directions, but three seemed especially intent on breaching the door. Steadying myself as best I could, I fired on them. I wounded two, the shock of injury causing them to lose command of the winds that buoyed them and sending them careening away into the tempest. The last, a wild-haired, calico-clad gentleman, rushed me as the hammer of my firearm clicked on an empty chamber, and only a sideways leap at the last possible second spared me a skewering from his wickedly serrated sabre. Recovering my footing, I cast about for a weapon suitable for close quarters and saw nothing but my walking stick. This I seized, just in time to knock aside a cut the pirate had aimed at my right shoulder. The exchange caused considerable damage to my cane, suggesting that as a long-term strategy for survival I would do well to consider alternatives.

I riposted with a blow to the pirate's wrist and was returning to a standing position when the floor rocked violently. My assailant was, of course, accustomed to doing battle in storm-tossed skies and, while I had some experience of fighting on shifting terrain, I stumbled, giving him the opening he needed to deliver a savage thrust to my face. I parried the attack hastily but, in so doing, caught my cane on the jagged edge of his blade, causing the two weapons to become momentarily locked. The unexpected break that this event introduced into the rhythm of our duel distracted my opponent for long enough that I was able to dart forward, driving my palm into the back of his extended elbow, twisting his body sharply away from me. I stamped heavily on the back of his exposed knee and brought the top of my cane down on the back of his head, following which the piratical gentleman had just enough wherewithal to drag himself to the door and throw himself again on the mercy of the winds. For his sake, I hope they brought him to a place of safety.

More felicitously, it appeared my assailant had lost his sabre in the tussle. I retrieved it and was thus able to better hold off the next wave of pirates as they descended upon the *Clouded Skipper*. Although I no longer had my pistol, between a blade, a better sense of the style in which the pirates could be expected to fight, and the narrow confines of the doorway, I was able to restrict my enemies' possible angles of attack, allowing me to defend myself against two opponents at once with reasonable efficacy. Matters were assisted by the inherently opportunistic nature of my opponents. When they had thought the vessel defenceless, they were eager to press their advantage, but, having seen two of their number shot down and a third bested in close battle, they approached now more hesitantly and would retreat in the face of a sharp countercut or stop-thrust.

Their numbers, however, began to prove challenging, as did the increasing instability of the vessel. But these difficulties may yet have proved surmountable had the ship not been struck by lightning and, moments later, ploughed into a mountainside.

My editor suggests that I leave off narration at this point, thereby creating an enticing mystery as to our survival such as might encourage the reader to seek out next month's edition of *The Strait* magazine. I am, however, sensible of the effect such suspense may have on persons of a nervous disposition and shall, therefore, elucidate. I had just seen off the most recent of my attackers, who had withdrawn when my riposte drew blood from her wrist, when I noticed that all of the pirates were pulling swiftly away from the *Clouded Skipper*. I felt a strange prickling in the air and the next thing I knew the world around me sheeted white. More learned friends have informed me since that I was very fortunate to be encased entirely within a steel box for, somewhat unintuitively, such places are, in fact, amongst the safest one can be in the event of a lightning strike. At the time, however, I had no such assurances and my sense of impending danger was only exacerbated by the realisation that Mr. Ngoie had lost control of the vessel and that we were, consequently, descending sharply.

The crash that followed was inelegant and painful, but the constructs of the Steel Magi are rightly as famed for their resilience as for their magnificence. Thus, neither Mr. Ngoie nor I perished in the collision.

We remained, however, in mortal peril.

❦

CHAPTER THIRTY-EIGHT

The Eye of the Storm

Readers who are familiar with Ms. Vandegrift-Osbourne's sky-pirate novel may remember the famous sequence in which the mutineers having seized control of the *Admiral Newton*, causing it to run aground atop the mysterious Skull Peak (whereon the traitorous quartermaster hopes to recover the treasure once buried by the legendary Captain Shale), the air at once grows very still, and it is this momentary calm within the storm that presages the arrival of the quartermaster's piratical allies. I can attest from personal experience that this scene also is remarkably accurate. As Mr. Ngoie and I emerged from the slightly battered *Clouded Skipper* we found the winds quiet around us. It was not reassuring.

Mr. Ngoie heaved a deep sigh. "Remind me why I allow Shaharazad to talk me into things."

"Did you not owe her a favour?"

"I repaid that debt long ago, but still I keep letting her drag me into her escapades."

"Well," I offered consolingly, as I reloaded my pistol, "I for one am very glad you did. And I'm sure Miss Beck will be glad also."

"Miss Beck may not have opportunity to be thankful. It will take me some while to repair the aerokinetic circuitry."

I looked up. Around a dozen figures were spiralling gracefully towards us. "Perhaps the circuitry is not the most pressing concern at this very moment."

"You mean them?" He pointed at the now quite rapidly descending pirates. "They should have known better than to damage the property of a Steel Magus."

And, without further comment, Mr. Ngoie placed a hand against one of the *Skipper*'s buckled wingtips. A wave of motion rippled across the whole surface of the vessel, much like a chain of dominoes falling, but substantially more complex. The scales on the machine began to flow up his arm, fusing with his robes and building intricate steel structures at whose function I could only guess. The whole process took less than a minute, but when it was complete both the *Clouded Skipper* and her pilot were gone, and in their place stood a gargantuan mechanical man.

"You know," said a metallic voice that shared a certain tonal similarity with Mr. Ngoie's but was much, much louder, "I really should have stayed in bed."

He stepped forward with reassuring precision, positioning himself directly above me and providing welcome shelter from our enemies. Then, with a deafening clang, he folded his arms, and called out to the sky, "You want my ship, you ———" And here he used language that, while it had probably not been the primary cause of his expulsion from the Steel Magi, may perhaps have been a contributing factor. ". . . come and take it."

This did, at least, answer the question of how we were to repel the pirates, although it also left me feeling ever so slightly surplus to requirements. A detachment of pirates swept down to attack us, but Mr. Ngoie's armour proved impervious to their weaponry and the wickedly sharp talons that tipped his gauntlets severely injured several of them before they retreated. One or two landed and made an effort to eliminate me instead. They were not successful in this endeavour, for between my pistol and my scavenged sabre, my armaments were quite the equal of theirs, and my morale was bolstered, rather than diminished, by the presence of the titanic construct that loomed above us.

When it had become apparent that swords would be of little use against a Steel Magus and that I, while more vulnerable, could not be so easily picked off as our enemies might have assumed, they retreated to a safe height, circling above us in a fashion distinctly too vulture-like to be comforting. It seemed for the moment that we stood at an impasse, they having the advantage of flight, and we the advantage of a sorcerous war engine. However, we had reckoned without their leader. From the roiling tempest descended a man wreathed in lightning, his scarlet coat billowing in the surging winds. As he stretched out a hand, a thunderbolt arced from the sky, splitting the ground some few feet from where I was standing. I hoped that this was an accurate reflection of the newcomer's aim, but I strongly suspected it was little more than a warning shot.

The pirate captain threw back his head, dark curls whipping about him, and laughed wildly. "Have at thee, kna—"

His neck snapped abruptly forward and his body plummeted the not inconsiderable distance from his prior vantage to the mountain-side, right next to us. There he lay, his limbs at terribly unpleasant angles, blood matting his hair, which I saw now was grey beneath the long black wig. The back of his skull bore the unmistakable mark of a bullet fired, if I was any judge, by a skilled marksman using a small-calibre handgun at moderate range. The storm was already fading and, as the remaining pirates fled for safety before the winds gave out beneath them, a bat-like, bird-like, ant-like creature burst from a cloud bank, Ms. Haas still upon its back, a revolver in her hand.

"There," she said, landing the scabrous beast a short distance away. "When in doubt, find the fellow with the biggest hat and shoot him in the head. It never fails."

Mr. Ngoie turned slowly to face her. "You got my ship struck by lightning."

"My dear man, I did not *get it* struck by lightning." My companion dismounted, then spoke a brief, blasphemous incantation and her erstwhile steed flapped away towards the gradually emerging stars. "It was incidentally struck by lightning while I was doing other things."

"Is the damage extensive?" I asked.

"The exposure to elemental forces has unbalanced her alchemical equilibrium." Mr. Ngoie flexed his razor-tipped fingers. "She can walk and swim and withstand the heat of a thousand suns but cannot fly."

At this, Ms. Haas flung up her hands in a gesture of inappropriate apathy. "Well, Captain. It appears Miss Beck will be eaten by a vampire after all. Blessing, do you think you could carry us?" She brightened considerably. "We should be down this mountain by sunset, through the ravine by midnight, and back in the foothills by sunrise. Where I'm sure there'll be a quaint little village where we can get breakfast, and perhaps some commemorative chocolates."

"Ms. Haas," I protested, "I do not wish to commemorate our failure with confectionery."

"Failure? I never fail. I just sometimes lack the impetus to pursue success as rigorously as I might."

Expecting no further concessions from Ms. Haas, I placed my hopes instead in the exiled magus of unknown capabilities in whose company I had spent less than twenty-four hours. "Is there no chance of repairing the *Skipper*?"

"Not quickly. And if I am to fix my ship, I'd rather not do it on a mountain. I would rather do it in a quaint village, preferably one with chocolates."

I slumped down in the snow, my old injury sending a sudden jolt of pain through my hip. "There must be something we can do. There must be something"—and here I glanced imploringly at Ms. Haas— "*you* can do. Can you call that creature back and, well, I don't know, get it to take the two of us?"

"Assuming it didn't eat you immediately, which it probably

would, it simply wouldn't make the journey in time. They're peculiar beasts, very suited to travel over vast distances and short distances, but not a lot in between."

"And there is no other sorcery you can perform?"

Ms. Haas grinned at me like a schoolchild who had caught her professor in an error. "You see? You're always complaining about how terribly illegal and unnatural my practices are, right up to the point you need them. Which, for what it's worth, is why I'm never concerned about being arrested. But, no, as it happens I have never studied the specific techniques that one would use in order to race a vampire across a mountain range and over several hundred miles of open country using only snow, rocks, dead pirates, and whatever you happen to have in your pockets."

At mention of the pirates, I stared a moment at the crumpled remains of their captain. "How did he manage it?" I enquired. "They travelled swiftly, and through the air, and must have done so with nothing more than they have about them now."

"They catch the wind in knots, then unleash it where useful. There's a sort of religious aspect but, like most religion, I suspect it's mostly for show."

Mr. Ngoie looked down at me. "This is another terrible idea. The sky-pirates stay in these mountains for a reason."

"You say that," drawled Ms. Haas, "but it's always struck me as evidence of a tremendous lack of vision."

"So we could fly a storm to Vedunia?" I endeavoured not to sound too hopeful.

To which Mr. Ngoie answered "no" and Ms. Haas, looking somewhat more engaged than she hitherto had, answered "possibly" at the same moment.

"Shaharazad," Mr. Ngoie continued, "even you would not be foolish enough to try to reverse engineer stolen magic and put it to a purpose for which it was never intended."

She gave him a haughty look. "I'm sorry, have we met? I'm exactly foolish enough to try to reverse engineer stolen magic and put it to a purpose for which it was never intended. And to think I didn't want to come on this journey."

With frankly unbecoming enthusiasm, Ms. Haas bounded over to the mangled corpse of the pirate captain and began rifling about his person.

"It . . . it was not my intent," I said hastily, "to suggest that you do anything reckless. To rescue Miss Beck would be honourable, but I'm not at all certain this is an appropriate course of action."

Ms. Haas was no longer listening. She had retrieved from the body a skein of knotted cord, which she now inspected with some interest. "Ah," she murmured. "Of course. I believe if I . . ." She teased one of the knots apart. The moment she began, I was conscious of a gathering chill, which grew deeper and more biting as she worked.

"Ms. Haas, I really think—" I got no further for, with the thread untied, a veritable gale swept across the mountainside, churning the snow into blinding flurries and snatching the breath from my lips. Then, all at once, the wind was gone as Ms. Haas retied the rope with commendable dexterity.

"How interesting." She tried another, and the skies darkened, bombarding us with rain that froze on contact. "Don't worry, I'm getting the hang of this."

A perfect bolt of forked lightning speared from the sky and struck the head of Mr. Ngoie's vast suit of mechanical armour, through which it was channelled harmlessly into the earth. Still, he did not seem best pleased. "You have not got the hang of it."

There was a brief shower of hail, a gust of surprisingly warm air, and then the clouds dispersed.

"No, no," said Ms. Haas briskly. "I definitely have. Come, Wyndham. To Vedunia."

Having inadvertently encouraged her towards this course of

action, I felt it would be both churlish and pointless to resist it now. Climbing to my feet, I brushed off the snow and joined her.

"I take it you won't be coming with us," I asked Mr. Ngoie.

Although the metallic face of the armoured statue was motionless, the look he gave me with it was staggeringly expressive. "No. Definitely not."

"And you will be able to return safely to Khelathra-Ven?"

"More certainly than you will."

Ms. Haas waved the cord impatiently. "Are you two finished? You do remember we're trying to save an innocent woman's life?"

Without giving either of us time to reply, she took three knots between her fingers and held them in a convoluted pattern. Gradually she began to draw them apart. The winds rose up around us and, rather more gently than I had feared, lifted us skywards.

CHAPTER THIRTY-NINE

Granny Liesl

Throughout my (though I say so myself) not uneventful life I have travelled by a bewildering variety of conveyances, but nothing has quite reached the unadulterated clarity of flying on a storm. Although at the time I was not wholly able to appreciate it, owing to my keen awareness of the possibility that we might at any moment plummet to our ignominious deaths. In retrospect, however, and secure in the knowledge of my survival, I look back with fondness on the journey. There was a great sense of liberty in moving swiftly, and unsupported, through the open air, unconstrained by propriety, society, or gravity.

We traversed the entire territory of Lothringar in record time and without incident, rolling hills and placid lakes sweeping beneath us at incredible speed. We soared above red-roofed towns with cobbled streets and, wary of the possibility of countersorcery against aerial incursion, skirted well clear of the impossibly delicate white palaces that nestled in the forests. As morning broke and we crossed the border into Nivale, I became increasingly aware that the winds around us were growing erratic.

Rain began to fall in intermittent bursts, and at least twice I saw lightning sheet from Ms. Haas's fingertips. Though I had not at that time known her long, I had already seen that my companion was skilled at concealing the degree to which her supernatural endeavours taxed her strength, will, and vitality. But given the ever-growing turbulence of our flight, I was forced to conclude that she was, indeed, feeling the strain quite acutely. I could only hope that our passage, marked as it now was by gale-force winds, a torrential downpour, and occasional thunderbolts, did not overly distress the sensibilities or damage the property of those Nivalians over whom we flew.

As the wooded vale that sheltered the city of Vedunia came into view, we began to lose height rapidly. What her sudden loss of control over the wind said about my companion's state of health I was not sure, and though I am ashamed to confess it, in the moment, my more pressing concern was the rapid approach of the ground. Some hundreds of feet from the forest floor, the winds failed entirely and we responded as might any pair of flightless organisms finding themselves abruptly unsupported and well above the treetops. That is to say, we plummeted earthwards, our garments and hair whipping about us as the wind (a phenomenon my more learned friends inform me was, in fact, caused by the air remaining motionless while we passed through it) grew ever stronger and the ground grew ever closer.

By some miracle of mental fortitude, Ms. Haas had just the wherewithal to break the last knot on her cord, bringing forth one final updraught, which retarded our descent sufficiently for us to at least reach the canopy. From there, we plunged rather ingloriously through a curtain of pine needles before tumbling to the moss below.

Having returned both literally and figuratively to earth, and reassured myself that my limbs and vital organs were relatively intact, my thoughts turned to the unacceptably shambolic figures we would cut as we entered Vedunia. We were both soaked to the skin, my doublet was torn in a dozen places, my hat was missing, I'd lost a buckle from one shoe and the entirety of the other, and my stockings were more run than they had any business being in public. Ms. Haas's attire, being altogether composed of more durable materials, had fared rather better, although she herself had not. She lay worryingly still, her hair matted, her fingertips charred, and blood running freely from a gash on her forehead. But she was, at least, breathing.

Finding myself unable to rouse her, and leery of the dangers inherent in leaving an unconscious woman alone in a foreign woodland, I took the rather uncomfortable and not altogether seemly decision to carry Ms. Haas to Vedunia. This proved less difficult than I had anticipated; I had some experience of lifting fallen comrades, and Ms. Haas, though taller than I, was lighter than she appeared, as I should perhaps have expected, given that she subsisted on a diet of oysters and laudanum.

I had some sense of the way to Vedunia and it did not take me too long to emerge from the forest onto the road. There I turned and walked towards the city in the hopes that I would soon pass some kind traveller who could assist me in conveying my friend to a place where we might find help. I had not gone very far at all when I heard hoofbeats behind me. And, standing aside to avoid making a nuisance of myself, soon I observed the approach of a low cart, drawn by a donkey and driven by a hunched old woman in a cloak. Setting Ms. Haas down, I attempted to attract the traveller's attention, a relatively simple matter, considering our current predicament.

She came to a stop beside us and eyed me speculatively from beneath her hood. "How can Granny help you, dearie?"

Her voice was peculiar in two ways. Firstly, it was possessed of an unnatural shrillness that made even the kindest of sentiments feel sinister. Secondly, she spoke in flawless Eyan. Despite these uncanny nuances, my circumstance was one of begging rather than choosing.

"My companion is injured," I said. "And I would be most grateful if you were to provide us with passage to town and directions both to a reputable apothecary and to somewhere we can rest."

"Come up beside me." The old woman shuffled over and patted

the seat next to her. "Whatever your heart desires, Granny will see you right."

I was beginning to suspect that this stranger would pose more problems than she would solve. "Madam, if I might ask, would you by any chance happen to be a witch?"

She grinned, displaying an impressive snaggletooth. "What cynical times we live in. I am but a harmless old woman on my way to market to sell a few simple herbs and trinkets."

I was not sure if the lady's intent was to confirm or allay my suspicions, but ultimately it made no matter. I lifted Ms. Haas again and transferred her as gently as I was able into the back of the cart. Not wishing to give this clearly untrustworthy person any opportunity to drive away with my insensible companion, I immediately hauled myself in as well, settling down against a bale of straw.

The witch turned in her seat and gave me a wounded look. "Why so nervous, dearie? Poor Granny means no harm to you or your pretty compan—oh." She paused, staring at Ms. Haas, and then went on in quite a different tone. "Who are you and why are you travelling with Shaharazad Haas?"

"My name is John Wyndham. Ms. Haas and I live together and are presently engaged on business of some urgency in Vedunia."

"And why is she unconscious?"

Once again, I was in the difficult position of wishing neither to lie nor to inadvertently give away information that might endanger others. "We fell from the sky."

"How like her." Then, before I could stay her, the witch snatched a handful of blackish powder from a nearby basket and cast it into Ms. Haas's face. "Shaharazad. Wake up, Shaharazad. Granny's got a bone to pick with you."

My companion's eyes flickered open. "Is that you, Liesl?" she murmured, still sounding somewhat fatigued. "I thought I'd killed you."

That made the old woman cackle. "Don't be silly, dearie. If I died every time a teenage girl stole my books, cut off my head, and set my cottage on fire, I'd have been gone centuries ago. It was very unimaginative of you. I hope you've done better since."

"I'm lying in a cart full of dung because my nauseatingly soft-hearted housemate convinced me to rescue a fishmonger from a vampire." She flung an arm across her forehead. "I've done magnificently."

There was a long silence.

"Well now," said the old woman finally. "Isn't it lucky Granny found you?"

Ms. Haas twitched her fingers wearily. "That rather depends on whether you're going to make another attempt to carve my still-beating heart out of my chest and eat it in front of me."

"Don't flatter yourself, Shaharazad. You're not the succulent young thing you once were."

I cleared my throat politely. "If you could just take us to Vedunia, that would be more than amply helpful."

"You, on the other hand"—Granny's glittering eyes alighted on me—"would make an excellent filling for a pie. So sweet and tender."

"That's terribly gratifying, but we really do need to get to Vedunia as soon as possible."

"Actually," Ms. Haas observed, "we likely have several hours before the train departs. Which is fortunate because I am not feeling quite myself. Besides, we have little hope of infiltrating the Austral Express looking like the last survivors of Sarnath."

Granny reached down and raked her fingernails through Ms. Haas's hair in a gesture that seemed strangely affectionate. "Not yourself? Why, Granny is just a simple old woman who lives in the woods and even she can see that you have a concussion, at least two cracked ribs, and a broken leg. To say nothing of the storm-shredded tatters you seem to have made of whatever passes for your soul."

"Don't fuss me, Liesl. I've fought dragons with worse."

"Ah, my pretty Shaharazad, you haven't changed in thirty years. Always wanting too much too quickly. Always thinking you can do everything."

"Well, I usually can."

"Then why don't you stand up, dearie. Show Granny how little you need her help."

"Ms. Haas," I said quickly, "I really wouldn't—"

I did not have time to complete my warning, although I doubt it would have made any difference. None of the others ever did. My companion steadied herself against the edge of the cart and rose to her feet with a grace that was quite breathtakingly impressive for the moments it lasted. But moments they were, and then she collapsed. I managed to catch her as she fell, returning her to the floor of the cart without too greatly exacerbating her existing injuries.

She propped herself up on her elbows and directed a torrent of remarks at myself and Granny Liesl that I shall forbear from repeating.

"Such harsh words," cooed Granny, "for somebody who has only ever wanted to look after you."

Probably I should have held my tongue, but I felt it only right to come to Ms. Haas's defence in this matter. "Did you not also try to eat her heart?"

"Yes, but only out of love. And a desire for immortality."

"I'm not sure I consider that kind of love entirely praiseworthy."

"Oh, dearie." She brushed a gnarled hand down the side of my face, in a manner that made me feel oddly violated. "So kind and yet so stern. But what use is your love or that of your blind, idiot god? Will it give your friend the strength she needs for the task that you have set her?"

Ms. Haas knocked the old woman's arm away. "Enough, Liesl. Only I am allowed to torment Mr. Wyndham. I will admit I need your help. Now help us."

Granny leaned over and reached into one of the many sacks that filled the back of the cart, producing at last a dusty bottle full of murky green liquid. "A potion"—she proffered the phial to Ms. Haas—"that will restore your strength, but only until the stroke of midnight."

Unstoppering the container, Ms. Haas sniffed cautiously at the fumes. "Asphodel, maiden's sorrow, bloodstone, and wolf's tooth stirred with a glass spike and sung over at moonrise." She resealed the bottle. "Not, I think, the correct potion."

"I'm sorry, dearie. Can't blame an old woman for trying."

She offered Ms. Haas a new draught. This one was red-brown in colour and sealed inside a round-bottomed flask. My companion repeated her inspection. "Deathwort, plague-fly wings, hangman's eye, hellblossom, needlefish eggs, and murderer's tears, boiled in a black cauldron by the light of a red candle. Now that's the stuff."

Ms. Haas raised the potion to her lips and, as my varsity friends were so fond of saying, downed it.

Granny smiled. "All better now?"

"For the moment. Although you know as well as I do that the side effects will be miserable."

"Everything has a price, Shaharazad. That was the first thing I taught you. Of course, now we'll need the second thing I taught you."

I was not altogether keen to learn the nature of any of the lessons that Granny Liesl had passed on to Ms. Haas. "I think you've done quite enough. Thank you so much for your kindness."

"Mr. Wyndham, would you like to know the third lesson I taught Shaharazad?"

"I would rather not, if it's all the same to you."

"It was, *never refuse a gift from a witch*. Now, let's do something about those wet clothes."

CHAPTER FORTY

The Cottage in the Woods

All of my instincts told me that permitting a self-confessed witch to lead us away from the road that we knew would take us to our destination and into an unknown part of a foreign woodland was most assuredly inadvisable. My misgivings were far from assuaged when I spied through the trees a low, ramshackle cottage decorated, I could not help but note, with human-seeming bones and supported above the ground by what appeared to be a pair of bird's legs.

"There now, love," Granny Liesl said to my companion. "Isn't it nice to be home?"

Ms. Haas curled her lip. "It wasn't nice thirty years ago. Now it's positively gauche. Nobody's hanging skulls from their eaves anymore and chicken feet are utterly impractical."

"Always so headstrong. Always so certain you know better than your elders. Granny was here long before you and she'll be here long after you're gone."

"And she'll still be talking about herself in the third person."

The witch smiled in a fashion that was hard to read, having all the character of affection but coming from a face designed for nothing but malice. "Ah, but you have learned some pretty words."

Ms. Haas responded to this with a few words that were not at all pretty, causing the old woman to laugh in a way that can only be described as cackling.

"There's the girl I knew. A workhouse brat, an alley cat, a starveling rat, but more than that." I was not certain I was following her train of thought any longer, but she seemed very much to be enjoying herself. "You have come far, Shaharazad. But not perhaps as far as you think."

This proved the first of the two and a half occasions on which Ms. Haas permitted another person to have the last word in an argument. The second would not come for some years.

Granny Liesl brought us inside her cottage, and I was struck at once by the unnerving similarity it bore to the sitting room at 221b Martyrs Walk. Its style of furnishing was, of course, wholly different, but it had the same air of barely corralled chaos, the same scent of unknown connotations, the same scattering of mysterious and forbidding artefacts. While Ms. Haas's chaise longue was the most striking feature of our own parlour, here it was a black and forbidding cauldron that occupied a central position atop a stack of firewood, currently unlit. I settled myself nervously onto a wooden stool and waited to see what our hostess would do next.

"One gift I have given you already." She raised a single bony finger. "Two more is customary, but you know that Granny hates it when people take and give nothing in return."

I was ill at ease with the turn events seemed to be taking, but out of deference for the long acquaintance between the two ladies and an awareness that my companion was far more qualified to understand the dangers of our predicament than I, I kept my peace.

"What do you want, Liesl?" she snapped.

Granny's eyes glittered. "A kiss, a wish, and a lock of your hair."

All of those things sounded terribly innocuous and, from what little I knew of magic, this suggested that they should in no circumstances be parted with. "If I might," I asked, "what are we to receive in return?"

"Oh, my dear sweet child." The old lady hobbled towards me, her fingers making acquisitive motions in the empty air. "Have you not been listening? You will receive nothing in return. I offer gifts to you. It is polite for you to offer gifts to me. You can choose to be impolite, and many have made just that choice."

I could not help but find my eyes drawn to the rows of skulls that decorated a number of the cottage's shelves and windowsills and thought it best that I return to my earlier policy of silence.

Ms. Haas strolled quite nonchalantly towards us, a manoeuvre which happened to place her physically between me and the witch. "I'd have thought," she remarked, "that you already had enough pieces of me to last a lifetime."

"One can never have too much of a good thing, my pretty."

There followed a long but very tense silence that reminded me uncomfortably of the last time I had spoken to my father. I was not certain, should the matter devolve into direct magical confrontation, which of the ladies would be victorious, an uncertainty which I suspected they shared.

At last Ms. Haas nodded. "Very well." She stepped forward, stooped, and kissed Granny Liesl gently on the lips, a gesture that—from my somewhat awkward vantage behind my companion—seemed almost to speak of genuine fondness. Then she retrieved one of the many, many knives that lay here and there throughout the room and cut off a lock of her hair, which she handed to the witch somewhat defiantly.

"And my wish?" The old woman had an almost triumphant air that did little to reassure me about either her nature or that of the present exchange.

For the first time since we had met, I saw my companion hesitate. Then at last she said, "I wish for the moon."

Granny Liesl gave her a look of exaggerated disappointment.

"I wish for a million wishes."

"Don't play games, my love. You know they only make Granny angry."

"Have it your way." Ms. Haas straightened her spine haughtily. "I wish that I regretted."

The witch nodded. "Acceptable."

"With apologies for my continued interruption," I said, increasingly eager to be anywhere but where I was, "what happens now?"

The witch clapped her hands and the wood beneath the cauldron caught light. "Well, we can't have you traipsing around Vedunia looking like two drowned rats in a pickle jar." I was very much aware that the detritus on a nearby table did, in fact, include two such animals in just such a receptacle. "And we can't have you running off to fight a vampire with nobody watching over you."

"I'm not entirely sure that answers my question."

"It wasn't intended to. Now hold still."

Granny Liesl began snatching ingredients from the nearby shelves and casting them into the cauldron. Ms. Haas, I observed, was watching her with an intense scrutiny—doubtless sensible that our hostess might be about to betray us utterly—but seemed to see nothing that gave her cause for concern.

As the cauldron began to boil, the witch cast in a pair of gossamer wings and a set of small, shrivelled objects that looked quite horribly like human fingers. She then began to chant in a low, guttural tone that rose ever louder as the ritual progressed. Smoke began to billow from the cauldron, and I became acutely aware of something crawling on my skin. I shivered, but resolved that I would take no actions unless my companion advised me to do so. I was not, after all, a witch hunter, and to act in panic when one is the subject of an unknown spell might doom one.

The room was now so filled with smoke that I could see nothing, but I felt dozens of sets of claws crawling over me, tiny teeth nibbling at my extremities. I was conscious of my garments falling away and of

246

their being replaced with something else, an experience I found singularly unsettling despite the relative lack of danger it posed to my actual person. Once the clouds had dispersed I found myself attired in a manner which, I presumed, was more appropriate for Vedunia and the Austral Express. It was not, however, at all in line with my personal sensibilities. While the colours Granny Liesl had chosen were appropriately modest, being for the most part blacks and silvers, she had chosen a luxurious fabric and an ostentatious style: a full-skirted velvet frock coat, decorated with the kind of delicate embroidery I had been raised to believe constituted the worst sort of frivolity. This she had combined with matching breeches, a white lace cravat, silk stockings, and black satin shoes. These last were ornamented with silver bows and small diamonds and had the elevated heels that were currently modish amongst the well-bred gentlemen of the Hundred Kingdoms, although they were considered somewhat old-fashioned in the south, and nothing short of a personal affront to the Creator in Ey. I found them most impractical.

Ms. Haas, for her part, was now dressed in a swirling gown of crimson silk, decorated with golden flowers. Something similarly extravagant had been done with her hair, the dark locks bound up with ribbons, feathers, and an elaborate structure on which perched a live jackdaw, its grey eyes seeming to watch me with a malign intelligence. She seemed far more at ease with her new wardrobe than I was with mine.

"There now," said Granny Liesl. "All ready to go to the ball."

I batted away an insistent raven that was trying to lower a powdered wig onto my head. "It isn't a ball; it's a train. And we are now even less appropriately dressed to fight a vampire."

"Oh, Captain." Ms. Haas extended her arms, allowing a small swarm of spiders to drag a pair of long gloves up her arms. "What is the point of doing battle against dark forces if you can't look your best while you're doing it?"

"And," added the old woman, "if you really think that a gift from a witch does nothing you can't see it doing, then you are a very stupid little boy."

I was, needless to say, quite affronted at this, since when people insult me they usually do so less directly, but I refrained from defending myself, if for no other reason than that the lady had a point and I was not entirely certain what power she might hold over me or my companion.

"There's just one thing missing." Granny tapped her talons together excitedly. "Two such pretty young creatures can hardly arrive in town in an old woman's cart."

She led us outside to a lone yew tree that stood a short way from the cottage. Stretching out a hand, she scratched the trunk, which oozed something that I was certain could not have been blood. Then the tree cracked, bent, and twisted, its bark distending and its branches distorting until it resolved itself into the shape of a dark-hued and ominous carriage, detailed with curling vines and death's heads. I was about to ask what manner of creature would pull it but then realised that I under no circumstances wanted to know the answer.

The door swung silently open and Ms. Haas entered without hesitation. And, first making certain to reassure myself that my clothes still housed my pistol and its ammunition, I followed her.

"Goodbye, dearies," called out Granny, as the carriage began to pull away under some mysterious power of its own. "And take heed, Shaharazad. My other gifts are yours to keep, but the potion will wear off at the stroke of midnight. And it wouldn't kill you to write occasionally."

Ms. Haas carefully leaned out of the window, her jackdaw flapping to keep its balance. "I thought you were dead. Also I hated you."

"You always were an ungrateful girl."

"And you were always a grasping, covetous, manipulative, iron-hearted . . ." My companion continued to hurl an increasingly inventive stream of pejoratives at Granny Liesl until she vanished out of sight. At which juncture she pulled her head back into the carriage, adjusted her gown, and said in quite a different tone, "You know, I did miss the dear old thing in a way."

I blinked. "She was flagrantly a monster."

"Aren't we all, Mr. Wyndham? Aren't we all?"

Then she settled back in her seat and closed her eyes contentedly. The jackdaw continued to stare at me in a manner I continued to find disturbing.

CHAPTER FORTY-ONE

❧

Vedunia

After some minutes, the carriage emerged onto the road and set a course that I fervently hoped would take us down the valley towards Vedunia. We would not, on this occasion, have a great deal of time in which to explore the many sites of historical and cultural interest that fine city has to offer. Readers who are interested in visiting Vedunia themselves may wish to purchase Ms. Zheng's excellent *Southern Aurwald and Nivale, including Guienne and Lothringar*, which, like all of the Zheng Guides, is a gold mine of practical advice for the commercial traveller.

For the purposes of this narrative, you need know only that it is a picturesque city of cobbled streets and golden spires with a spectacular cathedral in the architecturally lavish style of the Insular Church. It is renowned for its contributions to the worlds of patisserie and music, although its civic character took a turn for the melancholy after the strange and tragic fate of Crown Prince Florian, who, on his seventeenth birthday, ate of a poisoned apple and fell at once into a death-like slumber from which he has yet to stir. This unfortunate sequence of events has led to the rather peculiar local tradition of Kissing the Prince, popular amongst natives and tourists alike. Prince Florian's body lies in state in a glass coffin before the palace, where legend holds he may be awakened by a kiss from his true love. It is considered both good luck and a mark of respect for visitors to attempt to arouse the prince, although to date none have been successful. A fascinating peculiarity of Prince Florian's unusual condition is that, since he has not technically died, he remains crown prince of Nivale and, given that the enchantment under which he slumbers seems to have preserved his body from either age or decay, it is like that he will remain so in perpetuity. The consequence of this is that the Kaiserin of the Hundred Kingdoms now rules Nivale as queen regent, amongst her other titles.

It was late afternoon by the time we arrived in the city proper. And, while I was eager to start out at once in pursuit of Miss Viola and Miss Beck, my companion insisted that we had little to no hope of locating them by simply roaming the streets. The Austral Express included ample time for its passengers to experience the locations in which it stopped; we could be certain that the two ladies were currently loose in Vedunia but equally certain that they would return to the station in the evening, which would undoubtedly be the most efficacious way to intercept them. Therefore, Ms. Haas concluded with the triumphant air of one declaring mate in five moves, we had nothing to lose by going to dinner.

Thus, we repaired to a tiny restaurant in a somewhat obscure part of town, whose owner Ms. Haas had assisted with a matter of considerable personal delicacy some twenty-five years earlier. This left us somewhat overdressed for our environs, although, in truth, I felt far more comfortable with stripped wooden tables and rough benches than I did with my crushed velvet and silk hose. We dined on a local dish of thinly sliced veal coated in breadcrumbs, which, in the moment, seemed quite the finest meal I had ever taken, a reaction which may have owed something to my having subsisted on dried fruit and bottled water since leaving Khelathra-Ven some two days past. Ms. Haas ordered dessert before I had the chance to intervene.

"Are you honestly telling me," she said, when I questioned the necessity of the indulgence, "that your god took time out of its mighty works and divine labours in order to specifically prohibit its followers against eating chocolate desserts?"

"Oh yes, there are large sections of scripture devoted to the subject. We call it tort law."

She stared at me for a while, with her head quizzically cocked. "Was that a deliberate joke, Mr. Wyndham?"

"I'm sorry, I don't know what came over me."

"Well, since you've clearly committed yourself to a path of madcap frivolity, you might as have well have some cake."

"I'm not sure it's philosophically supportable to make one lapse excuse another."

"Were I inclined to take this debate seriously"—she plonked her elbows on the table—"I might advance the argument that if one violates an essentially arbitrary rule and in so doing finds it has precisely no negative consequences for oneself or for others, one might be not only justified but wise to conclude that there can be no harm in doing so again."

"I do not think," I replied, "that it is always correct to conclude that a thing which has been done safely once may safely be done with impunity."

"And that is why my life will always be far more interesting than yours. Now eat the dashed cake, man."

She did not say "dashed." I did, however, eat the cake. In truth, I found it rather rich for my tastes and its layers of apricot jam sat especially poorly with my day spent eating nothing but dried fruit on the *Clouded Skipper*. Nevertheless, the experience taken as a whole was so singular and strangely pleasant, despite the unfortunate circumstances of our visit, that I have been left ever since with a peculiar fondness for that variety of torte, and will seek it out in patisseries on special occasions.

We finished our meal at a pace I considered rather too leisurely given the urgency of our endeavour and departed shortly before sunset for the train station.

The Austral Express was a majestic blue-and-gold locomotive, every detail of whose design stood as testament to its unique marriage of technology and luxury. Passengers were already returning from their sojourn in Vedunia, some still milling about the platform making the most of the view over the hillside and others boarding the train with the unhurried ease of pleasure travellers. We made enquiries of the guard and were informed that Miss Viola and Miss Beck had not yet returned.

Taking up a position close to their cabin, it was not long before we espied the two ladies approaching, arm in arm. They both seemed relaxed and contented—even Miss Viola, despite the unrelaxing and discontenting circumstances that had led to their present holiday. That she showed no outward sign of the uncertainty she must have been feeling was testimony to either her deep affection for Miss Beck or her tremendous skill as a dissembler.

As they drew closer I realised that Miss Viola could on no account have failed to notice us, Ms. Haas being a recognisable figure even when she did not have a live jackdaw in her hair, and concluded therefore that her resolute failure to acknowledge our presence was a deliberate stratagem.

"Eirene," bellowed Ms. Haas. "We've got some very important news for you."

Miss Viola's smile faltered momentarily, and she bent down to whisper something to her fiancée before swiftly crossing the platform towards us. "This better not be one of your games, Shaharazad."

"Oh, it's a game, darling. But not mine."

"You have ten seconds," Miss Viola snapped, "to stop being gnomic. Or I put a pin in your eye and this time it's tipped with hagsbane."

Ms. Haas sighed. "Very well. Your former lover, and I appreciate that doesn't narrow it down, so your former lover the vampire, and in case *that* doesn't narrow it down either, your former lover the vampire

Contessa Ilona of Mircalla, is coming here right now to murder your girlfriend."

"Fiancée," I interjected.

"Because"—my companion rolled her eyes—"that little detail is so much more important than the erotically frenzied vampire who will be upon us any minute."

Miss Viola put her gloved fingers momentarily to Ms. Haas's lips, which had the somewhat unexpected effect of silencing her. "So, she's the one who wrote the letters?"

"Come now, Eirene, when was life ever that simple?"

"Are you really telling me that two completely different people are independently trying to ruin my life?"

"The question of whether the removal of Miss Beck would detract from your life or enhance it is still very much open to debate."

"Not to me," retorted Miss Viola.

Any continued defence she might have intended to make of her intended was interrupted by the sudden appearance at her elbow of the lady in question. "Eirene, what's going on?"

"This is Mr. Wyndham, who you know, and a friend of his from Khelathra-Ven. They were just leaving."

"I know it runs contrary to your nature," sneered Ms. Haas, "but this is one of those few situations in which telling the truth is actually safer than lying."

Miss Beck's eyes narrowed. "I'm not sure who you are, but I don't think I appreciate the tone you're taking with my fiancée."

"I am the sorceress Shaharazad Haas. And I am here to save your life."

"Much obliged, I'm sure." Miss Beck did not look at all obliged.

"I'm afraid," admitted Miss Viola, staring abashedly at the ground, "it's true . . . You know I haven't always lived the best kind of life."

Ms. Haas snorted. "You're too modest, Eirene. I'd argue that you've led the *very* best kind of life."

It was at this point that Miss Viola made certain remarks to the effect that Ms. Haas should keep her own counsel, but I shall not reproduce her exact phrasing for the sake of the lady's modesty.

"You know I don't care about any of that." Miss Beck slid a protective arm about Miss Viola's waist.

"There's a vampire coming to kill you," remarked Ms. Haas, wilfully ignoring, as ever, any suggestion that she refrain from comment. "You might start caring quite a lot, quite quickly."

"What? Why?" In context, I felt Miss Beck's reaction displayed commendable stoicism.

Ms. Haas opened her mouth to reply, but Miss Viola got in first. "We were lovers, Cora. Many years ago."

"And you're just mentioning this now?"

"I didn't want you to think less of me."

"It's a sweet sentiment, but if it gets me killed I'll be quite hacked off."

"Oh, Eirene." Ms. Haas clasped her hands over her heart with surprising sincerity. "She's delightful. I deeply regret calling her a dreary bourgeois kipper-peddling fart."

Miss Beck's generous mouth thinned a little. "I'm so glad I've got your blessing, though I'll have you know there's good money in kippers. Now can we get back to my being murdered?"

"We need to run, Cora," said Miss Viola, stepping clear of her fiancée's embrace and reaching for her hand instead. "I'm sure we can get lost in the city."

"I'm not sure that's going to work. I mean, she's tracked us this far and I don't want to spend my entire marriage running from an immortal."

Miss Viola cupped Miss Beck's face and drew her close. "Trust me, I've been doing this my whole life. There's a time to think about the next ten years and there's a time to think about the next ten minutes."

"Well, isn't this adorable," purred Ms. Haas. "But, have no fear. I didn't fly three hundred miles and let a witch destroy my best aeronautical jacket just to watch you get exsanguinated on a railway platform. I have a plan."

"Is part of the plan," asked Miss Beck, with the air of someone who has been troubled by something for a while and only just found the right opportunity to mention it, "having a bird on your head?"

"No, darling, that's just for fun. The plan involves Wyndham and I taking your place aboard the train while you two have a lovely romantic evening by the Verdun and take the first airship back to Khelathra-Ven in the morning."

"And what if your plan doesn't work?"

"Then we'll all be dead. What a silly question."

They took a little more persuading, but neither Miss Beck nor Miss Viola was able to raise any serious objections to Ms. Haas's proposed course of action. They surrendered their tickets to us and left the station, arm in arm once more, although no longer painting quite so ideal a picture of carefree young love. Ms. Haas and I, for our part, turned and boarded the Austral Express, there to settle ourselves into our cabin and await the coming of the vampire.

❧

CHAPTER FORTY-TWO

The Austral Express

It was perhaps a rather tragic condemnation of my lifestyle that the suite which we had taken over from Miss Viola and Miss Beck was substantially more pleasant than our lodgings at Martyrs Walk. Indeed, it was rather more pleasant than any of my prior residences, save the two terms at university when, owing to a clerical error, I was permitted to reside in one of the sets of rooms normally reserved for the masters. The cabin where we waited was oak panelled and sumptuously upholstered, with a double bed set into an alcove at the back of the room. Obviously, we did not make use of this particular item of furniture, as it would have been both unseemly and strategically unwise. Instead, I settled into a velvet-covered armchair and Ms. Haas, with no regard for the comfort or convenience of her resident jackdaw, stretched out on the sofa. The bird itself finally quit her hair and perched on the complimentary bottle of Avienese sparkling wine that had been set out in readiness for the couple's return.

We did not have to wait long before there was a hiss of steam and we pulled smoothly away from the station. Under different circumstances it could have been a quite charming experience, there being something almost magical in travelling so comfortably through the darkness that enfolded the valleys and rivers of the Nivalese countryside. But it was hard to enjoy the fairy-tale glimmer of the moonlight across the landscape when you knew that at any moment a night-stalking she-devil could fall upon you from the shadows.

I prepared for this eventuality by reloading my pistol with silver bullets and loosening the cap of the hip flask that contained the water of suspect holiness. Ms. Haas prepared by taking rather too much of the wine, to the chagrin of the jackdaw, which was forced to seek alternate lodgings on a corner shelf holding a variety of decorative objets d'art.

"Ms. Haas," I remarked as she poured herself a third drink, "should we perhaps be taking steps to secure the points of entry?"

"I agree that would ordinarily be sensible, but any ward I could place would not only rob us of the element of surprise but also reveal at once that we are not Eirene and her fishmonger."

"But surely we are at a significant disadvantage if we take no measures to limit our enemy's lines of attack."

Ms. Haas tossed back her beverage with an alacrity that did not trouble me at the time, but in retrospect I realise was a criminal waste of a fine vintage. "We're talking about a vampire, not a Marvosi raiding party. However she gets in, which I suspect will be either through the window or door, or percolating through the floor like mist, she will undoubtedly take a moment to savour the end of the hunt."

"I hope you are correct."

"I am always correct, Mr. Wyndham." She rearranged herself languidly on the sofa. "The Contessa is feeling betrayed and thwarted. She is seeking to confront her ex-lover as much as to eliminate a rival."

"Perhaps," I said slowly, "I am being overly romantic, but I do not quite understand how the Contessa expects that murdering Miss Viola's fiancée in front of her will be of assistance in winning back her affections."

Ms. Haas shrugged. "Vampire."

With that we both fell silent. Minutes passed, then hours, and my gaze kept returning to the small carriage clock that sat on the shelf next to the jackdaw. As its hands neared midnight I could not conceal my concerns any longer.

"Ms. Haas," I whispered, "if the Contessa does not arrive soon, Granny Liesl's potion will cease to be efficacious."

"That is a distinct possibility, but shh. The Contessa is almost certainly on the train already, and vampires have excellent hearing."

Despite what passed for my companion's reassurances, my unease only intensified until, on the stroke of twelve, the cabin door opened.

The figure who entered was at once magnificent and revolting. She was clad in a high-collared black gown, against which the unnatural pallor of her skin seemed almost to gleam. Her head was utterly bald, her ears tapering to animalistic points, and behind her voluptuously red lips her teeth were a jigsaw of needle points and jagged edges.

The figure of Ms. Haas upon the sofa caught her attention at once and the Contessa advanced towards her, taloned, too-long fingers grasping covetously at the empty air. Her shadow skittered across the wall, its movements not quite matching those of its owner. I thought it strange at the time that she did not notice me, for, while I was wearing black in a dark room, a vampire's night vision is as acute as its hearing. At the time I attributed her oversight to the passion of the moment but, on reflection, I suspect that the strange gifts of Granny Liesl played a part in the matter.

It took the vampiress only moments to realise that the lady she approached was neither Miss Beck nor Miss Viola, and she recoiled with a hiss. "What treachery is this?"

Ms. Haas propped herself up on her elbows and, even in the semi-darkness, I could see the effort it required. I hoped fervently that the intruder was not so attuned to the nuances of my companion's well-being as I. "It's not treachery. It's the oldest trick in the book. Now, are we going to talk like civilised people or do you wish to earn the ire of the sorceress Shaharazad Haas?"

"You are Shaharazad Haas? The woman who defeated the demon wyrm of Lakshmere? Who rescued the Princess Elisabet from Comte Korvin? Who burned Castle Zarovich to the ground?" The Contessa raised a heavy brow. "I thought you'd be taller."

"Well, I am lying down."

"A strange choice for one confronting a *vampyr*."

Ms. Haas put a hand to her mouth to stifle a yawn. "I'm very confident and very lazy."

"It is not"—the Contessa's shadow put a claw to its chin—"that you have injured yourself in pursuit of me, and now find yourself unable to stand?"

"That is certainly a possibility."

"Then what is stopping me from falling upon you right now and feasting on your heart's blood?"

"Maybe nothing. Or maybe"—Ms. Haas indicated the empty wineglass on the table opposite—"I have consumed an alchemical concoction that has transmuted my blood into the living fire of the mad god that some superstitiously revere as the Creator. And, should you bite me, it will be the last thing you do before you perish in a brief but exquisite moment of terrifying agony. Now admit it, that does sound more like me."

The Contessa paused for a moment. "You know, I think I'll take the risk."

"Oh, bother."

At this juncture, several things occurred simultaneously. The Contessa lunged for Ms. Haas, but the jackdaw, which had hitherto shown no signs of aggression, swooped from its perch and made a vicious attack against the vampire's eyes. This briefly arrested her attack, but in a matter of seconds she had slashed it from the air with a swipe of her talons. The poor creature tumbled to the ground, where it vanished in a billow of shadow and feathers. The distraction had been minor but afforded me just sufficient opportunity to snatch up my hip flask and empty its contents over the Contessa's head.

Wet, angry, and perhaps a little perplexed, she spun to face me. If she was presently experiencing the excoriating power of the Creator's wrath against her and all her benighted kind, she was doing a very good job of hiding it. "What the —— was that?"

I have removed an offending item from the Contessa's vocabulary but could find no appropriate substitute. Before I could make reply, her fingers closed around my throat and I was lifted bodily from the ground. The pressure on my carotid arteries, coupled with the general sense of disorientation that came of being picked up like a child's toy, limited my capacity to respond. I did, however, muster the where-withal to discharge my pistol into the Contessa's body. The silver bullets proved somewhat more efficacious than the flask of not-at-all-holy water I had been dutifully carrying since we had left Khelathra-Ven, although they were not so efficacious as to prevent my attacker from slamming me through the armchair I had just vacated.

When I had regained my senses sufficiently to be once more aware of what was happening around me, I saw Ms. Haas had, by some miracle, come to her feet and, swaying slightly, was once more chanting the private name of the Creator. Pale fire flickered in her eyes, but before she could complete the incantation the Contessa seized her by the hair and the waist and plunged her fangs into my companion's exposed throat.

To my horror, Ms. Haas went limp, her head falling back in an attitude of uncharacteristic surrender. I reached for my gun but found it nowhere to hand, and between the rigours of our journey and the exertions of the current battle, I was unable to rise in time to intervene. Just as I was coming to the perturbing realisation that this was likely the end of us both, the cabin door opened, revealing a man in a guard's uniform.

"Run," I cried, seeing no reason that an innocent railway employee should sacrifice himself for our doomed escapade.

Whereupon his image shimmered and in his place appeared a slight figure in a dark suit and a pallid mask. They raised a pistol and fired three shots into the Contessa's back. She crumpled to the floor, Ms. Haas doing likewise. I scrambled across the cabin to offer my companion what little protection I could and found her barely conscious, her dress dark with blood. Glancing up in the hope that our rescuer could offer further assistance, I realised they had vanished.

✿

CHAPTER FORTY-THREE

The Vampiress

There was little more I could do to aid Ms. Haas and so I thought it best to retrieve my pistol, which I eventually located underneath the table. I reloaded it and kept it trained on the Contessa, lest she recover her faculties before my companion and offer us mischief. Happily, Ms. Haas came to first. Dragging herself shakily to the sofa, she was silent for a troubling duration.

"Good shooting, Captain," she said at last.

"Thank you, but it was not my doing. We benefited from the unexpected apparition of a mysterious stranger."

Ms. Haas frowned. "Intriguing, but a matter best addressed after we have resolved the immediate problem of the Contessa."

It soon became apparent, however, that the Contessa was not our most immediate problem. The recent discharge of several rounds of shot, along with the rather extensive destruction of property, had attracted the attention of the actual guards, who appeared now in the doorway where the false guard had been only minutes earlier. To my surprise and relief, they were very understanding, accepting quite readily Ms. Haas's explanation that the firearms had been used in self-defence against the vampire who still lay on the floor of the cabin and who would, if not neutralised, have continued to pose a threat to the passengers of the train. Looking back I realise that, a railway guard being in no way qualified to do battle with either a mistress of the undead or a sorceress, they were likely more than happy to allow the one to take care of the other, any alternative course of action being, as the saying goes, *more than their job's worth.*

"Quickly," continued Ms. Haas when the attendants had departed, "pass me a piece of that wineglass."

I did as I was asked and at once regretted it when Ms. Haas took the shard I offered her and immediately began carving a sequence of blasphemous symbols into her forearm. "Are you certain that's quite necessary?"

"Not entirely. We could just cut her head off and burn the body."

This put me in something of a quandary. On the one hand, it was an obscure but axiomatic tenet of my faith that vampires were irredeemable abominations in the sight of the Creator. Further, I knew for a fact that the Contessa had murdered at least one person, probably several more, to say nothing of her choice of husbands, which I considered extremely tawdry. On the other hand, there seemed to be something fundamentally wrong in decapitating a defenceless woman, even if her defencelessness was worryingly temporary.

"What exactly are you doing?" I enquired.

"I wasn't entirely bluffing when I told the Contessa that biting me would be a bad idea. You'd think at her age she'd know better than to form an intimate connection with a powerful sorceress." She slid off the sofa and knelt by the Contessa's side, tracing in blood on the vampire's brow marks that mirrored the ones she had previously inscribed on her arm. "It won't give me very much control over her, but it will be enough to stop her coming after me or snapping your neck like a twig in an act of petty vengeance."

"Thank you. I'm most grateful."

"And at the very least, I should be able to compel her to hear us out on the subject of our dear Eirene." She sat back on her heels. "You know, even riddled with silver bullets I would have expected her to be stirring by now."

In the light of Ms. Haas's assurances, I lowered my weapon. "Is that not to our advantage?"

"It is never to our advantage for matters to run contrary to my expectations."

With that, Ms. Haas began a rather more intimate inspection of the Contessa's body, at which point I looked away so that I might not transgress the bounds of decency. What followed involved some inauspiciously fleshly sounds, on whose cause I did not, in the moment, like to speculate.

"Now, this is interesting," remarked my companion.

"What," came the Contessa's voice wearily, "is interesting?"

I turned around to see Ms. Haas, bloody to the wrists, holding a number of bullets in the palm of her hand, and the Contessa lying on the floor with her eyes open, wearing an expression of considerable displeasure.

Ms. Haas closed her fingers over the bullets and returned to the sofa. "None of your business. Let's talk about Eirene."

"That is none of *your* business." The Contessa folded her arms across her chest and, her body entirely rigid, swept up into a standing position. "I am a daughter of the immortal nobility of Mircalla and I will reclaim what is mine."

"I suppose you could, but why would you want to?"

An expression of bewilderment passed fleetingly over the Contessa's face. "What do you mean? Is this some kind of trickery?"

"No trickery. It's just that Eirene is a disaster who ruins everything she touches. Fabulous in bed, of course, but *so* high maintenance."

"What is this . . . high maintenance?"

Ms. Haas plucked one of the complimentary chocolates that had fallen to the floor during the kerfuffle and popped it into her mouth.

"Well, let's put it like this. We stumbled across your little murder plan because we were working our way down a list of people who might be looking for revenge against Eirene for all the ways she's stitched them up, set them up, screwed them over, or otherwise wrecked their lives."

"She has spirit," returned the Contessa. "I like a woman with spirit."

"Then get another one. I'm sure the world is full of independent-minded maidens who would love to be swept off their feet by a brooding aristocrat like you."

"My love for Eirene transcends eternity." The Contessa spread a clawed hand, then closed it acquisitively. "We are bound forever in blood and passion."

Ms. Haas uttered a long groan. "Oh, just stop it. You and I both know you're only interested in her now because you've suddenly realised you can't have her. You've had years to hunt her down and make her your immortal bride."

"I cannot allow her to defy me."

"You've met Eirene. Do you really think turning her into a vampire is going to stop her defying you?"

After a moment of thought, the Contessa hung her head and slumped onto the sofa next to Ms. Haas. "You know, this was so much easier eight hundred years ago. You'd just go down to the village and they'd tie a pretty girl to a stake for you."

"There are still places where they'll do that, many of them for a very reasonable fee."

"It's not the same. The people nowadays. They have all these crazy ideas. When I was a girl, peasants were happy to be peasants." The Contessa propped her cheek glumly against her hand. "To tell you the truth, the only reason I came back to Khelathra-Ven was because things weren't working out back home. One evening I say to my seneschal, 'Go out and get a baby and put it in a sack and bring it back to me so I can sate the hunger of my vile progeny.' And he says, 'Oh, mistress, we can't do that anymore. The burgomasters, they get very angry when we put the babies in the sacks. There'll be another revolution, mistress. Remember what happened in Pesh, mistress.'" She sighed. "What is the world coming to when you can't devour the children of your serfs?"

"Tell me about it," drawled Ms. Haas. "It's socioeconomic reform gone mad."

The conversation continued in this vein on and off the rest of the way to Liohtberg, Ms. Haas and the Contessa exchanging anecdotes about the iniquities of the modern world and the personal shortcomings of Eirene Viola. On this latter subject, their observations became increasingly intimate to the point that I felt compelled to leave the cabin. It was not, you understand, that I begrudged my companion the satisfaction she found in the society of the Contessa, but I fear that the ladies brought out the worst in each other, which was perhaps to be expected since one was a black-hearted creature of the night without compassion or remorse, and the other vampire. I make this observation with comical intent, my editor having expressed concerns that readers may consider me, in his words, stuffy. Besides, I believe Ms. Haas would have appreciated the comment and been gratified to know that at least some part of her sense of humour appears to have rubbed off on me.

In any case, the most immediate consequence of the two ladies' newfound (and mildly inappropriate) bonhomie was that I had cause to spend a lot of my time in the lounge car, since they grew increasingly comfortable in each other's company and chose to act upon that comfort in ways best transacted privately.

For my own part I was not unhappy with this outcome since the lavish appointments of the Austral Express afforded me an opportunity for relaxation such as I had not experienced in years. I made the acquaintance of several interesting travellers, played several stimulating games of chess, and read a variety of newspapers from across the Hundred Kingdoms and beyond. Thus, in our various ways, my companion and I passed an eminently satisfactory journey and arrived in Liohtberg.

✣

CHAPTER FORTY-FOUR

Aurwald Mail Flight 121

The remarkable luxury of the Austral Express threw into sharp relief the inconvenience we experienced when expediency and economy demanded that we return to Khelathra-Ven by mail coach. My companion complained bitterly of the necessity not only of sitting alongside commercial travellers but also, as she put it, being bundled into a box with the tedious correspondence of strangers. The carriage itself was miserably uncomfortable, although there was no denying the majesty of the four winged horses that drew it. Somewhat less majestic were the two other travellers with whom we were forced to share our three-day, four-stage journey. One was a large man from Hansea, a trader of sorts in exotic fauna who insisted upon bringing with him a box filled with live snakes. The other was a well-dressed lady who spoke with a slight Kendish accent and evinced the enviable capacity to sleep through literally anything, including a minor incident in which one of the snakes slithered free of its confines and was unceremoniously hurled out of the window by Ms. Haas, who declared herself quite out of patience with the whole situation.

Despite the utter lack of anything resembling privacy, Ms. Haas seemed entirely at ease discussing the latest points of information and evidence that had arisen as a consequence of our most recent adventure.

"These bullets," she said, ignoring the snoring Kendish woman and the ill-concealed interest of the merchant, "which I extracted from the Contessa's spine would seem to imply something very specific about the nature of your mysterious stranger. The peculiar metal of which they're cast, combined with the strange sigils on the casing, marks them out as Carcosan in origin. And when taken in conjunction with your description of our rescuer's attire and, indeed, with the broader fact that this whole affair hinges on the matter of blackmail, there is a very good chance that we're dealing with the Repairers of Reputations."

I leaned in and lowered my voice, in at least a token effort to avoid being overheard by the other passengers. "Forgive my ignorance, but I have little familiarity with the organisation in question."

"They are spies, Mr. Wyndham," announced my companion cheerfully. "Once the loyal enforcers of the crowned heads of Carcosa, they now serve the party with suspiciously similar fervour. And given that one of the names on Eirene's list happens to be a high-ranking member of the new order it seems we may at last have our man."

"But why would he rescue us from a vampire?"

"Firstly, it almost certainly wasn't him; it was one of his agents. Secondly, that agent probably didn't realise we'd pulled a switch at the station. Thirdly, if you're planning to ruin a woman's life, drag her away from her home, and force her into marriage, you don't really want to contend with a malicious, scheming immortal who has exactly the same plan."

I adjusted my cuffs, still unaccustomed to wearing so much lace. "Miss Viola certainly inspires strong reactions."

"In my experience, people tend to bring their reactions with them. It's certainly true that Eirene has been involved with some colossal ——" And here Ms. Haas used a disparaging colloquialism. "Myself included. But I think that says more about circumstances than her character. Though if you tell her I said so, I shall lay upon you the twice-blinding curse of Atlach-Nar."

"Fear not," I reassured her. "Nobody will ever learn that you once said something that wasn't entirely heartless and uncalled for."

Of course, in relating this incident in these pages I have now broken that promise. I take solace in the fact that it was largely made in jest, and that it represents one of only four times on which I have failed to keep my word to her.

CHAPTER FORTY-FIVE

Further Developments

As enjoyable as our sojourn aboard the Austral Express had been, there was nonetheless a certain warm sensation of homecoming associated with our return to 221b Martyrs Walk. The feeling was rather unexpected, putting me in mind of the time long ago when I had first said to my varsity friends that I was "going home" and meant returning to my room in college rather than returning to my parents' house in Ey. It was a sense of natural belonging that I had not felt in many years. My satisfaction was marred by the realisation that I would have to explain nearly a week's absence to my employers, and by the unexpected arrival of Miss Viola about ten minutes after I'd put the kettle on.

I emerged into the sitting room to find her standing over Ms. Haas, who, having shown no inclination to shed her Vedunian finery, was stretched across the chaise in a cascade of red satin.

"I would have thought," my companion was saying, "given the trivial detail that we saved your life a few days ago, you could show at least a little gratitude."

Miss Viola was dismissive of this notion in colourful terms. "Cora," she continued, "is going to the Myrmidons. She says it's company policy in cases of blackmail. I told her that I am not part of her company and, in the likely event that those upjumped hoodlums can't keep their mouths shut, that her parents will find out, they'll cancel the wedding, and whoever is doing this will get exactly what he, she, or they want."

"That's actually a rather interesting datum."

"Oh, I'm so glad"—Miss Viola attempted to kick Ms. Haas in the shins but made contact only with her voluminous skirts—"my incipient ruination is an interesting datum."

"Might I remind you that I am conducting this analysis for your benefit?"

"Then conduct it. What's interesting?"

Ms. Haas lit a pipe with the enthusiasm of one who has been denied access to tobacco for far too long. "Well, I can scarcely believe I have to point this out to you, but your blackmailer's behaviour is highly atypical. As you have just observed, the action into which this individual is attempting to coerce you—that is, the breaking off of your engagement with Miss Beck—is one into which you would necessarily be forced were they simply to reveal the information they have to Miss Beck's family. They are, in a sense, not asking you to do anything they couldn't do for you."

"And why," sighed Miss Viola, "is that so terribly intriguing to you?"

"It suggests your enemy is not your enemy, or not *simply* your enemy. Their goal is highly specific—the breaking off of your engagement to Miss Beck with the minimum possible level of collateral scandal. It was this rather obvious point that led me to suspect Miss Beck's associates, although I swiftly eliminated them after that silly matter at the ball. So now we are left with only two possibilities."

There was a silence, which Miss Viola seemed to find unreasonably provoking. "Which are?"

"Number one. That the culprit is, indeed, Citizen Icarius Castaigne of Carcosa and he wishes to force you to his side without rendering you an unsuitable wife or surrendering any leverage he might hold over you.

Number two is something rather more interesting." She paused again, smiling to herself. "Number two is a theorem not yet fully formed, but which I will share with you in the fullness of time."

Miss Viola did not appear to take this well and expressed her displeasure in no certain terms. I attempted to defuse the situation with tea and when that stratagem proved inefficacious endeavoured instead to change the subject. "Might it be possible," I asked, "to prevail upon the Myrmidons to treat the matter with discretion?"

Ms. Haas smirked through a haze of smoke. "You could write everything the Myrmidons know on the subject of discretion on the back of zero postcards."

"Which is why I am here," snarled Miss Viola. "This is your fault. You fix it."

"Darling, this is not at all my fault. The moral of this story is that you should address the issues in your relationship before they show up at railway stations trying to murder people."

"You are the last sentient being in this, or any other, world who is qualified to lecture me on maintaining a healthy love life."

"Yes, but"—and here Ms. Haas wagged her pipestem in a manner that even I, as a dispassionate third party, found condescending—"I'm not the one trying to marry a fishmonger. Now come along, let us see if we can persuade Lawson to leave this matter in more capable hands."

We took a hansom to New Arcadia Yard. Ordinarily one would not be permitted simply to walk in off the street and demand to speak to a ranking member of the Augurs. Ms. Haas, however, had little time for *ordinarily* and, after a certain amount of hectoring and no small amount of grandstanding, we were guided by a beleaguered constable to Second Augur Lawson's office. He seemed neither surprised nor pleased to see us. Miss Beck, who was already in the middle of explaining the situation to him, appeared to be more of one but less of the other.

There was a brief moment in which several persons exchanged

significant glances. Then Second Augur Lawson said, "Let me guess, Haas. This seemingly inconsequential case of blackmail is, in fact, the key to a deeper conspiracy with profound implications for civic security."

"On the contrary"—my companion casually knocked a pile of papers from the desk and perched herself in their place—"I suspect it is entirely personal. Which is why you should drop it."

Miss Viola put a hand on her fiancée's shoulder. "I told you I was having this handled."

"And I told you," returned Miss Beck, "that we had to go to the proper authorities. I mean no disrespect, Ms. Haas, and I'm sure you're very good at what you do, but this is a crime and it's a matter for the law."

Ms. Haas liberated a packet of tobacco from her décolletage and her pipe from somewhere beneath her skirts. "Good to know you're embarking on a lifetime together with absolutely no irreconcilable philosophical differences."

"Can we bring our attention back to the extortion?" suggested the Second Augur in some exasperation.

Miss Viola fixed him with her lambent gaze. "I'm sorry to have wasted your time, but I'm the victim here and I do not wish this matter to be pursued."

"I'm afraid it's not up to you, miss. Strange as it may seem, my job is not to protect you; it is to protect the city of Khelathra-Ven, and I can't let blackmailers run around making demands of upstanding citizens. It's you this week; it might be someone else next week."

"I assure you," put in Ms. Haas, "it will not be someone else next week. This is a very specific matter."

The Second Augur drummed his metal fingers against the arm of his chair. "Is it that time already, Haas? Go on, then. Tell me how I'm looking for a florid-faced man over six feet tall with unusually long fingernails."

"Right now you are looking for nobody it is within your power to prosecute. Although I am still entertaining a number of theories, I am certain that the blackmailer is a native of Carcosa and resides beyond your jurisdiction."

"How convenient for you."

"Mr. Lawson," Ms. Haas drawled, "you know full well I would never mislead the official force. To do so would be to pass up an opportunity to show you how infinitely superior my methods are to yours."

"I can talk to the authorities in Carcosa."

"In this situation, I suspect the authorities may be at least partially responsible."

The Second Augur rolled his eyes. "I know you said it wasn't, but it's beginning to sound a lot like this seemingly inconsequential case of blackmail is, in fact, the key to a deeper conspiracy with profound implications for civic security."

"Conspiracy yes. Security implications no."

Miss Beck put her hand on Miss Viola's and turned to look at her. "Conspiracies? What is this woman talking about?"

There was a tense silence, before Miss Viola replied, "When I was a child my parents arranged a betrothal for me. Shaharazad thinks he's still alive, has attained some status in the party, and may wish to exert a claim over me."

"So you only told me about the vampire because she tried to kill us. You only told me about the blackmail because nothing else would explain why these total strangers"—she gestured at Ms. Haas and myself—"turned up to save us. And you're only telling me you used to be engaged because I went to the Augurs and somebody else brought it up."

Miss Viola flushed. "I've done a lot of things I'm not proud of—"

"You're not joking."

"While I could watch your engagement implode all day," interrupted Ms. Haas, "I think the key point right now is that the prime suspect in this investigation is a foreign national with governmental immunity who lives in a city orbiting a distant star in an alien reality with which we have no extradition treaty. As such, and painful as I'm sure it is for him, the Second Augur must surely admit that I am far better placed to resolve this matter than he and his men will ever be. It's a sordid mess of sex and politics, Lawson, neither of which is your strong suit."

He blinked slowly. "I'll thank you not to pass comment on my suits, strong or otherwise. So here's what's going to happen. You"—he indicated Miss Viola—"are going to give me every item of correspondence you have received from this mysterious extortionist. I will pursue this case on the assumption that Ms. Haas's theory is correct and that we are dealing with agents of a foreign power. If Ms. Haas chooses to travel to Carcosa and pursue the matter more directly, that is up to her. Now will everyone kindly get the heck out of my office." He did not say "heck."

"I'm so glad you've seen reason. Come, Wyndham."

Ms. Haas swept out, her skirts disturbing several important-looking files as she did so. The other ladies followed in her wake, matters clearly unresolved between them. My sense of order and propriety, however, did not permit me to quit the office without making some effort to ameliorate the chaos that we had brought into it. I stooped and began gathering up the fallen papers.

"Mr. Wyndham," said the Second Augur, "are you attempting to unlawfully access privileged information?"

I stopped dead. "N-no. Absolutely not."

"You are a right berk, you know that?"

"I'm not sure I've ever heard it in those words, but others have expressed similar sentiments."

"A little bird tells me you were involved with that business on the Austral Express: Vampire Attack Thwarted by Heroic Travellers." The

Second Augur swung back in his chair and folded his hands behind his head. "No pictures and no names, of course, but for someone who claims to hate publicity, Haas is remarkably good at getting publicity."

"I'm sure the incident has been exaggerated. The confrontation was brief, and my involvement was minimal."

He huffed out a sigh. "I'm going to be very upset with Haas if she gets you killed."

"I thought you said your duty was to the city, not to its citizens."

"That I did." His eyes were steady on mine for a too-long moment. "Enjoy Carcosa."

Somewhat confused, I made my way to the hansom. Ms. Haas did not comment on my lateness but smiled at me enigmatically.

※

CHAPTER FORTY-SIX

The Coral Towers

The day we were to depart for Carcosa, Ms. Haas accosted me in my bedroom. She was wearing a crumpled suit that looked as if she had been wearing it for weeks, although I knew for a fact that she had not.

"Come, Wyndham," she said, "we have a submersible to catch and you will need to change clothes. We are to enter hostile territory undercover and if you persist in walking around dressed like an itinerant preacher at a harvest festival you will be severely compromising our ability to pass as innocuous travellers."

"Might my cover not be that I am an itinerant preacher en route to a harvest festival?"

"Don't be clever, Captain. Now change into this."

She threw a pile of clothes onto my bed. I was pleased to see that they were somewhat more conservative than the last set of garments into which our adventures had forced me, consisting as they did of a grey wool suit with a matching waistcoat, a white shirt, and a paisley print necktie that I personally found a little on the garish side.

Once my companion had decided that more important matters lay elsewhere, thus restoring to me my privacy, I swiftly reattired myself, completing the ensemble with an overcoat and narrow-brimmed felt hat. As disguises went, it at least made up in modesty what it lacked in honesty. I descended to the sitting room, where I found Ms. Haas waiting with her characteristic lack of patience. She extended towards me a document which, on inspection, proved to be a set of traveller's papers, asserting that I was Mr. Anthony Childers, a citizen of Athra, and that the Council of Interested Parties requested that I be allowed to travel freely without let or hindrance.

"It should go without saying," she remarked, "that what we are about to do is terribly illegal. On this side of the portals, it will get you into serious trouble with the Augurs. On the other, it will get you shot in the back of the head."

Neither of these outcomes appealed to me. "And I take it there is no better way to bring Citizen Castaigne to justice?"

"An interesting question. The difficulty, of course, lies in the fact that we have such radically different notions of what constitutes *better*. And, for that matter, of what constitutes justice. Now let's go, and remember that, once we reach Carcosa, I shall be going by Kim Greene."

"Are you quite certain," I asked, as we climbed into the waiting hansom, "that these papers will pass muster at the border?"

Ms. Haas settled herself into the corner of the cab, draping one leg languidly over the other. "Not especially. The documents you carry are designed to withstand casual inspection, not close scrutiny. Fortunately, I do not intend for that to be an issue. We will not enter the city by the conventional route."

"I was under the impression that there is only one way into Carcosa."

"My dear man," she said with a sigh, "there isn't only one way into anywhere. The cosmos is like a worm-riddled skirting board. It's simply a matter of wriggling through the right hole."

"And you can find the, um, right hole?"

"I can't, but I know someone who can. We have an appointment at the Coral Towers."

I had expected something less drastic, although, given what I had experienced since moving in with the sorceress Shaharazad Haas, I could not say why. The Coral Towers were the ancient palace-prisons of the Eternal Lords of Ven and one did not approach them without very good cause and without having exhausted all other possible recourse. To say that seeking the aid of a near-impotent, quasi-living sorcerer lord in order to infiltrate an alien city once ruled by a mad god and now governed by a populist bureaucracy famed for its efficient brutality seemed unwise would be, at the very least, an understatement. I had, however, learned by this point that questioning Ms. Haas's choices in these matters would prove utterly futile.

Thus, I found myself boarding a public submersible and descending to the depths of Ven for the second time that month. Although the Coral Towers were, in many ways, the most perilous part of Ven they were also one of the most accessible. The Eternal Lords, having no need to fear assault or invasion, and requiring the intervention of legates and messengers to make their presence felt in the outside world, had established the travel routes through Ven such that it is easier to pass close by the towers than to avoid them. Even the hermetically sealed pipes and passages used by the city's air-breathing inhabitants have connections to the Coral Towers. We were therefore able to disembark our submersible at an airlock station and make our way to our destination both dry and on foot.

An unfortunate fact of travel in these parts of Ven is that, since the habitable parts of the city are wholly self-contained, one never has the opportunity to admire the majesty of Ven proper, except through the occasional tiny and always crowded porthole. Indeed, there are many who find it rather disconcerting to be encased entirely in creaking, century-old steel, conscious with every unexpected drip and passing tremor of the great weight of water pressing down atop one. As a student, I found the whole experience a mixture of romantic and depressing, for there are few things that simultaneously engender those two contradictory emotions so completely as gazing out upon an impossibly delicate spire of pink coral and white marble through a grime-encrusted window in a leaky cabin from which you have singularly failed to banish the pervasive smell of damp.

Ms. Haas seemed as familiar with this place as she had with everywhere else we had been and led me with brisk, confident strides through the crowded walking tubes and to one specific tower, its entrance a mere fissure in the coral wall through which a small side tunnel had been rather inelegantly driven.

The gap seemed that it would barely accommodate us, and its sharp, rocky edges scraped at my hands and face as I squeezed through. On the other side was a sight most wondrous, but my editor informs me it will pleasurably heighten dramatic tension if I withhold my description of it until the next instalment of this narrative. He asks also that I remind the reader to be on the lookout for the next edition of *The Strait* magazine, in which he, she, ze, or they may vicariously experience my arrival in the domain of an Eternal Lord of Ven.

CHAPTER FORTY-SEVEN

❧

Walking Upwards Unmaking

My first thought on our emergence into the tower of the Eternal Lord was that I could see no way for us to go back. We stood on a platform of red coral some thirty feet across in the centre of which floated a decayed armillary sphere depicting an unfamiliar solar system. The sphere, the platform, and we ourselves were suspended in a vast and star-bestrewn void through which strange lights streamed like carnival ribbons in colours I cannot now recall but see sometimes in my dreams. Ms. Haas led me onto a staircase which arced out over empty space from where we stood and then curved upwards and backwards, leading to a second platform some way above us. The steps were barnacle-rough and kelp-slick, with neither handrails nor any visible means of support, which led me to proceed in a cautious fashion. Had I not served beyond the Unending Gate I would perhaps have found the experience more disorientating, but I had long developed the habit of focusing on the necessity of the task ahead, rather than peculiarities of the vistas around me. For all that it hovered unaided over a limitless starscape this was, after all, just a staircase.

At the summit, a woman sat upon a throne of shattered jade and tarnished silver. I say woman, but so human a term does not begin to capture the shifting nexus of past and future potentiality that was embodied in the being before us. To look upon an Eternal Lord of Ven is to witness all they are, have ever been, or may ever be, and so she was at once a laughing girl on the streets of a long-vanished city, a warrior queen in samite robes, a fish-eaten corpse in a drowned palace, and a vast, tentacled leviathan, dead and dreaming of forgotten glories. As we drew nearer, I saw her eyes across every version of herself were lightless wells of utter unbeing, and recognised the mark of the Empress of Nothing. Her name, I would later learn, was Walking Upwards Unmaking. This, too, was a scar from her battle against the Ruler of All That Is Not; the true names of the Eternal Lords having been taken along with their eyes and their empire.

She did not speak, but after she did not speak I remembered her having spoken. *What brings you to this moment, Shaharazad Haas?*

"I need a favour."

You need too many favours, Shaharazad Haas. In a thousand realities, I have already killed you.

"Well, that's fine," returned Ms. Haas rather warily. "As long as you're not going to do it in this one."

Walking Upwards Unmaking slowly turned over one childlike hand, one silver-gauntleted hand, one mouldering fleshless hand, and my companion clutched at her chest, a look of horror flashing across her face as she crumpled to her knees. And now the Eternal Lord held a human heart in her tightening fist, blood dripping between her fingers and seeping into the coral as the sorceress Shaharazad Haas died at my feet.

No. Not in this reality. And then none of that had happened.

Ms. Haas swallowed. Besides this and a subtle shifting of her balance, she gave surprisingly little indication of having just been struck dead in an alternate timeline. "Thank you." She bowed her head in a jarringly respectful manner. "But I need to travel to Carcosa and cannot go by the normal gates."

Walking Upwards Unmaking made no reply. And then time and space and memory shifted through ninety-five degrees. Dancers whirled in a ballroom while a figure in ragged yellow robes stood above them all. Pale, misshapen towers vanished into fog-choked skies. A stranger in a pale mask stared at me from an alley in an unknown city.

My companion and I stood on the shores of a grey and turbid lake. Across the water, twin suns set and black stars rose.

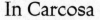

CHAPTER FORTY-EIGHT

In Carcosa

"That," observed my companion, "could have gone a lot worse."

"You died."

"I went to ask a favour from an Eternal Lord of Ven. My death was one of the least terrible possibilities."

"In all candour, I'm not sure why she assisted us at all."

Ms. Haas knelt down and dipped her fingertips gently in the lake. "It's not the first time she's helped me, insofar as 'first' has a meaning for such a being. My working hypothesis is that she believes I will be useful to her in some future scheme whose shape I cannot yet fathom, a thought that vexes me. And I suspect that Walking Upwards Unmaking also takes some pleasure in the knowledge of that vexation."

"That seems rather petty for somebody with so much power."

"My dear man." She laughed, as she rose from the waterside. "The whole point of having power is that you can be as petty as you like and nobody can stop you. Now come on. We need to get off the streets before the byakhees come out."

As it transpired, we had arrived on a relatively isolated spot along the shores of Lake Hali. A short walk up a sandbank and onto a narrow wooden jetty led us towards the city proper. The waterfront was entirely given over to industrial architecture, squat, square buildings from which a ceaseless stream of black smoke rose to choke the city in smog, casting a yellow pall over the sky through which even the impossible blackness of the stars struggled to penetrate.

I had never been to Carcosa, but I had seen pictures. The city's delicate spires, alien geometries, and strange moons featured prominently in the fever dreams and opium hazes of a certain sort of artist on many worlds, a peculiarity which had made the tourist trade a booming part of the Carcosan economy. The paintings tended to emphasise the bridges and towers and weird edifices of almost organic-looking stone. Later on our journey I would observe the city did, indeed, possess these features in abundance, but the facades of the factories spoke of dreams of quite a different sort. A brutalist vision of cement and steel, a triumph of collective will over individual sentiment. And it struck me that, while this was not the kind of madness that had made the city famed through a dozen realities, it was, perhaps, a madness nevertheless.

Ms. Haas curled her lip in disgust. "This used to be a charming little marina. Time was, you'd take a yacht out on the lake and make a blood offering to the Unspeakable One and then sail back in time for the masquerade at the court of the Yellow King. But now look at it." She paused in front of a poster depicting a proud Carcosan worker holding a hammer aloft, and indicated a slogan in a language I couldn't read. "'The Organisation of Consumer Cooperatives Strengthens the People's Army.' And to think Carcosan literature once drove readers mad with its beauty. What a waste."

A whistle blew, and from several of the factories, lines of labourers in dark overalls filed in and out as the shifts changed. Despite my companion's insistence that I eschew my traditional attire in favour of that which she had selected for me, I could not say that amongst the identically dressed proletarians I felt especially inconspicuous. Still, we attracted surprisingly little attention. Indeed, the Carcosan citizens seemed to go to some pains to avoid noticing us, rather pointedly averting their eyes as they passed. But in fairness to Ms. Haas, as we moved away from the lakeside towards the less modernised parts of the city our garments came to more closely resemble those of the general public, although I still saw wariness in the eyes of strangers.

Ms. Haas led me down a narrow flight of steps between two buildings, their walls fashioned from a rock-like substance that seemed somehow softer than such material ought to be, and into a shadowed, sloping alleyway. There she rapped sharply at a door, which, after a few moments, inched open. I should warn the reader now that since I speak no Carcosan and the majority of Carcosan citizens speak neither Khelish, Eyan, Athran, or Apostolic (this last being the common term for the set of mutually intelligible dialects spoken in the Hundred Kingdoms), much of what was said by both my companion and her contacts in Carcosa was quite beyond my comprehension. Whatever account she made of herself, the person upon whose door we had knocked apparently saw fit to allow us ingress into his chambers.

Our host was an old man, whose yellow-tinted eyes marked him as a native. He was clad in a sober outfit of brown trousers and a white shirt, accented with a yellow necktie and covered with a faded brocade dressing gown. After exchanging some further hushed words with Ms. Haas he took us into a tiny sitting room, filled with a variety of paraphernalia the origins and purpose of which I could not begin to guess.

My companion threw herself down on a sofa and I took a seat beside her. She and the gentleman continued to converse, and I did my best to avoid straying into impertinent inattention. Ms. Haas's prodigious talent for extended discourse meant that this proved rather more challenging than I had anticipated and, feeling quite excluded, my gaze began to wander to some of the artefacts around me. A disturbing array of decorative masks hung from the walls, all pale and queerly shaped, and surprisingly distinct from one another given their relative featurelessness. Well-stocked bookshelves boasted a number of slim volumes, whose titles I could not read and, open on the desk was some kind of genealogy the gentleman appeared to be compiling. On a nearby end table, I observed a delicate and rather beautiful onyx clasp, quaintly inlaid with a character in no script I could understand, but which I recalled having seen at several junctures on our journey through Carcosa.

I am not normally in the habit of handling the personal effects of strangers, especially those who are so kind as to invite me into their homes, but some eerie fascination drew me to the onyx clasp, and I rose from my seat and reached out to take it.

"I wouldn't do that if I were you," said Ms. Haas. "Not unless you want to be throttled by a dead man."

I sat down immediately, since I very much did not. My actions, however, had drawn the attention of our host, who became quite animated and addressed me with a stream of enthusiastic Carcosan.

"He says you have a good eye," my companion explained. "And he wishes to tell you some of the history of the piece. I would personally be grateful if you declined the offer, because I frankly can't be bothered to translate."

At this, the old gentleman seemed to take offence, although I am not certain how complete his understanding had been. Ms. Haas responded with similar sharpness and the two fell to bickering for some minutes. I made no further attempt to intrude upon their conversation and eventually it appeared that whatever business Ms. Haas had with the fellow was concluded. It was not until we had left that it occurred to me she had offered no introduction, and I felt an acute retrospective embarrassment at having had the ill manners to spend so extended a time in a person's company without endeavouring to learn his name. Ms. Haas, however, reassured me that this was for the best since it would mean that I would be unable to betray our contact in the likely event that we were apprehended and tortured by the Repairers of Reputations. This reassurance alleviated one set of concerns but exacerbated another.

My nerves were not aided by the fact that my companion then insisted upon undertaking a seemingly directionless ramble through the streets of Carcosa, a journey which encompassed two parks and a public fountain decorated with a grotesque antler-headed statue, looped back towards the lakeside factories, and ended in a small guesthouse in what I took to be one of the less wealthy parts of town. The language barrier still preventing my following any of the finer details of our interactions with the citizenry, it was not until we were making ready to retire for the night that I discovered we were to be sharing a room.

"Madam," I protested. "I must protest. This is unseemly."

"Mr. Wyndham, we are in an alien city-state attempting to reach out to subversive elements in the hope that they may put us in contact with a high-ranking member of the paranoid and oppressive political party that rules it. Is your greatest concern really that the locals might speculate as to the nature of our relationship?"

I resolutely avoided sitting on the bed. "I know you think me prudish, but I prefer to uphold certain standards."

"You can only call something a standard if it is demonstrably superior to the alternative. What you try to maintain are meaningless cultural taboos."

"I am, as you observe, in an alien city-state where I do not speak the language and I am hiding from the secret police in a small room on a street whose name I do not even know. Meaningless cultural taboos are all I really have right now."

Ms. Haas began to strip off her outerwear. "Well, that's as may be. But one room is all *we* have, so I hope you don't snore."

The night that followed was one of the most uncomfortable that I had ever passed. I, of course, allowed Ms. Haas to take the bed, not that there was really any question about the matter, for while I have known her to face near certain death in support of her friends or her clients I have never once known her willingly to compromise on a matter of personal comfort. I would, over time, grow more accustomed to sharing a room with my companion, something necessity would require that we do on several occasions over the course of our adventures. But that first evening the impropriety of it all left me feeling quite anxious, and I slept only fitfully. This, as it turned out, was fortunate, for Ms. Haas was in a talkative mood and would toss snippets of information in my direction seemingly at random throughout the hours that followed.

It was from these non sequiturs that I learned the substance of Ms. Haas's plan. We were to meet in the morning with a low-ranking party official sympathetic to counterrevolutionary causes. As part payment for certain services my companion had performed for the Carcosan resistance some years before, he would furnish us with a copy of Citizen Castaigne's itinerary, which should allow us to contrive a meeting in a relatively discreet location. Once in the gentleman's company, we were to rely upon Ms. Haas's powers of observation and persuasion to ascertain if it was, indeed, he who was responsible for the blackmail of Miss Viola. And, if it was, prevail upon him to desist.

❧

CHAPTER FORTY-NINE

Lost Carcosa

Ms. Haas had arranged to meet our contact at a pavement café on a cobbled street between two of the city's many bridges. The place was quiet, allowing us to secure a pleasant table by the door, and Ms. Haas ordered breakfast for us, which arrived in the form of an honestly slightly disappointing black coffee, some poorly cut bread, and a pot of bitter jam. Ms. Haas spoke animatedly to me in Carcosan and I did my best to respond appropriately to her nonverbal cues in order that I might conceal my utter ignorance of the language.

To my considerable discomfort, her manner grew increasingly flirtatious as she went on and, while I did my best to respond in kind, it was not a mode of intercourse with which I had a great deal of familiarity. Eventually, she took the opportunity to lean close and whisper in Eyan, "Something's wrong. Watch carefully and be ready to improvise."

Some minutes passed and a few other Carcosan citizens came in, took tables, and ordered refreshments. Close by us, to the right, a youngish man in a brown jacket sat sipping coffee, an unopened newspaper folded on the table beside him. A little farther away, a lady in a yellow patterned headscarf cradled a baby in her arms, while to our left a moustachioed gentleman in a threadbare suit argued with the waiter. From his gesticulations, it appeared he, too, had reservations about the quality of the coffee. Between the caffeine, my companion's warning, and my inability to understand what anyone was saying, my attitude to the entire tableau began to verge on the paranoid, a sensation that was further exacerbated when a woman in drab overalls began apathetically sweeping the street nearby. Her cap was pulled low over her eyes and her waste removal duties seemed to edge her ever closer to our location.

The argumentative gentleman left his table, and a bird-like creature landed in his place and began to peck at what was left of his pastry. The younger gentleman got up shortly afterwards, appearing to forget his newspaper. He started down the road at a brisk pace, but almost immediately, the waiter stepped out in front of him, blocking his exit. In a panic, the young man turned and attempted to flee in the opposite direction, only to find himself confronted by the street sweeper. I watched with a certain morbid fascination as she raised a hand to her chin and unhooked some strange and hidden mechanism. Her entire face came away, revealing itself to be a delicate porcelain mask with a second mask beneath, pallid and featureless. At the same time, she drew a pistol from within her overalls, a detail that I found less viscerally disturbing but more pertinent given our present situation.

My natural instinct was to intervene in this poor man's defence, but I was deeply sensible of the treacherous nature of our predicament. At that moment the only persons I knew for certain were not secretly Repairers of Reputations were myself and Ms. Haas and, when I looked to my companion for guidance, I found that she had gone.

A shot rang out. The waiter, too, had unmasked and discharged his own weapon into the young gentleman's back. Before the man even had the chance to fall to his knees, a great shriek echoed from above and a bat-winged creature, not quite ape and not quite vulture, swooped from the skies and seized him. Paying no heed to her adversary's piteous cries, the street sweeper turned her attention at once to the table at which he had sat, the table on which, I noted, there was no longer a newspaper. It was at this point that I became firmly convinced that it would be safest to leave at once.

I stood as calmly as I was able and did my best to walk away as if I had witnessed nothing untoward. A commanding voice shouted from behind me. Its words were Carcosan, but the tone was unmistakable. I turned and raised my hands cautiously. The waiter and the street sweeper both had their weapons trained firmly upon me, and the street sweeper appeared to be asking some manner of question or giving me some manner of instruction, although I could not have said which. Then I heard another shriek and a second of the strange bat-winged creatures swept down from the rooftops, wrapped its squamous talons around my shoulders, and hoisted me aloft.

CHAPTER FIFTY

Dim Carcosa

The flying creature brought me to a cell in a high yellow tower and there I was left for some days. They fed me enough that I retained the majority of my faculties, although the strange vistas visible through the narrow window, the ever-shifting patterns that marked the walls of my prison, and the peculiar behaviour of my captors caused me increasingly to doubt the strength of my grip on reality.

It began on perhaps the second day of my incarceration. The second or the third—early enough that time still had meaning but late enough that I was already losing track—I was led to an interrogation room, where two guards in black suits and pallid masks shackled me to a chair. A bright light shone in my eyes and opposite me I could just make out the silhouette of a slender man of aristocratic bearing.

"My name is Citizen Castaigne," he said in thickly accented Khelish, "and you will tell me everything."

I blinked against the glare. It was gratifying to have located our quarry, but I dearly wished it could have been under other circumstances. "I would be most happy to, but I have no information that would be useful to you."

One of the guards struck a blow to the back of my head, which dazed me sufficiently that I missed my interlocutor's next question. The necessity of repeating himself did not improve his mood.

"Why," he asked, apparently for the second time, "were you meeting with counterrevolutionaries?"

I considered the somewhat unenviable options before me. My ordinary instinct would be, of course, to offer my full cooperation, for I saw great value in upholding the social contracts that support an orderly society. I had also, however, grown up in a kingdom whose law enforcement agents were corrupt to the point that they could be considered unambiguously evil, being as they were primarily the un-living minions of a malevolent sorcerer king. The Repairers of Reputations put me more in mind of those beings than of the good and faithful Myrmidons who protected the citizens of Khelathra-Ven.

Be this as it may, I was also cognisant that my actions in Carcosa, although they had involved some peripheral contact with subversive elements, had not, in fact, posed any threat to the Carcosan state or its apparatus. And although it is rare for tyrants to believe the truth if it does not confirm their fears I nevertheless concluded that honesty, in this context, remained the best policy. "I am visiting from Khelathra-Ven in order to investigate the blackmail of a friend of mine. To this end, I needed to make contact with a high-ranking member of the party. More specifically, with you."

Mr. Castaigne leaned forward, leaving me uncertain whether I had made a clever choice or a foolish one. "Why would I be involved in the blackmail of a Khelathran?"

"You were betrothed as children. I thought it possible you might want her back."

"Your friend is one of the *former people*?"

"If you mean she's a refugee from the Carcosan revolution, then yes."

"So," sneered Mr. Castaigne, "you confess that you came to Carcosa as the agent of an enemy of the revolution and you believe that I am also in contact with this traitor."

"That seems like a mischaracterisation of my statement."

"Take him away."

The guards returned me roughly to my cell and I was sure the walls were closer together than when I had left, the ceiling tilting at an odd angle. In my dreams that night I saw black stars and heard a dreadful flapping in the darkness.

I do not know how long I slept, but on awakening I saw that my cell door had moved, and that I was no longer alone. Huddled against one wall was a dishevelled man in a grey suit. His face, which might once have been handsome, was gaunt and drawn, and his eyes sunk to dark circles. I asked him who he was, and he told me his name was Icarius Castaigne.

Looking closer, I could see that he did indeed have the same build as the man who had interrogated me earlier, although his demeanour lacked all of his former confidence. "But how did you come to be here?"

"The Repairers took me." His voice was thin and quavering, and he appeared almost on the verge of tears. "I am accused of consorting with an enemy of the people."

"Miss Viola?" Was this a consequence of my earlier confession? How long ago had it been? An hour? A day?

Citizen Castaigne gave an anguished laugh. "That's a name from another life."

"You are not attempting to destroy her marriage by means of blackmail, then?"

The man looked genuinely perplexed. "I didn't even know she was alive. I wish I still did not know. It is the knowing, you see, that they object to."

"Then I am sorry for what has happened to you." Outside I heard the beating of wings and the screaming of the strange not-birds. "But surely if this was all a misunderstanding they will let us go?"

"They see enemies everywhere. Without and within. They watch us always. *He* watches us always. The revolution was meant to end it, but I see the sign, I hear the awful dragging of His tattered robe. This is Carcosa, and ever will it be a place of—"

The door opened. Two guards seized him. Two guards in black suits and pale masks. The door closed and he was gone. Or perhaps he had never been there. I ran my hands over the floor where he had sat, looking for some sign that I had really seen him, that I had not imagined the frail man in grey or the opening and closing of the door. Or the world outside the cell. I closed my eyes and dreamed again.

A beating of wings. A ragged figure in a yellow robe. A cell that was smaller than it was. That was larger. Ever-shifting patterns on the wall. I was tied to a chair. I was locked in a room. I was alone on the shores of a lake under cold black stars.

I awoke. I thought I awoke. A light shone in my face and guards in pale masks stood on either side of me.

"You will tell me everything." By the shape of my interrogator's silhouette I was certain that it was Castaigne.

"You were not a captive at all, then?" He did not answer. Perhaps he was playing with my mind. Perhaps I was.

"Why," he asked, "were you meeting with counterrevolutionaries?"

"I am here on behalf of a woman who fled Carcosa as a child. She has no interest in your city or its politics, and neither do I."

"Your friend is one of the former people?"

"You know this. I have told you this."

The interrogator leaned forward. "Do you believe that Citizen Castaigne is in contact with this woman?"

This was preposterous. "*You* are Citizen Castaigne."

"You will answer my questions."

"I do not know how to."

A guard struck me, and the interrogator spoke again. "Do you believe that Citizen Castaigne is in contact with this woman?"

"You told me that you were not."

Another blow. I had known that it was not the answer he wanted. I did not know how to answer differently. I had been in the cell for two days. For five days. I had never been anywhere but the cell. I had never seen stars that were not black or a sky with only one sun.

"Take him away. I am growing tired of his impertinence."

The guards lifted me from my chair and dragged me down the corridor to my cell. It was the same cell as before. It was not the same cell as before. The floor had developed an unnatural smoothness. The air tasted of tin. In my dreams, cloud waves rolled across the surface of a great lake. On the far shore I saw a ragged figure in yellow robes.

I awoke in my cell with jaundiced sunlight filtering through the window. I awoke in my cell with the un-light from black stars prickling my face. I awoke to see Citizen Castaigne huddled against the wall. I awoke alone. The claws of a winged monster scrabbled at my window. Everything was silent. I could not sleep for the sound of the tattered robe dragging on the floors of an ancient castle. I slept and dreamed that my face was a porcelain mask.

I awoke in a cold chair, a bright light shining in my face. A hooded woman sat opposite me, and once more I heard that soft and now-familiar flapping, as of cloth against rock or leather against bone.

"If Castaigne is not the traitor, who is?"

"Perhaps," I suggested, "there is no traitor."

"There must always be traitors."

"Why?" I was not certain I wanted to know the answer. I could not help but ask the question. I had been there for three days. Two. Five.

"Because the shadows lengthen, and songs die unheard."

The guards took me back to my cell. It was the same cell. It was a different cell. A yellow sky. A black sky. Now I ate. Now I slept. Now I dreamed. Or perhaps I always dreamed. I awoke and the floor was unnaturally smooth. I awoke and the air tasted of tin. My skin felt smooth and dry, as if it would crack at the slightest pressure. I feared what I would find beneath. I heard the tearing of cloth and the beating of wings. I raised my hands to my face and dug my fingers into my skin. *Take off the mask. You must take off the mask.* The bird-things screamed outside.

I awoke, or thought I awoke, in my cell. The door had moved, and I was not alone.

"Mr. Castaigne."

He stared at me with wild, desperate eyes. "Tell them what you know. It's the only way to stop this."

I did not trust him, but then at that time I also did not entirely trust myself. "You have been interrogating me. You are as much one of them as anybody else."

"No longer. I have been found guilty. Guilty of betraying the Party and the People and the great City of Carcosa."

"I am sorry to hear that."

He giggled. It was perhaps the most disturbing sound I had ever heard a human make. "Do not be sorry for me. I am a traitor. I accused myself and tried myself and convicted myself. I am a spy. An agent for reactionary powers. And I will see myself hang for it."

"I am not certain that you are in a fit state to make such a judgement."

"The dreadful king whispers in my dreams. The shadows of my thoughts lengthen. How can I serve the people if I cannot trust even my own mind?"

The door opened, and he was taken away. The door opened, and I was taken away. I had been here for three days. Castaigne had been here for two days. He was a prisoner, a guard. I was a prisoner. I was a guard. I was Castaigne and I wore a yellow robe and a pale mask.

I sat in a cold chair, a bright light shining in my face. The silhouette opposite me was a hooded woman in a pallid mask.

"If Castaigne is not the traitor, who is?"

Focus, man. Keep to what you know. Tell them so you can tell yourself it is the only way to stay whole. "He told me that he was."

"These lies help no one."

"That may be, but I know what I saw." I did not know what I saw. "He was in my cell, only moments ago. He said that he had confessed, that he had been tried and convicted."

The lady sat quite motionless. "If that were the case, why would we still be interrogating you?"

"I do not know, but . . ." They are trying to break you. This is not supposed to make sense. You will never force it to make sense. Still I could not answer her.

"Why are you really here?" she asked, her tone unexpectedly gentle.

"I'm . . . I'm not sure I remember."

The guards took me back to my cell. I slept and I woke. Now I ate. Now I did not eat. I lay on the floor while the ceiling crawled and distorted above me.

"Whatever you do," whispered a voice I had half forgotten, "don't wake up."

"But I'm not asleep."

"Stop being tiresome, Wyndham."

The malign influence of that place still pressed into my head like thick yellow fog, but my companion's instantly recognisable tone brought me a good deal of the way back to myself. "Ms. Haas?"

"Yes. Now listen very carefully if you don't want to spend the rest of your short life watching your mind and spirit fracture under the unbearable weight of inexorable cosmic truths."

The prospect was not appealing. "If you have a means to free me from this place, I would be most grateful."

"Really, Captain. What do you think I've been doing for the past week? I can help you escape, but to do so I have had to invoke some quite explicitly unspeakable powers. Rather nostalgic, but terribly dangerous. In a moment, things are going to get very loud and very messy. I will need you to go through the door, keep moving, and when I tell you to do something, do it immediately and without question. Open your eyes when you hear the gunshots."

I heard gunshots and opened my eyes.

CHAPTER FIFTY-ONE

The Tatters of the King

Rising, I saw the door to my cell stood open. Beyond it, the hallway was deserted, and behind me I heard a sound like the tearing of cloth.

"What are you waiting for?" Ms. Haas's voice appeared to emanate from somewhere beside me, but she was not there when I looked. "Go."

I followed her instruction. The corridors of that tower were a maze of dead ends and blind passages, through which I wandered with no further direction from my companion. Disjointed laughter caught my attention and, in the absence of a clear alternative, I moved towards it. I found Mr. Castaigne in the wreckage of one of the interrogation rooms, crouched over the body of a slender man in a grey suit who I recognised as also being Mr. Castaigne.

"Dash it all, man," I exclaimed as I drew closer, "what have you done?"

He looked up at me, with an expression like a wounded fox. "It was him. It was him all along."

"No time for this," said an echo of Ms. Haas. "Get the mask."

I glanced between the dead man and his living double, neither of whom was masked. "What mask?"

"No mask," whispered Mr. Castaigne, rising and training a pistol upon me. "No mask."

Tired, disorientated, and half-starved as I was, my reflexes could have been swifter. But one did not survive long beyond the Unending Gate without learning to respond adequately in times of danger. I shifted my weight forward, bearing his weapon away with one hand and, at the same time, driving my opposite forearm into his throat. Mr. Castaigne fell, struggling to breathe, and dropped his gun.

I retrieved it and covered him. "Sir, for reasons I cannot explain, it is important that I acquire a mask. Please tell me where to find one."

But Mr. Castaigne was staring past me, his face a waxen veil of horror.

"If I were you," Ms. Haas said from nowhere, "I really wouldn't look over your shoulder."

Someone—something—rushed past me; a ragged creature in yellow robes, its presence at once glorious and vile. I did not watch as it engulfed Mr. Castaigne, but turned instead to flee.

"Mr. Wyndham. Wake up."

I opened my eyes. Rising, I saw the door to my cell stood open. Beyond it, the hallway was deserted, and behind me I heard a sound like the tearing of cloth.

"What are you waiting for?" said Ms. Haas. This all seemed familiar, but I couldn't think why. "Go."

I moved through the shadowed corridors as if tracing the steps of a half-forgotten dream. On the floor of one of the interrogation rooms, I found the body of Mr. Castaigne, his eyes wide and his visage a paroxysm of terror.

"Get the mask."

I saw none but, surrendering to the twisted logic of Carcosa, I knelt down and hooked my fingers behind the dead man's jaw. His face came away in my hands, becoming a shard of featureless alabaster and revealing beneath a thing of which my editor advises me I should not speak.

"Put it on and move quickly."

I followed her instruction and felt at once a cold and indefinable sense of violation. Returning to the tangled skein of corridors, I found now that my steps were drawn on by some will not entirely my own. My path led me up a spiral of broken stairs and out onto a ledge of scored and weathered stone. The sky roiled with sepia clouds and, far below, the ancient and famous city of Carcosa spilled forth its canals and its factories, its tenements and spires like the fever dream of a dying cartographer.

I found Mr. Castaigne standing perilously close to the edge, a few paces away from me.

"They are here," he said. "The enemies of the people are inside the tower. And, since only we two remain, it must be either you or I who betrayed us."

I considered my position. On the one hand, I could not help but feel some pity for this man whose loyalty to his cause seemed to have driven him so deeply into paranoia and whose predicament may have been at least in part my doing. On the other hand, he remained one of my captors and, therefore, ultimately my enemy. And it was this last factor that I deemed most pertinent to my current situation.

"That is so," I replied. "But we have no way of knowing which of us it was."

Mr. Castaigne curled his fingers despairingly into his hair. "Then we have failed."

The strategy to which I was about to commit was a gamble but, from what I had observed of Mr. Castaigne's state of mind, it seemed my best hope of overcoming him. "There is perhaps one hope. If we both cast ourselves from the tower, we shall be certain that the traitor is destroyed, and our lives are a small price to pay for the security of the party."

"You're right." His eyes began to fill with tears. "And had I not been compromised I would have thought of it immediately."

I felt more than a little guilty at this, but my own survival was at stake. "That does seem logical."

He stretched out a hand towards me. "Serve well, Citizen."

And then he stepped backwards into empty air, but before he could fall I felt a rush of wind and a sickness like joy as I watched a ragged thing in yellow robes snatch him up and consume him.

"Mr. Wyndham. Wake up."

I opened my eyes. Rising, I saw the door to my cell stood open. Beyond it, the hallway was deserted, and behind me I heard a sound like the tearing of cloth. In my left hand, I was still holding a chill, alabaster mask.

"What are you waiting for?" said Ms. Haas. I remembered this but I did not remember it. "Put the mask on and move quickly."

I did as instructed, and some will not quite my own led me swiftly through the not quite familiar corridors of that strange tower. On the broken steps of a twisting stair, I met a slender, aristocratic man with a wild look in his eyes. Castaigne. I should have been surprised to see him but could not recall why.

"The guards are dead." He caught my arm. "This way."

He took me higher to a narrow ledge overlooking the ancient and famous city of Carcosa.

"When you get back home"—he pulled a silver whistle from around his neck—"tell our friends that the Repairers are ours."

I briefly considered protesting that I really did have no connection to Carcosan counterrevolutionaries but felt that now would be a spectacularly bad time to mention that particular detail.

Raising the whistle to his lips, Mr. Castaigne blew a shrill note that tasted of blood and ichor.

"You have been incautious, Citizen Castaigne," a voice said. The masked and hooded woman from what I had thought was a dream emerged from a doorway that I was not sure had been there moments before.

"Citizen de Luca." Mr. Castaigne turned his pistol on me at once. "I have identified the traitor and am proceeding with his execution by winged messenger."

He pointed towards the horizon and I saw, approaching with great speed, one of the corpse-like, bat-like, mole-like beings that seemed to serve a variety of purposes within the Carcosan regime.

"A commendably quick lie, Citizen," returned the woman. "But a lie nonetheless. You have disappointed me, Castaigne, and my disappointment is never earned twice."

The flying creature was closer now, almost close enough that I could leap to it, though not so close that such a course of action would prove more than nominally survivable.

Castaigne produced a pistol from his jacket and pointed it at the stranger. "There's still time. The party is not what it was meant to be, but we can save it."

"So naive. There is nothing to save." Behind Miss de Luca, a figure in ragged yellow robes began to coalesce out of the fog. "The party, the monarchy, what came before, and what will come after, they are all just . . . masks."

The grim calculus by which I had been balancing the inherent perils of remaining on the ledge against those of pitching myself bodily into space, in the hope that some winged monster would break my fall, tilted sharply in favour of the latter option. I sprang with as much strength as I could muster out into the empty air, aiming as far as possible for the ape-bird-mosquito creature that was bearing down upon us. It shrieked in predatory delight as its talons closed about my outstretched wrist, its alien voice mingling horribly with Mr. Castaigne's scream of terrible and despairing apprehension. The beast swooped low as it carried me away over the spiderweb streets and shark-tooth roofs of the ancient and famous city of Carcosa.

"Mr. Wyndham. Wake up."

CHAPTER FIFTY-TWO

A Process of Elimination

I opened my eyes and found myself staring at the ceiling of my own bedroom at 221b Martyrs Walk. My left wrist ached sharply where the winged creature's talons had dug into it and in my right hand I held a delicate white mask.

"I doubt we shall have further use for that," said Ms. Haas, plucking the object from my unresisting fingers. "Although one can never be entirely certain with these things."

I blinked up at her in some bewilderment. "Am I still dreaming?"

"The distinction is often less relevant than you might imagine, but by most conventional standards, no, you are not dreaming, and yes, you are back in what it is useful to think of as the real world."

"What . . . how . . . I mean . . ."

Ms. Haas perched herself on the end of the bed, wiping the blood from her eyes. Her physical condition had deteriorated remarkably since I last saw her. I suspected she had been neither eating nor sleeping as she should have, and her movements seemed pained as I had never seen before. "Do you mean how did we get out of Carcosa, and indeed, were we ever truly there in the first place?"

"Something like that, yes."

"Carcosa is a strange place. Like a rainbow on an oil slick it exists on the border between delusion and reality. One may enter or leave by

a physical portal or by more dangerous and less reliable dream-paths involving certain meditations, incantations, and hallucinations. While it was vital that we enter physically in order that we might be functional on arrival, there were rather more options available to me when it came to the matter of extraction."

Sensible of the impropriety inherent in lying down before a lady, I endeavoured to sit up and realised that I was too fatigued to do so. "I'm not sure that explains how I went from a Carcosan holding cell to my own bed."

"Yes, well, your physical incarceration did rather rule out the portal option. Short of bombing the tower, there was no way I was getting your body out of there. So we had to dream our way to freedom, a task that could only be accomplished with the intervention of an unnameable god, best never invoked. I suspect I shall have a headache for some days."

"The guards were all devoured"—I laid my head back on the pillow, shut my eyes, and then immediately opened them, fearing what I might see—"by a spectre in yellow."

"That'll be him. Best not to talk about it, or think about it, or remember it."

"And if I do find myself talking about it, thinking about it, or remembering it?"

"In all honesty, that's probably unavoidable. Just steer clear of Carcosan theatre for a bit and if you wake up in the night and discover that you've drawn eldritch symbols all over your bedsheets maybe come and have a word with me. Oh, also keep your gun handy because there's a slim chance that the undying servants of the King Whom Emperors Serve will show up and try to claim your soul. Or mine. Probably mine, actually."

I wasn't entirely sure how to respond to that. I was equally uncertain whether I should be thanking my companion for rescuing me from the Repairers of Reputations or challenging her for the decision to abandon me to them. Suspecting that she would be equally dismissive of either sentiment, I elected to broach neither topic and, wishing to forestall sleep as long as possible, spoke instead of my encounters with Mr. Castaigne.

Ms. Haas shrugged, then winced. "A pitiable end for a pitiable man. After the unfortunate business at the café, I managed to track him down to a ghastly little flat in a concrete government building. Contrary to what my researches had led me to believe, he was clearly a man of no real influence, terrified of the Repairers, and willing to say or do anything to cling to what little property and liberty remained to him. Not at all the sort of person who would be able to arrange for a complex interdimensional espionage and extortion operation."

"Even so, he did not deserve the fate we led him to."

"Nor did he deserve the privilege into which he was born, the tumult that fell upon his people, or the pernicious and corrupting influence that emanates from the mystical Lake Hali and seeps, to one degree or another, into every soul in Carcosa. Sometimes bad things happen to uninteresting people. Now, excuse me, I've been living on opioids and water for the last three days and I need to pass out."

And, with that, she collapsed across the foot of my bed and did not stir for several hours. For the best part of the next week, my companion and I concerned ourselves primarily with convalescence. I gradually learned again to trust that reality would retain a consistent shape and that waking would remain broadly distinguishable from dreaming, although my dreams themselves were not wholly without visions of those black stars, those shrouded towers, and that lightless lake. And, indeed, such images remain with me, if infrequently, to this day. Ms. Haas, by contrast, mediated her recovery through her usual assortment of medication, relaxation, and nocturnal perambulation. I flatter myself that I was able to encourage her at least slightly in the direction of more wholesome pursuits, managing to persuade her to take breakfast on no less than three occasions.

As she had predicted, an unliving servant of the Yellow King did, eventually, come to our door, seeking to claim our lives and our essences in the forbidden name of its master. Ms. Haas and I both being somewhat indisposed, the monstrosity was met at the door by Mrs. Hive, who, although indignant at the intrusion, was pleased to discover that the entity—the livid and reanimated corpse of a local gravedigger—made a most suitable replacement for the stevedore whose body had, by this stage, decayed well past the point of viability. How she was able to overcome the animating will of the dread god the creature served I never asked, but it would not be the last time that I would be reminded that one should never try the resolve of our good landlady.

The day after this most startling interlude, the bloated cadaver shuffled into the sitting room to inform us, in Mrs. Hive's detached, droning way, that Second Augur Lawson was without and wished to speak with us. My companion's response was to declare loudly, and in no uncertain terms, that the Second Augur's presence was unwelcome, his aptitude suspect, and his parenthood likewise. To my mild embarrassment, he came in anyway.

"All right, then, Haas?" He lowered himself into the only remaining chair. "Meaning no disrespect to your good self, we checked the suspects that you had previously investigated and, on this occasion, the official force agrees with your assessment."

Ms. Haas, who had been insensible upon the chaise since breakfast, now propped herself on one elbow. "What uncommon wisdom you display."

"This leads us to the secondary line of enquiry, regarding the possibility of interference by Carcosan agents. Owing to the sensitive nature of investigations pertaining to foreign powers, the remainder of information on this matter comes by way of the Office of Augurs

Extraordinary, who assure us that while Carcosan agents do remain active in the city, as do agents of several nations, there is no indication that there was any organised effort by Carcosan intelligence to break up your client's wedding."

At this juncture, Mrs. Hive entered with a tray of tea things. She had taken to preparing refreshments while we had been too injured and exhausted to do so for ourselves, and I had never quite had the heart to tell her that the saprophytic flora that she routinely shed into the pot rendered the end product utterly undrinkable, at least to me. Ms. Haas seemed either unaware or indifferent. The Second Augur took the proffered cup and saucer politely but, I noted, made no effort to drink from them.

"Yes," returned Ms. Haas, poking the fungal bloom in her teacup speculatively. "That suspect proved to have rather less reach than we thought he did. Also, he's dead now."

"Not, I hope, as a consequence of your actions."

"Not directly. Besides, I'm sure the criminal element of this city is already taxing you quite to your limits."

The Second Augur tapped his metal fingers on the threadbare arm of the chair. "Oh, how I have missed our playful banter. Now, can you tell me anything else about this case or not?"

"The case is solved, Mr. Lawson. You don't need to worry your head about that."

"Solved?" I ejaculated. "But we've eliminated all possible suspects!"

"That, Captain," drawled Ms. Haas, with an air that it would not be uncharitable to describe as smug, "is precisely the point. When you've eliminated the possible, all that remains is the impossible, and I find that so much more satisfying to work with."

Demonstrating what in the circumstances constituted admirable restraint, the Second Augur asked, "So who was it, then?"

"I'm not telling you."

At this, the Second Augur's response was not so admirable, containing as it did only three words suitable for publication, those words being "for," "sake," and "you."

"Now, now, Mr. Lawson." Ms. Haas grinned with inappropriately sincere enjoyment. "While I would absolutely withhold information on a matter such as this just to annoy you, in this case I really am protecting my client. As I explained to you at some length before we left for Carcosa, this is a personal matter that cannot possibly impinge in any way on the safety of Khelathra-Ven or its citizens. You have done your job, Second Augur. Why don't you go chase a shoplifter?"

There was a none-too-pleasant silence, not aided by Mrs. Hive's provision of biscuits into which some of her larvae had crawled. This created something of a quandary of etiquette, there being no established convention as to whether it was less polite to turn down such an offering or to consume part of your host's gestalt body and consciousness.

"You know what," said Second Augur Lawson at last, "I'm going to pretend that I really think you've broken the habit of a lifetime and are trying to do what's right by another person." He rose, turning up the collar of his coat and putting his hat back on. "Good evening, Ms. Haas, Mr. Wyndham."

And he left.

After I heard the door close and was certain that the Second Augur was some way down the street, I turned to my companion. "You will at least tell me who the blackmailer is?"

"Captain, you disappoint me. I really thought you'd have worked it out for yourself."

"On the contrary, I am quite in the dark. We had five suspects at the start of this endeavour and now we have none."

Ms. Haas retrieved her packet of Valentino's Good Rough Shag, packed her pipe, and lit it. "Then that, surely, is our first deduction. The perpetrator is somebody we hitherto had no reason to suspect."

"That would seem," I ventured, "to narrow our list down from five to everybody in the universe."

"That is certainly a starting point, if—as we shall see later—a flawed one. But consider the other facts. When you analysed the letters, you saw no evidence that they had been handled by anybody but you, Eirene, and myself. The blackmailer clearly knows Eirene intimately, having shown quite startling knowledge of her personal habits and history. They expected, further, that Eirene would have similar familiarity with them, hence you will recall the effort made to disguise their handwriting." Ms. Haas paused to take a puff on her pipe. "But throughout this whole affair the miscreant has demonstrated an utterly idiosyncratic and very specific set of motivations. They seem to want one thing, and one thing only, which is for Eirene to end her engagement to Miss Beck of her own free will. Furthermore, they have gone to quite considerable lengths to ensure that no peripheral harm befalls either party."

I took an absentminded sip of tea and then immediately regretted it. "I confess that all of these details serve only to make the case more confusing to me."

"Then let me add to your confusion. It must have been the blackmailer who intervened in our defence on the Austral Express. But although they wore the guise of a Repairer of Reputations, Mr. Lawson's contacts confirm that no Carcosan agent was involved and, if you think carefully, you will realise that the details of the mechanism by which they disguised themselves as a guard do not match the magics employed by the Repairers in their adoption of false personas."

"I'm afraid none of this is proving helpful to me."

"Then"—Ms. Haas wagged her pipestem in my direction—"I shall give you one last clue. You said that our list of suspects had been narrowed down from five to everyone in the universe. As ever, your thinking is too limited. Now come, we should go find Eirene and set this matter to rest."

We called a hansom and set off into the night, Ms. Haas staring idly out of the window and smoking, while I did my best to sift through the clues she had laid before me. But, for the life of me, I could not imagine how my companion had pieced them together to discover the identity of the blackmailer.

❦

CHAPTER FIFTY-THREE

The Final Piece

Miss Viola had lodgings above a haberdasher's in Little Carcosa. She did not seem eager to speak to us, and it took a significant amount of hectoring on the part of Ms. Haas before she would consent to admit us. Once within, we found the lady's demeanour quite different from that to which I had become accustomed. While she had often displayed a somewhat tempestuous spirit, she had always presented herself with care and modesty. She greeted us now with her hair unbound and wearing nothing but a yellow silk dressing gown. Her room, which was small but decorated with a tasteful, feminine sensibility, was presently littered with empty wine bottles and reeked of cigarettes.

"Forgive the informality of my appearance," she said with a sigh, "but I appear to be utterly ruined." She did not say "ruined."

Ms. Haas clasped her hands to her breast. "Oh, Eirene, how I've missed you."

Miss Viola gave a reply that I cannot commit to print, and then cast herself tragically onto the bed, dislodging a sizable revolver from beneath a pillow as she did so. Given the lady's attire, I averted my eyes swiftly out of concern the situation would otherwise descend from inappropriate to salacious.

"So," said Ms. Haas, in a tone that I personally considered rather mean-spirited, "I take it the fishmonger isn't happy."

"She needs some time."

"Yes, dear. In my experience, that's code for 'I had no idea who you were, and now I know I am disgusted by it.'"

I risked looking up and saw, to my relief, that Miss Viola had wrapped herself in a blanket, thus preserving her modesty and my equilibrium. Ms. Haas was sitting beside her, patting her shoulder with a tenderness at variance with the sentiment she had just expressed.

Not seeming to appreciate the gesture, Miss Viola shrugged her off. "She said it wasn't the affairs, or the stealing, or the . . ." And here she listed a catalogue of transgressions of increasing severity that, for the sake of the lady's reputation and my readers' comfort, I shall elide. ". . . or even that I'd nearly got her killed by a vampire, but—"

"Let me guess," interrupted my companion, rolling her eyes. "She said it was the *lying*. Darling, that's what they always say. It's a convenient excuse that ordinary people fall back on when they realise we have dared to do things they lack the courage to even imagine."

This assertion on the part of Ms. Haas provoked a predictably intransigent response from Miss Viola and I have not to this day decided to my satisfaction whether that was, indeed, my companion's intent. "Just stop it, Shaharazad. You won't understand this, but I have actually been happy recently."

"Do you really want so little out of life?"

"You know"—Miss Viola stared wistfully at the ceiling—"it turns out I do. I've spent the past decade running from something or for something and—"

Ms. Haas laughed bitterly. "If you tell me you've realised that you had everything you needed all along, then I shall take up that gun"— she indicated Miss Viola's discarded firearm—"and shoot both of us."

"On the contrary, I realised I had nothing. Just stories and enemies. I mean, you're one of my closest and oldest friends, and we barely speak, I frequently hate you, and you're transparently a terrible human being."

"Is this the part where I remind you that, for the better part of this month, I've been risking my life and that of Mr. Wyndham entirely for your benefit?"

Miss Viola reached out and put her hand over Ms. Haas's. "I know, and I'm grateful. I really am. It's just right now it doesn't seem to have done me much good."

"Oh, come on, Eirene. You persuaded Lady Evangelina to take you back after she caught you in bed with both her sisters; Ambassador Tan carried on seeing you for six months after you told her that you were in the pay of Yue; I forgave you after you pushed me off the roof of the Vedunian Royal Opera House; and the high priestess of Thotek the Devourer discovered that you had seduced her only in order to steal the jewelled eyes of her altarpiece and let you get away without sacrificing you. You can certainly talk round a fishmonger, especially one who even I can see is disgustingly in love with you."

"Maybe I could, but"—and here Miss Viola pulled the blanket over her head, a gesture that exposed rather more of her ankles than I was comfortable with—"if we don't catch the blackmailer my whole past becomes public knowledge and Cora loses everything. I could never do that to her."

"Darling, we *have* caught the blackmailer. Didn't I mention?"

Miss Viola sat up quite violently. "No. No, you didn't, you utter ——" The language with which she described Ms. Haas was milder than some she had used earlier, but still not appropriate for print.

"I'm terribly sorry. It must have slipped my mind." Ms. Haas took Miss Viola by the chin and looked her dead in the eyes. "Now, listen very carefully because I need you to remember this exactly. I know who the blackmailer is and why they are doing what they are doing. You are to come to the Lake of Stars at midnight tomorrow, the last day of the seventh month, third year, Twenty-first Council."

Miss Viola pulled her head away sharply. "I know what day it is, Shaharazad. I'm not that drunk."

"Even so. Now, I will see you there. Tomorrow, at midnight exactly."

"Why tomorrow?" snapped Miss Viola. "Why not, for example, now?"

"Two reasons, my dear. Firstly, because although the board is set, the pieces are not entirely in place. And, secondly, have you even met me? Does telling you now plainly and clearly seem remotely like the sort of thing I would do?"

With that, Ms. Haas departed, narrowly avoiding the wine bottle that Miss Viola hurled after her as she left.

CHAPTER FIFTY-FOUR

The Lake of Stars

The next day, I returned home from work to find Ms. Haas soberly attired in a floor-length black skirt, embroidered tastefully with golden geometric designs in the Khelish style, a gentleman's white shirt, a black jacket, and a waistcoat accented with a gold watch chain.

"You are just in time, Wyndham," she remarked.

I had thought I would be early, for although I had worked late, I had not expected that we would be leaving for Little Carcosa before eleven. "Just in time for what?"

"I have invited Miss Beck to visit with us before we leave. It seems only right that she should be present at the denouement of this little drama."

"You will," I suggested firmly, "be nice to her?"

"What an unfair insinuation. I have never been anything but civil to the odious little shopkeeper."

"I think your definition of civility may be somewhat at odds with that commonly employed by others."

"Remind me, Captain. When did I last care what the rest of the world thinks?" She pulled out her pocket watch and checked it. "Do run along. You should have just long enough before the lady arrives to get changed into your least dreary outfit. I have left some cufflinks on your dresser that I fully expect you to ignore."

I did, indeed, ignore the cufflinks, which I found extravagant. But I did my best to attire myself in a manner at once modest and respectful of our guest's sensibilities and status. When I returned to the sitting room, I found Miss Beck had already arrived and was sitting in my usual chair, eyeing Ms. Haas somewhat warily.

"You better have a dashed good reason for dragging me across the city at this time of night." She did not say "dashed."

Ms. Haas was in the process of lighting her pipe. "I do nothing without good reason. I have summoned you here because I believe you have a vested interest in the case of Eirene's mysterious blackmailer."

"Actually, Ms. Haas, this case is exactly the sort of thing I don't want to be involved in."

"Oh, really?" My companion raised an eyebrow in a manner that Miss Beck could not have helped but find infuriating. "I thought it was just the lying you objected to."

"I definitely object to you interfering with my relationship behind my back."

"It seems to me you're not certain *what* you want. On the basis of this conversation alone, you appear to wish for Eirene to shield you from the reality of her lifestyle while also being entirely open with you about it, and for me to exclude you from my investigations into this affair while also keeping you fully informed about my interactions with the woman who, from what I can tell, you at once do and do not still consider to be your fiancée."

Miss Beck rose abruptly. "Let's be very clear, Ms. Haas. I profoundly dislike you. I know you saved my life, but you're still a condescending, reckless, arrogant witch. Now tell me something that profits me or I'm leaving."

"You know, I think in the right circumstances you could be rather fun." Ms. Haas's eyes gleamed. "If you ever feel like cheating on Eirene, give me a call."

"I'll give you a punch up the bracket if you don't stop fannying around and get to the point."

"You see. Fun. But since it seems to so preoccupy you, the point is this. Eirene will be meeting with her blackmailer at midnight tonight at the Lake of Stars in Little Carcosa. If you want to come with us, you may. If you don't, well, I think that answers some wider questions about your ability to sustain a relationship with a woman like Eirene."

Miss Beck sat back down and was silent for some minutes. To my surprise, Ms. Haas showed considerable forbearance during the interlude and resisted all further temptation to bait the lady, preferring instead to pace the floor and smoke the remainder of her packet of Valentino's Good Rough Shag.

Eventually, Miss Beck came to her decision. "Right," she said. "Let's go."

Ms. Haas had arranged for a hansom, into which the three of us squeezed in a manner that I found uncomfortable both physically and socially. Thankfully, the journey was of relatively limited duration, as the streets of Little Carcosa were narrow and we were required to walk for the final stretch.

The square around the Lake of Stars was quiet, its daytime businesses being closed and its more nocturnal inhabitants having decamped to those parts of the city with better nightlife. The lake itself was not, in fact, a lake per se but a largish water feature, which the first generation of Carcosan refugees had ensorcelled to reflect the night sky of their lost homeland. Having only recently escaped that place, I declined to gaze into the depths, for fear I would fall into a dream from which I might not awake.

Miss Viola awaited us on a bench. She had recovered her composure somewhat from the night before and was demurely attired in a dark gown, her hair twisted once more into its customary knots. On seeing Miss Beck, she started and then glowered at Ms. Haas. "You couldn't resist, could you?"

"Look," returned Ms. Haas, "the way I see it, we'll get everything out in the open and either she'll leave you or she won't."

Miss Beck pushed past us to put herself between Ms. Haas and Miss Viola. "She can talk for herself, thank you. Where's the ——" And here, again, her language became unbecoming of her station. ". . . blackmailer?"

"If I know her at all, and I flatter myself that I know her quite well, she's already here." Ms. Haas pulled out her pocket watch and checked the time. "She's probably just waiting to make an entrance, and I did tell her to be here at midnight precisely."

"When have I ever done what you told me, Shaharazad?" The voice from the shadows was familiar, though I could not place it exactly until its owner stepped into the light from one of the gas lamps. She was a handsome woman of some forty or fifty years, her auburn hair touched with grey, her golden eyes still startlingly intense. It was, unmistakably, Miss Viola.

Miss Beck was the first to speak, as she glanced between her present fiancée and the lady's doppelgänger. "This," she said, "is going to take some explaining."

Strolling over to the elder Miss Viola, my companion leaned nonchalantly against the lamppost. "Would you like to tell them, dear, or shall I?"

"Perhaps it would be better coming from me."

And so the elder Miss Viola told her story, a story that I relate here as best I am able from my recollections in the lady's own words.

CHAPTER FIFTY-FIVE

❧

The Blackmailer

The truth is, I'm not quite sure how to begin because, for me, this has all begun and ended many times already, and in many different ways. Which I suppose is fitting, for I have also lived many lives—a nobleman's daughter, a refugee, an actress, a thief, a murderer, an adventuress, a fishmonger's wife, and a blackmailer. If you asked my younger self which of these beginnings was the one that mattered and if she answered honestly (which knowing my nature I suspect she would not), she would say that it was the day she met Cora Beck. But the beginning that matters most to me came on the ninth day of the seventh month of the third year of the Twenty-first Council—a little under a month ago from our present position in our present timeline—when I received news that Cora had disappeared on the way back from Aturvash.

As much as I wanted to believe she was still alive and would return to me, I knew she would not. My parents had promised that we would be reunited in a new world and I never heard from them again. Friends and lovers down the years have vanished by choice or circumstance. Until Cora, I had long since stopped either seeking or offering assurances of fidelity, but she gave hers with such generosity that I forgot the lessons I'd taught myself. So as the days passed, and no news came from her, I realised that either I had been deceived or she was dead. I was not sure which I feared the most.

And then the Contessa Ilona paid me a visit. Oh, she made a great show of wanting to comfort me in my grief, but the comfort she offered was not to my taste and had not been for some years. Besides, the moment the vampire renewed her advances towards me I understood what had happened to Cora, and that I had brought it upon her. I had taken up with Ilona a few months after leaving Mise en Abyme and several years before meeting Cora. Shaharazad had already grown bored of me, as she does of everything, and the Repairers were still actively hunting the last survivors of the old nobility. The Contessa was rich, intriguing, powerfully charismatic, and strong enough to protect me. At the time, the intensity of her fascination for me was both flattering and reassuring. I eventually realised her affection was a prison and disentangled myself, or thought I had. But I should have known that while she could tolerate my leaving, she would never accept my giving myself to another. So in a sense, I killed Cora.

And knowing that almost killed me.

My first thought was for revenge. I knew it would be hollow, but I had survived on meaningless pleasures and fleeting victories before, and could do so again. But although I knew a little of how to kill a vampire—having lived with one for some while and having contacts in Little Carcosa who could provide me with some of the strange bullets that the People's Army used to fight the unnatural minions of the Yellow King—I knew also that I could not confront the Contessa alone.

And so I went to the home of my oldest friend in Khelathra-Ven, the one person in the city I was sure had the resources and the wherewithal to do battle with Ilona: the sorceress Shaharazad Haas.

"I fail to see," Shaharazad said, when I had finished telling her how the love of my life had been murdered, "why it profits either of us to pursue a blood feud against something immortal and demonstrably vindictive just for the sake of a dead fishmonger."

I responded as I always did at this stage in our arguments. I seized the heaviest and most fragile items I could lay my hands on and threw them at her. It is not a side of myself that I like, but it is a side of me that Shaharazad delights in provoking. Sometimes I wonder if she doesn't deliberately leave ammunition lying around in order to tempt me.

Her new housemate—a prim Eyan by the name of Wyndham who I disliked instantly—sanctimoniously reinforced Shaharazad's position with the observation that there was, indeed, nothing to be gained by throwing one's life away for the sake of retribution. "After all," he continued, "I know it sounds platitudinous, but it really won't bring her back."

"No." Shaharazad stirred on that awful threadbare chaise of hers with the stains I didn't like to think about. "If you wanted to bring her back, you'd need either necromancy or time travel, both of which are fascinatingly perilous, utterly forbidden, and have the potential to go quite disastrously wrong."

I lowered the paperweight I had been about to hurl at her. "But it can be done?"

"Well, yes. If you wanted to bargain with an Eternal Lord, and risk being erased from history, or with the Ossuary Bank, and risk losing your soul."

"Neither of which," put in Wyndham officiously, "you should on any account consider."

I ignored him. "If I were to do one, or both, of those things how would I start?"

"I do so love it when you're recklessly self-destructive." Shaharazad had that look in her eye that she got on the rare occasions when she decided she was going to care about me for a while. "If you wish to prevail upon the Ossuary Bank, then I would suggest speaking to Ptolemy Khan in Inadvisable Loans. He should be able to arrange matters at a price you may find almost bearable, and with hardly any ironic consequences."

"And if I wanted to go to an Eternal Lord?"

Shaharazad gave a sardonic laugh. "Frankly, your guess is as good as mine. They're all definitionally incomprehensible. Walking Upwards Unmaking has helped me in the past. I sometimes think she might secretly be a bit of a romantic. Of course, the rest of the time I'm just mortally terrified of her. And, if you want my honest advice—"

"When have I ever wanted that?"

"Well, I shall give it to you regardless. Your best bet is to take a staggeringly large quantity of drugs, hire an obscenely expensive courtesan, and try to forget everything, starting with your name and working from there."

I very much wanted to throw the paperweight, but I very much did not want to give her the satisfaction. Digging my nails into my palms, I said, "I don't know why I expected you to understand." And, with that, I left her to her drugs, her sorcery, and her bitterness.

Before the door had even closed behind me, I knew what I had to do. Dealing with the necromancers would be more straightforward, but if it went wrong it was likely that the consequences would fall on Cora's spirit instead of mine, and I couldn't risk that. So instead I sought an audience with Walking Upwards Unmaking.

People often think that it is difficult to meet with an Eternal Lord, but those people don't understand the difference between difficult and dangerous. I had lived in Ven for some while, and several of my former associates were able to put the right words into the right ears. And so, two days later, I was standing at the top of a coral stair before a throne of silver and jade.

My recollection of what happened next is disjointed—as, to some extent, are my memories of everything that I've told you already. After all, none of these things really happened. I made certain they didn't. But I do remember what Walking Upwards Unmaking asked of me and what I asked of her.

What brings you to this moment, Lady Eirene Viola Delhali? It's hard to describe what it's like to talk with an Eternal Lord of Ven. She spoke but she did not speak, and her voice echoed not in my mind but in my past.

"The woman I love is dead," I told her.

Death is meaningless.

"Not to me."

That is your limitation.

It was useless to be angry at a being so alien. You might as well be angry at the sky or the sea or time itself. But I've worked with limitations all my life, and I had no intention of being turned away. "And your tower is yours."

You are bold for so transient a being.

"I have no reason not to be. I've lost everything." I didn't know if I was begging her or defying her. "Help me. You can name your price."

What can you offer an Eternal Lord of Ven?

"You need agents. I can be a very good agent."

Your lover's death does not matter.

"Stop saying that. It matters to me."

So it does not matter if it is undone.

To this day, I'm not sure why she chose to help me. If there's a timeline where she has need of my services, it's not one I've yet inhabited, but I don't doubt that day will come.

Walking Upwards Unmaking directed me to a narrow chink in a ruined wall in the depths of Ven. When I passed through it and returned to the surface, I found that I had arrived a few days before Cora's trip to the salt mines. I wasted no time in tracking down a supply of Carcosan bullets and then, since my past self provided an unbreakable alibi, I stole a winged horse from the Hippocrene and flew to Aturvash. I arrived a full day before Cora, which gave me plenty of time to make enquiries and scout the roads.

I knew that Ilona would be laying an ambush, and that she would have to be lurking by day somewhere out of sunlight. A lonely road along the cliffside was the perfect place to waylay a traveller, and a cave a little way from the road the perfect place to hide. And, sure enough, there she was, asleep in a coffin full of soil. Vampires are terrifying creatures if they can fight you on their own terms. If they can't, they aren't. I shot her in the head and the heart without hesitation or remorse.

On my journey back to Khelathra-Ven I began to experience something strange—flashes of a different life, like the hazy recollection of a dream. I remembered Cora's return from Aturvash. The restaurant we had visited to celebrate her successful deal with the salt merchants. The night we shared afterwards. In that moment, I truly believed I had changed everything. And I had, everything except myself.

When I returned through the portal, by some Vennish magic I did not understand, I was reunited physically and mentally with the version of myself who had lived in the timeline I had created where Cora was alive. I suppose, in a way, I became her, and the memories of my other life—the life where Cora had died, where I had struck a bargain with an Eternal Lord and killed a woman I used to care for—began slowly to fade. It was hardest at the beginning. I still loved Cora with all my heart, but I also vividly remembered mourning for her. These shadows never entirely left me and it would be comforting if I could blame them for everything that happened afterwards. But I can't.

Cora and I married the following spring and, for a while, we were happy. Somehow I had convinced myself, or allowed Cora to convince me, that I could play the part of a company wife. That I could smile and make polite conversation at balls. That I could live respectably but frugally. That I would be content to wait through late meetings and long absences. I've always been an excellent actress, but it's different when you can't leave the stage. We began to argue, over small things at first, like curtains for the dining room—my tastes were too exotic for the Ubiquitous Company of Fishers—and then larger ones, like money, like the way I spoke to her colleagues, like whether we would have children. Eventually, we fought about everything. And, later, we stopped talking altogether.

I began my first affair a little after our ninth anniversary, an occasion we had both remembered but pretended we hadn't. For a while it helped. It made me feel free again and desired again. Like myself again. But none of it lasted, and afterwards it was worse. I was sure Cora knew, that I had confirmed all her fears and her parents' predictions about Carcosan women. Yet still she said nothing.

She said nothing about the next affair or the next. I lost count of the lovers I took. I felt little. They meant less. And now I hardly saw Cora at all. She was always working and usually travelling, while I was trapped in the shell of the life we'd made together. Out of loneliness, or resentment, or a mixture of the two, I began to invite strangers into our home. Even after fifteen years of marriage, I wasn't so cut off from my past that I couldn't surround myself with colour and chaos if I wanted to. And at last Cora took notice. But only because the Ubiquitous Company of Fishers did. A companywoman's wife could be as miserable as she pleased, but she could not be scandalous.

We fought terribly after that. Still, it was better than the silence and, in some strange way, we were closer than we had been for years. But spite is like any other stimulant—the more you depend on it, the larger the dose needs to be. And so my indiscretions grew ever more excessive, my excesses ever more indiscreet. Cora's progression within the company stalled as customers and trading partners began to shy away from her. She had a chance to redeem herself when, in our eighteenth year of marriage, she secured consideration from one of the most powerful trade clans in Seravia. Their khan came to Khelathra-Ven himself to finalise the terms of the deal. And then I seduced his wife.

The Ubiquitous Company of Fishers lost an opportunity worth four hundred full Seravic chants of commerce, and Cora was branded a liability and expelled. I had expected her to be angry at me, to rage and to scream and to curse me by every god and power in the multiverse. Instead she sat at the foot of the bed we had not shared in years and wept.

I left the next day. I took rooms in Ven and hid myself away from the world. And then unbidden dreams and buried memories led me back to the top of a coral stair and a throne of silver and jade.

What brings you to this moment, Lady Eirene Viola Delhali?

I did not know. "Have I been here before?"

A thousand times, a thousand ways, in a thousand worlds.

"I've destroyed the only person I ever loved." Saying it aloud almost killed me. I almost wanted it to.

Love is meaningless.

"That is the least true thing I've ever heard."

You are bold for so transient a being.

"I have no reason not to be. I've lost everything." I didn't know if I was begging her or defying her. "Help me. You can name your price."

You have already made this bargain.

Dimly, I remembered. "Then what can I do? I can't live like this."

Your life does not matter.

"I know."

So it does not matter if it is undone.

❦

CHAPTER FIFTY-SIX

The Conclusion

"And the rest," the elder Mrs. Viola said, "you know. I came out of a portal in Keeper's Shallows some twenty years in my past, I made my way to the surface, and I wrote the first letter. I knew it would hurt you both, but not nearly so much as a life together would."

Miss Viola put her fingers to her temples, murmuring in a despairing tone, "I knew I was messed up. I didn't know I was quite *this* messed up."

"Messed up," agreed Ms. Haas, "but terribly, terribly interesting. I'm starting to remember why I was quite so taken with you. I assume"—she turned to the elder lady, who I shall henceforth refer to as Mrs. Viola to distinguish her from the younger Miss Viola—"that was you on the train?"

"I knew Ilona was still out there, and I couldn't be certain you'd stop her."

"So were you trying to save *us*, or did you think that you and Cora were still on board?" enquired Ms. Haas, apparently far more interested in the finer points of time travel than in the possible ruination of two women's lives. "I'm not really sure how memory works when you come from a future that no longer exists."

"It's fuzzy. I remember a lot of things, and I know that some of them are true, and some of them aren't anymore."

Ms. Haas seemed quite unacceptably enthusiastic. "Well, isn't that fascinating? I have so much to ask you."

"Excuse me," interrupted Miss Beck, "can the quinquagenarians in the party focus on the fact that Eirene and I spend the next twenty years systematically destroying each other?"

"I'm sorry." The elder lady approached her and took her by the hand, but Miss Beck wrenched herself free.

"Don't you touch me. Don't you ever touch me."

Mrs. Viola swallowed, her voice hoarse with unshed tears. "I'm sorry. I'm so sorry. I've never wanted to hurt you."

"There's no point apologising to me. You haven't done anything yet. Maybe you should have had this conversation with the woman you cheated on for ten years."

"I tried. It was just too hard."

Miss Beck stormed over to the Lake of Stars and stared furiously into the water. "It was too hard for you to talk to your ——ing wife. But it wasn't too hard to rewrite the universe?"

"Oh, come on," interjected Ms. Haas. "Do you not think it's just a little bit romantic?"

"You are not helping, Shaharazad," shouted Mrs. and Miss Viola in unison.

"But that's the exact problem, isn't it?" Miss Beck whirled back round. "All of you, except maybe the boring man with the buckles, secretly, deep down thinks it's a little bit romantic."

"Actually," I offered, "I do think the gesture has a certain peculiar honour to it."

"You know what I think has a peculiar honour to it? Telling the truth and making a ——ing effort." Miss Beck looked somewhat confusedly between the two Eirene Violas. "Has it never occurred to you, Eirene, that I know who you are? I mean, I didn't know about the vampire or the jewellery heists or the man you fed to a mad god, but that's just details. You don't fall in love with a woman like you and expect her to be happy with dinner parties and weekends in Aviens."

Mrs. Viola folded her arms. "Actually, Cora, that's exactly what you expected."

"Did you ever ask me? Or did you just assume and start ———ing opera dancers?"

It was at this moment that Miss Viola burst extravagantly into tears.

"Oh, for pity's sake," growled Mrs. Viola, "now look what you've made me do."

Miss Viola glared at her future self. "Shut up, Eirene. I can't believe you've managed to ruin my life in two universes. And now you're arguing with my fiancée because you were too much of a coward to talk to your wife."

Miss Beck looked quite gratified by this. "Well said."

"And you're just as bad. You haven't even let me speak to *myself*. All you care about is how this affects *your* life and *your* career and *your* future and how this reflects on *you*."

Mrs. Viola let out a long breath. "I've wanted to say that for twenty years."

Miss Beck opened her mouth but closed it again immediately. And then a strange silence fell upon our strange company.

Finally, Miss Viola, having regained some of her composure, spread her hands in helpless despair. "So we're bad for each other? In multiple worlds, across multiple realities. What happens now?"

"Isn't it obvious?" replied Mrs. Viola. "You do what I've been trying to get you to do for the past month. You walk away."

Miss Beck fixed the future version of her future wife with a hard stare. "No offence, Eirene, but you are clearly a massive liability. There's no way I'm going to you for advice."

"But she's me." Miss Viola produced a handkerchief from some delicate recess and began dabbing at her face. "If you don't want to deal with her, you don't want to deal with either of us."

"No, she's not. She's you after twenty years in a failed marriage. You're you right now, and I'm in love with you."

This caused Miss Viola to shed fresh tears. "Don't be absurd. We're destined to hurt each other."

"Destiny"—Ms. Haas lit her pipe—"can go hang itself." She did not say "hang." "And, in my experience, everybody hurts everybody. The trick is picking the kind of hurt you want to live with."

Miss Viola reached for Miss Beck's hand. "You don't want my kind of hurt. You've seen what I'll do to you. You shouldn't have to go through that."

"So don't make me. All I've seen is what you'll do to me if you spend our whole life together thinking you've got to hide who you are."

"I'm afraid," said Miss Viola very softly, "you won't like who I am."

"I know who you are. And I love you."

"But what about your career? You can't be mistress of the Ubiquitous Company of Fishers before you're fifty if your wife attends Marvosi sex parties and steals paintings."

"Oh, blow my career." Miss Beck did not say "blow." "I don't want my position to come on the back of your sacrifices."

"And I don't want to take away everything you've worked for."

Miss Beck curled her fingers through a lock of hair that had made its escape from her fiancée's convoluted coiffure. "Most of what I've worked for has been making my family proud and other people rich, and I want to get the rewards of that one day, but until I met you, I didn't realise how much more there was in the world."

"Who could possibly have imagined"—Ms. Haas blew a contemptuous smoke ring in the direction of the ambiguously happy couple—"that there would be more to life than the price of halibut in Pesh."

"I'm beginning to think," said Miss Beck, "that we should continue this conversation in private. And by the way, Ms. Haas, it's one and two-eighths forints a pound."

Mrs. Viola stared at her younger self in open incredulity. "Are you seriously going to go through with this, despite everything I've done and everything I've told you?"

Miss Viola and Miss Beck exchanged a long, intensely private look.

"Yes." Miss Viola drew her fiancée's arm through her own. "I rather think that we are."

"Isn't young love grand?" remarked Ms. Haas. "And look at it this way, future Eirene, you'll have a lovely surprise, or at the very least a surprise, waiting for you when you go back through the portal. Now come along, Wyndham. We're done."

And we were, for thus concluded the affair of the mysterious letter.

EPILOGUE

Although we were well into the small hours of the morning by the time we returned to 221b Martyrs Walk and although I had work the following day, I was far too excited by the culmination of our recent adventure to retire immediately. I settled into the wingback chair, eager to reminiscence with my companion about the remarkable experience we had just shared.

"May I take this moment," I said, "to congratulate you on the truly extraordinary feats of deductive reasoning that allowed you to penetrate this seemingly impossible mystery?"

Ms. Haas did not even stir from her supine position on the chaise. "You may not."

"But however did you realise that the blackmailer was none other than Miss Viola herself?"

"My dear Wyndham, nothing could have been more . . ." She waved an apathetic hand. "What's the word?"

"Elementary?"

"Gods, no. Ghastly turn of phrase. *Obvious*. I think that's what I'm looking for."

I considered this. "You must think me very foolish, but I fail to see what was so very obvious about it."

"Crime is always tawdry and the criminal is usually someone

close to the victim and, really, who could have been closer? Or, for that matter"—Ms. Haas's lips twisted into something resembling a smile—"more tawdry."

"I thought her behaviour showed a commendable affection for Miss Beck."

"It showed a commendable affection for drama."

It would have been more politic to let this slide but, buoyed by our recent success, I spoke up. "Ms. Haas, during only this escapade you fought a necromancer at a company ball, were arrested twice, conjured unspeakable blasphemies in a street brawl, rode into Vedunia on a storm, made a scene of yourself at a literary salon, and, most recently, arranged for the resolution of our investigation to be played out at the stroke of midnight beside a magic puddle."

"As I said: commendable."

We were silent a little. "Madam," I remarked with some concern, "if you will forgive the observation, you do not seem very happy."

At this, she subjected me to one of her particularly withering looks. "You've been living with me for over a month and you've only just noticed?"

"I meant, in particular. Rather than in general. Are you, perhaps, upset about Miss Viola?"

"Do you mean, am I upset that an old friend may be about to repeat the worst mistake of her life? Or do you mean am I upset that my old friend has found contentment when I have not?"

"Both? Either? I hope you feel you can be open with me, Ms. Haas."

My companion, with some effort, levered herself into a sitting position. "Mr. Wyndham, in order that you may be under no illusions going forward let me explain to you how this relationship works. You may share these rooms with me at a reasonable rent for as long as you wish. I shall, from time to time, wish to consult with you on matters pertaining to the eclectic set of activities I call my work. On occasion,

I shall be bored and will call upon you to amuse me. But I am never, ever going to talk to you about my"—she grimaced—"*feelings.*"

"I quite understand. But, regardless, I should like you to know that despite its perils I have enjoyed our time together immensely."

"You are a strange man, Captain. But then, I have little time for ordinary people." And with that, Ms. Haas slumped back down into a position much like the one in which I had first found her. "Now make yourself useful and pass me that needle and the seven percent solution. There will be a new caller soon enough but, until then, I would rather be in any state of consciousness save the natural."

Though it ran contrary to my personal inclination and professional judgement, I did as she asked. Without further comment, she induced in herself a state of narcotic delirium and I, finding I could be of no further assistance to her, returned to my room, where, still too animated to sleep, I began to put down the notes from which, twenty years later, I have compiled this manuscript. This habit I continued throughout all of our many adventures, though my companion often mocked me for it. I am glad now that I did, for I miss her deeply and hope that these tales will stand as some small tribute to the extraordinary life of my dear friend, the sorceress Shaharazad Haas.

ACKNOWLEDGEMENTS

Thank you, as ever, to CMC, the best agent in this or any other universe. And to my utterly fabulous editor, RB, for her unflagging enthusiasm, insightful criticism, and frankly extraordinary patience, along with all the team at Ace for so thoroughly living up to the name of their imprint. You made me really feel like this book had found the right home. Finally, to friends and loved ones, particularly KR and KL, for putting up with me.

Alexis Hall is a pile of threadbare hats and used teacups given a semblance of life by forbidden sorcery. He has a degree in very hard sums from a university that should, by all rights, be fictional.

Ready to find
your next great read?

Let us help.

Visit prh.com/nextread

Penguin
Random
House